Lili

Lili

Abigail De Witt

W. W. Norton & Company
New York London

Published by arrangement with TriQuarterly Books, Northwestern University Press.
First published as a Norton paperback 2002.

The text of this book is composed in Sabon, with the display set in Nuptial Script.
Manufacturing by Haddon Craftsmen Inc.

ISBN 0-393-32318-8 pbk.

Library of Congress Cataloging-in-Publication Data

De Witt, Abigail.
    Lili / Abigail De Witt.
       p. cm.
    ISBN 0-8101-5100-6
    I. Title.
    PS3554.E92937 L55 2000
    813'.54—dc21   00-008058

W. W. Norton & Company, Inc.
500 Fifth Avenue, New York, N.Y. 10110
www.wwnorton.com

W. W. Norton & Company Ltd.
Castle House, 75/76 Wells Street, London W1T 3QT

1 2 3 4 5 6 7 8 9 0

For Cécile

For Paulette

. . . PURETÉ ET SOLITUDE SONT UN SEUL ET MÊME MALHEUR.

—Colette, *La Fin de Chéri*

ACKNOWLEDGMENTS

Several of the characters in *Lili* first appeared in an excerpt published in *The Journal*.

For support during the writing of this book, I would like to thank James Michener and the Copernicus Society of America. Many thanks also to my agent, Jennifer Lyons, and her assistants, Hannah Tinti and Heather Currier, for their generosity and wisdom; to Susan Betz, Josh Hooten, Kim Maselli, Maria Vettese, and everyone at Northwestern University Press; and to Amy Cherry and W. W. Norton for the wonderful welcome they have given me. Diana Donovan, Cécile Docherty, Chris De Witt, Rob Perkins, Jim Grant, Paul Feldman, and all my family and friends provided great help, support, and encouragement in various ways, and I am grateful to them all.

To Susan Monsky, Carolyn Coman, Janet Shea—thank you for everything you have given me, thank you for my writing life.

PART ONE

One

Long ago, Lili believed in God. She lay in the crook of her mother's arm, in her mother's warm, sweat-smelling embrace, a smell like hay, like overripe peaches, and that was God. Her mother's arms were fat, browner than Lili's, and her gown was like silk. Lili warmed her hands on Maman's neck, curled her knees in the fabric of her gown. If she was careful and quick, she could slip her hand inside and touch Maman's breast before Maman caught her wrist and scolded her. "Sh-sh, Lili. *Ça suffit.* Go to sleep now, little cabbage. Go to sleep."

But outside it was bright: pale threads of light slipped through the cracks in the shutters, the heavy brown curtains which did not close all the way. She could hear the birds in her father's garden, the older children in the street on the other side of the house.

When she grew up she would be a nun, and when she died she would go straight to God. But it was important to learn all the words to all the prayers, to forget none—

"Hail Mary,"

"Hush, Lili."

"Hail—"

"That's enough, Lili. You'll have to nap in your own bed."

She lay perfectly still; she did not even breathe. After her nap there would be *goûter,* chocolate and bread. The fruit of thy womb was a ripe, red pear.

She slept, and when she awoke Maman's eyes had closed and her mouth had fallen open. She did not want to take her hand out of Maman's because Maman would awaken then and put on her hat and go down to church, and even though there would be *goûter* Lili would have to eat it alone with André and Maurice. In the afternoon she wasn't

3

allowed in church; that was when Maman confessed her sins and needed to be alone, with her eyes closed.

"*Arrête!*"

"*Mais! C'est toi—*"

"*Arrête!*"

Maman rolled over, away from Lili, and sat up. She got off the
bed, pulled off her gown, fastened her stays and put on her black dress.
Then she went to the vanity and put on her hat with the veil. She did
all of this in the half dark and she did not hurry although the boys were
fighting more and more loudly in the hallway.

At last she flung open the door and Lili heard her slap them and
only André cried though he was eight and Maurice was four and a half.
Maurice was Lili's twin. He was supposed to nap in his own bed,
because he was a boy, but he never lay still. He came and stood in the
doorway and stared at Lili. He couldn't read but Lili could. André was
still crying and Maman said she would slap him again if he wasn't
quiet. Maurice came in and climbed up on the bed next to Lili. They
knelt facing each other, but they did not speak.

Then Maman came back in and scooped Lili into her arms and
kissed her and said that she must go down now and have her *goûter*
and Maman was going to church. Be a good girl—if the boys fight
again tell the cook or Mademoiselle Duroc or Papa, Papa will be very
angry if he's disturbed while he's working.

But Papa and Mademoiselle Duroc were in the garden. Mademoiselle
Duroc was the most beautiful woman Lili had ever seen. She had
blond hair wound around the top of her head and ruffles on her dress
the color of the sky. They let the children eat their bread and chocolate at the garden table until Papa told André to practice his Latin and
not to come down again until he could do better than yesterday.
André's face turned red. He got up and stood behind his chair and his
eyes met Lili's. They were always shining, as if he were about to cry.
Then he shrugged and went toward the house and all of a sudden he
started to sing for no reason at all, but Papa told him to be quiet and
get to work.

Maurice reached across the table toward the chocolate.

"That's enough, Maurice. *Ça suffit*—he's getting to be as fat as I
am," Papa said.

Maurice stared at the chocolate for a while, then he slid off his chair and walked slowly over the grass and along the path between the flower beds and then behind the rosebushes where nobody could see him.

Lili's chocolate was still in her mouth; she did not let her teeth touch it because it was the Body of Christ, *Corpus Domini nostri Jesu Christi;* she knelt in the chair with her eyes closed but she was not sorry that André had to do his Latin because he always wanted to carry her like a baby and she didn't like it.

Mademoiselle Duroc laughed and Lili opened her eyes: when Mademoiselle laughed she bowed her head and covered her face with her hands, like someone crying. Papa threw his head back and his cheeks shook, red like apples, like the color of Mademoiselle's lips. Mademoiselle was Papa's secretary.

"Come here, Lili," Mademoiselle said. "Come and let Mademoiselle give you a *canard.*" Mademoiselle dipped a sugar cube in her coffee and gave it to Lili. In Lili's mouth it fell apart, sweet and grainy and warm, and then Mademoiselle pulled her close and said, "What do you think, Lili? Your father tells me André is lazy and Maurice is turning into a glutton—can you be the little man of the family?"

Lili looked up at her and then at Papa, but Papa did not see her. He was staring at Mademoiselle.

"*Allez, va,*" Mademoiselle said suddenly, patting Lili's bottom. "*Va, mon petit. . . .*"

"I might have to try one more time," Papa said. "This one's engaged to the Church. One more time if I close my eyes and think of something else."

"Oh, Monsieur!"

Lili walked across the garden, the way Maurice had gone. The sun was hot and bright, and she lifted her arms like a bird. Then she ran, and the breeze filled her dress. She stopped and ran again, stopped and ran, stopped and ran. I am learning to fly, she thought; and then it came to her for the first time that she was alive, that once she hadn't been and now she was and she stood completely still; she did not make any sound at all.

Lili, come. . . .

Maurice did not speak. He told her to come without saying anything, without even looking around the bushes at her: he was kneeling in the soft dirt, watching a slug make its way toward the roses. The slug left a trail in the ground and Lili wondered if it knew it was alive. Maurice cleared the leaves and twigs out of the slug's way and Lili helped him. They made a wide path for the slug, a boulevard all the way to the roses, and then they lengthened it so that the path looped from bush to bush. They worked hard, smoothing the path over and over, and when they were done, Maurice patted the slug's head with the tip of his finger. The slug trembled. Maurice stared at it for a moment and then he touched it again. It trembled again. He tried again and again and each time the slug trembled. Then he took one of the sticks they had cleared away and poked it. "Don't," Lili said, but Maurice poked it over and over, and Lili didn't say anything else; she went to find her doll carriage and pushed it around the birdbath in the middle of the garden. If she closed her eyes partway, all she saw, circling around, were streaks of red and purple and gold. But she wasn't happy anymore. She went around and around, as fast as she could, counting in a whisper until she reached four hundred and seven, and there at last was Maman, and Lili ran straight into her knees—

"There, there, little cabbage."

"I'll finish those papers now, Monsieur," Mademoiselle said, and she stood up and went inside the house.

"Did you pray for me?" Papa said, looking at Maman, and then he stood up too and went to the garden shed and came out with his straw hat. He knelt by a bed of pansies and pulled weeds, and Maman sat in his chair and lifted Lili onto her lap. Lili leaned in close to her and Maman scratched her scalp gently, looking for nits.

"Maurice?" Maman said, and Maurice peeked out from behind the rosebushes. "What are you doing, my big boy?"

"Playing," Maurice said.

"Good boy," said Maman, and her hand moved more and more slowly until Lili could tell she was sleeping. But Lili did not sleep. She watched André come out; he stood in the middle of the garden and stared at her and Maman and then at Papa. Papa kept weeding. André had black hair and white skin and his ears were too big.

"Want to play?"

Lili shook her head and nuzzled closer to Maman.

"I'll carry you."

Lili shook her head again.

André shrugged and went around behind the rosebushes.

They did not start fighting right away and she thought maybe now they would play nicely, but André came out screaming: Maurice had thrown the slug at him and it had landed on his shoulder. He was screaming so loudly that the neighbors would come soon if he didn't hush. Papa rose slowly, shaking his head. Maman was awake now, watching him, and he went behind the rosebushes.

"My eldest son. My eldest son! We had a name for boys like you, back when I was in the army."

"There, there, little cabbage," Maman said. "He'll be all right. He's a big strong boy. Don't cry, *chérie*. He has to learn to toughen up somehow."

But just then Tante Alice and Claude-François burst through the garden gate.

"Well," said Tante Alice. She was Maman's sister, but she did not look like Maman. She was tall and thin and she wasn't married, though Claude-François was her son. They lived in Paris, in a little apartment. "It seems I've come just in time."

André and Maurice ran out from behind the roses. Papa followed them with his hand in the air, then let it drop. He stared at Tante Alice, but he did not say anything.

Tante Alice kissed the top of André's head and she bent down and shook Maurice's hand, since he did not like kisses. She gave each boy a chocolate and she kissed Maman and Lili and gave Lili a chocolate, too.

"Now children," she said, lifting Lili out of Maman's arms. "Run along and play nicely and I'll give you more chocolates later on. I need to talk to your mother. André and Claude-François, you two are big enough; hold the little ones' hands and you can all go to the park."

"Well, if you're going to have a regular little gossip, I'll go inside," Papa announced, but Maman didn't answer him.

Claude-François was a year older than André. He had curly hair and knew how to whistle. He showed them how to make their mouths very small and blow the air out, but only André could do it.

"I'll be the leader," he said. "And André is my second in command. You two little ones will be our scouts."

He showed them a place where they could climb over the wall of the park and into the vines and shrubs that led down to the valley. In the distance, they could see Paris.

"Now you two little ones, Lili and Maurice, if you see anyone coming, any grown-ups or any big people who might be grown-ups, you sing the 'Marseillaise.' That will be our code. Keep a sharp lookout."

He lay down against the creeping vines and reached into his pocket and pulled out two cigarettes and a match. "When you suck in, you swallow," he said. "Then you can blow the smoke out your nose." André coughed and coughed, but Claude-François kept patting his back and saying it was OK, it took practice, did he want to try again? He never got mad at André, or laughed at him.

There were swallows circling above the blackberry brambles, swallows circling out toward Paris, rising and falling, and the tiny leaves of the vines were thick and cool beneath Lili and she remembered it, *I am alive.*

"Try again," Claude-François said. "It's tricky at first, but once you get the hang of it, it's fun."

"All right," André said. He was still coughing. "I'll try."

"Good going! That's the way. Just don't suck in so hard, gently, gently, it's all right. Stop—stop. We'll rest for a minute."

They practiced until the sun went down and the sky over Paris turned red, and then they had to run as fast as they could back to the house.

"I don't want your father to hit me!" Claude-François said, but he was laughing. He held Lili's and Maurice's hands and they ran so fast it hurt, so fast that for a minute Lili and Maurice were lifted straight into the air and they were flying, flying in the warm evening, with Claude-François's hands on theirs.

From time to time it came to her again, that she was alive: in the midst of a game with her friends, on her way home from school, when she knelt for communion. It struck her on Holy Thursday the year she was twelve as she was preparing for her confirmation. All through mass, with Maman's heavy, dark body next to hers, with the rank smell of coffee on Maman's breath that Lili loved, she had been fixated on the body of Christ hanging above the altar: it seemed to her as if it would lift off and fly. Even his hands, his feet nailed together, the painted blood that so often made her heart pound with terror—even these could not change her impression of the open, outstretched arms, the arcing chest; for what were they but the shape of a body in flight? And seeing this, seeing Christ poised above the priest, she began to tremble. I, too, am alive, she thought. I, too. God has allowed me, created me—

She did not wait for Maman, who stopped after mass to talk to the baker's wife. She walked home alone, dazed, not paying attention to where she was going, and even the thickness of the gray, warm morning seemed beautiful to her.

But Claude-François was standing outside her house, talking to André. She stopped short, blushed, as if she had been caught at something. Claude-François teased her every time he saw her for being vague and distracted, for thinking too much. He was seventeen now, and they hardly ever saw him since he went to boarding school. She did not like to act stupid around him.

"Hey, Lili."

"Good morning—"

André stood next to Claude-François, his big ears shining; he was as thin and stiff as a toy soldier.

"We're going to the park for a smoke," Claude-François said. "Come with us."

Lili looked down. She tried to think of Jesus in flight, but she had lost her sense of it. She knew the boys smoked whenever they could, but not in front of her, not since she'd begun going to confession.

"Come, Lili." He touched her arm and she couldn't speak. All of the housewives had put their window boxes out, a hundred geraniums lighting the gray walls of the houses.

"Oh come on, Lili."

It was André who had spoken this time and Lili glanced at him sharply. "You know—" But if she reprimanded him, she was reprimanding Claude-François, too. "Let's not smoke," she said. "Let's—" *What?*

Claude-François laughed. "*We're* not going to smoke, little one. André and I are."

"Well, of course, I know—"

"Sh-sh, come with us."

"Come on, Lili," André said. "Maman will be home soon."

For Lent she had made a special effort to be kind to André. Sometimes she dreamed that Maman had killed him, and no one minded. He had been so difficult—she woke terrified, heartsick, unable to eat until she told herself that it was only a dream, a stupid dream.

Claude-François put his arm around her. "Come, Lili. I won't see you this summer. I've got to study for my *bachot*." He led her along the narrow, cobbled street with its geraniums, down toward the park where the trees were budding, a green veil beneath the white sky. "You won't see much of your brother either," he added suddenly. "He's got to study so he won't fail again."

9

André blushed, a pale bruise on his pale cheeks, but Claude-François just laughed. "What do you care, old boy?"

"It's true," André stammered. "I—"

"Who cares? You worry too much, just like our little Lili."

"She's first in her class," André said sullenly.

"Oh, you're like peas in a pod. Who else throws up before exams?"

Lili caught her breath, but Claude-François liked André—he was the only person in the world who did—he hadn't meant to insult her. Still, he couldn't be quite right: it was true that she was thin and nervous, but she had a pretty face, friends, *elle avait du charme*—did Claude-François not see it? But he wasn't paying attention to her now.

"André, listen to me. What do you care about exams? First of all, when you're eighteen you can join the army. You'll go off to war and be a hero and it won't matter what kind of grades you made. Second, you can sing. You've got the best voice I know. Hell, you could be an opera singer. If I had your voice, I'd give up school right now."

Lili stared at André; she had never realized that his voice was unusual. But André began to giggle, a high-pitched, nervous laugh, and it made Lili think of how, when they were younger, he used to ask her to smell his shorts after he had gas.

They were in the park now: mothers pushed their infants in carriages along the wide dirt paths, and through the trees Lili could see Nellie Charpentier chasing her hoop. "Look," she said, for she must not watch the boys smoking, "look, there's Madame Roussel, with her new baby. Let's—"

Claude-François didn't hear her. "You could," he was saying, "you could be rich and famous and you could sing all day. It's funny that everyone else in your family is tone deaf."

But when had Claude-François ever heard her sing?

André giggled again. "Lili sings like a cow."

"I didn't mean—"

"She does, she does! She sings to her dolls and she sings just like a cow. I'm sorry, Lili, but it's the truth. You're not offended, are you?"

"Of course not," Lili said. Her voice was high and thin and André was still laughing, sputtering, standing in the middle of the path with his white, white skin and his too-big ears and his greasy hair.

"I like the way Lili sings," Claude-François said. "It's not always on key, but it's—passionate. Let's play messenger." He turned to Lili and leaned down. Then he whispered, "I love you. You might be too little to understand, but don't forget, all right? Now pretend that what I said was *The cows are loose.*"

"I don't want to play." But she let Claude-François take her hand, let him help her over the wall; she let him sit close to her while he smoked: she was shaking. She kept her gaze fixed on Paris and tried not to think of anything.

"Do you like me a little?" Claude-François asked when André went behind a bush to pee.

Lili didn't say anything.

"Look at your hands," he said; she could not hide their trembling. "I think that means you like me."

She shook her head, but she didn't speak. She didn't speak the whole rest of that morning, and in the afternoon, when Tante Alice and Claude-François were on their way back to Paris, she hid in her room so they would not have to kiss good-bye. She heard him looking for her, but she was flat on her stomach under the bed.

She did not come out until it was almost evening, and when she went downstairs and opened the door to look out—as if Tante Alice and Claude-François might still be there—the street was empty; not even the neighbors' children were around. She leaned against the wall of her house and stared at the geraniums, the soft red petals and the round leaves, thinking, Claude-François loves me, a boy loves me, I am almost grown-up.

André was coming toward her in the dusk. "You won't tell, will you?"

"Tell what?" she asked sharply, looking around.

"You know."

"I don't."

"About our smoking," he whispered. "Where have you wandered to?"

"Oh. That's a sin, you know."

"Well, pray for me," he said, rolling his eyes.

"I might tell," she said, suddenly angry. "I might. You can't just run around doing whatever you want, you know. Maman and Papa—"

His eyes filled with tears. "Please, Lili. Please don't tell. I'll—"

She did not know which was the worse sin, to be mean to him or to deceive Maman and Papa. Papa might beat him, but wasn't it his own fault? The street was full of shadows, but she could still see his face, contorted now, his eyes wide and shining.

"You shouldn't be doing it," she said.

"Just please don't tell, Lili. Please." His voice rose and she knew that soon he would be crying, a sixteen-year-old boy, and as if the other children in the neighborhood could smell it, as if he carried his fear of them like a piece of rotten flesh, they appeared, high-spirited, laughing.

"I won't tell," she whispered quickly, and she saw his face relax, but it didn't matter: he was lazy and ugly, a crybaby, no one could leave him alone.

"Hey, big ears—" It was the Duasé boy, a big strong fourteen-year-old. "Hey, dog turd. Your mother must've cried when you came out and she saw the size of your ears!" The other children burst out in peals of laughter and ran off, on to other games, drinking in the last bit of warmth, of fading light; they meant no harm. André stood, perfectly still, tears streaming down his face.

"They're idiots," Lili said, but she was miserable. She hated to be seen with him, and her heart felt as small and cool as a stone. It was Good Friday tomorrow; the Sunday after Easter she would be confirmed, and she was full of sin.

Claude-François did not tell her again he loved her until she was fifteen. It was the end of summer, hot and beautiful, and they were at war with Germany. Maman and Tante Alice were on the love seat in the parlor, weeping; Papa stood near the French doors. He was looking out into the garden, brokenhearted to be so old and fat; he would have loved to fight. Baby Thérèse, three years old, sat in Maman's lap and clutched her doll. Lili and Maurice sat awkwardly, watching the grown-ups. Only Mademoiselle Duroc and the new soldiers, André and Claude-François, were absent. Maurice was as brokenhearted as Papa, jealous beyond words. He was certain the war would not last long enough for him to fight. And André with all the glory! Plump and unpopular though Maurice was, he had never been a laughingstock like André. He had joined in whenever he could with whatever taunting was taking place, done all that was possible to be better than André—and now this! He kept his eyes fixed on the ceiling, as if he were bored.

It surprised Lili that Maman was crying. She was relieved—here, after all, was proof Maman loved André—and yet André would have friends now, and in his uniform he was almost handsome.

Maman and Tante Alice wept afresh, blowing their noses, loud and unrestrained, and Claude-François burst in, looked at them all, and laughed. He kissed Tante Alice, kissed baby Thérèse—"Your turn will come before you know it, Maurice"—and, leaning down toward Lili, pretending to kiss her, he whispered to her to meet him in the attic in a few minutes.

The attic was hot and dusty and Claude-François was struggling with the round window in the roof.

"You have to pull it toward you," she said. "Then you can unlock it."

He did, and he turned to her and smiled. "Cigarette?" he offered.

"Oh, no. No thank you."

He laughed. "Such a good girl."

She did not know what to say.

"It's all right. It's nice. Pray for us all while we're away, will you?"

"Oh, I will. Of course I will. I do already, I—"

"What makes it interesting is that you're smart, too. I've never seen that, someone who's smart and devout. I don't mean school smart. Lots of girls are school smart and devout, but you see things. You're not easily fooled."

"So maybe piety isn't foolish."

He laughed.

"Oh, I don't mean that I'm so pious. I—I'm like anybody else, I—"

"Sh-sh, Lili, hush. What did you almost commit? The sin of pride? It's all right. Sin away, I won't tell."

"But I—"

"Oh, Lili. I'm sorry. You really do believe. That's hard for me to believe. What do you think? That no one's actually going to die in this war? That we'll all either go to eternal bliss or eternal suffering?"

"I will pray for you, Claude-François. I will pray for you every minute."

"Oh, sweet Lili. Sweet God, Lili. I still love you, you know."

She looked away.

"Does it embarrass you?"

She shook her head.

"I've always loved you. You're the only girl I've ever loved."

"Why?"

He laughed again. "You would think to ask. Because you're smart. Because you know nothing. Because you believe in God. May I kiss you?"

She looked away again and suddenly his mouth was on hers and she was shaking the way she had when she was twelve, but she didn't stop him. The priest himself said that in wartime people did all kinds of things that might be sins otherwise; that the rules were not exactly the same now.

"You're too young, Lili," Claude-François said, but he kept kissing her. "God, look how beautiful you are—these thin arms and all this long hair. Come, come here. Will you lie down with me?"

He pulled her onto the dusty floor and she lay flat on her back, shaking, her gaze fixed on the circle of blue cut from the ceiling. There were cobwebs everywhere, the rafters were filthy, but the sky was as clean as she had ever seen it, a distant, blue, radiant host. Claude-François lay on top of her and it was hard to breathe; he was kissing her, murmuring things she couldn't quite catch, and then he was crying. "I don't want to die, Lili, I want to marry you—will you please let your hair out of your braids? I want—shit." He rolled away from her suddenly, doubled up, and she did not know what she had done wrong.

When he sat up and looked at her, he was bright red. "Will you?" he asked thickly. "Will you marry me?"

"Yes," she said, without thinking, and she began to shake again, and she was so glad that it was wartime; she had never been so happy in her life. She wanted him to come back and kiss her again and again.

But he died; he hardly fought the war at all. Claude-François Terrasse, second lieutenant in the Twenty-third Artillery Regiment, was shot getting out of the trenches. Lili and Maurice were in the garden, eating *goûter*—they had no chocolate, but there was still bread—when Tante Alice appeared. Her face was so hideous—all white except the red eyes—that even Maurice gasped, glancing around helplessly as if she had come to injure them. She was struggling with an enormous trunk and she dropped it at Lili's feet. "You can tell your mother—"

"Alice, *chérie, mon Dieu*—" Maman came out, her arms wide open, but Tante Alice wouldn't touch her.

"I won't have you praying over me, Jeanine. The trunk's for Lili. He was crazy about her, you know—"

And what Lili felt at that moment was mortification: that everyone should know Claude-François had loved her.

Tante Alice took the train to Florence that evening. It was Papa who carried the trunk into Lili's room, and two years later, when she was admitted to Sèvres to study philosophy and spent five days a week in the pension, he moved it again. No one ever spoke to Lili about it or asked what was in it. There was everything: childhood diaries, a train set, trousers and shorts and socks and underwear, a wool jacket, Claude-François's torn uniform, his helmet. The helmet had a bullet hole in it, just above where his right ear would have been.

It made Lili long for the company of soldiers, but only the wounded. She began to bicycle whenever she could from the pension to the Hôpital des Invalides, to sit by the soldiers' bedsides and tell them stories. She murmured on and on, her voice cheerful, light, as if they were not half naked, as if they were not lying beside her with stumps for legs, with mangled faces, with the loud, torn breath of old men. It's the will of God, she told herself, but the words sounded rote, and that little crack in her conviction was the sole discomfort she felt.

She would have kissed each man on the mouth, taken off all her clothes, if any man had asked. She wasn't even hungry then; it was the only time she didn't think obsessively about food.

But at last the nurses told her to leave. She'd been very helpful, but she was too thin, her color was bad; they couldn't be taking care of sick girls.

Her fever rose, and even the pension didn't want her; she went home and lay all day on the couch in the parlor where she could watch the dining room table and see the family sit down to it; over and over and over, it seemed to her; they seemed to do nothing else, though there was never anything to eat and there were times when she thought deliriously, That is faith, nothing to eat, until at last she fell asleep.

But she was awake when they were at the table and the army messenger came to tell them that André was dead. No one answered him, and after a while he cleared his throat, mumbled his apologies, fled. And still no one spoke; they stared into their bowls of turnip water.

At last Thérèse began to cry, softly, and then Maman was screaming and Papa pushed himself away from the table, knocking over his chair, and went out through the parlor and into the moonless garden. He stood there all night, perfectly still, as if he were at attention.

But Lili did not die as people had thought she might. Her fever broke and Maman could grieve her eldest child in peace. She went back to her old habit of spending half the day in church, and so it was that Lili was alone six weeks later when André's letter arrived. She was emaciated, weak, but she had not coughed in days, and everything was so bright, vivid, even the sound of the postman ringing the bell, even the smooth banister beneath her hand. She went down the steps slowly, the wood hard beneath her slippers, and there on the floor was a lost letter from André.

She was shaking as she opened it, her hands drenched with sweat.

Dear Lili,

You are the only one who ever loved me. Don't believe what the army tells you: I am going to kill myself. I don't want someone else killing me, I'm tired of doing what other people want. Don't tell the others—I want my name on whatever monument goes up.

You were such a cute little girl and always so sweet. I'll meet you in the next world and I'll carry you like I used to do when you were a baby—do you remember?

Je t'embrasse,
André

She tore up the letter, pulled herself back upstairs, knelt by her bed, and prayed. Five Our Fathers, fifty Hail Marys; she did her rosary aloud until she was hoarse. And then she was shouting, her throat like an open sore now, *T'es un salaud, seigneur, t'es un connard*—she had never used words like that before—until at last she began to weep. Of course there was no God. He was a fantasy—what else? What else when Lili had lain passionately on Maman's breast while André was cowering, flushed, glassy eyed, when night upon night she dreamed of Maman killing André, and Papa was asleep with Mademoiselle Duroc? André had loved her. He had loved her and she had refused him and so she would marry Claude-François and it would be as if she had loved André because Claude-François had—but Claude-François was dead. She didn't know how André had managed it, if he had gone off by himself or done it publicly. The telegram called him a hero; did they call everyone a hero? *Oh my André, I didn't love you, you must not imagine that, not imagine anything, anything, but I will never, never again burrow into Maman's soft fanatical body to get away from you, I will never do that.*

She was still kneeling when Maman came home. Lili said nothing. She was feeling better, yes. Yes, a tisane, that would be nice. Thank you, Maman.

How long ago that was—how long ago it all was, everything. The war had come and gone and she had lost all sense of time. There were afternoons when even the morning seemed impossibly remote. Claude-

François was dead, André, the Duasé boy. All dead, yes, but only fourteen years ago? Were fourteen years a lot? A little?

Now it was the end of November 1928. She was sitting on a marble bench at the Sorbonne, alone in the Great Hall with the list of the dead: TO THE STUDENTS AND FORMER STUDENTS OF THE FACULTY OF LETTERS WHO DIED FOR FRANCE 1914–1918. Dozens of brown marble plaques with gold names.

They were dead and she was alive. She closed her eyes and lit a cigarette. She was small and when she leaned back her feet did not reach the floor. If only she could weep! She opened her eyes and stared down at her shoes, scuffed and worn and with laces that did not quite match; she shrugged. She was not a good dresser. She had taken to wearing Claude-François's old jacket, though it swallowed her as if she were a child.

She stared at his name—Claude-François Terrasse—twelfth down in the fourth column from the right. Sunday and Thursday for two months now she had been coming here, staring at it.

But it was a bad habit! She was a member of the faculty of the Lycée Victor Duruy, a onetime protégée of the late, famous professor Cartier; she had work to do, exams to grade, correspondence to attend to. . . .

Sometimes she almost ran. She left her breakfast half eaten on her bed—the two small rooms she rented on rue Madame a perpetual shambles—and raced through the Luxembourg as if she might miss something. As if, if she were quick enough, she might still catch sight of him.

She wore his jacket; sometimes, as faithful as a widow, she even wore his socks and underwear, but in truth—this was the terrible thing, the shameful thing, that memory closes over, becomes smooth, simple—there were things about Claude-François she could no longer imagine. She could see quite clearly the blond curls, the high cheekbones—but the shape of his mouth? The way he walked?

She shrugged again, lit a new cigarette off the end of the other, though she had barely smoked it, and let the first one dangle from her free hand, burning itself out.

It offended her suddenly that André's name was not on the wall; he was not among the students and former students of the faculty of letters. In the fifth column from the right were the R's—Jean-Pierre Ruelle, Alexandre Rocher, Bertrand Renaud—but no Ravaudet, André Paul Ravaudet, last in his class, skinny, and large eared. She was being ridiculous. Every list was exclusive—the boys of this neighborhood, that school, our village—wasn't his name in Saint-Germain, carved into the ugly granite obelisk in the center of town?

Every day Maman stopped at the obelisk on her way home from church. She told anyone who would listen about her son, who died in the war. A true hero, she would say, pointing to his name. A hero for his country.

A group of students burst into the hall with the names of the dead. They swept past Lili, their dark cloaks swelling, heads bent passionately in debate; they made her think of a flock of crows, and on they went into the Cour d'Honneur, where the sky shone like blue glass. They had not seen Lili, but their suddenness startled her, made her self-conscious. She noticed with surprise that both cigarettes had burned themselves out, slipped out of her grasp, and she stared blankly at her hands, the stained fingertips, the veins.

How old were those young men? Twenty? Twenty-one? Her own students were sixteen, and she thought of them as children, but these boys frightened her. They might have come to replace the dead, she thought, and then their innocence overwhelmed her, and she was suddenly ravenously hungry. She thought of her breakfast waiting for her on her pillow—half a bar of chocolate, a *ficelle*, a tin of sardines—and she lit a fresh cigarette. If she went home, she would have to correct exams. Or I could go out to Saint-Germain, visit Maman and Papa—she shrugged. She hardly ever went out there anymore. Thérèse came in, seventeen years old now, bringing gifts from Maman—a cake, wool stockings, a basket of fruit—but of course Lili was terribly busy, she worked so hard, she didn't take care of herself. Lili worked; André was a hero.

Oh André, André chéri—

She wondered if he had held the gun to his temple, or his mouth—

She sat up straight, her eyes fixed hard on Claude-François's name as if suddenly she would see how his features fit together, it would all come back to her, and he would cover her body with kisses.

She remembered André's face perfectly, every expression, every angle.

She sat for another hour, motionless, her back perfectly straight, and if the students passed her again she didn't notice. She wasn't thinking now;

she was just still. Finally she murmured, "You'd better get your work done," and she slid off the bench, went down a narrow corridor and back outside. It was cold and windy. She pulled Claude-François's jacket closed and hurried toward the Luxembourg. No one there seemed bothered by the wind. The old men read their fluttering newspapers undisturbed and the boats sailed more swiftly around the fountain. She nearly ran to warm herself, but on the far side of the Luxembourg, near rue Guynemer, a gardener was pushing a wheelbarrow full of dying flowers he had just pulled up. There were pansies, geraniums, chrysanthemums, faded and spotted but still colorful, and she stopped and asked, "May I?" He looked at her suspiciously but shrugged, "*Comme vous voulez,*" and she gathered up an armload of flowers and carried them home, leaving a trail of dirt and petals behind her.

At home, with the door closed, she surveyed the dirty cups everywhere, the ashtrays, the books on the floor—she liked it. She put the flowers in jars and set the jars randomly around her bedroom, and then if she glanced at everything quickly, in a blur, it was like a lovely garden going to seed. An orange kimono lay draped across a chair; through the door to the kitchen she could see a purple cabbage on the kitchen counter. She imagined Claude-François finding her here—how he would laugh at her untidiness; he would light them both cigarettes—for the truth was, she never wore the orange kimono: she left it out on the chair in case he should come, to charm him with her colorful mess. It was a stale fantasy, but what could she do except repeat it over and over?

Claude-François's trunk was next to the window; besides that she had only a narrow bed, a bookcase, a desk. The desk had nothing at all colorful about it: on one side, crisscrossed so that she could find each one quickly, were more than a dozen versions of the opening chapter of a book she meant to write. Halfway between the two piles were three pens, lined up next to one another, and a bottle of ink. It was as perfectly organized as a schoolgirl's desk, and she looked at the stack of exams now with a heavy heart, sat down on her bed, and ate the sardines with her hands. Then she licked her fingers, ate all of the bread, the chocolate, and went to sit on the floor by the trunk. She opened it, took out Claude-François's helmet, and held it up to the window. Through the ragged bullet hole she could see the polished sky. It seemed to dissolve and flow through the windowpane, through the bullet hole, into the empty helmet. She kept staring, fascinated by the blue sky, by the rusted, curling edges of the wound; it was like holding his death in her hand.

They never received André's helmet; no doubt he wasn't wearing it when he shot himself.

André—

She kept staring through Claude-François's bullet hole, tracing her fingers along the edge. She did it over and over, slowly, pressing her fingertips into the sharp metal. There was something luxurious in what she did, some secret, erotic consolation.

Two

The next Sunday, woken by the afternoon bells from Saint-Sulpice—
for she had stayed up until four in the morning grading exams and
then gone to sleep—her first thought was that she wouldn't go to the
list of the dead. She would do everything differently today, would act
as if she had never lost a soul. Thérèse had brought her a red wool
dress, claiming it didn't fit anymore since her fiancé had been bringing
her chocolates every week; Lili rose, put it on, and stared at herself in
the mirror: she looked almost fashionable. If she pinned back her
hair—which was thick and tangled—found matching shoelaces, and
wore her own coat instead of Claude-François's, she might look prop-
erly bourgeois.

She had no doubt that the dress still fit Thérèse. Thérèse was
always giving her clothes—soft, lovely things that Mademoiselle Duroc
herself might have chosen—because it pained her to see how badly Lili
dressed. *Of course you haven't time to think about things like clothes
. . . if only we could persuade you not to work so hard. It's your students who should be working, not you!*

Lili works so hard, André—

She closed her eyes. She would comb her hair, buy some proper
food, clean the apartment, and when she was done, she would work on
her book. It was intended to be a study of nineteenth-century atheists,
one chapter for each man, but for the most part she had simply written and rewritten the introduction, in which she explained her own
ideas. Today she would write the entire first chapter, "The Father of
Modern Atheism."

She had, however, no other shoelaces. Nor was her coat as warm
as Claude-François's. Still, she kept the red dress, took her wallet, and
did not run when she went down the stairs of her building and out into
the pealing bells, the cold, bright air.

At the corner of rue Madame and rue d'Assas, she realized she had not brought a shopping bag, had done nothing with her hair. She stood for a moment, paralyzed—it was so difficult to be comme il faut, to look like everyone else, to stick to one's own small tasks—and here, in the middle of the street, with two girls skating past her hand in hand, where it was not possible, it must not happen, she nearly burst into tears. She had been impeccable as a child! She took hold of herself; she would not give in. What did it matter if her hair was uncombed? The point was to eat a proper meal, to do her work, not to spend her free days like a madwoman at the Sorbonne.

There was a line outside the *boucherie-charcuterie* on rue de Fleurus, housewives buying their Sunday roasts, and Lili stood behind them, her mind fixed on Feuerbach's theory of projection.

"So I told Marie-Louise she could have the day off, I was appalled, simply appalled . . . and the price of sugar, well, if he had come into my house that way—no, of course not, no absolutely not! I told her, I said, 'I don't think that color suits you'—two hundred francs for a plain beret!"

Lili stared at a large, pink mole trembling on the neck of the woman in front of her—it was Madame Dupuis. She glanced at Lili, gave her a thin smile, and leaned in more closely to Madame Arnaud to finish her story. They were like bees, with their urgent whispering, their tight, round bodies trembling with importance—Lili lit a cigarette. Madame Dupuis swung her head around, glared at Lili this time, and once more returned to Madame Arnaud. Hers was the story of the two-hundred-franc beret, and Lili realized suddenly that her first year of teaching she had had Madame Dupuis's daughter and had nearly failed her. The worst passing essay I ever read, Lili thought triumphantly, though in fact she had pitied poor little Claire Dupuis. Madame Dupuis had abandoned the beret, was whispering about Lili instead. "I think it's frankly ugly when a woman smokes, I think—" But the door to the butcher shop opened and Mesdames Arnaud and Dupuis disappeared inside.

Lili turned away. Once more her eyes welled up with tears and she saw, shimmering, a boy in shorts run toward the Luxembourg, the two skaters circling around and around, their arms out at their sides—

"And with that?"

"That's all."

"Thank you, Madame."

A young woman came out of the butcher shop and Lili stepped inside, ground her cigarette under her heel, and for a moment all her misery left her, for she loved the butcher. He was a young man with a heavy body and broad hands. His eyes swam behind a pair of spectacles, but he moved with the grace of a dancer among the slabs of beef and ham, the calves' heads, entrails; he slipped his hand under a glossy brown liver and, holding it out in his palm, offered it for inspection to Madame Arnaud.

"Yes," she shouted, for in fact she was deaf and had likely heard nothing about the beret or the ugliness of Lili's habits, "yes, that will do."

The butcher sliced through the liver as if it were butter. "And with that?"

"That's all."

"*Merci*, Madame."

The butcher's wife—a small, pretty woman with bad teeth—handled the money. The butcher had already turned back to his meats and was holding up a string of blood sausages for Madame Dupuis. Lili glanced at the butcher's wife, with her basket of clean white eggs at her side, and her lovely stained smile, and then at the butcher's heavy forearms, and she imagined him a kind, generous husband. No one—not the greengrocer, not the pâtissier, not the fishmonger—was as graceful as he, as provident, *Here, this will nourish you, this is the meat for your table*. No one else broke the rules of his trade—keeping pork and beef and poultry all together—or handled his wares so lovingly. And Lili imagined how, at the end of the day, with his apron discarded, his hands and arms washed, he would turn to his wife, and though he would still smell of raw meat, for it infused him like smoke, he would see only her fine hands.

It was Lili's turn. Madame Dupuis, laden with three blood sausages, a whole calf's tongue, and part of its brain as well, edged her way past Lili, gave her one last disapproving smile, and went to finger the eggs by the cash register.

Lili could not meet the butcher's gaze. She could not think of what to order. "Three thin slices of smoked ham, please," she said, all in a rush. It was what she bought every time, and she was embarrassed. But nothing else occurred to her—she hated cooking. He sliced through the ham, wrapped it in a matter of seconds—for though he moved without haste, not a single gesture was wasted—and gave her the small brown parcel. Their eyes met for an instant—how forgiving was his half-blind gaze!—then she went to the butcher's wife, and onto the small table with its basket of eggs she poured all the love that she felt for the butcher himself: she smiled at the butcher's wife, said how nice the day was, wished her a good afternoon, poured too much money out of her purse—

She was out on the street again, with the door chiming behind her, and without thinking at all, she walked as quickly as she could to the Sorbonne.

She sat for a long time with the parcel of smoked ham in her lap, lighting one cigarette off the end of the other. Every now and then a group of students burst into the room from one of several doors leading to the classrooms and vanished through another door or out into the Cour d'Honneur. Their voices filled the hall for a moment and then dissolved, as if they'd never been. They didn't notice Lili, with her cigarette upon cigarette. It's as if I were invisible, she thought. And if I am invisible, I am nearly dead, but not quite—and it is that small gap that causes all the misery.

Her fantasy now was this: Claude-François, who had, in the chaos of the war, been mistaken for someone else, found her here, before the list of the dead. (He'd been in Alsace-Lorraine for the last fourteen years, recuperating from his war wounds.) Naturally he knew right where to find her, just as he knew exactly where her apartment was. At the sight of her, so disheveled, so sad, he fell to his knees (or lifted her to her feet?); she wept; she told him that André had killed himself, and he forgave her—yes, this was the part of the fantasy that she loved, that she imagined over and over, the one part that hadn't worn thin—he forgave her, yes, again and again, *You were only a child, Lili.*

The scene of forgiveness underwent infinite subtle variations, but the scene before it—of confession—was always the same: her heart beat painfully in her throat and the words came out loud and quick and she couldn't see anything.

She inhaled her cigarette, blew the smoke out in one strong gust, felt her longing to weep as passionate and futile as her longing for a lover—then she shrugged and, like a child, kicked her heels against the base of the marble bench.

A man wandered in from the Cour d'Honneur—too old for a student but without the garb of a professor—stood for a few minutes in front of the brown marble plaques, and sat down next to Lili. An arm's length away. She focused her gaze on the wall and read all of the names, every one, column by column. He seemed to be reading them with her. Obviously she could get up and leave, but this was her spot. She didn't want to give way.

She stopped reading, dangling her cigarette over the edge of her knees. The package of ham lay in her lap as soft and warm as a child's hand. The room was suddenly heavy, silent, and she seemed to have gone blind except in her right peripheral vision, where the stranger sat.

At last her cigarette became a thin column of ash and she lifted the end of it quickly and scattered the ashes across the floor.

The man stared at her.

Without thinking, she held out her cigarettes. "Do you smoke?"

He kept staring at her. Then he took a cigarette and asked, "Why do you keep coming here?"

She gasped. "Excuse me?" But she could see that he was guileless. He was not telling her to leave.

He rose, stood in front of her, and bowed. "May I introduce myself? Pierre Larat."

She didn't understand if he was mocking her or meant to be friendly. Obviously he had no more business here than she did, but she had never noticed him before, had no idea how many times he had seen her come. He had a heavy provincial accent, so perhaps he simply didn't know how to act.

"Your brother?" he asked, indicating the wall.

"Yes."

"Ah," he said, nodding. Then he sat down again. "All you women. Mourning the dead. The dead are happy. It's the living who suffer. A living man fights, he manages to stay alive, and the whole time women are just waiting for him to come home and get back to work."

She stared at him; he was a lunatic.

"I was going to return to my village," he continued. "Do you know Auvergne? I was going to marry a beautiful girl."

The fact that he was mad softened her. She nodded and asked, "Did you know André Ravaudet?"

He shook his head, scanning the list. "But he isn't there—"

"I don't like to make small talk," she said sharply, but it wasn't small talk. How had she grown so rude? From disuse, she thought. I hardly talk to anyone. . . .

He didn't seem to mind. He was shrugging, continuing his train of thought. "All these monuments to the dead, and the automobiles, and the streets with American names. . . . I find them exhausting. But it's impossible to imagine the way things used to be. The simple happiness!"

"It never was."

"But in Auvergne. . . ." He rose abruptly and ground out his cigarette. "Sorry to have disturbed you."

"Oh," she began, but he had already turned from her; he was a tall man with a long, loose stride, the gait of a peasant going back out into the fields.

She ate her three slices of ham and suddenly she was painfully aware of how dirty her hair was, how thin and angular her body inside the oversize jacket and the soft, damp wool. It was cold in the room with the names, but streams of sweat rolled down her sides.

The next Thursday she ran to the list of the dead as soon as she awoke. She wondered if the stranger would come again, and when he didn't, she was both relieved and disappointed. But just as she was about to leave, he appeared, tipped his hat to her, and sat down without speaking. His face was broader and simpler than she remembered. But his failure to speak rattled her, and when, after a while, he began to whistle, she got up and left.

At home, she went straight to her desk and wrote a letter:

My dear Tante Alice,

Sometimes I think of crossing the Alps to find you. Do you remember that summer my family went to Haute-Savoie? How beautiful it was. . . . I would like to cross the glaciers, the blinding snow, go down into Italy, and find you at last sitting near an olive grove, the dry sun putting you half to sleep. Of course we are neither of us the same anymore, nothing is the same. Don't worry: I would never disturb your solitude, though I write like a spoiled, insatiable child.

There is no news here: my students are rather dull this term, with—thank God—one merciful exception: a bright, witty, red-haired girl.

Je t'embrasse de tout mon cœur,
ta petite Lili

They wrote to each other once a week, she and Tante Alice, but they never mentioned Claude-François.

❧

The next time Lili went to the list of the dead, the stranger appeared right away. He tipped his hat to her and sat down closer than he needed to: a large, blurry presence in the corner of her eye.

Sunday and Thursday he was always there now, and always without an overcoat, regardless of the weather. He tipped his hat, but they never spoke anymore.

Then one day, instead of going to the Sorbonne, she went to the memorial at l'Ecole Normale. It was a smaller room, quieter and darker, and for that reason she hardly ever went. There were no benches to sit on, no way to pretend that she was there for any reason other than to view the names: the smaller, more exclusive list, the very best students. But what could she do? The man at the Sorbonne distracted her. She wanted to stare at Claude-François's name in peace. It was raining outside and she crouched in front of the wall, hugging her damp knees to her chest. She was almost level with the statue lying at the bottom of the wall, the lovely black marble boy, composite of all dead boys who had aced exams, had shown great promise—she reached out to touch the cold, smooth hip, and just then she heard steps, and, jumping up, her heart pounding, she found herself face-to-face with the man from the Sorbonne. He was soaking wet.

"For God's sake," she said.

"I'm sorry," he said, stepping back quickly, as if she had spat on him. "Really I am. I haven't meant to bother you. But I'll leave you alone now. I won't come back."

She said nothing. Again she felt the longing to weep, the impossibility of it.

"I would like to say, though, Mademoiselle—it wasn't to get you in bed. The city is full of prostitutes and I like prostitutes."

She smiled suddenly. He was a remarkable conversationalist; it didn't matter, then, how odd she was with him, how rude she'd grown in her solitude. "Good-bye," she said softly, and though she didn't rise, she extended her hand.

"Good-bye," he said. His hand was wet and cold against hers and she didn't want to let it go. It was the size of his hand, the strength of it, and most of all that it was so cold and drenched—she had not touched another person's skin in months.

He tugged gently as if he were pulling her up, to hold her, and without thinking, she rose.

He was staring down at her hand, laughing slightly; he only wanted her to let go.

A wave of heat washed through her body. Of course. Look at her—she was a mess. She wanted to hit him, for her humiliation.

"Would you like to join me for a bite to eat?" he asked.

He was patronizing her. She wasn't even pretty. But the chill of his hand. I want to touch him again, even if I am not pretty.

They ate in a small, basement-level café and he asked her questions as if he were conducting an interview. He was especially interested in the book she was writing. It must be a fascinating document, to be taking so long.

She laughed. "I've written the first chapter twenty or thirty times."

"You've written thirty different proofs of the nonexistence of God?"

"There are subtle variations." She laughed again. Then she asked, "Don't you have any friends?" to change the subject.

"Actually, no."

"You've been here ten years and you don't have any friends?" He had told her this: he had stayed in Paris after the war, had failed to return to his village and marry his fiancée, had passed his *agrégation* and become a geography professor at the Lycée Henri Quatre. He had never been back to Auvergne, where his abandoned fiancée was still unmarried, ruined, and his older sisters waited daily for his return.

"No," he said simply. "No friends."

"Have you tried this way before? Inviting strangers to dinner?"

He smiled, the warm broad smile of a farmer. "No. You're the only person I've been drawn to."

She laughed nervously. "What do you mean 'drawn'?"

"Physically. Oh, but more than that. Because, as I said, I didn't want to go to bed with you. I kept imagining you naked, that's all. I didn't imagine kissing you or making love to you. I just kept trying to picture you without your clothes."

She smiled. "Shall I unbutton my blouse?"

He looked down, as if she were still clutching his hand and he wanted to get away. "No. No, of course not. I didn't mean—"

She looked down at her *rillettes*. All her desire to touch his hand drained out of her. She couldn't make sense of him, with his frankness and prudishness all mixed together. She smeared some *rillettes* on a piece of bread, devouring the salty, greasy fleshiness of it. She thought of Tante Alice and was overcome with a longing to see her. But this man, Pierre, was staring at her, waiting for a response to something he had said. She stared back at him, blankly, waiting for him to repeat himself.

"I was wondering about your family," he said at last, his voice newly shy and formal.

"Well perhaps our fathers should meet," she said dryly, though of course he hadn't meant it that way; he wasn't talking about courtship, but she had no idea how to answer him except absurdly. "Perhaps they should decide if they're interested in each other—which I doubt—and then. Oh, well. Since your parents are dead, you should address yourself directly to my father—a grim business, I'm afraid. Though, of course, he might simply be relieved at your expressed interest. Farmer's son or not, he might be overjoyed to learn of your interest in seeing me naked. And I have quite a dowry, should you decide to legitimize your viewings—" Why was she talking to this man about marriage? His interest in her was purely intellectual, as if she were a curiosity. And my interest in him? she wondered. Oh, I am lonely. It isn't fair to take up his time out of loneliness.

"Excuse me," he said. "I seem to have annoyed you."

"Well, you baffle me." She put down her napkin and rose. "One minute you're saying you'd like to undress me and the next you're asking me with the solemnity of a schoolboy about my family. It seems backward, don't you think?"

"No." He put his hand over hers to stay her. His skin was warm now. "No, I don't think so. They're different subjects. One is your body, which I would love to see, and the other is your family. I was simply curious who your family is, where your family is from. I forget about families. Since the war. But then I remembered. The truth is I spent most of the war in an asylum."

"Oh," she said, and her heart contracted. She had forgotten that he had seemed mad to her at first. "You're better now?"

He shrugged, withdrew his hand. "I'm not afraid anymore. I don't wish to talk about it. I'm a good teacher, and I obey the law."

She was stung by his tone and said nothing: He guards his madness. The taciturn farmer.

Around their silence, the din of the café resumed itself. Their lamb chops arrived and they ate wordlessly, their knives and forks scraping loudly against the china. She watched his large, square hands, the crude way he gripped his knife.

She thought how, despite his stay in the asylum, he looked handsome in the dullest, most ordinary way. He was recovering well; soon he would pass into the realm of cold, masculine normalcy. He would marry a girl from his village—perhaps the one he'd left behind—and he'd say nothing about his years in Paris, the asylum, the prostitutes. He would not even remember this meal.

"Why, suddenly, were you interested in someone?" she asked. "Naked or otherwise?"

He shrugged. "Your wrists are very thin. The sight of them touched me. You wear a man's jacket, smoke like a man, you even have a deep voice—but then such small wrists! And your feet don't even reach the ground when you sit. It's an amusing sight, I suppose, but it made me sad. I felt that I did not have to feign anything in your presence. It reminded me, if you want to know the truth, of the way I felt with the other patients in the asylum. Some of them. Some of them were as horrifying as what you see on a battlefield. But then I learn that you're about to become a famous philosopher. You don't need a former lunatic's sympathy."

"I'm not sure I need anyone's sympathy."

"No, of course not. Certainly not! I apologize. But do tell me, who is your family? It's difficult to imagine you having any, Mademoiselle."

She laughed, gave in to him. "We are old bourgeoisie, Normands. A stern, disappointed father—disappointed in most of us, his children. A sad, disappointed mother—disappointed in him, though he has always provided well for her. I have a twin brother, Maurice, who was born an angel. But now he is fat and mean. He has moved to Germany . . . no one understands it. And I've a younger sister, Thérèse, who is quite beautiful. She is charming and lovely and everyone adores her. I adore her. She will be married next year to a kind wisp of a man in the civil service. She is my parents' consolation. But I'm afraid they often forget her—forget to be consoled by her—so busy are they trying to decide which of us to be more embarrassed by, my brother or me. I showed such promise; I was such a good girl, so serious. And tidy. And now"—she gestured toward her unbrushed hair—"I've let myself go. I'm unmarried."

"Why?"

"Well"—she shrugged—"I can't quite see the point." Then she added, "I also had the brother who died, of whom we are all quite proud. There were four of us originally."

"André," Pierre said, nodding.

"And the girl you left behind in Auvergne? What was she like?"

"There isn't much to say." He waved suddenly for the bill, turning away from her.

And again he seemed suddenly normal, dull, handsome.

But she let him accompany her to her rooms on rue Madame. It was past eight and the rain had stopped. The sky was cold and black, awash with stars; she drew Claude-François's jacket around her shoulders. She thought of this man's fiancée, still waiting for him, and of his desire to see her, Lili, naked. She shrugged, and out of despair—she didn't want to have wasted the evening; she wanted something to happen to her, a shock—she invited him upstairs.

"Shall I undress?" she asked, but he shook his head. He was looking around the small, cluttered room, taking in the piles of books, the ashtray, the orange kimono.

"May I kiss you?" he asked, looking down at her.

She started. She had reconciled herself to undressing for him, to the strangeness of standing naked in front of a strange man who would forget her. But to let him kiss her! It must be only an experiment, to see if anyone else kissed as Claude-François had.

He leaned down toward her slowly and she could see his lips, pale and full, and her chest tightened: he was nothing like Claude-François. He brushed his fingers along her elbows, the lightest of touches, and her chest was so tight she thought it would explode, like glass. Then she knew that it was too late: he had already hurt her and she would have to suffer now. She reached up and kissed him, clasping his head between her hands with a kind of fury that, she could tell, aroused him.

Three

He did not ask to go to bed with her. He stayed, stroking her thin arms, her neck, until two in the morning, but suddenly he left—quietly, so he wouldn't wake the concierge. He disturbed her; it was impossible to see clearly when he was in the room, but she had wanted him to stay. It offended her that he had not gone anywhere near her bed, had not even asked to see her again.

She taught badly the next day. She was tired, and the high, windowed classroom seemed desolate, joyless. A cold light streamed in, full of chalk dust, and she could not keep her notes in order. But the girls stared at her obediently, terrified and dull as always. Only Jeanine Roussel, with her red hair and her freckled face, seemed to notice that anything was wrong. She knit her pale eyebrows and frowned, the way she did when she was struggling to understand something, though today's lesson was a review of concepts she had mastered weeks ago.

"Pity," Lili heard herself say dully, automatically. "In what way do Schopenhauer and Kant differ, first in their estimations of, and second in their definitions of, pity?"

She waited for Jeanine to raise her hand, but Jeanine simply stared, and for a moment Lili was terrified that she had just asked that very question a minute ago. "Mademoiselle Laruelle," Lili said sharply, and poor Marie-Claire Laruelle jumped to her feet and stood by her desk, unable to say a word.

Lili sighed. "It doesn't matter," she said in a voice so soft and forgiving that Marie-Claire gasped. "There is too much terror and boredom in this classroom. Do try to pay attention. It will go easier for you if you do well in school. You may have some hope of independence then . . . and you will have developed a strong intellect, which will serve you in ways you cannot even imagine now, from perils you have not yet dreamed of. But try to replace your abject terror with desire.

It's a desire that requires cultivation: the more you think, the more you'll wish to think. Now, Mademoiselle Roussel, Kant on pity?"

Jeanine rose, lovely, plump, freckled, but still frowning, so that Lili wondered if she'd buttoned her blouse wrong. "Like Plato, Spinoza, and La Rochefoucauld, Madame, Kant thought it valueless."

Valueless, oh yes, but the day would never end, and why had Pierre Larat kept her up so late and never said when he'd be back?

He came to her apartment that evening. She called out to him to come in, but she did not rise from her desk; she could barely look at him.

"I hope . . . ?" he began, then he fell silent. He stared at her and suddenly she stared back, taking him in more fully than she had before, her heart beating too rapidly. He had lilac eyes, and she wondered why she had not noticed this. She realized that, despite the color of his eyes, he was not as handsome as she had thought. He was tall and broad shouldered, with hair the color of sand and a broad face, which gave him the appearance of being frank and open, but his features were thick, almost crude—a short, blunt nose; rough skin—and she thought, The whole is one thing, but the pieces are quite another. He came around behind her desk, lifted her out of her chair, asked if he could kiss her again, and then she could not see clearly anymore—eyes, nose, anything—there was only the painful beating of her heart and the odd, dark sensation of his mouth open against hers.

"I hope you don't mind that I simply came over like this."

"You didn't say anything last night, whether you would come or not." Her voice was accusing, and her eyes stung.

He laughed. "Oh, Lili, you didn't invite me."

"Well!" she said, throwing her hands in the air. He caught them, still laughing.

"You had only to invite me."

"How was I to know?" It was terrible to want a person this way, to care what he did with his time.

He picked her up and held her in his arms as if she were a child. "I'll come, if you invite me." His face was too close to hers; he was blurry, oversize; she could not rein herself in.

"And if I invite you to make love to me?"

He smiled. "But I don't think you want me to make love to you."

She was afraid again that she would cry when she didn't want to. But Pierre was still laughing, kissing the inside of her wrist. "I thought of you all day," he said, sitting on the edge of the desk and holding her on his lap. It was difficult to have a conversation, so close together. "You are like a fierce little animal, like a fox with a sore foot," he said, "and despite myself—despite my preference for fat, overripe, languid women—I am smitten. What do you make of it?"

"I don't know why I've let you in."

And again he kissed her, and it was like being pulled underwater.

"You are the first woman I have kissed for free in years," he said, and his face had grown soft, like a child's—he wasn't laughing anymore, and she was not so afraid of him now.

"Why?" she asked kindly. "Why have you always preferred prostitutes?"

"Because it's simpler," he said. "There isn't the terrible complication of emotions. Jealousies, suspicions, guilt. You spend an evening with a prostitute, you have a nice time, it's friendly, even affectionate—even, at times, passionate—and then it's over. There's a certain purity. . . ." But his voice trailed off and he began kissing her arm again.

"And with me?" she asked. "Would you have come back tonight if you'd paid me last night?"

"Ah, with you," he said soberly, meeting her eyes. "With you I am afraid."

"Are you?" she asked, and the sudden eagerness in her voice embarrassed her.

He burst out laughing and pulled her close. "You'd like me to be, wouldn't you, Lili? Yes, you would! Already we're at war—we were at war before we'd even kissed. That's why I like you—one of the reasons. I am afraid and yet there's nothing to be afraid of. You were jealous and guarded from the start. There was no preliminary coyness, no drowsing effect. Yes, perhaps that's what I can't stand with other women: the hidden danger . . . all the misery that awaits you behind their lovely softness, their feigned stupidity, their kindness. It wears you down in the end, all that gentle, soft, loveliness—and that is when they come, sharp as tacks, exacting their price. My fiancée, all her waiting. . . . Better to pay by the night."

"What you're saying is loathsome."

He shrugged sadly. "But you see, Lili, with you. . . ." He shrugged again. "There is a point when all the caution in the world is useless. You go along, paying every night, keeping your accounts in order, avoiding disaster—and suddenly there is this small, wild woman who won't meet your gaze, who snaps at you one moment and is warm the

34

next, and you must see her again, and again, and she isn't one who accepts money."

"I want you to make love to me," she said.

"Not yet," he said. "Not quite yet." But he touched her breasts through her blouse and kissed her neck. She was shocked by how certain his gestures were, how practiced and confident. Her heart began to race again and she pulled away.

"Your fiancée?" she asked. "What is she like?"

He looked away. "I haven't seen her in fourteen years," he said, and his voice was suddenly cold, the way it had been the day before when she'd asked him about the asylum. She noticed that it was when his tone was unfriendly that he looked the most handsome. When he spoke of being afraid, his face looked ravaged, unformed.

She wanted to ask him again: Who was the girl? What was her name, and why, really, had he failed to return to her? Why did he grow so cold when Lili asked about her? But what right did she have? She barely knew him, though he was here, in her apartment, kissing her.

They went down into the street and he put his arm around her and tried to keep her warm, and they walked all the way to the river. He talked about Auvergne, how beautiful and wild it was, about the goats his family kept and how hard the little ones sucked on a human finger when they were hungry. He took Lili's index finger and sucked hard on it to show her. He described the intoxicating smell of the cheese house and how he could not bear to buy a single, overpriced *crottin* from a Paris *crémerie*.

She risked his coldness and asked, "If you love it so there, why have you stayed away?"

But he didn't pull back. He simply shrugged, leaning over the railing of the Pont Saint-Michel. Beneath them the water was swift and cold and black. "Oh, you know. . . ." He shook his head, revealing nothing but turning toward her and pulling her against him, holding her close in the black, frozen air. He spoke above her head.

"Why *does* one do things? It is such beautiful country, Lili," and he described it further: the steep escarpments, the river, the narrow road that cut through the village. She was only slightly interested in what he was saying, but she loved the strength of his arms around her, the heat of his chest against her face. His scenic descriptions floated out into the night, and she thought, surprised, He thinks the world is a physical place. Abstractions mean nothing to him.

This impression of him—of a man who apprehended the world

through his senses alone, like an animal—excited and repelled her. How much more surely he knew the world than she did, and yet how ignorant he was, how lacking in perspective. She realized that he was truly interested in what he was saying—it wasn't simply small talk—and this amazed her. He was utterly foreign to her. And yet he had seen something in her, when he described her fragile wrists, her fury, some tender and secret part of her.

"It's a good place to be born," he was saying. "And a good place to die. My mother died in her garden; my father died milking the goats."

She smiled, thinking, That is almost an abstract thought, "a good place to die." She was oddly thrilled, as if she had discovered something unexpected, and it occurred to her that what attracts a person to her opposite are moments of recognition, sameness, delicious because they are rare.

"Come home with me now," she said. "Come and spend the night."

"Not yet." He laughed. "There is all the time in the world for that." She felt embarrassed and tried to pull away from him.

"What's the hurry?" he said, lightly.

"Oh," she said, her body rigid, afraid. "To get it over with." But it wasn't that. She simply wanted him.

He laughed again, softly. "How strange you are, Lili. Come, it's time to go home. You have your tests to grade, and so, in fact, do I. May I see you on Thursday?"

"Not tomorrow? Not Wednesday?"

"I have to go to bed at a reasonable hour tomorrow and Wednesday, so that on Thursday—"

"What?"

"I don't know. Perhaps we'll go on a picnic."

"In the middle of winter?"

All day the next day, she wanted to weep, to laugh. She smoked incessantly. And in the evening, after all, he came again. His eyes looked feverish and he kept swallowing, as if he were parched. He did not want to make love. Only to lie in her bed and rest while she worked at her desk. Then he left, abruptly, and she was so happy because he hadn't been able to resist seeing her.

On Thursday, they rode their bicycles out toward Versailles and back, pedaling hard to keep warm. It was a clear, icy day and the fields on the side of the road were the same color as his hair.

"Will you undress for me?" he asked. They were standing in the middle of her apartment, still breathless from riding.

She stared up at him without answering.

He shook his head, embarrassed. "I just want to see you," he said.

"To make love to me?" she asked.

"Yes, of course, only not yet. Not quite yet. But if I could just see you once, in the meantime. Just see you. Not to touch, not yet."

"Why not?"

"Because everything takes time, Lili. There is nothing that doesn't take time."

She kept staring at him: his face looked softer, clumsier, than she had ever seen it, as if he would weep, and his large, square hands hung, lost, at his sides. He was still flushed from the ride, his eyes red.

She unfastened her shoes. Then, hurriedly, artlessly, she pulled her dress and her slip over her head, unfastened her stockings, pulled off her underwear. She stood naked, arms crossed, a little cool, damp with sweat. She watched him watching her, and her heart thundered in her ears. He stood across the room from her, perfectly still, with his red, anguished face, his violet eyes. She let her arms fall to her sides. After a long time, she turned around, so he could see her from behind. Then she bent over and picked up her clothes and put them on again.

They did not speak for the rest of the afternoon. He sat on the floor, leaning against Claude-François's trunk, his head flung back against the curved lid, weeping. She lay on her side on the bed; it was her turn to watch him now. The shuddering rise of his chest, his heavy, helpless, outflung arms.

When he left at last, after nightfall, he only kissed her hands. "I love you so much," he said. "So much."

He left, and she did not move from the bed. She lit cigarette after cigarette, and she could not stop crying. She watched the watery smoke float up toward the ceiling and dissolve, and she thought of Tante Alice, of crossing the Alps to find her. For she had not been this happy in years. He was stranger than anything she could have imagined, and yet he was exactly what she wanted.

She fell asleep, smoking, and burned herself awake with the embers. And suddenly alert, watchful, in the darkness of her room, she felt a pang of guilt for not having been to the list of the dead. And she thought how it is like believing in God, to be in love: it makes you forgetful, heedless. . . .

Seventeen years ago, when she was twelve, she had waded naked at dawn into an alpine lake while the rest of her family slept in an old chalet. It was the first time since she was a baby that she had been completely naked, because Maman had taught her to bathe without ever removing all of her clothes. They had gone to Haute-Savoie that summer, instead of the ocean as they usually did. . . . She couldn't remember why. Because Mademoiselle Duroc had had tuberculosis?

The mountains were beautiful: the white, suspended peaks and the Aiguilles, dark and jagged as their name, the Needles. Below was all soft, rich meadows, birch trees, blueberries. The chalet sat alone in a field, beside a stream. It was dusty and filled with mouse droppings. Maurice flicked the droppings at André, and André screamed; Lili hated them both—

At night she climbed out onto a low window ledge and sat in the chill darkness, her bare legs dangling into nothingness. She could smell the fog and the old wood, and nearby she could hear the cold rush of the stream. One night, she saw stars and, hoping the sky would stay clear and the morning not be blind with fog, she stayed awake, waiting. It was like sitting at the bottom of a cold, black lake, and the night went on and on, interminable. After a while she couldn't feel her legs or hands anymore and still the darkness was deep, impenetrable, unfading. She stared at the dense, brilliant stars which failed to light the earth, and eventually they seemed to move, to bleed together into streams of light. Then the darkness grew thinner. When the sky was almost gray, she slid down the splintery side of the chalet: the grass was cold and drenched and she ran quickly through it, toward the stream and along its edge, following the swift, rushing water, until she began to warm up, to sweat in her nightgown though her feet were wet and numb. When she reached the pool where the stream collected, she looked up, her face and scalp damp, the nightgown clinging to her skin, and the top of Mont Blanc was bathed in light. She knelt in the wet grass—a child, still, with a child's straight, innocent body—and thanked God for this proof of his existence, because what else could explain such height, such blinding snow, the murderous Aiguilles? Then she pulled off her nightgown and waded into the water so she could feel the cold more fully, could feel the snowcapped peaks here, where they dissolved into a pool of clear darkness. All the rest of that day, back at the chalet, she picked blueberries and made dollhouses in the roots of the trees. It was a warm, sunny day and every time she saw the white tops of the mountains suspended above the earth, she thought she was looking at God. She did not worry that no one loved André; she barely noticed him that day.

That was what it was to believe in God: to stand, naked and exposed, yes, and that was good; but was it good to believe that the Alps mattered more than a boy's misery? Was it good to be so infatuated with that blinding snow that you forgot everything else?

Still, with Pierre, even knowing that she must not forget the unhappiness of the world, she forgot: she stopped going to the list of the dead, stopped writing to Tante Alice. She did not drape the orange kimono at the foot of her bed anymore.

He told her more about Auvergne than she'd ever wanted to know: which mountains were to the east, which to the west, whose garden grew the best tomatoes. But it was the pressure of his thick arms, the helplessness of his face, that she loved. And his laughter, always directed at her, as if she were the most amusing sight.

He did not make love to her until February, and when he did, he was so slow, so patient, she thought she would go mad. When he was done, she would not wipe the spray of semen from her stomach—how it had surprised her, so thick and foamy!—but let it turn to a glaze across her skin.

In the morning, the concierge—an old, thin, black-haired woman who had been miraculously discreet for months—was waiting for them at the bottom of the stairs, her pale eyes cold with rage.

Lili smiled warmly at her. "Bonjour, Madame Bouts!" she said, and her voice was filled with Pierre's laughter, as if she had swallowed it into her lungs.

Four

Then, for weeks, she hardly thought at all anymore, she was so drenched in sex. All night long, she lay with him in her narrow bed and her skin ached. Her fingers were cold. Her mouth was thick and numb and she laughed too easily. It was difficult to form words, though they talked for hours, coiled together like twins, and it was impossible to tell when they were making love and when they weren't, they were so restless.

When the sky grew light, he would say, *We should sleep,* and though she was so tired she wanted to cry, she couldn't rest. She lay on her side, watching his eyes close, his mouth fall open, and with her eyes open, she slept. From the depth of her dreams, she felt his mouth on her breasts, his sleeping hands reach into her thighs.

In class, she was sick with impatience for the day to be done, for Thursday or Sunday, for Pierre to come over and wash her, limb by limb, in the bath. She was sure that Jeanine Roussel could smell her lovemaking. Poor Jeanine Roussel! For years, no doubt, she had heard how difficult and inspiring Mademoiselle Ravaudet was—and what did she find? A woman who forgot, midsentence, what she was saying, who was perpetually sore with love.

In the evenings, she ran down to the river, to the Pont Saint-Michel. She hung over the railing of the bridge and gazed at her own hand, reaching toward the water, veiny and thin, with a cigarette held loosely between two fingers; and she loved her hand for having touched Pierre.

Then, looking up suddenly, she would see him on the quay, emerging from the crowd of people, still in his schoolteacher's jacket, walking eagerly, head raised, searching for her. She ran to him, cigarette in her mouth, dimly aware of how scuffed her shoes were, how the hem of her skirt had fallen out.

"Lili!" he would cry, lifting her up to his height. "My God I thought the day would never end. . . ."

But sometimes, watching him walk naked across the bare floorboards of her room, she wanted to look away. There was something terrible in the sight of him, the way flesh and bones worked together beneath his skin: his long, solid legs, his broad back with the mole beneath his right shoulder blade. That he should have a body—something so specific, with such particular details—shocked her; she went to him, pulled him back into bed, for only lovemaking could obliterate what she had seen.

One day, he asked her again about her family. It was March: the river was raw and full, the earth swollen, and she could smell it all, the rain, the dirt, the green veil that covered everything. She burrowed her face in the crook of his arm and inhaled, for he, too, smelled different now, richer and warmer.

"You never speak of them," he insisted.

"Oh, my family! What? What is it you want to know?"

"You never visit them."

"Well! They're far away," she said, though the train ride was only an hour.

"I'd like to meet them," he said.

"Oh, Pierre!"

"I would like to know them."

"That's ridiculous," she said. She swung herself off the bed and went into the kitchen. She had not told him about André. *Have I mentioned there's suicide in my family?* She had not told him how cruel she had been as a child. To speak of it would ruin everything. She lit the stove under a pot of water and leaned, naked, against the sink. She didn't want any coffee; it was just something to do: make the water boil.

Pierre came up behind her and put his arms around her. She felt his stomach against her back and she wanted him, and was afraid. What they had—this comfort in each other's bodies—was infinitely precarious. Even if she didn't tell him about André—about her own meanness—real life, with all its tedium, would sooner or later reassert itself: Pierre would remember his fiancée. She imagined him leaving, putting on his clothes one last time and saying—what? Would there be anything to say, after all?

41

In the immensity of the city, they might never see each other again. She would forget the feel of his skin against her skin. A moment's revelation had brought them together, but now they must close everything off, keep out anything that could upset the delicate, erotic balance.

"What is it?" he asked. "What's wrong with your family?"

She sighed, thinking, After all, he has his own madness—but it was no comfort.

"The part about André I didn't tell you"—her voice was filled with dull, despairing laughter—"is that he committed suicide."

Pierre didn't answer, and, emboldened, she went on, "My father mocked him and my mother—my mother sat and watched. I was mean to him, too, when I was a little girl, but he told me I was his favorite. Somehow, by accident, my meanness didn't add up to the others'. Once or twice I did tell the other children to leave him alone. I must have—"

She paused. "My family doesn't know how he died, and they don't know that I don't believe in God. I see them as little as possible. I don't know why you'd want to meet them."

He tightened his arms around her chest and rocked slightly, back and forth. For a long time he didn't say anything and she was aware of nothing except the slight dampness of his skin against her skin, the hair on his chest pressing into her shoulder blades.

"Poor Lili," he said at last. "They are yours. Your family."

She laughed. "Yes, mine. I have stared at my mother for hours, trying to decide—what? If she loved him? If . . ." She shrugged. Pierre would not leave her because of this and she felt at once relieved and oppressed. She wanted him to let go of her, but she did not want to seem ungrateful. Through the grimy kitchen window she stared at the street below: at the strange, insectlike tops of the automobiles and now and then a woman's hat with a cluster of bright feathers on the brim. She tried to picture André's face and she wanted to scream, to tear the wallpaper into shreds.

The water was boiling and she reached over brusquely and shut it off. She laughed; that's all one's fury amounted to in the end: one shut the stove off brusquely. She should have clawed herself until she bled when she received André's letter.

She pulled away from Pierre and went into the bedroom, to the tall, narrow window above the courtyard. "Let's go to dinner," she called out. "And let's not discuss my family anymore, shall we?"

"Lili—!" He followed her into the bedroom, then stopped, flustered. "Lili, you're standing naked where anyone can see you."

42

"Yes." She laughed. "So I am. Would you make love to me here, where anyone can see us?"

"No." He smiled, but she could see that she had shocked him, and that made her smile. She hadn't shocked him with André's suicide, with her childhood cruelty, but with this, her desire to make love in front of the window. To stand naked and passionate where everyone could see her. To be dismissed from the lycée, reviled. To be set free.

"Let's get drunk," she said when they had dressed and gone down into the street. It had rained earlier, but the evening was light now, filled with the smell of water.

"You want me to give in and make love publicly!" He laughed.

No, she thought. I want to get drunk and smash my hand through a window, but she let him put his arm around her and lead her into a bar.

"I might," he said. "If I drink enough."

Instead, drunk, they went dancing. She had never danced before and Pierre had to teach her all the steps. She was too drunk to follow, and she laughed uncontrollably, but she loved the music, the heat of the bodies.

At the end of June, after the distribution of prizes, he asked her again about her family. He was solemn about it and this time it made her laugh.

"Lili—"

"Oh, for God's sake. Why don't we go to your little village and visit your sisters while we're at it? If we're going to get up out of this bed and go somewhere, let's go somewhere interesting. Let's go to Haute-Savoie."

"I want to meet your family."

"What is this obsession? Do you think that because we are lovers, introductions are in order? Really, let's start with your family."

"That's not possible."

"Because of the girl?" she asked, and his heart, resting beneath her hand, began to race.

She sat up, covering herself with the sheet.

"It isn't fair to go back as long as she isn't married." His voice was cool, formal.

"You're still in love with her."

43

"I want to marry you," he said, but his voice was remote, strained. "That's why I want to meet—"

"Oh for God's sake." She rose, taking the sheet with her, wrapped it around herself, and opened the window. She stood outside, on the narrow balcony. Everything was confused, broken by the bright, shifting light. She could feel his heartbeat still, beneath her hand. Who was this girl? What did she look like? She imagined some big peasant girl with yellow braids, but maybe she wasn't like that at all, maybe she was small and dark—*I want to marry you. That's why*—when he made love to the girl, did he clutch her shoulders, did the same look of desperation cross his face as when he made love to Lili? But he wanted to marry her. Marry Lili. *He wants to marry me.*

"Marry me, then," she said, but she felt as if he had emptied her out, taken something from her that she would always be trying to retrieve. *He wants me to marry him while he still loves the other girl. And I will. I will do anything.*

She went back to bed and lay motionless beside him.

He drew her toward him hungrily, and she said, "Your heart beat more quickly when I spoke of your fiancée."

His voice was suddenly easy, careless. "I'm not in love with her, Lili."

She thought, *That is possible. It's possible, but I will never know. Either he's lying and my whole life I will be made a fool of, or he's telling the truth and I ruin us both by my refusal to believe. I don't know which is worse.*

They made love and even the lightest brush of his fingers against her thighs hurt her; and her throat ached with the desire to cry.

The next day she took the train to Saint-Germain to visit her family. It was a warm, clear day, and she walked the long way from the station, through the park. She paused for a while, looking out toward the city, toward Pierre, and she was overcome with longing for him. She had the terrible feeling that she would never make it back there . . . then she laughed. She could smell Pierre still on her skin; of course she would go back. A quick lunch with Maman, Papa, Thérèse—she would just say what she had to say to them, make it short and simple—and she would leave.

It was Mademoiselle Duroc who answered the door. "Well, Lili! This is a surprise. I'll have to tell the cook—we weren't expecting you. Thérèse and Jean-Louis have just gone out, what a pity, it's just the old

44

folks at home today. This is a surprise. . . ." She babbled on, kissing the air beside Lili's cheeks, taking her coat. She dyed her hair and wore so much rouge now that, from a distance, she looked no more than thirty, though up close you could see the sag of her cheeks, the worn skin of her neck.

Lili glanced past her, her heart aching, toward the dining room. How still it was, with the golden, dusty light from the garden falling across the table and the three white soup plates, the six glasses: three for Bordeaux, three for water.

"Monsieur, your daughter is here." Mademoiselle still addressed Papa as *vous,* and Lili imagined that even at the height of passion they used the formal address.

Papa was sitting in the parlor, on the sofa where Lili had lain when she was sick, where all day she had watched the family sit down to an empty table until at last the messenger came with news of André. Papa was old now, with the red, shattered face of an alcoholic. He lowered his newspaper, pushed himself out of his seat, and said, "Well." He grabbed Lili's shoulders and, like Mademoiselle, briefly kissed the air around her face. "What brings you out so unexpectedly," he said, but there was no inflection in his voice. He reminded Lili of a child who has learned to say "please" and "thank you" but who has no feeling about the words yet. He sat down, cleared his throat, and took up his paper again. She sat in the chair beside him and lit a cigarette. How quiet the house was! Maman was still napping and Mademoiselle Duroc had vanished into the kitchen to tell the cook to make more soup. Lili watched Papa's liver-spotted hands holding the newspaper and her own stream of smoke dissolving in the air. Her whole body ached. Everything was so empty and motionless; it seemed as if nothing would ever happen, as if she would sit there in silence with Papa until he died.

She wished Maman would wake up, and for a moment the longing to be with her was as aching and passionate as it had been when she was a child. She wanted Maman to take her in her bed, in her soft, brown, flabby arms.

"Lili," Papa said, and suddenly he put down his newspaper again and patted her on the knee. "I'm glad to see you." He left his hand on her knee and stared at her, his eyes pale and old.

She looked away. You are a cruel man, she thought, driving your son to suicide.

She wanted to put her hand on his, to hold it to her cheek.

At lunch, Maman sat timidly at the head of the table, passing the leek soup, the bread, the wine, the roast and potatoes. She looked small and worn to Lili, her eyes dark rimmed, though she was still fat, her face youthful. Youthful and infinitely tired. She asked anxiously after the health of Lili's colleagues and students, as if she knew them personally, commented on the price of string beans and on the priest, who had a cold.

Papa sighed and burped and wiped his mouth often, but he did not join in the conversation. It was Mademoiselle Duroc, giving her opinion of the beans and the priest, who answered Maman, and Lili imagined it was always like this now: the two women giving their parallel reports of the world while their husband and lover sat wordlessly between them, making a great, noisy show of his old age. *Maman*, she wanted to say, *Maman*—what? Nothing, she didn't want to say anything. She wanted to curl up next to her on the bed.

"You've got good color in your cheeks," Maman said.

"That's what I said," said Mademoiselle Duroc.

"Are you still eating at the nice little restaurant down the street?" Maman asked. "You work so hard. It's important to eat well when you're working hard. Be sure to take some of the cook's flan with you when you go back. She makes such good flan."

"It's not as good as the baker's," said Mademoiselle Duroc.

"That's not true at all," said Maman.

"You always get it when it's a day old," said Mademoiselle Duroc. "That's the problem. You're always saving money. Your mother is always saving! On my day off I always go and have a slice of flan and a hot chocolate—"

"Saving on the little things gives you money for the big things."

"What big things? At our age! The baker's flan is so delicious when it's fresh, and with a nice bowl of chocolate. . . ."

When they were young, the two women barely spoke to each other; now they sat the whole day bickering.

"You never did tell us why you came out," said Mademoiselle Duroc. "Thérèse will be so disappointed to have missed you."

"Thérèse can take the train in to see her," Maman said. "We're the ones who are deprived of her company."

"The reason I came," Lili said, and Maman and Mademoiselle Duroc stared at her, as if her answering surprised them, "is to tell you something." She paused, terrified. She did not know what to say. "I

46

don't go to church anymore. I haven't gone in years. I don't believe in God."

Maman covered her mouth with her hand. Her face seemed to collapse, as if Lili had risen and struck her for no reason. Her gaze was as wide and frightened as a child's. "My God," she murmured, and her eyes darkened. She put down her napkin and left the table.

Papa seemed on the point of rising and following her, then he looked over at Lili. "You should have stayed in Paris."

He looked down at his plate of roast pork and potatoes as if it were something foreign and disgusting. He speared a potato, put it in his mouth, chewed, burped, and speared another. He ate methodically, one potato after another, his gaze never leaving his plate.

Mademoiselle Duroc leaned over to Lili. "It's only going to upset your mother more if you stay," she murmured.

A small, hard sound tore from the back of Lili's throat, like a sob, like laughter.

"Come back another day," Mademoiselle Duroc suggested. "And none of us will mention this again."

Mademoiselle Duroc was an idiot, but she was right. They must pretend Lili hadn't said anything. She might as well have murdered Thérèse, and then what was there to say?

Oh, Maman, I'm sorry. But surely there are other things we can talk about? Other points of interest? She rose. "Good-bye, Papa."

Mademoiselle Duroc followed her out. At the door she whispered, "But why did you have to say anything? Of course I don't care. I've never believed in God myself. And I knew perfectly well you didn't—but why couldn't it just be our little secret?"

Lili stared at her for a minute, at her small pursed mouth, the lipstick oddly threadbare—was she still Papa's mistress? it was impossible to imagine her naked under any circumstances—and felt a wave of disgust.

She wanted to run upstairs to Maman's room, to throw herself at Maman's feet and beg forgiveness. *Maman, I love you. I have always loved you.*

But what was the use? Nothing Lili could say would make up for her disbelief.

She refused Mademoiselle's hand and left.

The train was rocking, throwing her from side to side, the wheels turning over and over, through the green, blossoming countryside and back into the city. Now we're even, she thought. Now. . . . She dug her fingers into the leather seat and leaned her head against the cold, dirty window. She felt the way she did in dreams when she realized that she had killed someone. It was never André who died anymore. It was strangers, children, stray dogs. But she would awaken filled with the same inconsolable grief.

Pierre was waiting outside her apartment building. He ran toward her, to kiss her, then stopped. "Lili, what is it? You look terrible."

"They hardly saw it as a cause for rejoicing."

His face fell. "Because I'm a farmer's son?"

"What?"

"Is that why they were upset? Because I'm not—"

"What do you have to do with it?"

"You didn't tell them that we're getting married?"

She laughed. "I told them I was an atheist."

"But, Lili—"

"What?" She wanted to hit him. "You don't think I should have told them? You think I simply should have kept lying for the rest of my life?"

"No, Lili—no." He was embarrassed to be arguing in the street; she could see that. He didn't like to make a scene, to offend in any way. She had been that way herself once, and yet now—now? She couldn't bear all the little niceties. It was pointless to get married to him, to anyone. He didn't even love her as much as he had loved his fiancée. "Lili. Lili, of course you should have told them. I simply thought you would also tell them that we—"

"Oh, Pierre." All her fury drained out of her. She was tired. "I had to tell them I was an atheist first. So they wouldn't expect a religious ceremony." She spoke slowly, as if she were explaining something to a child. And of course it was a lie. She had gone to Saint-Germain to tell them about André. That was all she had been thinking. And then she had told them about God instead.

"Come on," she said, pushing open the door of the building—the concierge was mercifully out. "Let's go upstairs. Let's rest. Later we can go for a bicycle ride. It will still be light."

"Yes," he said. "I should have realized that. I hadn't thought about a ceremony."

48

She pulled the curtains and took off all her clothes. Then she climbed into bed. She heard his breath catch with desire, but she turned away from him, so that he would curl up behind her. "Sleep," she murmured, so heavy and weak with exhaustion that she could not shut her mouth.

When they awoke, it was dusk, and at first she did not know where she was, what she was.

Then she remembered: We are lovers, we are getting married.

And then: Lili. Pierre. We've slept all afternoon.

Neither of them had the strength to sit up; she could not even lift her head, her body was so drugged, but her heart was pounding with fear.

"Pierre," she whispered.

"Yes."

"I am a difficult person."

"Yes."

"Why do you love me?"

"You're interesting."

"Oh."

They lay together, awake and motionless, until the room grew dark and one of them spoke again.

"We should eat."

Three weeks later, they were married. She wasn't sure why they did it—why they didn't simply go on being lovers; it wouldn't have shocked anyone any more than her being an atheist—but she felt compelled to do it, to go with him in her scuffed shoes and her worn skirt down to the Mairie, to borrow a pair of witnesses from the couple in line behind them.

Lili almost laughed, saying her vows in the cool, dusty office. Everyone's voices echoed off the stone. Her mouth trembled and she was afraid.

Then Pierre was holding her hand, leading her back toward the light of the street, away from the grim, underfed court clerk, and past the Mairie's sad statue of Adam and Eve.

Outside, the day was bright and warm. They went to a café and sat for a long time, drinking coffee and smoking. He didn't usually smoke, but today he did. They didn't speak; she tried but couldn't think of a word to say.

She was as dazed and light as if she had not slept in weeks.

"When I was a little girl," she said, "we went to the ocean every summer. To Brittany. Pornic."

So they walked down to the Gare d'Orsay and bought two tickets for Pornic, for a honeymoon. They could stay there all summer, if they wanted. In the fall she would introduce Pierre to her family; in the winter, maybe, she would announce that she was getting married.

Five

In the gray light, fishermen left and entered the harbor, hoisting their sails, dragging their nets full of wild, flapping fish up toward the marketplace. The air was tangy and cold, though it would be hot by noon. Lili stood on a low wall beyond the harbor, staring at the seaweed tangled in the restless nets, at the sky turning violet, turning a blue so pale she could not breathe. Pierre stood on the ground behind her, resting his chin on her shoulder, holding her arms straight out at her sides like a dancer's.

They had been in Pornic for three weeks, and their hair had grown coarse, their skin brown and salty and tight. She wore a hat to keep the sun out, so she would not feel stupid in the midday heat, but it was no use: the sun came in anyway, and all day long she was stupid and simple-minded. She grew fat and she forgot her work, Maman, the way Pierre's heart raced when she mentioned his fiancée. She was overcome with pleasure at times and at other times filled with despair, and she never knew why she felt either.

It was their lovemaking that made her so simple, lovemaking and the hot sun and the cool morning air that washed over her like water. She fell backward off the wall, into his arms.

He laughed. "Shall I carry you to the beach?" But she jumped down and ran ahead of him, toward the ragged, barnacle-covered rocks over-looking the sea. On the way they stopped and bought two crepes from a woman at the edge of the market. Lili devoured hers in three bites and licked the sugar from her fingers, as hungry as a child. She realized that she was pregnant, but the realization had no effect on her; it came to her as information does in a dream: *Then I was pregnant, and we were walking along the rocks.*

They held their arms open for balance and the sky turned pink. The surface of the water, shimmery as the scales of fish, flashed violet and silver.

I was pregnant, she thought, trying to understand it, but she was distracted by the beach below. It was low tide, and the wet, rippled sand glistened with its endless pools and rivulets. The edge of the water was littered with the dregs of sea foam.

"Pierre," she began.

"Hm?"

"Nothing." She didn't want to tell him yet. She would save it, tell him when they were making love. Yes, then she would understand: *Now you are always inside me. It is not just this moment but always.*

Once, jumping from rock to rock as a girl, she had seen a couple embracing in the sand. She couldn't tear her eyes from them. She was not sure what they were doing and wondered if they might need help, clinging to each other down near the water. . . . Her mother and Tante Alice came up behind her, gossiping, and she ran ahead, hopping from rock to rock.

Oh, Maman, she thought. I'm pregnant. She was afraid she would weep, but Pierre slipped into a narrow fissure between two rocks, and she scrambled after him, not wanting to lose sight of him. She let him catch her as she jumped into the narrow cove, let him wrap his arms around her and pull her down into the sand. They had seen no one since they left the village and they made love right there, rolling over and over and over until their mouths and hair were full of sand. But she did not tell him. She didn't know what she would do with a child, but she was wildly, inexplicably happy.

Afterward, the sky was simple and blue; the vivid chaos of dawn drained away. Pierre walked along the beach collecting shells. He did this every day, and when he had made a big enough pile, he set them back in the sand, arranging them in the shapes of letters. He spelled out words—LILI, SEA, FISH, PEACE—the way children do. He had lots of games—he built castles, dug rivers out of the sand—and his earnest concentration filled her with love, but the games themselves bored her beyond words. He wanted her to join him, but after a clamshell or two, a moat, she found herself standing perfectly still, stupefied, desperate for the game to be over.

She walked to the edge of the sand and sat in the freezing water in her skirt, lit a cigarette, and blew smoke out across the sea. Pregnant, she thought, over and over, until the word dissolved into meaningless syllables.

How I would sit on the beach between your legs, Maman, in the endless hot sun. She remembered being alone on the beach with Maman. She did not know where the others were. She ran naked in the sand and Maman, sitting with her legs straight out in front of her, unbuttoned her dress, laughing. She remembered Maman's large, dark nipple, how delicious it was to sit in Maman's lap and drink. She must have been three years old. Maman fell asleep, finally, with her head beneath a parasol. Lili stood over her and watched her chest strain against the black fabric of her dress, its skirt tangled in her heavy legs, the lacy shadow of the parasol falling across her throat. Her mouth hung open, dark and rich, and she was covered with fine white grains of sand. It was like looking at a statue of the Virgin. You could stare and stare, and no one would tell you to stop. Then Maman opened her eyes.

"Are you married to God?" Lili asked.

"Hardly!" Maman laughed.

How amazing to think that Maman had had a sense of humor. If I had only remembered, she thought. But what? What then? Would Lili have made them laugh together before saying, lightly, perhaps, *Oh, Maman, I don't believe in him a bit.* And would Maman still have laughed? *Well, Lili! Who can blame you? What a funny, clever girl you are!*

She kept picturing them, laughing together, making fun. She threw the end of her cigarette into the waves, watched it bob for a moment and then go under. The cold water pulled and slapped at her bottom, her ankles, and the fabric of her dress clung heavily to her skin. Oh, Maman. She didn't want to laugh with her; she wanted to lie with her in her big bed, in her fat arms. I love her more than anyone in the world, she thought, appalled, and she rose abruptly, drenched from the waist down, and ran along the littered beach to Pierre.

He held up a tiny, perfect conch.

"I'm . . . ," she began, but she could not say the word.

"You're—?"

"Bored." She laughed. "I'm bored, Pierre."

"Do I bore you, darling?"

"No, not you. Not you. But all these projects, all day long."

"They're not projects, they're games. Didn't you learn to play games as a child, poor Lili?"

"Yes, as a child. But now—"

"Now—?"

"All I want is for you to hold me."

He laughed, putting his shells on the ground. Then he lifted her into his arms as if she were a baby. "You are insatiable." He laughed again, kissing her on the lips. "Insatiable."

"I have something to tell you," she said.

"Tell me," he said, still carrying her.

But it was impossible. What did the word mean, "pregnant"? She wanted to tell Maman first, then Pierre.

"I love my mother," she said solemnly.

"Well, naturally!"

"More than I knew."

He laughed. "You are the oddest girl I ever met."

She slipped out of his arms, into the sand. "Tell me about your fiancée," she said, suddenly remembering her, and she concentrated as hard as she could to recall everything she'd thought before the sun and his body and her pregnancy had made her so stupid.

He must tell her about his fiancée, the asylum, everything. Yes, he must reveal himself to her; then she would tell him that she was pregnant. "Tell me about how you loved your fiancée."

"Oh, Lili." He smiled. "Why don't you sing me a song instead?"

"What?"

"A song. Any song. Sing to me."

"But I've just asked you a question."

"I'll answer it later. Sing to me and then I'll answer anything you like."

"I'm tone deaf."

"Tone deaf?"

"Yes."

"But if I'd known—" He stopped.

She was suddenly, absurdly, afraid. "You wouldn't have married me?"

"Why, no. It's not that. Well! It doesn't matter. Sing to me anyway."

"Could your fiancée sing?"

"Oh, Lili. Probably. It doesn't matter."

"I can't sing."

"Nonsense, Lili. Everyone can sing."

"When the tide comes in," she said, her eyes burning. She felt, now, that she had to sing to him, however much it would humiliate her. "When the tide comes in and it's good and noisy."

She ran down into the water to be alone. She went far, far out until the water reached her waist. She was still in her skirt, and she moved slowly, heavily. After she sang to him, he would have to answer her questions, and then she would tell him. The water came up to her breasts, stinging and cold, and he was behind her, grabbing her arm: she couldn't swim and she had never been out this far before. She had no intention of letting herself drown, certainly not now, not pregnant, but he didn't know, so she let him rescue her. He took her back in his arms and carried her, his hands wet and slippery against her skin. When they reached the shore, they lay on the cold, wet sand, and she kissed his hands.

"You came to save my life," she murmured gratefully, and she thought that perhaps she would not have to beat the truth out of him after all. Perhaps it was simply enough that he loved her.

He sat up. "I don't want to have to do it again."

She gasped. How quickly happiness came and went! "I'm sorry," she said. "I didn't mean to frighten you, I was only—"

"Just don't expect me next time."

She stared at him. His face was as cool and handsome as she had ever seen it.

She stood up, her arms across her chest. She was shivering from the sea, despite the sun. "I wasn't going to go any farther," she said coldly. "Suicide doesn't run in my family."

"Oh, Lili," he said, looking up at her, his face as clumsy and soft as a child's now. "I forgot. I didn't mean it that way. Who would I be to speak of heredity?" He rose and took her hands in his. "Let's run back to the hotel and get warm. It will be lunch soon."

But what did you mean? she wondered, following him back onto the rocks, scrambling behind him. *What did you—?*

He stopped. "I've never liked chivalry," he said apologetically. "I've never been any good at it."

"Oh," she said, relieved. "If that's all. You needn't worry about that with me. I always take care of myself."

"Yes," he said. "That's why I love you."

She was so happy to hear those words; she wanted to hear them again and again, *I love you I love you I love you.* She didn't worry about the rest of it.

"I'm pregnant," she whispered, watching the muscles in his back as he leaped ahead of her, arms outstretched, from rock to rock. He didn't hear her but kept jumping, first to the right, then to the left, nimble as a child. She put her hand on her stomach and walked gingerly behind him. She stopped for a moment and was perfectly still, as if, if she were quiet enough, she might hear something.

"Coming?" he asked, turning around, and she jumped across the rocks to him. Midair, light as a girl, she laughed. How incredible to think that he was always inside her now, and how delicious these surges of pleasure.

The hotel keeper in the village, Madame Latour, remembered Lili from before the war—from the days of Maman and Papa and Mademoiselle Duroc—and she'd given them her best room, one with its very own bath.

For lunch she served them plates of oysters, shrimp, bread with sweet white butter. Lili devoured the oysters and the shrimp, but the sight of the butter, so smooth and greasy, made her feel as if she would throw up. Madame Latour, old and whiskered, smiled knowingly at her, and Lili had to look away, so close to tears was she.

They made love again, in the hotel room, after lunch.

"You don't have to pull out," she said, weeping, but he didn't understand; he simply thought it was a safe time, thought she was crying with passion. And she was: to be so sought after, to have her body explored this way, to see his face above his strong, thick shoulders dissolve. . . .

Exhausted, sore, they washed together. They sat face-to-face in the tub, her legs thrown over his, and he washed her arms, her throat, her swollen breasts.

"Your fiancée," she said. "Was it because you'd been in an asylum that you didn't go back to her? Did you think she wouldn't have you?"

"The asylum's all finished," he answered brusquely, getting out of the tub.

"Yes, of course," she said quickly. "But then why—"

"In the fables, Lili, curiosity always kills."

"This isn't a fable. Please."

"For God's sake, Lili." Then, rubbing himself with the towel, he gave an odd, disjointed laugh. "I've already told you. I didn't go back to her for the simple reason that she was waiting. I couldn't bear it."

Oh, she thought, realizing that he had been explaining himself to her, right from the beginning. He hated weakness; that was all. That was easy to understand, perfectly natural.

"I'm pregnant," she said, standing up in the tub.

"Lili!" He turned and burst out laughing and took her in his arms and suddenly all the day's odd tension dissolved. He swung her by the waist, still laughing; she had never seen him like this, and she imagined that this was a peasant's laugh, that in promising him a child, she was restoring to him his village, his mountains, his river. "That's why you've been so strange," he said happily. "Why you've gotten fat."

And though she thought, *I've always been strange, Pierre,* she laughed with him.

"You'll be a good mother, Lili."

She laughed again, happily, for he should know, he who had delivered goats and cows with his own hands.

She wanted to run back down to the ocean and have him carry her in the water. Just for the pleasure of it this time, not because he thought she was drowning.

He did carry her, and this time they were naked, and his arms and legs slipped against hers in the cold, salty water. She stood and let the waves knock her down; she made him laugh. She ran onto the shore and offered to build a sand castle or collect shells, anything. She could feel him watching her, looking at her differently.

A good mother, she thought. He was unchivalrous, but he loved her, Lili. Loved in her the things that should have repelled him—her sharpness, her strength—knew that those qualities would take them farther than prettiness.

When the tide came in, they scrambled onto the sage-covered hill and watched the ocean pound against the rocks. The water seemed miserable, beating itself on the stone, and Lili drew her knees to her chin, wrapping her arms around herself.

"Now," Pierre said. "You promised."

"Promised?"

"That you would sing."

"Oh, Pierre," she said. "I don't want to."

"You'll have to learn, for a baby."

"Surely you don't expect me to be a conventional mother!" She laughed. But the truth was she wanted to sing; she had always wanted to, ever since she was a little girl.

"Please," he said.

So she closed her eyes, and, still curled up, with her arms around her knees, she sang, as quietly as possible, *Fais dodo, Colin mon p'tit frère, fais dodo, t'auras du lolo.* . . . She was hot with embarrassment, but he joined her, singing the lullaby in a low, deep voice that made her want to weep. It was like André's voice, only heavier. Even off-key, she thought, even off-key, he loves me.

But he would not save her life.

She stopped, midverse, staring out at the violent water. Dusk was coming on, purple and gray, the darkness falling over them like rain, and Pierre kept singing, on and on above the sound of the waves: *Maman est en haut, elle fait du gâteau, Papa est en bas, il fait du chocolat. Fais dodo, Colin.* . . . Perhaps, after all, he didn't love her. He wanted her all the time, he covered her with kisses, and yet—how suddenly he grew cold, blank. She watched him growing dark as the darkness surrounded them; he could vanish midsentence almost, his body still there but his voice and eyes empty, and she wondered if he had always been that way or if it was madness, the war, that had done it to him: as if there were parts of him that had been erased. And yet when he returned, laughing, swinging her around—there was no one in the world like him, then, no one so frank, so unembarrassed, so true.

Six

Two years later, Lili woke sharply in the middle of the night, as she often did now, to the feel of Pierre's hands on her: hungry, ungentle, kneading. She waited a moment, heart pounding, her eyes open in the dark, and soon he stopped, his hands resting loosely on her stomach. Then he rolled over, away from her, and began to snore. She curled up in the opposite direction, her arms and thighs trembling, knees pressed hard against her lips. This was all that was left of their love-making, these nocturnal gropings, from which Pierre did not waken and of which he claimed no memory in the morning. If she roused him, *Yes, Pierre, yes, make love to me,* he jerked awake, frightened, did not know what she was talking about, hated her for disturbing his sleep. Otherwise, he didn't touch her at all.

She uncurled herself, reached hungrily for her cigarettes on the bedside table, sat up. Moonlight forced its way through the cracks in the shutters, its pale threads falling over Claude's crib.

"I'll leave you," Lili said aloud. Her hands were still trembling. "Soon, any day now, Claude and I will go away." Pierre's ribs rose and fell evenly, undisturbed. "Or maybe I will simply take a lover, bring him into our bed. We could make love right beside you; I'll bet you wouldn't even notice." He slept on, and she could feel that if she kept talking she would weep, so she shut up. It was the moment of her sleep that he had caught her in—some dream, something—that had made her respond so instantly to his hands. Sometimes, when he reached for her, she was only angry that she had been awakened for nothing. But tonight his fingers pulling on her breasts, jabbing clumsily between her legs, had made her feel as if she were dying, and wanted to die, wanted him to break her in half—then she woke, realized he was only dreaming, waited, stunned, for him to roll off her.

"I would have married the butcher," she whispered, "if he hadn't already been spoken for." His snoring caught for a moment, and then resumed. Nothing would wake him now, not even Claude, if Claude should suddenly decide to cry. But Claude wouldn't. He never cried at night, though right now she wished he would, wished he would scream and scream, just to distract her, to give her something to do with her body.

Even as an infant, Claude was quiet for nine, ten hours at a stretch. So it wasn't because they were tired that they never made love anymore; it wasn't even because her body was so changed: in her ninth month of pregnancy, when she stood, swollen and helpless, in the doorway of her study, weeping at the prospect of motherhood—it was her new study in the six-room flat they had moved into on rue Guynemer—he couldn't stop making love to her. "It will be fine," he'd said, stroking her hard, taut belly, running his hands along her varicose-veined legs.

"You'll be a good mother, Lili." She wept all the more loudly, choking on her sobs. She didn't want to be a good mother; she didn't want to be any kind of mother at all. She stared dully at her boxes of papers, journals, ashtrays, books that she had not found the strength to unpack, and she blamed Pierre, as if it were he himself who inhabited her, making her sick and slow and stupid. Naturally, she thought, he was more in love with her than he'd ever been: she could barely construct a complete sentence. When the baby came, she'd be too exhausted to think at all anymore. The cooking and cleaning would take it out of her; she'd be as numb as a factory worker.

"Hush, Lili," he murmured. "You'll be a wonderful mother."

"Leave me alone!" she begged, but her eyes were dry now, emptied out.

"It's all right, Lili. Sh-sh."

"Suppose I told you I don't want the child?"

He smiled anxiously. "I'm sure that's not an uncommon feeling, Lili."

She shut her eyes. The depth of her egotism filled her with shame. But there it was: all she wanted was solitude, the purity of memory, like the clean, voluptuous lines of sculpture. She pictured herself the instant before she fell in love with Pierre: slender and agile and bright, crouched before the dark, reclining statue at the memorial at l'Ecole Normale; if she had only touched the black marble instead of Pierre.

He began to kiss the back of her neck, her shoulders, and it took all her strength not to push him away, but that was the one cruelty she wouldn't allow herself: because as soon as he began to make love to her, his face grew soft and helpless. Impossible to suspect him! He kept touching her and she let him lead her down onto the square of carpet, and then there was no difference between the feel of his hands and the feel of her own despair: he could still arouse her, still make her hunger for this; so perhaps, after all, she would have child after child. She had given an abortionist in rue de Vaugirard a hundred-franc down payment, but she hadn't been able to go through with it. An old sense of sin came over her, and the fear of death, for she was a coward; and she fled.

She knelt above him, huge and swollen, thirsting—too late—for the cool, dark courtyard where she had waited outside the doctor's door—it was neatly swept, with a potted geranium in the corner—she pictured her pale, swollen hand on the doorknob and felt the weight of Pierre's hands on her back, the pull of his mouth: it was like drowning, and she could not resist. She was too cowardly to die, and the pressure of his hand behind her neck was so delicious. . . .

Now, as she sat in the dark with her cigarette, the memory of his hand curved around her neck was like a foul smell: something gone bad, rotting. He had not made love to her in more than a year. She got up, went to the window, and opened the shutters. Moonlight flooded the room, and she walked to the crib, lifted Claude into her arms. He was fifteen months old, a thin, pale, beautiful baby, and he let her lift him without resisting. His eyes fluttered, and he lay limp and wet in her arms. She changed his diaper and carried him back to bed with her.

How she adored Claude, after all! He was pulled out of her and she was torn open down to her feet; she heard herself scream, heard herself beg Pierre to save her, and then it was over. Claude hung upside down in the harsh air, the bright light; tiny, bloodied, his arms and legs moving like sea grass. And that was all she needed: to bring him into the light. The doctor put him on her breast, and her heart broke, it flowed into her milk, and she was not surprised to feel such passion; it was the very passion she had felt as a child when her mother's arms seemed to her the embrace of God. The invisible membrane that holds the world together dissolved, exploded.

She was happy beyond words, beyond thought. It was the very thing she had feared the most—a brainless, witless peace—but even now, fifteen months later, her mind restored (the sham of her marriage revealed!), she did not begrudge that early bliss; she had had the spring term off from the lycée (the directrice had been decent; even her parents had been decent: at least she was married—hastily, secretly— thank God she was married), and she sat all day in front of the bedroom window with Claude, her bare toes curled on the lip of the windowsill. When her arms grew tired, she lay him on a pillow on her lap and brushed her fingers across the soft, sparse strands of his hair, across his moist skin. He was beautiful and pale from the first, not red like other infants, and his eyes were the color of Pierre's, the blue of lilacs. She didn't read, or talk. She simply sat, holding a cigarette and watching the smoke and the sunlight move across his small, still body. Behind her, the bed was warm and disheveled, the sheets all wrinkled— the bed of lovers—and that was their world: from bed to armchair and back again. She did not even bother to brush her hair; she would have had to put him down too long to do it, and she was afraid that he would stop breathing then.

She didn't question why Pierre stopped kissing her after the night Claude was born, stopped touching her except through her clothes: light, fraternal pats on the sleeve of her kimono. It seemed simply a matter of politeness; she was so bruised still. And then, too, she'd been distracted by her own sudden lack of interest in him. She tried to hide how she felt; every evening, as soon as he came home from work, she told him how much she loved him.

What a fool she'd been, how innocent! It wasn't politeness; it was distaste. What else? But she didn't know that then. She didn't know anything in those early days.

She couldn't keep track of the days of the week, sitting there before the bedroom window, watching Claude sleep. The pale March sun washed over them both, and when he awoke, she put out her cigarette, let the old orange kimono fall open, and lifted him to her breast. Her nipple stung at first, and then, after a while, she could feel his suckling through her whole body, as if he were drinking from her belly, her thighs. *Oui, mon chou, tête.* . . .

And still it was not enough. His lips kept pulling, drinking in more and more. The small of her back dissolved, flowed into her breasts.

She could not imagine ever desiring a man again.

❧

She laughed softly, brutally. She couldn't imagine being free of desire now. She stroked the silk of Claude's hair, gazed at the endless rise and fall of Pierre's ribs. A big man. She couldn't stand to look at his shoulders, at the breadth of his back, at his head flung back against the pillow—to smell his sweat and his night breath—couldn't stand it and couldn't resist. She drank him in furiously. She almost touched him—she wanted to run her finger along his naked side, just to see if it would hurt her to do it—she closed her eyes instead, brushed her forehead against Claude's. Claude, still sound asleep, grabbed weakly for her, as if he were underwater.

Once, when Claude was three weeks old, when Lili still didn't want Pierre, when she still had no thoughts, Pierre had held Claude in the palm of one hand. Lili's heart beat painfully and her eyes welled up with tears, her breasts began to leak. But she forced herself to be kind, because of how cool her love for Pierre had grown, because it wasn't his fault that she had found something better. She didn't say, *Put him down, be careful, he's mine!* She said, "What a good father he has. We both love you, you know." It was André who had taught her to lie this way, to hide the ruthlessness of her heart.

She laughed softly again, bitterly, letting Claude explore her underarm, the loose skin of her elbow, the crook of her arm. At least Pierre is honest, she thought. At least he doesn't try to spare my feelings.

When Claude was three months old, Lili began to have thoughts again. It was like waking up from an anesthetic: at first she simply felt distressed, dimly aware that something was missing. Then she began to dream about the study at the end of the hall—it had been ransacked; someone had gone in and remodeled it into a sitting room; it was filled with ornate satin-covered chairs and glass figurines—she woke afraid, thinking, But what about atheism? and then, her mind springing into action, leaping forth like some young girl who has been casually napping in a field, she thought, Of course. This, what Claude and I have, this is what people confuse with God, because they lose it. And lacking the skill to find it again, they make it into something intangible and unattainable—but always waiting just around the corner: *When I am old, I shall know the love of God; when I am dead—*

and let their human relations degenerate into pettiness and cruelty. "Come, *chéri*," she murmured, lifting Claude from his crib, "let's go visit the study."

It was dusty, but it was hers, with its promising boxes of ashtrays and philosophical journals, its naked squares of sunlight.

"We've got to get to work," she whispered, and she put Claude on a cushion on the desk, fell to her knees, and tore open the boxes. She lit a cigarette and began to write.

When Claude awoke, she put down her pen and unfastened her blouse, but she kept smoking, sitting at her desk while he suckled, reading over what she'd written.

"Yes, darling, drink," she murmured, and she reached across his tiny, pale body and wrote the title for the hundredth time, *The Peril of Faith*. He sucked harder and harder and she thought that at last she could write what she had to without bitterness. So much awaited a person when he acknowledged the absence of God: the unequivocal pleasure of the body, the love of human beings.

"That's a good boy," she whispered, and she watched the words swim across the page, her body dissolving into his mouth.

All that summer, she kept him beside her; she wrote and hummed to him, wrote and nursed him, wrote and held him against her heart. She who had always needed absolute solitude just to think. But he was a good baby. He barely cried.

It was then, during the summer when she was finishing her book, that Pierre began to reach for her during the night. The first time she didn't realize that he was asleep, and she began dutifully to respond. After a few seconds he rolled off her. He knows my heart isn't in it, she thought, and she lay awake, unable to move or speak. As it turned out, of course, he wasn't awake. She realized this the second time and now she thought, He'll only touch me accidentally, in his sleep, until I want him again. And even in his sleep he stops himself. She was relieved that he did and so sorry for her relief that she brought him coffee in bed in the morning and kissed his forehead over and over.

Then it was September. Rain dripped down the gutter all day, and the walls of her study were unpleasantly cool and damp.

She had finished her book. She laid her head on her desk, her arms outstretched, and shut her eyes. She felt the way she did at the end of an examination: her heart beat rapidly, her mouth tasted foul, she couldn't move. *If I could weep!*

Claude lay in a basket on the floor beside her chair. Such a good baby. Even now, at six months, he slept most of the time. He didn't cry.

The edge of the desk dug into her breasts and her hands were loose and damp; her pen rested in the crook of her thumb. She was paralyzed with exhaustion, with terror. But she had shown parts of the book to Monsieur Girard at the Presses Universitaires, and he had promised her an advance.

Claude's eyes opened and she reached mechanically into the basket, lifted her blouse. *Yes, Claude. Yes.* But she was crying now, despite the comfort of his small, sucking mouth. Tears streamed into her ear, the hollow of her throat, onto his warm, blond head.

"I'm so exhausted," she murmured, and her voice was the voice of a child. "I'm hungry." She reached across the desk for a cigarette and lit it with her free hand. Now she was better. She stopped crying and she could feel her heart begin to quiet.

"I'm done," she whispered, stroking Claude's head. "We're done, *chéri*." His hair had filled out, but his eyes were still the pale blue-violet of his father's. She stared down at the tiny blue veins on his forehead and ears, around his throat, inside his arms. . . .

She would dedicate the book to him. Lying in her arms, drinking from her body, he had nourished her, given her the conviction she needed. She shut her eyes again. She must dedicate it to Pierre, to the one she had ignored, forgotten. Yes. Because that, after all, was the first hint of God's absence: the failure of love.

"Oh, *chéri*," she said, looking down into Claude's violet eyes. "If there is any hope for the whole miserable human race, it is in this kind of love, yours and mine."

She ought to play games with him—make faces and sounds, bounce him on her knee—but he didn't get excited about that sort of thing. Wagging tongues bored him.

Because you're too smart for that, she thought, grateful that he never responded to the idiotic squealings of the passersby.

She'd read to him from her manuscript, to entertain him, and she imagined that that would be his earliest memory: that the sound of certain phrases—*free of the insatiable desire for a god . . . the true morality of the atheist*—would always be linked with an image of light coming through naked windows and the smell of ink, of milk. He lay quietly in her arms, taking it all in.

He fell asleep, still sucking, but she did not put him down. Pierre was in the living room, no doubt, reading the paper. She ought to get up and tell him that she had finished the book. She might go out and get a bottle of champagne to celebrate.

She didn't move. What was there, really, to celebrate? Who could tell, until a hundred years had passed, if the book was any good? What was good was to sit in this room, with Claude, with the windows open and the light and the breeze falling over them. To be writing a book, that was good, naturally, because then people left you alone, and you got a bit of mental exercise while you were at it—but to have written a book? A few hundred pages that would be read—if they were read at all!—only by those who agreed with it at the outset? How sweet it had been to spend the summer in this narrow, light-filled room with the one she loved—but the school year began in two weeks. In a week the au pair girl from England that Pierre had hired was arriving. Lili put Claude back in his basket and rested her face in the palms of her hands. She was so tired. She had worked so hard, for so many years, to write this book, and now it was over and no one would read it and Claude would spend the days in the Luxembourg with an English girl. If she could have kept writing and crossing out forever, if the fall had never come. *Oh, Claude . . .*

She picked him up brusquely and went into the living room.

Pierre lowered his newspaper and smiled at them.

"I'm done," she said, tonelessly.

"Done?"

"With the book. I finished it."

"Lili—!" He rose and went toward her, but she turned away from him, sat down on the sofa.

"Lili!" he repeated. "That's wonderful news. You must be—"

"Exhausted," she said. "I am exhausted."

"Of course," he murmured. "Naturally . . . let me take the baby from you—"

"No!" she cried sharply, and Claude's eyes opened, but he did not even whimper at being woken. *Such a good baby. . . .* She shrugged miserably. "I have to give him up eventually, don't I?" She held him out to Pierre. "Take him."

"Lili?"

"Take him," she repeated, holding Claude in her outstretched arms.

66

She was afraid of what she might do—she was so tired, so numb, and no matter how hard you worked, it was never enough, everything was taken from you in the end, handed over and then snatched back—Monsieur Girard had praised her book for twenty solid minutes. That was all she had ever wanted—to finish her book and have it praised. She would have thrown herself out of a window eventually if she hadn't finished it. Yes. Yes. I should be grateful. I am grateful, oh my God. . . .

"Please take him," she whispered, her arms shaking.

And still Claude didn't cry, though he shook in the air. He lay in her trembling hands, limp, indifferent, and Pierre gathered him up, rocked him, and it changed nothing. He did not care who held him, Lili or Pierre or some English girl. He never cried for her, never reached his arms toward her, and that's why he was such a good baby. She could have left him alone all day in the dusty little study and it wouldn't have bothered him as long as someone fed him; he did care about food. But it wasn't her presence, her murmuring voice as she read her manuscript to him, that kept him peaceful. Because it wasn't peace. It was something else, more terrifying.

Pierre was rocking him, cooing at him, and she could see that he was still limp and expressionless. Like a sleeping baby, though his eyes were open.

"What is it, Pierre? Why doesn't he react to things?"

"He's fine," Pierre murmured. "Fine. He's a good baby."

"I've had such a fantasy, that we were working together on the book—that I was teaching him philosophy!"

"Well, that's a bit much, Lili! He's six months old—"

"He doesn't roll over yet—"

"Of course he does!" Pierre said, rolling Claude over on his lap. Claude let himself be positioned, as passive and remote as a rag doll. "He's a good roly-poly baby—"

"Oh, Pierre." She knelt beside his chair and put her head in his lap. A wave of gratitude washed over her: he was, in fact, a good father, a good man. She remembered how she had loved him in the beginning, with what fear and hunger. And then she had had Claude and in her heart of hearts she discarded Pierre. But he was a good man. If she could learn to love him simply, gratefully.

"I have been so self-centered," she murmured. "My baby, my book, my pregnancy."

"Why Lili," he said, patting her head. "I don't know what you mean. You're a wonderful mother. Just as I predicted!"

She looked up at him, grateful even for his lack of insight. She noticed the fine, hairline cracks around his eyes and thought, My God, how suddenly youth disappears, and she wanted to spend the rest of the afternoon in bed with him and Claude; to have this day, wholly and without haste. In the quiet of their bedroom, with Claude asleep beside them, they would make love, and she would not be false with him.

"Shall we go to bed?" she said.

"To bed?" Pierre laughed. "It's the middle of the day."

"Oh, Pierre, I didn't mean to sleep. I meant to make love. I have been a poor lover to you."

He blushed. "But the baby—"

"He'll nap," Lili said lightly.

"It's the middle of the day, Lili."

"What of it?"

"Actually. . . ." He looked away. "I have some preparations to do for my classes."

"What?" she asked.

She still remembered the sound of her voice—*What?*—light, almost lilting, a voice of such innocence, *What did you say?* knowing the answer before the words were even out of her mouth: *He doesn't want me. He hasn't noticed anything because he has no interest in me anymore.* It was in his eyes, in the way he held his body: stiff, a little pulled back. She rose quickly, took Claude, and sat in the chair across from him.

"Yes, of course," she said politely. "I'd forgotten how soon classes start."

In the night, he must not know who she was. He must think she was someone else. Her body felt loose and ugly, and she pressed Claude tightly to her heart. He allowed himself to be squeezed, but he did not respond, and Lili began to weep, she was so tired, tired and confused. . . .

"What is it, Lili?" Pierre's voice was frightened, guilty.

"School," she said. She didn't know what else to say.

"Oh, Lili." He laughed, relieved. "You'd hate to give up teaching. You must be exhausted from writing your book. You get so carried away with things. We need to celebrate, that's what we need to do. You've finished your book!"

She gestured helplessly. "I thought you had work to do."

It was as if she'd slapped him. "I do," he stammered. "But this is important. Your *book*."

"Well," she said with a sudden, terrible cheer, "I'd like to celebrate by making love."

"Oh, Lili," he said, and he looked back down at his newspaper, smoothing the crease against his thigh.

Then he rose, took Claude from her arms, carried him back to his crib, returned to Lili, pulled her up from her chair, and kissed her. His lips were dry, thin. She turned away.

He sighed. "What, then? What do you want?"

"For you to want—"

He let go of her, dropping his arms to his sides. "I don't know . . . ," he began, then he gave up. He sat back down and shook out his newspaper.

She went to the bedroom and locked the door, leaning against it as if he were pursuing her, as if she must escape him. She thought of his fiancée, still waiting for him in Auvergne—Lili might wait as long in the end. In despair, she lifted Claude out of his crib and buried her face in his hair. He didn't respond. They were both indifferent to her, Claude and Pierre, and she didn't know why, what she had done wrong.

Now, in the moonlight, she kissed the sleeping palms of Claude's hands. He wasn't indifferent to her—what an idea! He was simply deeper, subtler than other children. He wasn't a monster like other boys, running everywhere, breaking things; he did not walk yet—but boys often walked late!—he pulled himself from place to place like a slender sea otter. Yes, an otter, a sea angel, with his gentle, waving limbs, his lavender eyes. He was happy enough during the day with Mary, the English girl, but when Lili came home from work, what a flood of infant babble, what wild, uncontrollable smiles. Other boys might talk and walk at fifteen months, and look what they grew into: cold, conventional men. Claude was wiser, lovelier, than any of them. As soon as she came home, he reached for her and buried his face against her breasts. Hurriedly, she unbuttoned her blouse, unfastened her brassiere. "Was he good?" Lili would ask. "He is good," Mary would answer, looking away, her pale cheeks reddening. Mary was a nice girl, tall and thin with long black hair, but she was deeply British. She couldn't bear the sight of Lili nursing.

"You should have married an Englishwoman," Lili murmured, laughing, her laughter lost in Pierre's snore. But it wasn't an

Englishwoman he needed; it wasn't prudishness that had driven him away.

At first, after that day in the living room, the day she had finished her book and discovered that Pierre didn't want her, she wanted to make love with him because she thought their bodies simply needed reminding; once they held each other naked they would remember everything: the way skin felt at the beginning, sore and hungry. That was when she began to wake him when he reached for her during the night, and he jerked away from her, *Lili! What is it, what are you?* Then from thinking about it so much, maybe, she simply wanted him. Seven times this year she'd asked him to make love to her, and each time he refused. It was as if she'd asked him to do something absurd and distasteful, like defecate in the street.

But Claude was a good boy. Claude was good and Mary was good and even her students were good this year. Pierre, in his way, was good: he was kind to Lili, solicitous of her. He simply didn't want to make love with her. She still didn't know why. It was nearly summer vacation; he had been refusing her for so long now, and she had studied him, searching for signs of another woman, a man, despair, something; he gave no clues. He told her the facts—*I was in an asylum, I was supposed to marry a girl, I don't want to make love, I am unchivalrous*—but he explained nothing.

All year, he had come home in the evening at the usual time, had sung to Claude, without complaint had eaten the dinners Lili made—boiled cabbage, sardines, a slab of pâté—and spent the night calmly correcting papers. He never expressed the slightest irritation with this dullest of tasks but simply sat at his desk, writing "false" over and over in the margins in his neat, even handwriting. He was a good teacher; he obeyed the law.

Once a week, on Sunday, he took a brief, perfunctory bath. He stood in the enamel tub with a sponge in his hand, washing beneath his arms, beneath his testicles, quickly; rubbing himself with a towel while Lili stood, leaning up toward the mirror above the sink, touching the skin around her eyes, her mouth; she pretended to be examining herself for wrinkles, though her eyes were glazed: she simply wanted to stand in the bathroom with him while he washed.

She hated him and would have left him but for the way he treated Claude. He held Claude so carefully, and his face grew soft and clumsy, the way it used to do when he was first in love with Lili—how could she not want him then? One night she saw him leaning over Claude's crib—the broad shoulders, the large, square hands—his back was trembling and she heard him catch his breath: he was weeping. She stood in the doorway, transfixed, and she drew her breath in to cry out: Why was he weeping? What was there to weep about? And then she remembered how he wept when he loved, how he had wept when she undressed for him.

"Sweet darling," she whispered, blowing against Claude's face. She put her breast to his lips, but he really was sound asleep; he didn't want to nurse. So she rocked him some more, watching her cigarette smoke dissolve in the moonlight. Claude smelled sweet and warm, like her own milk, like the faint sweat of her armpit where he rested. But there was another smell, too, wholly his, something animal, like the ground in spring. She put her nose in the crook of his neck to smell him better; for a moment the pleasure she took in his small, pale body became confused with her desire for Pierre, and she thought, desperately, I could make love with Claude. She rose hastily and put Claude back in his crib. There was something rotten at the heart of her life. She was no different from André, taking love wherever she could find it; an older boy once accused André of fornicating with a chicken, because the one who should have loved him didn't—Maman would stiffen slightly when André went to kiss her.

But Pierre had asked to marry her. He had loved her once. Something had happened to him the night Claude was born, but she didn't know what. Had he lost interest in her simply because she had begged him to save her? Or was it something else? The sight of her covered with blood? The realization that he couldn't abandon her now, even if he wanted to? She had to do something—seduce him, kill him—or she would lose her mind.

She curled back up in the bed, her knees pressed once more against her lips, and shut her eyes so she wouldn't see the summer moonlight, the crib, Pierre's wide, naked back. She wouldn't sleep, but she wouldn't be tired either. When he woke her like this, she stayed alert for days.

She might try to be seductive, like other women, if she could overcome her sense of the ridiculous. Overcome her horror. What? A lace brassiere? Some lipstick? She laughed silently, furiously. No one in her family except André ever begged for love. Her mother lived side by side with Mademoiselle Duroc and never groveled once. Only André kept trying; morning after morning he had thrown his arms around Maman's neck, stupider than a dog.

She imagined pulling Pierre's head so far back that it snapped in two. Over and over she pictured it, till she was dreaming, and the bells from Saint-Sulpice woke her to the brilliant, cloudless blue of the whole morning pouring in over the balcony.

Seven

After breakfast, brazenly, giddily, dully, she put Claude in his carriage and took him with her to a hairdresser on rue de Rennes. She had never been to a hairdresser before, and the young man eyed her with obvious disdain.

"What a pretty baby," he said in a flat voice, glancing quickly and distastefully into the carriage.

"Oh, do hold him up," squealed a woman two chairs down who was having her hair curled by another young man. "Let me see!"

"He's sleeping," Lili said, wondering if she would be able to go through with this after all—to have to sit in this scented salon with these two cold young men and an idiot woman! "I'm afraid I'd wake him." Claude wasn't a bit asleep, in fact: he was simply lying on his back, gazing peacefully at the ceiling.

Her hairdresser saw this but said nothing, whipping out a long bib and fastening it quickly around Lili's neck as if he'd caught her. He took Lili's head between his hands and pointed her straight at the mirror.

"What would you like?" he asked, still in that same flat voice.

She could not meet her own gaze. "Something romantic," she whispered, staring down at the litter of scissors and pomades on the counter. "With allure." Then she smiled. How easily she fell into acting stupid, she thought. Perhaps that's why so many people did it. It was so simple, so effortless . . . she might do it more often.

"With allure," the young man said flatly.

"Yes, allure," she repeated more loudly, emboldened, enjoying the charade: they were all pretending, as if they were children.

"A bob," the young man said. "Some curl, I suppose."

"Exactly," Lili said.

"Oh, yes," said the woman two seats down. "That's what I'm having done."

"Really?" Lili murmured, as if half of Paris didn't have its hair bobbed.

"It will require maintenance," her hairdresser warned, his hands still clasped around her head.

"Oh," Lili said. "How much?"

"Every week."

She hesitated—but why not, after all? It wouldn't kill her. And she couldn't imagine that missing a week now and then would be so terrible.

Afterward, he gave her her hair—which he admitted was lovely—in an envelope. She promised to be back in a week. The sight of herself with her short, curly hair was strange, but it had no effect on her. She felt, still, as if she were in a child's game and soon it would be time to stop, to go inside and rest.

She bought dark red lipstick, some perfume, an ivory-colored sundress, and matching ivory sandals. Through it all, Claude lay on his back, staring up peacefully as sky turned to ceiling and back again to sky.

It was almost noon when Lili returned home, and Pierre was in the living room, reading. He did not look up when she came in and she went straight to Mary's room.

"Would you be so good as to take him to the Luxembourg for a few hours?"

Mary looked up from the French grammar book she was reading, saw Lili's outfit, heard her request, and blushed. *These French,* she seemed to think. *At any hour . . . !* She left quickly, as if afraid the lovemaking might begin before she was out the door.

Lili stood in the living room, waiting for Pierre to stop reading.

"There's a smell . . . ," he began, and then he looked up. "Well! Look at you."

She turned around self-consciously. "Do you like it?"

"It's a little frivolous," he said. "But it's not bad. Is that perfume you're wearing?"

"Yes," she said, turning to face him again, thinking, I must not lose heart. . . .

"It's a bit strong," he said.

"Would you like to wash it off me?" she asked, but now her ears were ringing; her palms were cold and wet.

"What?"

"Would you like to give me a bath?"

"But you've just gotten all dressed in your new outfit—"

She would not give up, no matter what. She went to him and knelt beside his chair, took his hand, and laid it in the space between her breasts. "I could get undressed," she said, but her voice was trembling, uncertain. His hand lay coldly on her heart.

"Lili, Mary and Claude might come in at any minute—"

"I sent them away for a few hours."

"Why?"

"Because I want you." Her voice was hoarse and garbled, but she could see that he had no trouble understanding her: his face was drawn, his shoulders slumped. As if I had beaten him, she thought, her eyes burning.

"I'm tired," he said finally. "Hungry."

She rose, trembling, let out a short, hard laugh, and ran down into the street.

The butcher's wife was just locking the door for the afternoon, but, seeing Lili, she opened up again. The butcher refastened his apron and leaned nearsightedly toward Lili. They both watched her, smiling their soft, provident smiles, waiting for her order.

"It's a lovely haircut," the butcher's wife said.

"Thank you," Lili answered, unable to look at them. "Thank you for staying open."

"What can I give you?" the butcher asked.

"Tongue," Lili said, her gaze still fixed on the sawdust that covered the floor, absorbing the day's drops of blood. "A whole calf's tongue."

"Ah," said the butcher warmly, "guests?"

"Yes." Lili glanced at him briefly and smiled. But the butcher had already turned from her, his large, heavy hands clasping the meat.

"And with that?"

"A blood sausage."

"And with that?"

"A roast."

"And with that?"

"A kilo of smoked ham."

At last the butcher paused. "Have you an icebox, Madame? Meat

75

doesn't keep, you know." He spoke to Lili as gently as if she were a child, but if she looked at him again she would weep.

"Yes," she said in a new, strange, shrill voice, her eyes fixed on the upside-down gaze of a veal calf. "An icebox." Then she turned and poured a hundred francs into the hands of the butcher's wife. "Thank you. Thank you. Good afternoon!" she cried, letting the door chime closed behind her. If she had stayed a moment longer, she would have embraced them.

Pierre was sitting at the dining room table, his head in his hands. He looked up when she came in, his eyes full of pain, of a kind of grief. Neither of them spoke.

She unloaded the raw meat and the ham onto the table, and he did not move, but he watched her, his eyes following her hands.

"Eat," she whispered. "Eat if you are so hungry."

He hesitated, then he reached for the parcel of ham, unwrapped it, took out his pocketknife, and cut off a piece. He slipped the ham from his knife into his mouth, like a peasant, and he chewed slowly, cutting off bite after bite, his gestures slow and deliberate.

She sat opposite him, lighting one cigarette off the end of another until he had eaten the entire kilo of ham.

Then he wiped the back of his hand across his mouth and stared beyond her, toward the windows that faced rue Guynemer and the Luxembourg.

"I'm sorry I've disappointed you," he said at last, flatly.

"For God's sake—"

"I am sorry," he repeated more sincerely, looking at her now.

"Just tell me why. What is it? What have I done?"

"Why is it so important?"

"Important?" she cried. "What? To make love? To love one another? To desire? What is it exactly that you think is not important?"

He shrugged. "The act itself—like animals."

"Oh, God, Pierre." She looked away from him, stunned. "What if it is? Is that evil?"

"You're the one who celebrates the intellect. 'Let animals, who lack our intellectual capacity, console themselves with the notion of God—' "

"That isn't what I wrote. What I wrote was that man invented God to—"

"Yes, yes," Pierre interrupted. "You protest too much with your atheism, Lili."

"Fine! I protest too much, I desire too much. What of it? If you can no longer see the appeal of making love, why must you make it evil?"

"I didn't say it was evil, only unimportant."

Her arm struck his cheek, and she clutched violently at his hair, the way she used to clutch at Maurice's hair when they were little—he stopped her.

"For God's sake, Lili. Do you think we need another child?"

"What?"

"Another child." He sat down heavily and for a moment he seemed as if he would weep.

"But what are you talking about?" she cried.

"Lili," he said. "Oh for God's sake, Lili. We—you, *you* have more than you can handle already—"

She hit him again, her arm swinging against the side of his face like a stick. He did not resist her, letting her hit him until she saw that his face was bruised, and she stopped. "I don't know what you mean," she said. She was breathing heavily and the new ivory-colored sundress was damp with sweat. "Whether you think I am a deficient mother or he is a difficult child—but there is nothing wrong with either of us. I'll tell you the truth. You haven't touched me since the day he was born, for the same reason you never returned to your fiancée, the reason you went into an asylum: you're a coward. You can't kill anyone, you can't love—"

He was gone. She barely saw him leave, only the chair skidding across the floor, the terrible clatter of wood on wood, the door slamming; the apartment was perfectly silent.

She went, numbly, to pick up his chair, to put it back in its place. Then she knelt on the floor and laid her cheek on the hard wooden seat. Her breath still came too rapidly, and she was drenched with sweat.

I'm ugly, she thought. It's as simple as that. I am hard and without charm. And then: *Of course. He has returned to his prostitutes.* The realization was so simple, so obvious, that it came to her like actual evidence: a love letter left in his coat pocket, the smell of another woman on his clothes.

She felt sick. Naturally, there were plenty of occasions for him to slip out for an hour or so. She had searched so carefully for signs of a single other woman—someone he might have been in love with, who would beg him to stay an extra fifteen minutes—that she had forgotten the possibility of a hundred, who would leave no individual traces, cause no disturbance. It was no comfort to think that he had not fallen in love with anyone; he loved a way of life, loved the anonymity of whores.

But behind her despair—how could she compete with a prostitute; she, who watched him wash, who shared his bed?—she was afraid: Didn't he want more children? He had spoken of children the way a man, running from wild dogs, throws off a piece of clothing to distract his pursuers—and yet didn't he want any more? Didn't he? She couldn't think about that. Doing so was like staring wide eyed at the sun. Besides, she must compete with the prostitutes; there must be something she could learn from them: an attitude, a gesture, something. . . .

The front door opened. Pierre was talking to Mary in a friendly, animated voice, asking her questions about the south of England. They had run into each other at the end of the street and Pierre had come back upstairs to help her with the carriage. Lili rose and greeted them warmly in the hallway.

"Did you have a nice time in the Luxembourg?" she asked, taking Claude from Mary's arms. "Did you, *chéri?*" He leaned his soft, pale head into her shoulder. "Did you have a nice time, Mary?"

"Oh, yes, Madame," Mary answered brightly.

Pierre stood, towering above them all, smiling as brightly as Mary was. They were all smiling, as if everything were perfectly fine, as if Pierre's cheekbone were not blue and swollen.

I will visit a whorehouse, she thought. Why not? I've nothing to lose. It will be more interesting than going to the hairdresser.

In the evening, after Claude had gone to sleep, she left the apartment without a word. It was past ten and the street lamps floated like yellow fish in a dark blue pool. She took the *métro* at Saint-Michel, changed at Strasbourg–Saint-Denis, and went to rue Montmartre. She had never actually been on this side of the National Library before, and suddenly she was afraid to go aboveground. As if, up there, the girls from the Folies Bergères danced in the street, and the onlookers wore no clothes; as if she might see Pierre—whom she had left in the living room, engrossed in Alain-Fournier's correspondence with Jacques Rivière—making love on a street corner.

She stood at the bottom of the stairs, hesitating: if only she could find a fat, aging prostitute who would take her in and . . . what? What did she expect to learn from a single encounter? No, she would have to come here again and again, to make it her world as it was his—and then? Then maybe he would love her again. Then everything would be all right. They would be a family, finally. Not like other families, but more irreverent, more profound. Did Pierre not understand how much subtler and more interesting Claude was than other children?

Still, she was shy about going up. Years ago, out of curiosity, she'd bought a copy of *Le Sourire*. It was full of badly written tales of adultery, advertisements for aphrodisiacs, racy jokes, sketches of women wearing nothing but slippers. She'd been struck, at the time, by the friendly tone of the little monthly. Of course it was cheap and tawdry, but there was a warmth to its humor, a sort of collegial friendliness in the letters between women advising one another on their extramarital affairs. There was even an advertisement for a dentist, and Lili had wondered why a dentist would advertise in such a magazine; she imagined his waiting room filled with heavily painted, half-dressed women, all moaning with toothaches. But of course prostitutes had toothaches, colds, liver ailments, like anyone else. They were just women; there was no reason to be shy.

But she was afraid of derisive laughter behind delicate painted fingernails. *What is* she *doing here? Who does she think she is?* She had changed from her sundress and sandals into her ordinary clothes; everyone would know her for a schoolteacher.

She was surprised, finally, climbing up into the balmy gaslit street, at how ordinary the neighborhood seemed. Ordinary men and women sauntered past the *métro* station with folded newspapers, parcels; with loose, lovely hands; with the weariness of a day's labor in their necks. Lili turned down a side street, clutching her jacket—Claude-François's jacket—though she hardly needed it. She passed a bar, and through the window she could see the men at the counter, smoking and drinking, laughing loudly among themselves, the way they would in any bar in the city: unhurried, cheerful, continually putting off the moment when they must put on their coats and hats and venture alone into the night, back to their wives, their families, their homes, where there were no funny stories, just children with colds, and bills to be paid, a million things to do and everybody tired and dissatisfied. . . . So someone would tell one more joke and another man would respond, telling a story, revealing more than he would like to, but it was important to keep laughing, not to pause long enough for any man to say *I've got to get going, boys. . . .*

Beyond the bar was a newspaper and magazine shop and across from that, on the right, a dusty-looking pâtisserie with a few tired pastries in the window. The windows of the newspaper and magazine shop were filled with scandal sheets and girlie pictures, and bits of litter floated in the gutter, but over the shop was a lovely curved balcony and a lace curtain.

Two boys ran past her down the street, chasing each other. She watched them disappear around a corner, and looking at her feet, she saw a thin red stream in the gutter. She stopped, thinking it was blood; but it was only the reflection of a red lamp shining into the brackish water from a window above. She stared at the red-lit window and forced herself to press the bell—then, like a schoolboy playing a prank, she ran as fast as she could.

She turned on one street, then turned again, going more slowly, dawdling even. She saw another red light, and another, but she did not press the houses' bells. She realized that if she wanted to see more energetic commerce she should go to the place Pigalle, but she liked these quiet streets with their occasional red lights between rows of ordinary houses. Now and then a housewife reached out to close a shutter or call brusquely to a child and disappeared inside.

She walked down a narrow, dimly lit street in which no one seemed to live or work at all. She was about to turn when she saw, on the other side of a large, street-level window, like something displayed in a shop, a half-naked woman sitting in an armchair. Lili stopped. The woman wore only a pair of black net stockings and a yellow shawl, which barely covered her breasts and gathered in a silky fringed pool between her legs. She stared blankly into the street, her legs spread, her ringless hands resting on the arms of the chair. She did not seem to see Lili at all. It's rude to stare, Lili thought, but she could not tear herself away. The woman was fat—her bare, pale stomach fell over the silk fringe, her thighs spread across the edge of the chair—and she did not move at all, her gaze fixed somewhere above Lili's head.

Lili's heart beat painfully, and she wanted to keep staring as long as possible, to understand, to gaze without haste at every fold, curve, wrinkle—

The woman's hair, piled messily into a bun, was artificially blond, but there was, still, a deep, inflexible plainness about her: she wore no necklaces, had no beauty marks, had applied no lipstick, and in her broad face, her eyes look red and almost lashless.

There was something forbidding and judgmental in her refusal to adorn herself. She is like a nun, Lili thought, inviting fascination with her ugliness. Yes, like nuns, whose terrible secrets—the baldness, the celibacy—they proclaim everywhere, revealing nothing. Lili could stare for hours at those white, naked thighs and come no closer to understanding than she'd ever been. The woman was as removed from ordinary life, as hidden behind her dull gaze, as if she'd worn a habit.

And then again, she was offered up to the gaping stare of any passerby: that immobile body. She was at once brazen and vulnerable, so that Lili flushed with a strange excitement, with the simultaneous desire to be her and to hurt her—she looked up and saw again the woman's soft, aging face and she wanted to throw herself on the sidewalk and beg forgiveness, to turn her back to her and guard her privacy. But just then the woman moved her fat, bare hand down between her legs, lifted the fringe for a fraction of a second so that Lili saw nothing but darkness, and returned to her original position. Her eyes did not move at all.

Lili turned to leave, the blood pounding in her ears, but her way was blocked by another woman, even fatter than the one in the window and very short, with the same blond hair and pale, empty face. This one wore a red dressing gown. "So?" she said, her voice low and harsh.

"I'm sorry," Lili stammered. She wanted to weep. "I shouldn't have—" but she did not know what to say, and she could not make her voice rise above a whisper.

"So?" the woman repeated. "What is it you want here?"

She wanted to leave, to run away; she was so ashamed that someone had found her.

"We don't serve lesbians," the woman hissed in her deep, gravelly voice.

"I'm not . . . ," Lili began.

"Well come in," the madam said, apparently changing her mind. "There's one who'll do it. But she charges double."

She opened the door to her house, and Lili, despairing, followed her. This is what I came for, after all. And her own curiosity, mixed with an inability to say no to the madam, sickened her. Yes, it is like being with nuns, the fear and the shame, their superior knowledge.

The madam led her down a narrow, dimly lit hallway filled with the stale odor of alcohol and wet wool.

"The woman in the window," Lili began, and the madam laughed shortly.

"She's busy." She threw open a door, and Lili found herself in a room of a dozen or so half-dressed women sitting on benches. The room was lonely and bare, like a country train station. One of the girls glanced coldly at Lili; the others spoke secretly among themselves, ignoring her.

"Mélanie," the madam barked. "A lesbian."

Lili stood straight, with her hands at her sides, in her old oversize jacket, her brown skirt, sensible shoes.

A small dark-haired girl—she couldn't have been more than fifteen or sixteen—rose from among the cluster of women and came toward Lili, her gaze on the floor.

"Oh!" Lili gasped. The girl was as small as Lili, her breasts barely formed, her hips shallow and smooth. She was dressed in some ridiculous Egyptian costume, and she wore a fringed headband over her short black hair. "She ought to be in school," Lili said severely.

The girl glanced helplessly at the madam.

"I'm sorry," Lili said, and she reached into her coat pocket and took out a fifty-franc note. "I'm sorry, I've made a mistake." She put the money in the girl's hand and the girl looked at her for the first time, her eyes round and dark and impenetrable. How small and cool her hand was! Lili wanted to take the girl home and explain to her the significance of the Enlightenment, she wanted to give her a good meal, but the girl was already seated back among the other whores.

The madam laughed again, her short, low laugh, like a bark. "You'll come around," she said. "You unhappy woman. You'll come around."

"I'm sorry," Lili said, and she fled from the room, down the long, stale-smelling hallway, back into the clear, cold air of the street. She ran all the way back to the *métro*, her heart tight and painful.

On the train she lit a cigarette and stared at her reflection in the grimy window. She had to hold her eyes wide open to keep from crying, and the effort took all her concentration.

Only when she was back in the studious side streets of the Latin Quarter did she relax. She walked alongside the closed iron gates of the Luxembourg and wept. She wept quietly, without restraint and without wiping the tears from her face. She wept until her throat was raw, until she was exhausted, and then she leaned against a wall, her head flung against the stone, and let the mild, dark night wash over her.

She laughed sadly: she could feel the old aching desire to kneel in a confessional and be absolved; to hear the murmur of a priest's voice through the grate; to be reassured that she was right to feel helpless, that within her impotence resided the very innocence she mourned. *Lord I am not worthy I lusted for Claude I paid a child prostitute only say the word and I shall be healed.* Yes, like sleep, like Maman's hand on my forehead: *Take away my sins, take away the sins of the world.*

She turned to go home, then stopped: for the first time since she'd entered the whorehouse, she thought of Pierre standing in a roomful of women, selecting one—maybe a child, like Mélanie—going into some windowless bedroom with the girl. Her heart beat painfully again and she turned toward rue Guynemer, walking quickly and deliberately to the heavy, wooden doors of their apartment building.

He was standing in the vestibule, smoking and pacing. He seemed infinitely distant to her, like something seen at the bottom of a pool. He began to exclaim over her: *Lili I was so worried, what were you doing you didn't leave a note—*

She had no idea what time it was. She walked past him into the dining room—she could smell the odor of cooked meat, so he had done something with the tongue and the roast; he wouldn't let it go to waste; he was a good man—she opened the window, pushed open the shutters, and stared down into the dark, empty street, its yellow globes suspended in the murk.

"I went to a whorehouse."

"Lili?"

"Do you sleep with children? There were children there, is that what you do?"

He sat down at the table and put his head in his hands. For a long time they were silent. She leaned out the window, and now and then a car passed noisily on rue de Fleurus. She hated the sound of cars. How much gentler the night had been when there were only carriages.

At last he said, "Lili, I've never been unfaithful to you."

She laughed. "If this is what you call fidelity!" But she heard in his voice that he was telling the truth: he didn't visit prostitutes anymore. Her trip to Montmartre had been a waste, as wasted as her morning at the hairdresser and the dress shop. The truth was something blanker, more silent, more incomprehensible. But she kept on: "For God's sake, Pierre, I don't care what you do. Fornicate with whomever you please. Only make sure that she has stopped growing. Promise me that at least. Tell me that you've never slept with a little girl—"

"I didn't ask the ages of the prostitutes I slept with," he said quietly, behind her.

She closed her eyes, shut out everything except the feel of the cold iron rail against her hands. Then she heard his chair scrape back, heard him walk slowly down the hall toward their bedroom.

She closed the windows and sat down in the chair he had been sitting in, laid her head down on the table.

She awoke suddenly, out of no dream, to the sound of the clock ticking on the mantelpiece: for a moment she remembered no one—neither Pierre nor the prostitute—she was conscious only of Claude's existence, that he was asleep in another room and she wanted him, wanted to feel his smooth baby skin against her face. Then she remembered it all: Pierre didn't want another child, but that wasn't why he didn't want her; that much she knew, though she knew nothing.

She pushed herself up from the table, and she was afraid, seeing before her—as if she were there, in the shadows of the dining room—the naked woman from the whorehouse. Lili closed her eyes and saw the woman's dull, blank stare, her pale nakedness; and it seemed to Lili as if everything were random, fragile, breaking.

She felt her way down the hall to the bathroom and, turning on the light, she laughed sadly at the sight of herself, with her short, bobbed hair. She left her skirt and blouse and underwear on the floor of the bathroom, walked naked across the hall to the bedroom, opened the shutters to let the moonlight in—what comfort to stand naked on the iron balcony, in the mild summer night—gathered Claude into her arms, and laid him between her and Pierre. As long as Claude was in the bed, Pierre wouldn't reach for her; she wouldn't be startled awake for nothing. In his sleep, Pierre, who sensed so little in his waking life, knew if they were alone, knew how to arouse her and how to discard her. She sat up, smoking, watching the rise and fall of his chest, his slack, sleeping face, and beside him, pale and beautiful, Claude moving like a fish in his sleep, his thin arms waving slowly, smoothly over the sheets.

Eight

Claude turned two without learning to speak or walk. Lili knew then that something was wrong. She knew it and Pierre knew it and between them was a kind of dread, a waiting for the moment when they would have to give it a name. There was tenderness at the heart of the waiting, a tenderness so extreme it was painful, like something swollen you did not dare touch.

They did not make love, and they did not fight anymore either. She did not provoke any fights. She felt, suddenly, like Pierre, content to let things be, not to question anything, not to go digging around where she didn't have to.

In the evenings, after she put Claude in the exact middle of their bed—after his *bouillie* and rice pudding, because, though he had teeth, he could not make sense of how to use them—she sat in the living room with Pierre and discussed the news, the books they were reading. They discussed these things—the strikes, a new translation of Blake—the way people do who must avoid other subjects: the way people gossip.

I wonder what Freud makes of Blake, he might say.

Oh, Freud, she'd answer. *He's too pat.*

Yes, perhaps. Give me a cigarette, will you?

On the other hand, he is compelling. Poetic in his own way.

Well, yes. That's why I wonder what he makes of Blake.

Yes.

They exhausted their subjects quickly and sat awhile without speaking. She thought of nothing, then, listening to the sound of their sucking breaths, watching their two thin streams of smoke mingle in the air. When they'd finished their cigarettes, they went to the bedroom and climbed in on either side of Claude.

❦

One night, the summer after Claude's third birthday, restless with dread because they had promised to go out to Saint-Germain the following day, it came to her with a sudden, terrible clarity that she should have had braces put on Claude's legs long ago. Talking would take care of itself—there was the Deauville boy who'd done so well at l'Ecole Polytechnique, who didn't speak till he was four—but without braces Claude might never walk. It might already be too late, she thought, and her heart began to race, as if she should dress him right now and take him to the doctor in the middle of the night. Then it occurred to her that Pierre would never agree to braces—he hated doctors—so she would have to take Claude alone, secretly.

She reached for a cigarette, and in the flash of light from the match, she saw Claude's thin, pale body caught in its endless night-swimming, the top of his pajamas pushed up over his stomach. Beyond him, Pierre slept on his back, his chest and neck arched upward and his head flung back, like some beautiful, reclining statue: an image of death. It was a hot night, a last breath of summer, and the sheets were knotted at his ankles: he lay naked in the darkness. Yes, she thought, you are beautiful, but you cannot help me.

She was sticky and swollen from the heat; it was like being sick, her heart beating too quickly inside her sluggish body. And although she felt she should take Claude now, in the middle of the night—but to whom? which doctor? what should she say?—she didn't move. She sat, perfectly still, until her cigarette smoked itself and the ashes fell onto the mattress; only when it began to burn her fingers did she reach to put it out.

She was still sitting up, unmoving, when the room grew light and Pierre began to stretch, to nuzzle his face into Claude's head. Lili's eyes ached, but she could not close them, and her heart began to race again. She thought, Now. I'll take him to the doctor now. I'll say we're going for a walk.

But she merely watched as Pierre swung himself out of bed and into his robe, lifting Claude up. "Oof, you're a smelly boy. Time to change your diaper, little cabbage. Smelly little cabbage." He blew against Claude's stomach and Claude laughed a high, soft laugh, his eyes fluttering sleepily. "You look dazed, Lili. Bad night?"

She did not move until she heard them leave the bathroom and go toward the kitchen, Pierre singing *Il était un petit navire,* cheerfully, lightly, as if everything were all right: as if Claude's legs were fine, as if he, Pierre, were simply looking forward to going to Saint-Germain. As if he'd never been crazy, as if he still loved his wife. *I will tell you the truth Pierre if we don't get braces now it will be too late you can go on to Saint-Germain yourself if you want I am going to fix his legs.*

Pierre was in the dining room, feeding Claude the last of a mashed banana. She stared at them, her arms and neck heavy with sleeplessness, but said nothing. She felt confused, unsteady; as if at last she *were* sleeping and this was a dream, and she couldn't make sense of how to do the simplest things.

"Come, *chéri*," she murmured finally, taking Claude from Pierre's lap. How heavy he was, impossible to carry: she put him on the living room floor. He clucked happily, obliviously, crawling from chair to chair, stringing together syllables that meant nothing. His pink, full lips were shiny with spit and he looked up at Lili and laughed. She closed her eyes to weep, but found herself laughing with him instead, suddenly, inexplicably, happy. "What is it, *chéri?* What is it that's so funny?"

His eyes grew as expressionless as pools of water: he didn't recognize her. He stopped moving, lulled to stillness by the sun coming through the window. The light played across the surface of his blue, watery eyes as if he were blind.

"Look at me," she whispered, dropping down to her knees, bringing her face close to his. "Look at me."

His eyes remained frozen, unblinking.

"Claude," she said, her voice low and urgent. "Claude!" And she lifted him under his arms so that he hung straight in front of her, her fingers digging into his thin light bones, and his eyes refocused, startled. He cried out—her nails were scraping his skin—and she heard her own voice, pinched and anguished, and then he was in her arms, sobbing against her throat. She was on her knees, rocking him. "Claude. Claude. *Mon petit chou-fleur chéri.* Oh my God, you are just a baby. A baby."

He stopped crying, nuzzling against her breast, and she lifted her blouse hurriedly, unclasping her brassiere. "Yes, darling. Yes." His teeth hurt her, and he suckled so rarely now that she had only a faint thread of milk to give him, but still it was like the old days, in front of the bedroom window, the blood coursing into her breasts, his lips strong and certain. "A baby," she murmured, stroking his hair. "How ridiculous to imagine braces on a baby!"

She pushed herself up to her feet, still holding Claude to her breast, and went toward the bedroom. "Come, *mon chou*, we have to get you dressed. We have to go out to Saint-Germain today."

She knocked on the door of the spare room, where Enid, the new au pair slept. Enid was sitting at her desk, writing postcards. Poor Enid. She had a flat, red face, and her eyes were always red rimmed. She must be very homesick. But Lili always spoke to her briskly, quickly, so that no gap opened up in their conversation in which Enid might say, *I was wondering about Claude, Madame.* . . .

"We'll be leaving shortly," Lili said, standing in the doorway with her blouse pushed up, distracted by the sharpness of Claude's teeth, the waves of painful pleasure that washed through her. "We're going to visit my family. You should take yourself out and have a good time; we won't be back till the evening. Good-bye, then!"

Enid's eyes grew redder, as if she might burst into tears. Poor Enid, Lili thought. You're so alone. I'd invite you to join us for the day— you'd like Thérèse and she'd take you shopping some afternoon—but I can't, Enid. I can't. . . . And she shut the door briskly behind her.

She never let anyone say too much anymore. In line at the butcher shop, holding Claude in her arms, she talked incessantly: the strikes, the weather, Léon Blum. On and on she prattled, and all Madame Dupuis and Madame Arnaud could manage to say was *Yes, yes— awfully warm—no—I hadn't.* . . . Only when Lili was inside the shop itself did she shut up. And then it was as if the world grew silent, and the butcher did his hushed ballet among the slabs of meat, and she was safe, until she must leave again, passing the stream of housewives, all itching to comment and pass judgment—*He's three now, isn't he, Madame Larat?*—but she wouldn't let them; she smiled broadly: *Madame Charpentier, hello, awfully warm today, isn't it? Good news for the textile union, oh but of course you're not prounion, I forgot, pity. Well, good-bye, mesdames!*

"Pierre!" she called out. "I'm going to dress Claude. Will you be ready soon?" She heard the water running in the bathroom and went in: he was standing in the tub, soaping his chest. It startled her to see him, as if she didn't watch him bathe every Sunday. But she had learned over the years to look at him numbly. Only now and then a memory of desire washed over her, sudden and quick.

"I'm going to dress him," she repeated. She looked up at his face, and having met his simple, violet gaze, she did not break away from it.

She could see that his arms were moving, but she imagined that he did not have a body.

They had bought an automobile and they drove to Saint-Germain. They went there once a month now, though it was worse than ever now that Maurice was back from Germany. But Claude loved the garden in back of the house where he could crawl all afternoon without hurting himself. He loved his grandmother, who held him for hours in her old, brown arms.

They had to pick up Jean-Louis on their way. He and Thérèse were married and had an apartment in the Ninth Arrondissement, but Thérèse still spent half the week in Saint-Germain.

He sat in the front, a thin, slight man with bourgeois manners and expensive suits but with his votes cast solidly to the left. Lili and Claude sat in back; Claude's legs dangled across hers. He looked up at her, his head flung back against her arms. She stared into his light violet eyes, and their gaze held, as if nothing else existed: the car, Pierre, Jean-Louis's too-thick cologne. Her face was not a hand's length from Claude's. The violet of his eyes was filled with different colors: flecks of yellow, green, gray. He looked at her intently, as if they were speaking. At first it was as if she were reassuring him—he was so small still and the world to him was chaos—and then it seemed as if he were the old one, with his soft, watery eyes, reassuring her. But of what? They stared at each other, their breathing slow and in unison, and in the hand's width between their faces, sight dissolved, so that she was no longer thinking, His eyes, his face: she had become his face.

Then his mouth fell open and he uttered a sharp, ragged little cry. She thought he was beginning to laugh, and she started to join him, but the sound ended abruptly: it was not a laugh at all.

"What is it, Claude?" she whispered. "What's wrong?"

Jean-Louis and Pierre were discussing the economy.

Claude's mouth hung open, pink and shiny and silent. Then it came again, a high tuneless cry that she had never heard before.

He leaned his head farther back, stretching his long white neck—too long a neck for a baby—and his eyes rolled in his head. She tried to pull him forward, but all his strength was in his neck, and he resisted her. His mouth still hung open slackly, and at regular intervals that strange, shapeless sound flew out of him: a single, sustained *ahhh,* one rasping note.

"He's restless," she murmured. "He's impatient to get to Saint-Germain!" She forced a laugh. "We'll be there soon enough, *chéri*— you can't wait to see Grand-mère, can you?" But her chest was unbearably sore, as if her heart were lodged in it incorrectly.

Then he stopped. His mouth closed and his eyelids fluttered, as if he would sleep.

They had left Paris. Outside, the countryside, rich and tarnished with the end of summer, sped past them. She glanced up at the plane trees, the heavy golden wheat fields, and closed her eyes. She rested his small silken hand in her own veiny tobacco-stained one and threw it gently into the air, caught it, threw it up again.

"People don't realize," Jean-Louis was insisting.

"All the same," said Pierre, holding the steering wheel easily, casually, as if he had been born to it. "France isn't going to suffer like other places. The franc's in much better shape."

"But if no one keeps his promises—"

"All the same," Pierre repeated. "I've got faith in Briand."

Claude opened his mouth again and now the *ahhh* went on and on—five seconds, ten—and stopped.

Lili rolled down the window, and the air seemed to rush in and fill her body: she felt as if she did not exist, as if there were no barrier between herself and anything else; everything came rushing in, the warm August afternoon, Pierre's voice, the weight of Claude's hand, all pouring in on her indiscriminately, the sounds of the automobile as rich and terrifying as Claude's tiny, inhuman cries. Her bones were like water and her skin was thin, so thin she could see right through it. She was shaking.

"Are you all right, Lili?" Jean-Louis was looking over his shoulder and his face was all sincerity, chivalry, concern.

Pierre turned his head sharply and saw that Lili's face was drenched with tears. He caught his breath and said, too cheerfully, "It's nothing. A little cold, that's all."

"Well," Lili said, and her own voice surprised her: she could not control the pitch and it seemed to go up and down and up and down in the space of a single word. "Well," she repeated. "I'm very happy, that's all. I'm just very happy." Unbelievably happy, she thought, desperately. What was she supposed to say?

Claude cried out in her arms—sustained, meaningless, a sound neither of pain nor of joy—and the two men were silent, as if, if no one spoke, the moment might cease to exist.

"I do think," Pierre said, his voice a little too loud, too certain, "that Briand knows how to deal with them. He won't back down."

"Back down?" Lili interjected brightly. "Oh, absolutely not—he'd never back down," she went on, forgetting who it was they were talking about. She lifted Claude's hand to her lips and kissed it, blew against his fingertips: Claude laughed, the light, unmistakable laugh of a three-year-old boy.

"Oh, my big boy. My big, big boy!" Maman took Claude in her arms and kissed him. Her skin hung on her in tiny folds, and she was practically blind. Old age had come to her almost overnight, but the dark circles around her eyes had vanished: as if it were seeing that had exhausted her all these years, as if the white film over her irises were a gift. She held her loose, flabby arms out to Lili. "Give him to me. Give me that big, handsome boy," and Lili gave Claude to her, his eyes fluttering, the slender stalk of his neck thrown back. "Such a big, big boy," Maman murmured, and then she turned to Pierre, and Pierre leaned down and kissed her tenderly. "Such a handsome man," Maman said to Lili. "A big, handsome man."

Lili did not answer, staring at the thread of spit that shone on Claude's chin. "*Mon amour,*" Lili whispered. And she leaned toward him and licked it off, letting the warm, sourish saliva dissolve in her mouth. Claude's eyes widened for a second, the way they did when Lili tickled him, and then once more they were empty, expressionless, like pools of violet water.

"A handsome man," Maman repeated, as if she wanted to make sure that Lili appreciated what she had.

At the dining room table, Thérèse sat dreamily, huge and beautiful as a Rubens. She was in her tenth month of pregnancy, but she did not seem miserable, only dazed. She tried to rise from her chair, gave up, and indicated the parlor with her head. "Papa's asleep," she said, lifting her face to Jean-Louis so he could kiss her.

In the parlor, Papa was snoring next to Mademoiselle Duroc. Mademoiselle Duroc finished counting the stitches on her knitting needle, looked up, and shook Papa's arm. "They're here, Monsieur." She still made up her face, but her features had dissolved completely and you couldn't tell that she had ever been pretty. Lili remembered her suddenly on the beach at Pornic, when Papa held up a towel for her to change behind. Papa stared right over the top of the towel while

Mademoiselle Duroc undressed; Maman sat apart, beneath the shade of the umbrella, not needing to change her clothes because she didn't know how to swim: she'd stared glumly out at the ocean, at Lili and Maurice running from the waves, at André, nine or ten, whining because there was sand between his toes. At last she walked away from her children, tired of watching over them. "I'll hold Mademoiselle Duroc's towel," she had said and, taking it from Papa—he gave in to her, laughing, playing the henpecked husband—she, too, refused to avert her eyes but stared over the top of the towel at the young, smooth body of her husband's lover.

They must have stopped being lovers years ago, Lili thought, watching Mademoiselle Duroc push herself up from her chair: she would have stayed on because she had nowhere else to go—she had no family—and they kept her, Maman and Papa, as they would have kept a spinster aunt: she peeled potatoes for the cook, did the dusting that Maman hated, took care, now that both Maman's and Papa's eyes were weak, of all the correspondence.

Papa rose groggily—a large man still but oddly fragile—and now everyone was standing, even Thérèse, embracing, *Hello, hello, hello,* their bodies, their voices filling the room: everything seemed fractured and confused, *How are you, Monsieur Ravaudet, sit down, Thérèse, sit down you mustn't be on your feet.* Maman stood apart, holding Claude in her arms. "My big boy," she murmured. "My big, big boy." Maman did not seem to notice anything unusual about him, as if she had forgotten about babies—when they learn to walk, to speak. She held him so tightly in her arms, so proudly.

But Lili felt lost, disoriented. She could not bear to spend the afternoon here. She wanted to go upstairs and lie down with Claude, to talk to him, tell him—what?

She turned away from them all so that they would not see her. She unlatched the French doors and stepped out into the garden—she had played here long ago, hiding between the rosebushes and the wall, cradling her clown doll in her arms, and singing lullabies cheerfully off-key—there was Maurice, sitting at the round table beneath the chestnut tree, reading the newspaper.

"Well, Lili," he said. "So you've come for your monthly visit." He was an unattractive man, overweight, with an ugly little goatee and small, dull eyes. She couldn't believe that she had grown in her mother's womb with him, and yet, for all that she could hardly stand him, she felt an odd comfort in his presence. The misery he caused her was deeper and truer than anything else she knew. He sees right through me, she thought.

She lit a cigarette. "Yes," she said. "My monthly visit." They did not kiss hello. She sat down next to him at the little table, but she faced away from him, out into the garden: everything was still so meticulously laid out, the chrysanthemums and the marguerites, the marigolds. At the far end of the lawn, a few dark, overblown roses clung to the vines, but their smell no longer filled the garden the way it had a month ago. The heavy dark leaves of the chestnut tree seemed as if they would only get darker and greener—it was impossible to imagine that this rich sky would ever turn cold and thin, but it would: it would be winter again before long, with everyone huddled inside and the endless cold, dark, wet afternoons.

"Well," Maurice said. "The trade unionists are staging another strike. What do you think of that, Madame la Marxiste?"

"Oh, Maurice," she said. "I don't feel like talking politics."

"But that's right, isn't it? You atheists are Marxists, too, aren't you?" Maurice had figured out on his own, when Lili did not have a religious wedding, that she had ceased to believe, and he hounded her with it every time he saw her.

She did not answer. She wanted to take Claude from her mother and run away, to the ocean, to North America, to Africa, anywhere.

But Maurice was lecturing her about the trade unions. ". . . You'd have to agree, wouldn't you? They do get in the way of work. That's a fact, isn't it? Work, Lili. You wouldn't have much of a civilization without it. Would you, Lili?"

"Please," she said. "Please." She lit one cigarette off the end of another and ground the old one into the dirt. "I don't feel like talking."

Maurice laughed. "Well, that's something new! What have you done? Taken a vow of silence?" He laughed again, amused by his own joke. "Yes, that's very good—a vow of silence! The atheist Carmelite!"

The French doors opened and the rest of the family poured into the garden. Lili jumped up and took Claude from Maman's arms. "It's time for his nap," she said. "I need to put him down for his nap." But Claude began to whimper, seeing the grass. He wanted to get down and crawl.

"Oh, *chéri*," she whispered into his head. "I want to go away, I want—"

But Claude only whimpered, straining his pale, slack face toward the ground.

"It's nothing, *chéri*, nothing, hush. . . ." She could not refuse him.

"But over here, by the bushes, *mon chou.*" She carried him to the other side of the garden, but he did not want that either. He wanted to crawl in the grass at the grown-ups' feet, surrounded by their bright, deep, nonsensical voices.

Pierre and Jean-Louis brought more chairs into the garden: they were going to have *goûter* outside. The heat affected Thérèse badly: she would be better off inside, in the cool of the house, but she hated to be alone. She was fanning herself with a page of Maurice's newspaper, and Maurice was patting her hand. The shade of the chestnut tree fell unevenly across them, like veils of light.

She would have beautiful children, Lili thought. Beautiful, healthy children, and she would clap for them at the end of every school year, at the distribution of prizes. She felt bitter and hard, and then, overcome with shame, with the strange, almost painful passion she felt for Claude, she dropped down to the ground beside him and crawled with him, over to the rest of the family. He moved in a straight line, clutching the grass as he went, and she moved alongside him. He did not seem to notice her, so intent was he on his destination, and she wanted to stop him, to gather him in her arms and hold him there. She kept crawling. The grass pressed into her palms, and her skirt bunched up around her knees. She lowered her head, all her attention focused on his pale, slender, straining hands.

But at last the others' feet came into view. She must get up now, smile, take one of the miniature pastries that Mademoiselle Duroc had brought out on the silver tray, make some pretense of enjoying the afternoon. Pierre glanced down at Claude, smiled, but he did not look at Lili at all. He was not avoiding her gaze; he was simply absorbed, so happy to be talking to Jean-Louis. She thought of him that morning, soaping himself in the bath. How terrible it had been to stand there, watching him touch his thighs, his underarms, his neck, as he would never let her do.

She lifted Claude and put a dab of crème anglaise in his mouth, but he wanted the ground. "There, *chéri.* . . ." She set him down again, redirecting him into the garden, and he crawled back the way he had come. Then she dragged one of the chairs from the table, out of the shade of the chestnut tree, into the strange, bright heat. She sat, facing away from the others, watching his slow, determined progress. When he reached the marigolds, she would turn him back.

The rest of the family sat in the shade all through the long afternoon. Maman, Mademoiselle Duroc, and Thérèse knit infant-sized sweaters and socks, discussing the price of things, the news from the neighbors, their voices low and murmuring, punctuated occasionally by a laugh from Thérèse, a momentary sharpness between Maman and Mademoiselle Duroc. Now and then Maman put down her knitting, rose, and went to whatever part of the garden Claude was crawling in, knelt down beside him, and stroked his head. Papa snored gently; Pierre and Jean-Louis discussed Lausanne. Maurice sat on the other side of them, trying to join in the men's conversation, but his remarks were so pointless, so deliberately reactionary, that Pierre and Jean-Louis would merely pause for him to finish saying what he had to say and then resume their own discussion. He is like André now, Lili thought. No one wants to talk to him. She loathed his stupid comments, and at the same time her heart ached, and she wanted to yell at Pierre and Jean-Louis: *You are a pair of snobs, both of you! If you'd be a little nicer to him, he wouldn't act like such an idiot.* But she knew it wasn't true. He would act like an idiot no matter what.

She kept her chair turned away so that she could watch over Claude, so that they could not see her face. Behind her, their voices rose and fell, a chorus of syllables in which she did not even try to make out any words: it was not necessary. The pattern of their confidences, their assurances, their little cruelties, was perfectly clear without the words themselves. She knew when Thérèse grew suddenly vague, distracted, then came to, laughing at herself; when Mademoiselle Duroc was disagreeing with Maman; when Pierre and Jean-Louis were waiting for Maurice to finish. Now and then a phrase rose clearly above the others, as if one of the chorus were having a solo or had lost the rhythm: *But I. . . . Oh yes, yes! . . . Sugar. . . . No I don't think. . . . higher than. . . . Yes! Yes, absolutely!*

Before her, the garden wavered, lost its outlines, became a pool of color—green and blood red, gold, orange, and, farther on, a band of grayish violet. Then everything resumed its shape, and there were the beds of autumn flowers, the grass, the mauve shadows of the garden wall.

And Claude, in the little sailor outfit that Thérèse had given him, the grass and the dirt staining his skin, his clothes. His full pink mouth hung open, drooling slightly. Naturally none of the others would let their children crawl for so long and in such a nice outfit, but no one ever tried to advise Lili on how to raise her son. It was remarkable, really, given the pleasure they took in giving advice, in criticizing and correcting one another. They didn't even comment when he tugged on the flowers. They said nothing, she assumed, because he wasn't baptized: he was past hope.

He had crawled to the base of the birdbath, and for a moment he couldn't figure out how to get around it. A blue jay flew down beside him and pecked in the grass near his hands. He was startled, and deep in his throat he made again the high, raw sound that was neither laughing nor crying. Then he began to babble, murmuring without words, his lips moving steadily, wetly. He pawed at the base of the birdbath, frustrated by the obstruction, and Lili ran to him, her heart pounding.

"Oh *chéri*," she said, moving his hands. "Over here. Over here the way is clear." She could smell that his diaper needed to be changed, but he would scream if she tried to lift him off the grass, so she let him be. She sat down beside him, and he crawled onto her lap and stayed there, butting his soft, warm head against her breasts.

"Oh my little Claude," she murmured. "*Mon petit chou, mon petit chou-fleur.*" She turned him around so that he was sitting in her lap, and she rocked him from side to side, holding him tightly in her arms.

Maurice had come and stood above them, looking down. She glanced up at him—at his soft, round belly, his suspenders, his little goatee—and then looked away, fixing her gaze on the last of the roses.

Claude crawled off her and toward the ragged circle of shade cast by the chestnut tree; he moved steadily, back toward the grown-ups' feet, the iron legs of the garden table.

She felt that she should get up, talk to Maurice, but she didn't want to. She wanted to be left alone. She lit a cigarette.

"Well, Lili," Maurice said. "Don't you think you're a bit old for that? For crawling around in the grass?"

She rolled her eyes and said nothing. Everything he said was so astonishingly stupid, as if he missed half of every equation: she hadn't exactly crawled around in the grass by herself.

"What is the matter with him, Lili? He should be walking by now, shouldn't he?"

There was a high, thin whine, as if a wire were vibrating. . . .

"Is he crippled or something?" Maurice asked.

She laughed: a soft, light tremor that began at the bottom of her belly and rose through her chest, collecting in her throat so that her neck trembled violently, but she did not make a sound.

"Well, is he?"

And still she could not stop the trembling, the soundless laughter.

"Maurice!" murmured Thérèse from the other side of the garden, her voice full of disapproval. "Maurice!"

"Well, someone's got to say it," Maurice went on, his voice loud and booming and solitary. "Some sort of provision has got to be made. A wheelchair or something."

She was sitting in the grass with her back to them all: she couldn't see any of them. Her legs shook and she put her palms firmly on her thighs, but they kept shaking.

Eventually, the others would go away. If she sat long enough, she would at last sense that they had gone and she would be able to get up. She would put her palms down in the grass and push herself up. Then she would walk straight through the garden to the side gate and out into rue Thiers, left onto rue du Président Wilson, straight to the end of town. She could picture her hands, the little indentations of grass and rocks left in her palms, after she had pushed herself up.

"I'm sorry, Lili." Thérèse's voice hung in the garden, pale and transparent and lovely. "You know how he is. . . ."

"Well, what?" Maurice asked. "What?"

"That's enough," said Maman suddenly, sharply. "You don't know what you're talking about, Maurice."

How cruel she is to him, Lili thought, and for a moment her heart was so sore she couldn't bear it.

"Well, if I can't say *anything,*" Maurice said, and Lili heard him walk heavily, slowly, toward the house. She could hear the French doors open and close, and then he was gone. No one said anything.

She turned her head slightly, and there was Claude, crawling away from her, toward the others. She wanted to pull him back toward her, to hold him tightly against the beating of her heart, but her arms could not reach that far: he made his way slowly, steadily toward the shade. She was still trembling, but she pushed herself up.

They all stared at her, all except Papa, who was still dozing, and Mademoiselle Duroc, bent discreetly over her knitting. Maman and Thérèse looked at Lili anxiously, their eyes dark and worried. Her legs were soft, unsteady, and in the unsteady shade of the chestnut tree, Pierre sat, stunned, his pale lilac eyes shot with pain. She glanced at him for a moment and then looked away, as if she'd seen something she wasn't meant to.

"Maurice doesn't know what he's talking about," Maman repeated harshly.

"Of course not," murmured Thérèse. "Come and sit with us, Lili."

But she walked over to Claude and gathered him in her arms. He began to cry out, to gasp in his longing for the ground, but she held on to him tightly, pressing his tiny, beating heart against her own.

"We have to go," she said, and once more that afternoon the sound of her voice, thin and empty, surprised her. "Come on, Pierre. We have to go now."

"So soon?" Maman asked.

"I can't stand it here," Lili said, and she watched Maman flinch, draw back as if Lili had slapped her. She wanted to say it again and again, until Maman collapsed, until she couldn't breathe.

Lili moved quickly, jerkily, grabbing their belongings with her free hand: Claude's little cap, her purse, her book. . . .

It was still light when they returned to Paris. The day's heat had accumulated in the pavement, in the trunks of the plane trees, the walls of the buildings. The heat breathed back upon them as they walked down the street, and she wanted more than anything to rest—to sit on the sidewalk and lean back against the warm stone of the neighboring building—but Pierre walked on ahead, carrying Claude in his arms. They had driven back without speaking, the sound of Claude's strange, toneless cries washing over them again and again, insistent and meaningless. She had closed her eyes, letting the sound vibrate in her heart, her lungs, as if it were her own voice that made it.

But now, out in the street, negotiating the few hundred steps between car and door, she felt lost, drunk. She wanted Pierre to stop and wait for her. She felt sick—afraid, on the way up the stairs, that she would throw up. It was hard to see after the light of the street. She followed Pierre into the apartment and down the hall to the bathroom—she put her hand out to steady herself—past the living room on the left and Enid's room on the right: no doubt Enid was in there, writing postcards. Enid would have lifted her head for a moment, hearing them return, and then resumed her scribbling, her telegraphic cries of homesickness on the backs of pictures of the Eiffel Tower, Notre Dame, the Louvre. Poor Enid, Lili thought, but I cannot help you. And she moved on, steadying herself against the wall.

In the bathroom, she leaned against the door and watched mutely as Pierre turned on the water, began peeling off Claude's dirt- and grass-stained clothes. She was so dizzy that she thought at any moment she might faint. She stared past them at the round frosted window at the foot of the tub.

"He's retarded," she said.

"Yes," Pierre said, and their eyes met, raw and helpless, above Claude's head.

"Retarded," she said again. "How long have you known that he's retarded," she said softly, but it wasn't a question. She was drunk with the sound of their voices: they were still their voices, the same voices they had always used, to talk about Blake, to argue, even to love. "We've always known, haven't we?"

"We've known a long time," he said.

"Shall we call the doctor?" she asked, and her heart beat painfully.

"Oh, Lili," Pierre said, "there's nothing a doctor can do." He added bitterly, "He'll predict an early death, give us the name of an institution, and reassure us that we can have others."

She cried out, as if he'd hit her.

He turned away from her and knelt in front of the enamel tub, lowering Claude's long, pale body into the water. She watched the muscles in Pierre's back, the expert way he leaned over and washed the dirt and grass from Claude's body. The floor beneath her feet was soft, dissolving, and the walls of the bathroom spun slightly, then stopped. She could hear his thin, small limbs splashing in the water, the smooth soap falling to the bottom of the tub.

"Take off your clothes, Lili."

Yes, it was the same voice, deep and slow, like a farmer's.

"Take off your clothes." He was looking at her over his shoulder now, staring at her. "Your blouse. Unbutton your blouse." She felt the smooth, hard buttons and she did as he said, removing each garment as he told her to do—blouse, brassiere, shoes, socks, skirt, slip, underpants—until she was standing behind him, completely naked, her skin a little cold. He was still looking over his shoulder and she was self-conscious. She slumped her shoulders a little, as if that would hide her nearly empty breasts, the mound of her pubic hair.

"Climb in the bath," he said softly, and she did, stepping carefully into the water, taking Claude's wet, warm body in her arms. She lay down in the tub, holding Claude on her stomach, and Pierre washed them both, using just his hands, no washcloth. His slick, soapy fingers glided over her thighs, under the crook of her knees, down to her ankles. He washed each of her toes, the arches of her feet, and then back up, across her thighs, across Claude's tiny buttocks and back. He lifted each of her breasts between his hands and washed them as carefully as he had done her feet.

Claude cried out, tuneless and plaintive, and then he grew silent, nuzzling Lili's breast, sucking the last, faint drop of milk from her body.

She watched Pierre's large hand glide along her skin and Claude's, washing them both patiently, carefully. Kneeling over the tub, his shirt-sleeves rolled up over his strong, thick arms, he was as intent as a man at prayer.

Nine

Later, when she was dressed, they went for a walk in the Luxembourg. The sun was slipping down behind the tops of the buildings, but the flower beds were still drenched with light.

Claude lay in his carriage, staring soundlessly at the blue evening sky. His mouth was barely open, the pink wet lips only slightly parted. It was a big carriage, but he filled it completely; they'd have to find something else to carry him in soon.

Lili watched the lengthening shadows of the trees, like pools of clear, dark water, and the watery shadows fell across her back, across the nape of her neck, where the hair clung damply to her skin.

And still, beyond the shade, the earth glowed, the sun soaked the grass. . . .

She felt inexplicably light, peaceful. She was damp in places from the bath, and the old silk dress of Thérèse's she wore stuck to her underarms, her hips; slipped dryly against her belly. It was like going to a party, walking with Pierre and Claude down the wide, straight path toward the fountain, the silk rustling between her legs.

I am so happy, she thought, without knowing what she meant. Happy? Happy? What is that?

A mother and her two sons appeared out of nowhere, on their way home for supper. The mother leaned forward from the waist, as if she were walking against a strong wind. The boys dragged behind, carrying their toy boats under their arms.

"Come on!" the mother said, wheeling around. "Gerard. François!"

"Are you disappointed?" Lili asked suddenly.

Pierre caught his breath sharply.

"I'm sorry," she said. "I am sorry." But it isn't really possible to hurt him. She thought this without resentment, only a kind of relief: He won't say what it hurts him to say. She reached over and took his hand, brought it to rest on the carriage handle next to hers. *I asked him because I am not disappointed,* she realized.

"Maurice is a brute," Pierre said, changing the subject.

Her eyes filled suddenly with tears: she understood that he could not talk about Claude; he would never be able to talk about him, any more than he could explain his lack of passion or describe his months in the asylum. He could not talk, but he was honest. He wouldn't put his son in an institution, and he would never make love to a woman out of obligation. They were not what he had hoped for, she and Claude, but he had washed them. He washed them carefully, gently.

"He can't help it," Lili said. "Maurice is the way André used to be. Seeking disaster. . . . Anyway," she said softly. "I'm relieved actually."

"Yes," Pierre said. "Yes, it is a relief."

He squeezed her hand and again she felt light, peaceful. They walked slowly, so slowly she could see the silver and violet breasts of the pigeons. The garden smelled old and dry: the packed earth, the dusty bark of the trees, the heavy green leaves. She could hear the leaves rustling and the constant trilling and calling of the birds and laughter, far away: a cluster of lycéens gossiping in the path. And this was all she was aware of, the sounds of the Luxembourg, the yellow bamboo handle of the carriage. She was aware of Pierre's hand on hers, of the mothlike flutter of Claude's eyelids.

And how did she know, anyway, that they were not what he had hoped for? *Maybe,* she thought, *we are all Pierre has ever wanted, Claude and I. I don't know and I assume the worst. The truth is only that I know nothing.*

She did not feel the usual terror that accompanied the possibility of ignorance, and her own calm surprised her.

His thick hands had slipped through the water, brushing her skin, Claude's. Washing our feet, he didn't look me in the eyes, his gaze was so intent on our bodies, the way he'd care for an animal he loved, until the end, and then so quickly, his lilac eyes like Claude's, resting on mine just for a second, a moment of recognition—You were my lover once—then he lifted us out of the warm water and dried us. If I let myself feel any desire for you now, it will ruin everything, I'll get mean and the water was so warm, your hands so soft. . . .

To distract herself from wanting Pierre, she began to hum the four notes she'd hummed to Claude when he was a baby. Pierre smiled, hummed along with her.

Claude's eyes had closed completely—pale, veiny lids stretched over his lilac eyes—and his mouth hung wide open, breathing in the trembling blue of the evening air.

But now, as they reached the fountain, the peace was abruptly shattered: lovers were piled onto each other on the small green chairs— a blond woman sat on a man's lap, her face buried in his; another pair pecked lightly at each other, like birds. Children knelt over the edge of the fountain, pushing their boats; mothers scolded, grew bored, turned away, and gossiped with each other; old men read: so many people, all of them doing what they did every summer evening—the Luxembourg, the fountain, the carousel for the children, and the mothers gossiping. Nothing had changed for any of them.

Yes, I never thought of that, how the rest of the world would keep going. Of course! It makes no difference to them that some child is retarded. What's most important to them is still whether the charcutier has a nice suckling pig left, whether there'll be a chance to go and buy that pretty hat tomorrow. I didn't notice this when André killed himself—how the world goes on—because I didn't pay any attention to the world that time until I'd begun to care myself whether there'd be time to go and buy an éclair before class. . . .

She felt alone and miserable again. They sat down on two of the wooden chairs, with the carriage in front of them, and stared at the cool gray surface of the water. The boats got tangled up with each other in the spray, had to be retrieved with sticks, and all around them the earth still held the light, golden and radiant. She couldn't stand these little boys with their brown, muscular legs, shouting at their boats, already arrogant. "That's not how it's done, stupid, I'll show you!" How cruel they would be to Claude if they knew, if they peered inside the carriage and saw that he was nearly as big as they. And the mothers, oh the mothers. They might fawn over him now, but what prissy recoil when he grew big and misshapen and still made his terrifying sounds.

She sat limply in her chair. *Take me away from here, Pierre.* But she said nothing; he sat peacefully, with his hands resting on the side of the carriage, his eyes half closed, as if he were, actually, utterly content.

And again she thought of him washing her, his thick, smooth hands: Washing me and drying me and then I chose my dress myself, this purple silk, because I was happy. What was it I was so happy about; it was more than Pierre, it was a feeling of freedom. Yes, it's that I'm free of all this.

I don't have to worry what people think of me anymore. The gossiping mothers with their petty morality, the authoritarian children. For all my oddness, I've always wanted it to be clear that I could be like the others if I chose—

But everyone will see us, Claude, and know that you are mine, my heart, and they'll never again imagine that I could be one of them.

She closed her eyes and thought of André, of his name carved only on the obelisk in Saint-Germain.

He had sat on the beach at Pornic, crying. A big boy, sitting cross-legged, trying to rub the sand out from between his toes. He had been sitting there for a long time, in the full sun, and he was burning. Maman said he could go ahead and burn if he liked. She'd had enough of his sandy toes; he was a big boy: *Look at Lili and Maurice. Maybe burning will teach you a lesson and you won't whine so much.* Lili was five years old. Papa and Mademoiselle Duroc were in the waves, laughing. "Come on, André," Lili touched his shoulder. She wanted to go in the waves with Papa. "We'll wash your feet in the ocean." "It's OK, Lili," he said, and he kept rubbing his toes raw, crying.

Another family came and set up an umbrella and stared at André. "He's going to burn to a crisp," the mother muttered, but Lili heard. "Look at him. A big boy."

Lili walked over to the family and threw up her hands in despair, like a grown-up. "He's just a big baby," she explained. "He whines all the time. Burning will teach him a lesson."

"Honestly!" the mother said, shaking her head. She wouldn't meet Lili's eyes. Behind her, Lili could hear Maman scolding André, dragging him up to the shade of the umbrella. André screamed and screamed.

But Claude would save her from the terrible world of adults. She would be a freak now and alive: forever on the edge, far from the cruel, conventional center of things. What was that center anyway? The love of the Father. *Come in the waves,* Papa said. *Come. Come with Mademoiselle Duroc and me. Such a bright girl, isn't she? Much brighter than her brothers—look at that one: what an idiot, crying over a little bit of sand. Come, Lili. . . .*

You cannot be at the center and at the same time open your heart.

When she looked up again, the light had faded out of the grass. The children were pulling their boats back in, hooking them with long, thin poles.

"Jacques! Cécile! Jean-Marie! Come on. Time to go home. Bernard!" The mothers droned on, hands on their hips, finishing conversations with each other in the pauses between their chants: "Cécile! Come on! So, yes, finally I didn't know what to say—Cécile! I just looked at her and laughed, you can't expect me to—Cécile!—what? Oh no, no, not at all—come on, Cécile. I'm counting to three—yes, isn't it the most ridiculous thing you ever heard of? Honestly! That's enough, Cécile, you come right here." The mother strode to the fountain, grabbed the pole out of the little girl's clumsy hand, dragged the boat in brutally, and clasped her daughter by the wrist. "So, yes, there's more to it, of course. You wouldn't believe! Yes, yes, absolutely ridiculous! Well, dear, good-bye. Cécile, say good-bye to Madame Carré. Speak up! Honestly, she's such a little dullard. Good-bye, dear. . . ."

The old men read on, undisturbed. They heard, saw, nothing, so preoccupied were they with staying informed.

And the blond lovers drank in each other's bodies, tongues darting, roaming; a button undone; a sleeve pushed down over a white shoulder; a brassiere bunched up beneath the light fabric of her dress. *Oh my darling, my darling!* The bird lovers dozed on separate chairs, their fingers loosely entwined, and a new pair had joined the scene, kissing each other lazily, dreamily, motionless almost: they could have been a statue.

Oh Pierre. Why won't you—? Our secret, our little secret. No one would ever guess there's no passion between us.

She thought briefly of how he had tried to blame his lack of desire on Claude. How long ago that was, that day at the hairdresser, the whorehouse! Yes, they had known even then that something was wrong—of course! But they did not know when Claude was born; they did not know that anything was wrong the night that Pierre turned from Lili. All he knew then, she thought, was that I was more fragile than he had realized.

Pierre still sat with his hand on the carriage, his eyes half opened, in a kind of trance. And Claude, his mouth insatiable, drank in the evening air. Any minute now the guard would announce that the garden was closing. The sky deepened, and the gray, light air seemed to tremble. There was no gold left in the garden, only violet, gray, green, as if a tide were coming in.

"Lili!"

She started and looked around.

"Lili Ravaudet!"

A woman with black curls, wearing a fashionable red dress, circled around the fountain toward her. A tall boy with the same black curls followed her.

"Lili!" the woman called, waving. "Lili!"

Who in the world—?

She clasped Lili's hands, out of breath, and looked expectantly at Pierre. Then she laughed. "Of course! You don't know who I am. I was fat and wore long hair in a bun. At Sèvres."

"Paule Jacob?" Lili remembered a shy, fat Jewess with enormous eyes. Her gaze had always made Lili uncomfortable.

"Yes, yes, that's me. Can you believe it? This is my little brother, Marcel."

The boy, who could have been anywhere between twelve and fifteen, hung shyly behind his sister. His hand darted out, and Lili took it briefly in hers—such a light, dry hand but carefully sculpted, his fingers long and bony—he buried his hands in his pockets and stared at the ground.

"My husband," Lili murmured, "Pierre Larat." And Pierre rose, tall and limber and gracious. "*Enchanté,* Madame—Mademoiselle—?"

"Oh, Mademoiselle!" Paule Jacob laughed. "Mademoiselle!"

But will I have to talk to her? Lili thought. What a bore. But really she wasn't bored. She was intrigued by this suddenly beautiful woman—she'd been in literature, hadn't she?—and her shy little brother with his dry, muscular hand.

"Do you know how I recognized you?" Paule said, smiling. "Shall we tell her, Marcel?"

Marcel shrugged, visibly embarrassed by his sister's exuberance.

Paule dropped her voice. "I was staring at those two"—she indicated the blond couple with her head—"so un-Russian. And even here, usually it's a bit more restrained, or at least one's view of it is obstructed by a few bushes. But this! I was curious what they were going to do with themselves, finally. One can't simply go on pawing the ground forever."

Lili could feel Pierre blushing beside her.

"And then Marcel—he hates it when I stare at people. He's still young enough to get embarrassed by things. . . ."

As if in illustration, Marcel turned bright red.

"Marcel said they were probably doing it for my benefit. 'No one else is looking at them,' he said, and so I looked around the garden and there you were, staring at everyone—just gazing from person to person, as if you were in a museum, and that's what made me recognize you, you always used to do that at school—I hope I haven't offended you! But really, what's the use of life if you can't look around a bit? It's so good to see you, Lili. Where are you teaching? I ought to know, but I never read the newsletters—"

106

Lili flushed. "I wasn't aware that I stared so much."

"No," Paule said, sitting down suddenly beside Lili. "No, of course not. Most of the time you're probably worlds away."

Pierre laughed, a deep, generous laugh. "Yes, she is. She is!"

Lili was flustered by this suddenly intimate conversation—she looked at poor Marcel, no doubt dying to get away—and yet it was exciting, too; it made her feel young, as if, at any moment, they might all get up and have a drink somewhere. They might laugh loudly and raucously, as if they owned the bar—

"When she talks to you"—Pierre laughed—"she's always having twelve conversations at once: one with you, one with herself, and ten with imaginary companions. . . ."

"Better than someone who talks to you and isn't really talking to anyone at all," Paule said.

Yes, Lili thought. It's like being a student again.

"And he's yours?" Paule asked, indicating the carriage. "May I look in? Oh, he's lovely . . . so fair. . . ."

Lili's heart began to beat too heavily—but there was nothing to be afraid of: she was perfectly friendly, this Paule Jacob.

"How old is he?" Paule asked.

"Three," Lili said, and her heart grew heavier and duller. "He's three years old." Then, not knowing why, she asked, "Would you like to hold him?"

"If I won't wake him," Paule murmured.

"Lili . . . ," Pierre began, but Lili was determined—to find someone to love Claude or to bring disaster on them all; she did not know what impulse drove her—and she reached into the carriage, lifted Claude's limp, sweet, heavy body, and handed him to Paule.

Claude opened his eyes, only mildly startled, and Paule cooed at him. "Cuckoo, my big boy. Cuckoo! Are you a sleepy boy?"

Claude burrowed into her neck, as if he had always known her, and Lili thought, There! Yes, yes I was right!

So quietly Lili almost didn't hear him, Marcel Jacob murmured to his sister, in Russian, *That baby is an idiot,* and Lili hit him, hard, her palm flat against his jawbone. She did it so quickly, so instinctively, there was a kind of pleasure in it.

"Lili!" Pierre protested, but Lili grabbed Claude, now whimpering, from Paule's arms, and Paule and Marcel stared at her, their eyes wide and round, as if they didn't understand, until Paule said sharply, "Marcel!"

"But all I—"

"I'm sorry," Paule said, interrupting him. "He's always doing that—speaking in Russian—it's terribly rude, of course. He didn't mean anything, he always tells me—apologize, Marcel—"

But Marcel turned and dashed off. Paule hesitated, frozen, and then she ran after him, and the two identical dark heads disappeared swiftly into the shadows of the trees.

Lili stood trembling, holding Claude's body against her own.

"What do you imagine he said?" Pierre asked softly. "He told her not to treat babies like idiots."

"Oh," Lili said, devastated. She had felt like a student again, as if they might all go to a bar together and laugh. "Oh," she repeated. "I could always look them up. I could look them up and invite them over for a drink."

Ten

She did invite them for a drink, and they came, and no one mentioned that Lili had slapped Marcel. As it happened, Lili had nothing for them to drink when they arrived, so she brought out some bread and chocolate, a plate of sardines on toast.

"Oh, no," Pierre said, as if that hadn't been their daily menu for years. "We've got to do better than this." And he ran out for brandy and pastries.

Lili was stung, as if her behavior in the Luxembourg cast everything she did in a dark light: if she hadn't slapped Marcel, Pierre would have laughed at her sardines, but now it wasn't funny; it was embarrassing; it must be rectified; they must do everything possible to appear normal and civilized. She bowed her head over the tiny glistening silver-black fish, arranged them in concentric circles, and offered them politely to her guests, who politely refused them. She spoke for several minutes about the weather, which, in fact, she hadn't noticed at all today, but she did not glance over at the window for help. She looked straight at Paule and Marcel, trying not to cry, for they were obviously repelled by sardines. And she thought longingly of Claude's sweet, pale body, napping in the bedroom, but she couldn't, after all, simply leave her guests: *I'm sorry, it was a mistake to have invited you, my son is napping he needs me—*

Politely, she asked about Paule's post at the Lycée Fénelon, about Marcel's studies—he was fifteen; he wanted to prepare for the National Academy of Fine Arts. But why? Why was she straining at all for a semblance of normalcy?

Hadn't she realized just before she met these two that never again would she be mistaken for a normal person? And hadn't it been the sweetest revelation of her life? Besides, Paule herself hardly seemed normal. She was laughing at nothing, looking around the apartment, her attention so unfocused she seemed witless.

"What—? Oh, my family. . . ." Paule rose, went to the bookcase, ran her finger along the spine of some book, turned back around, laughed. "Yes. Oh! There's just my mother and Marcel and me. The rest are still in Russia." She laughed again, pointlessly, then sat down and smoothed her skirt over her knees, sat perfectly still and straight-backed for a moment, her eyes glittering, rapt.

She's off in the head, Lili thought warmly, and she offered Paule a cigarette, but Paule pointed to her mouth, indicating the piece of chocolate she had just taken. Then she smiled. "I like to hold it in my mouth till it dissolves completely," Paule explained. "The way children do. It's so delicious, letting the chocolate turn to liquor in your mouth . . . yes, now I'd love a cigarette."

Marcel, though, sat perfectly still, quiet, his eyes downcast. Every now and then a blush spread across his cheeks, like a memory of Lili's handprint.

Lili, chastened, asked if he wasn't bored; she had some books he might like, art books.

Paule laughed again, putting her hand on Marcel's knee. "Oh, he's happy. He's an odd one—he likes to be around grown-ups. He hasn't any friends his own age."

"You're not too well behaved, are you?" Lili asked. "It doesn't pay to behave well."

"No, Madame," Marcel murmured, staring crimson cheeked at his own fingers.

"Oh," Lili said again, throwing her hands up helplessly. "You'll grow out of it, I suppose." She reached to trace her finger along his cheekbone. "You must forgive my outburst yesterday—"

"He's forgotten it." Paule laughed.

"May I look at your art books, Madame?" Marcel said, rising suddenly and going to the bookcase.

Paule stretched her arms above her head and half a dozen silver bracelets slipped from her wrists to her elbows. "How nice to be here, Lili. How nice of you to invite us. . . . I was so happy to get your note . . . so happy to see you yesterday. I don't keep in touch with anyone, you know. And I never would have expected—I thought you'd go to a convent."

"A convent?"

"Well, yes. After Sèvres. Is that done? Would a girl join a convent after Sèvres? Or would she have too much education by then? Forgive me for being so ignorant."

"But I don't even believe in God." Lili laughed.

"Don't you?"

"Not at all."

"Oh, but you did," Paule insisted. "You did. I remember—"

"You're confusing me with someone else," Lili said lightly.

"No, no. I remember—you were terribly devout. And judgmental. I thought you held me personally responsible for the death of Jesus."

Lili laughed again. "Well, if I seemed devout—I don't remember—I was just pretending. I never believed in any of it."

Paule stared at her, perfectly serious. "How odd. I was so certain."

Lili forced a smile; she had no idea why she was lying. "You haven't converted, have you?"

"Oh, no—"

"Not sorry you came to the house of a heathen?"

"No, no," Paule murmured. "Only I really thought. . . ." She looked around again. She wandered to where Marcel was standing, tousled his hair, laughed. "It's nice to go out, isn't it, Marcel?" She glanced back at Lili with her dark, rapt eyes. "Shall we go for a walk? We could go down and look in the windows of the houseboats on the Seine. Have you ever done that?"

"Pierre will be back any minute, with the brandy—"

"Oh," Paule said, and she sat back down and folded her hands in her lap. "And yet I have such a craving to go for a walk!" she exclaimed, rising again. "You'll give our regrets to him, won't you?"

And they were gone. Lili, watching them from the dining room balcony as they hurried down rue Guynemer, laughed softly to herself. I could be friends with her—but that poor, shy boy, so accommodating, so obedient!

But to Lili's relief, Marcel stopped at the end of the street and threw his hands in the air in a gesture of exasperation. They stood for a moment at the corner of rue Guynemer and rue de Fleurus, arguing about something—Lili could not tell what, though she hung over the balcony, staring frankly at them—and now Marcel had the upper hand, now Paule. He wasn't meek at all anymore; he wasn't even childlike: the two seemed like a pair of lovers, arguing energetically but without heat; then they locked arms and disappeared around the corner.

"Smell," Paule said, holding out a tomato. Lili put her nose to it, breathed in: it was just a tomato. It was a Sunday in midsummer, three years after they had run into each other in the Luxembourg. They were standing in the middle of the market, with Claude in his miniature wheelchair between them, and Paule was holding in her arms a bag of ripe red tomatoes.

"You smell," Paule said, crouching so that she was eye level with Claude and holding the tomato to his nose. But Claude craned his neck away and made a faint moaning sound. "Oh, *chéri*, I'm sorry," Paule said. "Here. You want it in your hand, don't you? That's all right. You don't need to have it shoved in your face." She wrapped his thin, pale hands around the tomato and kissed the top of his head, and he sat happily now, thin and hunched, grinning at his tomato.

"But you," Paule said, straightening. "You. . . ." She held another tomato out for Lili. "Have you ever seen anything more beautiful, Lili? So red and full, smooth as a baby's bottom. Look"—she held the tomato up toward the sky—"look how the light shines through it and yet how it catches the light." She rubbed the tomato against Lili's cheek. "It's enough to make you weep, how smooth it is."

Lili laughed, exasperated. "Come on. We have other things to buy besides tomatoes."

"Suppose I did all the shopping, in a little while? Suppose I came over and made supper for you?"

"You don't like my cooking?"

Paule shrugged. "It's food."

They spent every day together in the summertime, inseparable as schoolgirls. Pierre was writing a book on the history of Auvergne; he'd begun it the same day Paule had neglected to wait for his brandy. Drunk and maudlin after three glasses of it—"I haven't tasted anything so sweet in years"—he took to his study and began writing a rambling and totally unscientific history of his own village. But the next day, sober, he kept at it, and now he was nearly done. He rarely came to bed before one or two in the morning; sometimes he forgot to eat all day. And the light in his eyes, the leanness of his face, made him all the more beautiful, made Lili hate him.

Lili herself couldn't work at all. Of course there was Claude, but even with the au pairs to help her, it was useless. She was waiting for a revelation. She wanted a single, perfectly formed argument she could offer to the world: a proof of God's nonexistence that could not be softened by anything, not even by the notion of mystery.

Paule, too, was incapable of working. She tried to write poetry, but it was laughable, she said, and she wouldn't show it to anyone.

And so they spent all day together—Failures, Lili thought—and yet, oddly, not unhappy. They ought to be unhappy, Lili felt. She herself at least ought to be—she did not have the faintest glimmer of an approaching revelation—but it was so easy to be in Paule's company. It was an odd friendship: except for Paule's admission about her poetry, they had never spoken of anything intimate, and yet they were as comfortable as children with each other. Marcel joined them sometimes, and even he had become easy, familiar, affectionate. He lived with his mother near the Bois de Boulogne, but he often slept at Paule's, and once, having drunk too much and stayed up too late, Paule and Marcel spent the night in Lili and Pierre's spare bedroom. Lili rose in the middle of the night and stood in the doorway, watching them. They were both in the bed, and Paule's arm was flung across Marcel's chest, as comfortably as if they slept together every night. And perhaps they did. Lili could not fathom them. Marcel had filled out, grown taller, but he was still oddly mute. He spoke only of how things *looked*, and he watched everything, his dark eyes roaming and staring, as if at any moment he would make a pronouncement, tell them, in the arrogant, certain way of youth, what they really were.

"Will you?" Paule asked. "Will you let me make supper for you?"

All around them, housewives swarmed through the marketplace, and the men and women selling fruits and vegetables and fish and entrails and eggs and live chickens and dresses and scarves stood with their red arms open, cajoling, demanding.

"As a matter of fact," Lili said, lighting a cigarette, "I put a lot of effort into my cooking."

"Oh, Lili. That's heartbreaking."

"I didn't even used to come to the market. I make much more of an effort, now that you practically live with us, to get the nicest vegetables."

"Oh, Lili."

"Because you seem to care," Lili went on. "Pierre doesn't care and God knows I don't and Claude doesn't—but you do. So I let you drag me to the market and I don't settle for the oldest head of lettuce. Not just because you care, but because apparently I have nothing better to do. I never used to come to the market. Never!"

"Oh, Lili. *Chérie*. Don't you like coming to the market? Don't you like just smelling it all? Suppose you let me cook from now on, since I do practically live with you. You're a terrible cook. The merchants must weep to sell you their food. And I'm quite good at it. *Pauvre chérie.* It doesn't matter. We all adore you anyway—"

"But to have nothing better to do," Lili said. "That's what horrifies me. Not that, after all this time, it turns out you hate my cooking. But that I've bothered. Why? How have I turned into this, an old bourgeoise who goes to the market?"

"You said you did it for me." Paule smiled at Lili, showing her small, perfect teeth.

Lili laughed shortly. "What an idea! I should have psychoanalysis before my mind rots completely."

Paule laughed, too, reaching for one of Lili's cigarettes. "I'll cook, *chérie,* and you sit in your study and think. You put that famous mind to use again. But right now, taste." She held the tomato to Lili's mouth, and Lili took a bite of it. "It is dust and heat and salt—"

"Poet!" Lili laughed.

"Is that an insult?"

"Only if we'd been lovers, and if you'd spurned me—isn't that how the story goes?"

Paule blushed the way she did at any off-color comment. It was a bit of prudery that baffled Lili and convinced her, somehow, of the darkness and strangeness of Paule's intimate life. "I don't believe you don't like the market," Paule said. "How can you see these mounds of tomatoes, peaches, these baskets of strawberries, and not feel your soul expanding?"

"Oh, well!" Lili said. "My *soul.* If I believed in its expansion, I'd probably believe in God."

"Do you never lose yourself," Paule asked, "in the smell of a tomato?"

"I try not to lose myself," Lili answered. "I should think I'd lost enough. . . ." She stopped, embarrassed. "I mean *one* loses enough, without trying, over the years. One loses everything, eventually, without the slightest effort."

"I don't mean—"

But just then, Claude, who had been grinning all this time at his tomato, defecated and began to cry, and Lili wheeled him out of the marketplace.

"I'll finish shopping then," Paule called after her. "And I'll come over and make supper."

Lili nodded vaguely, irritably, thinking, Well, naturally I've had my expansive moments, like anyone else. Of course she had, as a child.

What of it? She would be having them still, no doubt, if André hadn't written her, if she hadn't imagined his brains exploding—like what? A tomato? A clod of dirt? The way dust explodes silently in the air, a fine spray: it wasn't that at all. It was blood, so much blood her arms could never hold so much. Imagine the thick salt taste of his blood, the gray meat of his brains.

Yes, she would be having them still, no doubt.

They had oysters for the first course.

Pierre, lean and distracted, devoured his half dozen without looking up.

Paule laughed her bright, easy laugh. "The poor man is starving, Lili! Look at him!"

"He always eats like a peasant," Lili said, and she sucked the cool, round creature into her mouth. She loved the wetness of it, the grit of the shell.

"You see, Paule"—he and Paule still addressed each other as *vous*—"she's not the egalitarian you think she is. She has her aristocratic judgments."

"I'm not sure what I think she is," Paule said. "I am studying her."

Lili smiled, lifted another oyster to her mouth, pressed the curved, ragged shell to her lips, tilted it so that the taste of the ocean flowed into her mouth, and then the soft, raw animal. "These are delicious," she said.

"Aren't they?" said Paule. "Aren't you glad I made supper?"

"Delighted," said Pierre, tearing into a piece of bread.

"Look at the color," Paule said, holding an oyster in front of her. "This gray and white, how it trembles and catches the light. One doesn't think of oysters as beautiful, but they are, really. Look at it!" She shook the oyster slightly, and it shimmered, catching the overhead light on its glossy surface.

Pierre was watching Paule, and Lili thought how she and Pierre had not eaten oysters since their trip to Pornic seven years ago.

"I've never fully appreciated oysters till now," Pierre said.

Paule smiled, showing her tiny, white teeth, and rose to collect the plates. Lili put out a hand to stop her, but Paule shook her off. "No—no. I want to serve you! Please."

Pierre's gaze followed Paule to the kitchen door: she had a small, trim body, but there was a lusciousness to it, like the body of an Oriental woman. Like a ripe apricot, Lili thought.

"Let's go to Pornic again," she said, while Paule was in the kitchen. Her voice was thin and dry. "The oysters there are the best."

"Not a bad idea," Pierre said, and when Paule returned from the kitchen, he asked, "Will you join us for a trip to Pornic? We'll eat oysters every day. I wonder if Claude could learn to swim. . . . He makes swimming motions all night long, you know. It makes it hard to fall asleep, sometimes, with a fish in the bed!"

Lili caught her breath: he had spoken of their sleeping arrangement as if it were common knowledge, as if he had already discussed it with Paule! Her heart beat furiously, and she imagined them all on the beach, Pierre holding Paule's towel for her while Paule undressed, and Paule laughing, her stupid, witless laugh—

"I've always thought it would be nice to go to Brittany," Paule said, passing a slice of salmon to Pierre, "though I don't swim well. I've only been to the ocean once in my life. We went to the Black Sea when I was four or five. I barely remember it."

Lili's heart slowed: there was no intimacy between Pierre and Paule; no desire, even, on Paule's part. She simply appreciated whatever was before her: a man's appetite, the prospect of a trip to the sea, the texture of an oyster, the blush of tomatoes.

It is we who desire you, Lili thought, startled. For it was not just Pierre who gazed at Paule; it was Lili herself. She almost laughed. It's like being a child, she thought, with a crush on my schoolmate. But she knew that it was not like that at all; this was something new, something more disturbing than a schoolgirl's crush. She imagined herself holding the towel for Paule, imagined seeing Paule's smooth, olive skin. How lovely her breasts must be, Lili thought, and she flushed violently.

But who is it you want, Lili wondered. What is it? You who are everything we have ceased to be: alive, passionate. . . . Is there a man you love? Some boy long ago?

Claude cried out from the bedroom, and as Lili rose to comfort him, she felt a flood of gratitude toward Paule for having betrayed no interest in the fact that Claude slept with them all night long. Gratitude and embarrassment, because she could not stop imagining Paule naked, on the beach.

"What am I becoming?" She laughed nervously into the crook of Claude's neck—he whimpered, sighed heavily, and fell back asleep. "Who would have thought . . . ?"

And then again, perhaps she only wanted Paule because Pierre did.

Perhaps Maman, all those years, had been dreaming of Mademoiselle Duroc.

Late the following morning, Paule, who had gone to her own apartment after supper—to sleep? to meet someone?—arrived at Lili's, lay down on the living room floor, and promptly fell asleep. She did this all the time, like someone afflicted with narcolepsy, and she never offered the slightest explanation.

On the other side of the living room floor, Claude crawled on his hands and knees, pursuing a red rubber ball. Lili sat on her haunches between them, staring at Paule: she was curled into the fetal position, her hair falling over her eyes, a fist balled up between her thighs.

Claude squealed suddenly: he had caught the red ball. Lili should have gone to him, kissed him, kissed the ball itself, but she did not move; all her attention was fixed on Paule's blouse, on the small white buttons that strained slightly each time Paule inhaled. How surrendered she was, sleeping so soundly there on the floor. . . . And how given over I am, Lili thought, watching her, as if I had nothing better to do. It annoyed her that she was so content just to watch Paule while she slept and that Paule herself did not make more of an effort to stay awake and talk to her. What did Paule think, coming over here and collapsing on the floor all the time? She was like a cat, luxuriating in her own body.

Again Lili tried to fathom Paule's life away from them, when she was alone in her apartment. She imagined an assignation with a tall, lean man—some sort of artist—a man with bad teeth and heavy lips. Perhaps Paule had shown him a poem and the man had scoffed at it. It shocked Lili to imagine Paule suffering in the ordinary way of lovers, and yet Paule must; everyone must.

She didn't often go to Paule's apartment—it was easier, with Claude, to have Paule over—but she was struck, when she did, by what a dark little cave it was. It was just one room with a nook for the bed. A heavy green curtain meant to hide the bed from view was always pulled back slightly, revealing more of the same dark green fabric sewn into a coverlet. The bedclothes were lumpy beneath the cover, and books were spread-eagled everywhere. A cave within a cave, Lili thought. The same oppressive green cloth had been nailed over the windows; the paneling was dark, the lights dim. Within one minute, Lili was desperate to leave, but inevitably she sat down at the small, cheap table which, along with the bed, was the only furniture besides an armchair buried beneath Paule's clothes. She lit a cigarette, accepted the glass of wine Paule offered her, and felt herself sinking into the darkness. . . . She felt as if she would never get up, never emerge from that cave into the light. Until Paule, as always, said, "Let's get up. Let's go look at the streets." Maybe, after all, Paule needed the dark, needed relief from the acuteness of her vision.

She slid across the floor and lifted a strand of hair out of Paule's eye. Her hand was trembling; she was so afraid of waking Paule, of being discovered. I could just lean over and kiss her. . . . She was kneeling at Paule's back, leaning over her. She lowered her face toward Paule's—how dark her lips were—

She leaned back suddenly, her heart pounding, and there was Claude, still clutching his ball, still making his small, faint cries of delight. "Claude," she murmured, scrambling to her feet and going to him. "Claude, *mon chou*—what a beautiful red ball." She bent down and kissed it. What had come over her just now? What had she thought? Leaning over a sleeping woman, and with Claude right there!

Paule opened her eyes and smiled. "Did you catch the ball?" she murmured sleepily. "Did you, Claude?"

"Yes," Lili said. "Yes, you caught it, didn't you?"

Claude laughed, squeezing the ball with all his strength: his fingers turned white. His loose, lopsided mouth hung open, and when he breathed out, a web of spittle caught on his lips. Lili wanted to gather him in her arms, but he might lose the ball if she picked him up. And what had he thought of her, leaning over Paule like that? *Oh Claude, what do you think? Do you think?*

She looked again at Paule, lying on her back and stretching her arms over her head, arching the small of her back. If she knew, Lili thought, she would just smile. It would be nothing to her with her pantheistic vision. *Of course I should want to kiss her, as I should want to smell and fondle all the vegetables in the market. No doubt she has a dozen lovers.* And then she was filled with the old despair, to be married to such a handsome, physical man, who would not make love to her.

She looked back at Claude and wanted to hold him as she used to, nursing him, his hand curled against her heart. And she felt monstrous for wanting so much: that sleepy woman, this big, crippled boy. She looked down at herself, sitting between Paule and Claude, in her brown pleated skirt, her masculine shoes. She was so skinny, with her long ink- and tobacco-stained fingers, her straight, fleshless calves. Skinny and monstrous in her desire.

Eleven

A few weeks later, Lili stood rummaging in her closet for something to wear to Maurice's wedding.

"Don't go," Pierre said. He was sitting on the edge of the bed, with Claude in his arms, staring at her. His eyes were hollow and glittering, and they barely spoke to each other now, since he'd begun the final revisions of his book. The sound of his voice startled her. He was so thin, obsessed with the history of Auvergne, the agony of writing about a region he'd exiled himself from—because of a girl! Woman, she'd be a woman by now, middle-aged. *Do you realize that, Pierre? A* book drenched in romanticism, no doubt, a portrait of Auvergne as a young girl. *But she's changed since you left her, Pierre. The whole world has changed. Or did you stop at 1914?* She expected his voice to be ragged, suffering, but it wasn't. It was the same slow, deep voice as ever. She did not know how many days it had been since she had heard him speak. She'd written him a note the night before—he was still in his study, working—*It's Maurice's wedding tomorrow. Shall I ask Paule to watch over Claude?* In the morning, when she awoke, she found his answer on the bedside table. *I'll watch him. Tell me when you leave.* He didn't seem to have come to bed at all.

But now he was watching her dress, as if he had nothing better to do. Had he finished his book during the night? This morning, he hadn't waited for her to knock on the door of his study. He had simply come in, gathered Claude into his arms without a word, and sat down on the bed.

"Don't go," he repeated. The sound of his voice, so rich and soft, emerging from his lean face, that face of obsession and concentration, and the voice so paradoxically soft, easy, caught her off guard, made her flush with desire; she reached brusquely for the skirt nearest her— it was gray and had a stain near the hem—and slipped it on. The momentary longing filled her with shame: it wasn't, after all, for the pleasure of her company that he wanted her to stay. It was because Claude wasn't invited, because it made Pierre think less of her that she would attend an event from which Claude had been excluded. He himself wouldn't dream of going.

She fastened a strand of pearls around her neck to compensate for the stained skirt. Months ago, when Pierre first told her to avoid the wedding, she argued with him until she was hoarse. That he would accuse her of betraying Claude!

She wasn't angry anymore. Secretly, it pleased her that he refused to go. But she had to go, out of pity for Maurice and because Tante Alice might be there; she had said she might!

Claude gurgled, deep in his throat, happy to be in his father's arms.

Lili sighed; she was dressed. "Maurice is like a boy throwing rocks for attention. He's so much like André, if you had known André— what would you do if it was your sister's wedding?"

"My sister would adore Claude."

At the sound of his own name, Claude's face broke into a wide lopsided grin.

Lili smiled back at him, leaned down, and kissed the top of his head. She could smell the sour, sleepless smell of Pierre's clothes, his breath.

She straightened and shrugged. "Well, then. You see—your family isn't barbaric like mine. If I were always to be consistent, true to what I believe, I should—what? Kill Maurice?"

"I'm not asking you to kill him, Lili. I'm asking you to stay home from his wedding."

Are you asking me, Pierre? Are you asking me? Because if you would ask me something, anything, I would be so happy—

She gestured hopelessly. "If I thought this actually had anything to do with Claude, I would spit on it. But it's just . . . Maurice's way of competing with André." She laughed sadly. "This expensive, elaborate wedding with no sign of anything . . . imperfect. He can't stand it that André is a hero, when he, Maurice, was supposed to be the favored son. If there's a flower out of place at his wedding, Maurice will be destroyed! He must be torn up about the prospect of my presence there! No doubt he's praying for a sudden illness to befall me. But if I choose not to go, he'll be offended. I won't do that. I won't even pretend to get sick to make everybody happy. We are what we are, the

Ravaudet family. And really, I'm as much of an embarrassment to Maurice as Claude is. In a way . . . it's on Claude's behalf that I have to go. On behalf of embarrassments."

"No, Lili." And again it was that slow, deep voice that filled her with longing. "I don't see that. I see only that you can't stay away from this."

And it was true, she thought, watching the small, silky waves of fabric around the women's calves—rose and peach and dark blue dotted swiss—she had come to this little brightly colored nightmare in her parents' garden the way an addict went to an opium den. She couldn't resist it. She must stand among them and join in the false cheer . . . even in her stained, drab skirt with her hair falling out of its bun. . . . She held her glass of champagne with both hands and smiled over at Tante Christine, Maman's oldest cousin, almost one hundred years old. And there was Papa, drunk, his face vivid with all its burst capillaries, wandering jovially among the company, holding up a bottle of champagne. "Have a bit more? Another drop?" Maman, in an old silk dress, wove slowly in and out of the guests, as if they weren't there at all, as if she were searching for someone else. And Mademoiselle Duroc, in all her light blue finery, stood with Papa's old business associates, laughing, covering her round little mouth with her hand, flirting.

Lili must watch them all, wait to see how badly it hurt just to *see*. I will dig my fingernails into my own flesh, scrape the arches of my feet along the razor edges of the mussel shells littering the beach.

She could hear the buzz of voices all around, a dozen different conversations to drive you mad.

Everyone stood with a glass of champagne, waiting for the cake to be cut: Maman's cousins and school friends, friends of Thérèse and Jean-Louis, Papa's colleagues. Maurice had no friends of his own, but he wandered, like Papa, from cluster to cluster, offering champagne. He was flushed, sweating, a little bulldog dressed up in a tuxedo, wildly drunk. "I didn't marry her for her intelligence—!" He was leaning confidentially toward some younger man Lili didn't know, laughing. The man was smiling weakly.

His bride, a seventeen-year-old German girl whom he had met six months before in Hanover, stood quietly by herself near the cake, smiling at it as if it were a friend. Helga—Helga who? Lili had never seen the girl before today.

She was a pretty girl, with rich, auburn hair and a smooth, wide, innocent face. She looked exactly like a doll, except that her breasts were too big—so big it was startling to see them there, beneath that bland, childlike face: as if she'd been violated not by Maurice with his goatee and his loose belly but by nature itself; as if Maurice had merely walked in after a battle and gathered the spoils into his arms.

I should talk to her, Lili thought, and she made her way through the guests to the other side of the garden. "Excuse me," she murmured. "Excuse me." She pushed past the young, chic couples—how they rustled when she brushed against them—and the old women Maman had invited, as if this were a school reunion. They were all nearly identical, Maman's friends, with their gray birdlike faces, holding their champagne glasses weakly—why had no one provided chairs? The day was white and glaring, and they needed to sit in the shade. But Lili hurried past them to the bride. She felt sorrier and sorrier for the girl, who had unwittingly landed in this scene. Maurice had finally gone to collect her from Hanover just last week. She must be terrified.

"Helga," Lili said, taking the girl's soft, moist hands in hers. "I'm so glad to have a chance to talk to you finally."

The girl stared at her with round, soft eyes and said nothing.

"How was your trip? Was the trip all right?"

Helga didn't answer. She was taller than Lili, with long, plump arms. But she was too white. The day was white and the bright silk of her dress hurt Lili's eyes.

"It must be exhausting," Lili said. "To have just arrived last week and now to have this wedding!"

Helga stole a glance at the cake and then looked down silently at Lili again.

"You can cut it whenever you like," Lili said. "I think it's up to you. I didn't have a proper wedding myself, but I believe it's the bride's prerogative. You have only to say the word—shall I get Maurice?"

Still the girl said nothing.

Good Lord, Lili thought. He—

"Do you . . . ?" She hesitated; she didn't want to hurt her feelings. "Do you speak French?"

Helga obviously didn't.

"And I can't pronounce German," Lili said. "What a bastard you've married, poor thing." Her voice was soft and murmuring, as if she were consoling Claude for a bruise. "And you so want a piece of that cake. . . . But how did he get you here? Had he even met you six months ago or had

122

he simply decided that he would go to Germany this summer and find a child?" She took a pencil out of her purse and wrote on the back of a pack of cigarettes, in German, "Would you like to eat the cake now?"

Helga took the pack of cigarettes without reading the question, looked inside, and then handed it back to Lili, as if to say, *No, thank you. I don't smoke dark tobacco.*

Lili lit one herself. She's illiterate. "Well." She sighed. "Well. . . ." She pointed to the cake, to the gleaming knife lying beside it. She mimed herself cutting the cake, offering a piece to Helga.

Helga shrugged.

"I'll find Maurice," Lili murmured. "I'll tell him you want some cake now."

She walked away, back toward the clusters of guests. Then she stopped. She turned back to Helga, to smile at her. *I'll be back; I'll bring Maurice.* But Helga was staring coldly at her now, at her skirt, her hair, her unfashionable shoes, eyeing her with the cool disdain of a shop girl.

Lili flushed and turned away. Who did she think she was, going to a wedding in this skirt, her hair uncombed? She should have worn one of Thérèse's dresses. But she looked even more ridiculous in all of Thérèse's silks, her crepes de chines . . . a madwoman all dressed up, with her stained fingers, her hair that she could never comb right, her single pair of ugly, comfortable shoes.

But where was Tante Alice? Lili looked around for her desperately. She had caught a glimpse of her during mass—the interminable kneeling and chest beating—during which Lili sat alone, at the back, like someone paralyzed, the smell of incense catching painfully in her throat the way it always had; she'd slipped out finally and had a smoke on the church steps, but she hadn't seen Tante Alice since. She might already have fled, revolted by this family she'd not seen in more than twenty years. "You've always been a delight," she'd written to Lili once when Lili had asked to visit her, "but I can't see you any more than I can see the others. There are some things that supersede even the affection I feel for you and your mother. You mustn't imagine that we share the same pain. Each person's pain is unique, however much we all wish to mourn together. . . . Or, rather, I should say that I personally have never been comforted by the misery of others." She was a brutal woman and Lili adored her.

But there was Maurice now, and Helga still alone, waiting for her cake. She tapped Maurice on the shoulder and he turned to her, beaming, crimson, drenched with sweat—then he saw her and frowned.

"Whatever you've got to say to me, I don't want to hear it. I know you, Lili. You've just come to spoil my wedding, haven't you?"

"I . . . ," she began, but he was already walking away from her.

"Maurice," she called out after him. "Your wife. She's all alone. She doesn't know anyone. I think she's hungry—"

A few people she didn't know turned to stare at her—but where were Maman, Thérèse, Tante Alice? How was it possible, in this small garden, to lose so many people? The glare, the champagne—she heard Mademoiselle Duroc's gay laughter nearby; Maurice, too, was laughing. "Well, then, let her eat cake! Let the bride eat cake—ha, ha, that's good, isn't it, Lili? Even you, you old snob, who never laugh at anything you'll have to admit. . . ." He looked over at Helga. *"Elle est belle, n'est-ce pas? Il faut l'admettre. . . .* You've got to admit I've got a beautiful wife." He began to walk toward Helga, holding his bottle of champagne aloft like a prize, but there were too many clusters of people along the way and he had to lean into each one with his fermented breath, his wide, florid face: *Elle est belle, n'est-ce pas? N'est-ce pas?*

What was the use?

At last she saw Tante Alice through the French doors in the living room. She was sitting and laughing with Thérèse, who'd spent the whole wedding chasing after her children. There were three of them now—one a year: Yvonne, Bernard, Nicolas—all invited to the wedding, all dressed in matching sailor outfits. Plump and matronly, Thérèse still wore exquisite clothes, still laughed like an adolescent.

Lili waved to them through the French doors and Tante Alice, seeing her, rose suddenly and came out into the garden.

"There you are!" Tante Alice exclaimed. She gathered Lili into her long, strong arms and Lili caught her smell, the same smell she'd always had, of perfume and tobacco, but changed, too: she had lost the rich, ammoniac smell of her own sweat; old age had made her dryer, cooler, and then she released Lili; it was an embrace almost cold, it was so quick. She shuddered, laughing in a deep voice. "What are we doing here, Lili? Come, give us a cigarette." She led Lili away into a corner of the garden, far from the other guests.

She lit two cigarettes in her mouth at the same time and then handed one to Lili, exactly as Lili had seen Claude-François do with André. So it was she who had taught him to do that, and for the first time it occurred to Lili that, living alone together, mother and son, they'd had an intimacy she couldn't even imagine.

"I do hate this sort of thing," Tante Alice whispered in her hoarse, masculine voice, indicating the wedding party. "I'm so glad you're here, though. What a pleasure to see you . . . and I'm leaving tonight on the night train, so there'd be no other chance."

"So soon? I'd love for you to meet Pierre and—"

"*Oui, mon chou.*" She did not even want to hear the name, *Claude.* "But this whole nation makes me crazy. I've got to get out of here. I really don't know why I came. Why didn't you bring your husband and son with you today?"

"They're not welcome. I mean my son isn't."

Tante Alice shook her head. "That poor man," she said, meaning Maurice. "He's even more difficult than André was. Well, I'm sorry. I would have liked to have met him."

Claude, Lili thought. *Not Pierre. She isn't interested in meeting Pierre. She'd have thought better of me if I'd had my Claude out of wedlock, too.*

"Anyway, I am glad you came at least. I wasn't sure if you would. I wasn't sure if I would!"

Lili smiled. "I was surprised, actually, that you did. It always seemed to me you were free of the family—you did what you wanted. I've always admired that in you."

"Hah!" Tante Alice snorted. "There's no such thing. I'd have moved to Ethiopia a hundred years ago if that were the case. Love is the sickening thing that keeps us bound. If only it were possible not to love. Your idiot mother wanted me to come—so hurt that I didn't come to Thérèse's wedding—but look at you! You're all grown up. You even have a couple of gray hairs. I always picture you as a schoolgirl with long braids, writing me about your book, your sweet retarded son. Yes, I always see you sitting at a school desk . . . ! But there is even the faint suggestion of wrinkles about your face. It's very nice. And do you like being married, Lili? It's a state I can't begin to imagine."

Her voice was rough, abrasive—*sand against my heart*—but Lili craved her, wanted her to hold her against her breast and say it was all right. *Of course you had to get married, to come here even when your son wasn't welcome. Of course! Claude-François would love you still, if he could see you, with your gray hairs, your new faint wrinkles, naturally you had to come. . . .*

"Oh, marriage," Lili began. "It isn't easy."

But Tante Alice did not actually want to know about it. She wasn't interested in comforting people anymore. She'd given that up when she discovered there was no such thing as comfort. Only a resurrection would make any difference to her now.

I should return his clothes to her, his helmet. Lili flushed, embarrassed that she hadn't done it years ago, when she'd gotten married. She wrote to Tante Alice once a month and never had it occurred to her to return the clothes.

Tante Alice was laughing, her low, hoarse laugh, like a man's. "Well," she said. "You could always try your sister's solution."

"Thérèse's?" Lili asked. "What solution?"

"A lover!" Tante Alice exclaimed, too loudly.

"A lover?" Lili asked.

"Just look at those children. They don't look a bit like either one. Not a bit. Nor like anyone in either family. There's clearly a third party involved."

"A lover?" Lili repeated stupidly.

"Don't tell me you didn't know."

"Good God, I never guessed. . . ."

Tante Alice laughed. "Well now you know, *chérie*."

"But she's so—"

"Pious?" Tante Alice asked, and she laughed heartily. "Come now, Lili, don't tell me you disapprove."

"No, of course not, but—"

"Or that you think there's the slightest connection between religion and virtue?"

"No, no . . . only she's so young."

Tante Alice laughed again. "She's a big girl now, Lili. She can love whom she pleases. You ought to try it, Lili."

"Try—?"

"Taking a lover."

Lili blushed. "But—how do you know I haven't?" She laughed awkwardly.

"Oh, Lili. It's painfully obvious. Whatever else you have in your life, you don't have a man who loves you. No doubt he's a good man, your husband. But he doesn't love you. And why should he? It isn't his duty. A husband's duty is to be good to his wife, not to love her. I have to go now, *chérie*. I have to go and talk to your mother for a while before I catch the train. Why I still feel compelled to take care of her, I don't know . . . I hate taking care of her. But she clings so."

She kissed Lili warmly on both cheeks. "Yes, *chérie*. A lover. You seem to have given up on love, too, when you gave up on God. They're not one and the same." She laughed, turning and making her way into the crowd.

Lili watched her tall, straight back, the proud way she walked. And then she imagined Claude-François, his blond curls, his high, flushed cheeks, the small, wet kisses he planted on Lili's eyes, her cheeks, her neck. How the light streamed in through the hole in his helmet—!

I will return his clothes to her—but she didn't move, standing rooted in the spot where Tante Alice had left her. Twice, Tante Alice had brought Claude-François to Pornic for the summer. Lili had lain between Tante Alice's long, slender legs, and Tante Alice buried her in the sand. She might have been eight, nine, ten. All I wanted was to clasp that brown thigh, to throw my arms around it. I wanted to run away with Tante Alice and Claude-François, and never see André or Maurice again.

But Claude-François had died and Tante Alice had left and Lili had married a man who didn't love her. Such a big man, with his strong farmer's hands, holding the second Claude in his arms.

She shuddered and went toward the house. And again she must pass through the crowd—*Excuse me, hello, yes a beautiful day*—they were all holding pieces of cake now, as if a little miracle had occurred while Lili wasn't noticing: the wine had turned into cake. Helga was still at the far end of the garden, but Jean-Louis, poor cuckold, was standing beside her, making her nod and laugh, though he couldn't speak German any better than Lili could. So trim and precise he was, in his black suit, perhaps he didn't mind being cuckolded. There were Maman and Tante Alice, clasping hands and whispering to each other like children. The other old women had vanished, dissolved, it seemed, into the glaring light, and the young ones—Jean-Louis's and Thérèse's friends—had lost their chic to the heat and the alcohol.

Thérèse was still in the living room, surrounded by her children. She was nursing Nicolas and fixing something on Yvonne's collar at the same time.

"Thérèse," Lili said, pushing open the doors. How dark and peaceful the house was after the garden.

"Oh, Lili." Thérèse smiled. "I'm so glad to see you." She put a bag of diapers on the floor to make room on the sofa for Lili.

Lili sat down, automatically gathering Bernard into her arms. He was a fat, sweet baby. She stared at his little red sensual mouth, his olive skin. He looked, actually, like a baby wrestler . . . Jean-Louis and Thérèse had fine, small bones. But who could tell anything at this age?

Who could tell anything, ever? Pierre *might* love her.

"Is he Jean-Louis's?" she asked abruptly.

Thérèse blushed, but she answered immediately, as if she'd been asked the question a dozen times. "I honestly couldn't tell you."

Lili laughed suddenly, warmly. "Who's the other possibility, then?"

"Oh, Lili, I haven't a clue. There are three or four other possibilities." She was speaking without a trace of guilt, as if this confusion were inevitable and only the delicacy of the subject matter as a whole—reproduction—made her blush.

"Three or four!" Lili exclaimed, laughing. "How do you manage it?"

"How does one avoid it?" Thérèse asked, shrugging. "Before I was married, of course, I was. . . there were no . . . no opportunities. Everyone seemed to respect that I was affianced. But don't you find, Lili, that since you've been married, all of Pierre's friends . . . ? And how can one refuse? They're so desperate, the poor things."

"And your religion?" Lili asked weakly. "You must really slow down traffic at the confessional."

Thérèse winced, and her face drained of light, as if Lili had slapped her. "Don't, Lili. Just because you don't believe." She made no attempt to explain the contradiction, only adding defensively, "It might seem to you that things are simpler without any faith. But I don't think so. I don't think, in the long run, that things will be any easier for you."

"Oh, *chérie.* I'm sorry. I didn't mean to make fun. It's only because I still think of you as a child and it's difficult for me to imagine. . . . Forgive me. I've no right. Really, I'm sorry."

Thérèse didn't answer. Yvonne began to whine—she wanted to go outdoors and play—and Thérèse snapped at her. "Be quiet, Yvonne! I can't be in twelve places at once."

"I could take her," Lili offered. "Do you want to go outside and play, Yvonne?"

But Yvonne wanted her mother. The whole world wanted Thérèse, and she could not refuse anyone.

"I am really sorry, Thérèse."

"It's all right," Thérèse said finally, in a wounded voice. She changed the subject: "That poor girl doesn't speak a word of French. I hope Maurice'll be decent to her."

Lili threw up her hands sadly. "She'll be in your prayers, at least."

❧

Afterward, in the hot, still afternoon, she walked slowly from the *métro* station toward rue Guynemer. A brief rain shower had broken up the cloud cover, and the sky was blue and glittering. Her feet were heavy and the pearls were uncomfortable around her neck. "A lover," she murmured aloud, into the early afternoon silence of her street. "But who, Tante Alice? The butcher? He loves his wife." The concierge's husband, who played the flute, had a roaming eye, but it wasn't a kind eye. She thought of Paule and blushed. Paule was too indiscriminate to be anyone's real lover. She wasn't capable of such single-minded focus.

And I do want a man. . . . But maybe that's the trouble, the specificity of my desire. If I could just take everything in, colors and sounds and tastes, like Paule. If I were not so determined and aggressive, wanting Pierre, in the end, only Pierre. Who would not sully himself today.

She thought of him as he had been that morning, sitting on the edge of the bed, watching her. His lean, exhausted face and still that deep voice.

"You bastard," she whispered, and she turned around, away from rue Guynemer, back toward the *métro*.

Paule and Marcel were leaning over the tiny balcony of Paule's apartment when Lili walked up.

"Lili!" Paule called out. "How was the wedding? Come and tell us everything!"

Lili climbed the narrow stairway. She held on to the cool iron railing like an old woman; it was night inside the stairwell and barely lighter in Paule's apartment.

"It's as if you live underwater."

"Underwater?" Paule said, kissing her. Lili shook Marcel's hand. She could feel his knuckles, the strong, dry fingers.

"So dark," Lili said, and Marcel grinned suddenly, conspiratorially.

"It's a hiding place," Paule said, lowering her voice seductively. "A sanctuary. But we could go outdoors."

"No," Lili said, sitting down at the small square table. The end of a baguette and half a bottle of wine sat on the table among envelopes, pages of the newspaper, a comb, an address book, an ashtray. "I need a little hiding place right now."

"Yes," Paule said. Her hands were searching the table for something, like a blind person's, like two pale birds. They alighted finally on the bottle of wine and she emptied it into three questionable-looking glasses. "They're clean. A hiding place. Tell us everything about that awful wedding."

Lili lit a cigarette and offered one to Paule, who rolled it appreciatively between her fingers before putting it into her mouth.

Marcel pulled out his own pack.

"You're smoking now?" Lili asked.

"Isn't it awful?" Paule said, inhaling hungrily on her own.

"Well." Lili shrugged. "He's older than I was when I started."

Marcel said nothing, watching Lili with his wide, dark eyes. He held the cigarette lightly between his fingers, as if he'd been smoking in secret for years. Lili smiled at him and he blushed.

"How is your work coming?" she asked him gently. There was a fragile quality about him that made her lower her voice whenever she talked to him.

He shrugged shyly, and Paule said, "He's given up on his eggs." He had spent six months sketching nothing but eggs. "He wants to do people now—not just their hands, the whole person, naked."

Marcel frowned.

"Oh, Marcel," Paule said. "It's just the thought of you alone in a room with a naked woman—"

"It doesn't have to be a woman," he said irritably. He rose and pulled the dark green curtain aside and stared down into the street. "Man, woman, child—they're all interesting, Paule. The muscles, the fat—!"

"He's cross because I treat him like a five-year-old," Paule murmured, shaking her head. "And who can blame him? I don't treat him like an artist, but like a little boy who mustn't see certain things. It's nauseating . . . I'm so condescending."

Lili smiled, but she tore her eyes away from Paule and looked up at Marcel. "Have you any models?"

"One," Marcel said gratefully, turning back and facing them.

"Ah," said Paule. "You see, *she* understands that you're an artist, not a kid."

"Well," Lili said. "I was rude to Thérèse at the wedding."

"*La petite* Thérèse?" Paule asked. "What has she been up to?"

Lili glanced at Marcel. "It's nothing. . . ."

"I can leave," Marcel said resentfully. "If the two of you—"

"No, no. Stay," Lili said, catching herself. "Really, I haven't any business talking about it to anyone, you or Paule." She wanted to keep her friendship with Paule honest, not to spoil it with the false electricity of shared secrets. "It's nothing—only that she surprised me. She's twenty-five years old, and still I'm amazed that she can tie her own shoes."

Paule laughed, throwing her head back and showing her teeth. "Well, how were the others? This bride—Helga?—have you discovered why she's marrying Maurice?"

"Oh," Lili said. "Oh—she's your age, Marcel. And she doesn't speak a word of French—"

"The poor thing," Paule murmured.

"She's illiterate."

"How do you know?"

"I wrote her a note in German. She didn't even try to read it."

"So then—?" Paule asked.

"I suppose he met her on the street. She's quite pretty."

"Is she a prostitute?" Marcel asked.

"Oh, I don't know," Lili said. "I didn't mean that. Perhaps . . ."

"She doesn't have to be a prostitute," Paule said irritably; she was often impatient with Marcel, though she adored him. "There are plenty of hungry German girls to be had as wives, I imagine. Oh, but the poor thing . . . what can one do for her?"

Lili shrugged. "I tried to talk to her, but I'm afraid she was rather put off by me."

"By you?" Paule exclaimed.

"Well"—Lili laughed—"This outfit, my hair. . . ."

"Your hair?" Marcel asked. He was speaking more than Lili had ever known him to. "What's wrong with your hair?"

Paule laughed. "The outfit, we'll grant you, is not the most stunning! Not that that's a reason to be anything but utterly charmed by you . . . but your hair?"

Lili laughed again, nervously. "It's a mess . . . I didn't even comb it."

"You have beautiful hair," Marcel said simply.

"Of course you do," Paule said. "It's so thick and glossy. It's lovely the way it's always falling loose, as if you'd just come out of the wind." She reached over and brushed her fingers quickly through Lili's hair. "What else could the girl want on her wedding day besides a charming, windblown sister-in-law?"

Lili's face burned. "I can think of a few things . . . ! Really, I think the poor girl just wanted a piece of cake . . . a cake and nice men asking her to dance, and there were Maurice and my father, both completely drunk and ignoring her. No one danced at all. Though maybe she didn't even want to dance. Maybe she just wanted to sit in the shade in her lovely gown, dressing and undressing her dolls."

"Oh, how miserable," Paule said. "We'll have to take her under our wings. I don't believe she was put off by you—that isn't possible! You are startling at first, in your rags and your deep voice, but one has only to look at your eyes, your smile. . . ."

"Let's go for a walk," Lili said, standing. Her heart was racing, and she kept wanting to laugh for no reason.

"Oh," Paule said. "A walk. All right." She seemed suddenly disappointed. "It is too dark in here for you, isn't it?"

"It's a tomb!" Marcel cried, jumping up. "Let's go to the Bois de Boulogne, and I'll sketch you both, clothed, leaning against a tree, holding eggs, since you miss my eggs so much, Paule."

"What's come over you?" Paule murmured gloomily. "I don't think a portrait is a good idea. Lili will never sit still long enough for a portrait."

"Well, let's go to the Bois de Boulogne anyway," Marcel said. "I need to be heading home. I told Maman I'd have supper with her."

Paule rose abruptly as if she were offended and gathered her things—her cigarettes, the crust of bread, a bar of chocolate—into a bag, scraping them off the table with her slender, delicate fingers, her head bowed, not looking at either of them. Her spine showed through her white dress, and she seemed to Lili suddenly small and fragile. What was it? Lili wondered. Why was she unhappy?

In a grassy part of the Bois de Boulogne, Paule stretched out and went to sleep. She did not even try to stay awake and talk to them.

"She has sleeping sickness." Marcel laughed, sitting down against an elm tree near Lili.

Clouds were coming in, and the air was gray again. The prospect of a rainy evening fading into dusk saddened Lili, but the grass still felt warm, and she could smell the dusty barks of the trees. It had been a strange, changeable day, and all without wind, the sky filling up and emptying itself silently. She watched Marcel's strong agile fingers lighting a cigarette. He was a beautiful child, even if he thought he was all grown-up. She smiled sadly: he was as old as Claude-François had been when he was shot, as André when he shot himself. As old as Helga. They were all children, and how serious and tragic their lives already were. It was incomprehensible that she had ever been so young herself.

She looked down at Paule, lying on her side, facing Lili, at the faint wrinkles around her mouth, the roughness of her slender hands. If they'd not come to the Bois de Boulogne, Marcel would have gone home for supper eventually and she and Paule would have been alone. Her heart beat quickly, absurdly, at the sudden fantasy that Paule had wanted that . . . Paule's back rose and fell with her sleeping—she was far gone now—and her mouth hung open slightly.

All around them, the woods was full of lovers, and Lili was suddenly self-conscious to be here with these two, the three of them on their separate plots of grass. Her arms ached, and she felt herself give way: she could not help staring at Paule. But Marcel was leaning back beside her, smoking, and Lili felt—or imagined—his eyes just grazing her from time to time. She could feel her own heart going too fast, the embarrassment of desire, *What would you think, Marcel, if I leaned over and kissed your sister right now?*

Paule jerked and rolled on her back, and again her breathing was deep, slow, regular, her breasts rising and falling beneath the white cotton of her dress. Lili thought of Pierre watching her that morning as she dressed. He would be wondering where she was by now. Anxious, no doubt, after his day alone with Claude, to get back to work.

Maybe it is all Pierre, Lili thought, though her arms still ached. Pierre who is too painful to want. But the thought did nothing to lessen the trembling in her hands, how she wanted to brush her fingers over the faint mound of Paule's stomach. The thin, white fabric revealed almost everything: her hipbones, the roundness of her thighs, the shape of her knees. *It's you who are teaching me to see this way: the shadows in the folds of your dress, in the hollow of your neck. How I would love to touch your throat; it's like a pool of water there, where the shade collects.*

"Your hair really is beautiful," Marcel said suddenly.

"Oh!" Lili exclaimed, blushing; he was such a child.

Twelve

It appeared to be the year for weddings. A few days after Maurice and Helga's, Pierre—who had, in fact, finished his book and taken it to an editor, and who spent all day eating and sleeping now—received a letter from his sisters saying that the coast was clear: the girl he'd left behind had survived after all; she'd married a widower and could hold her head high again.

"It means we can go home now," Pierre said, holding his sisters' letter in one hand and a *saucisson* in the other.

"Home?"

"Yes. God, Lili, I've missed it."

Lili was sitting on the living room floor. She was in her nightgown, her hair unbrushed, and Claude was naked except for a diaper. Home, she thought, enviously: it was as if all he'd had to do to set himself free, to set the girl free, was write a book. How simple! Her own book had sold twelve copies, and she had nearly wept with gratitude for each of its twelve readers; but it had bought her nothing, had granted her no wishes. Home, she thought again. What was that? Her old, bare apartment on rue Madame?

Pierre reached out his hand, as if he wanted to pull Lili to her feet; he bent down and stroked Claude's hair instead.

"You'll like it, Claude," Pierre murmured. He squatted to Claude's level, and Claude reached for Pierre's thick, strong fingers. "The rocks," Pierre said. "Wait till you see the rocks!"

Claude pulled on Pierre's fingers, over and over, as if amazed that they did not come off.

"What do you say we leave this afternoon, Lili?" Pierre turned his face toward her and she realized that she had never seen him so happy: his eyes were damp and he was smiling uncontrollably. She remembered how the sun fell onto the floor of her old apartment in two long rectangles, how the orange kimono draped across her bed caught the light; and she felt a violent distaste for Auvergne, this region she had never seen.

"What about Pornic?" she said. "I thought we were going to go to Pornic when you finished your book."

"But Lili." He stopped, stared at her, and when he spoke again, his enthusiasm was restrained, cooled. "I haven't been home in more than twenty years."

"Of course," she murmured guiltily. "I—"

"And anyway, we were going to go to Pornic with Paule, weren't we? You said last week her Russian cousins were visiting for the rest of the month."

She was hurt by his obvious infatuation with Paule, and irritated: Paule was hers. "Yes," she said coldly. "Of course we have to go to Sauxillanges. Only I can't leave today."

"But why not?" he asked, happy again, oblivious of her tone; all that mattered was that she say yes. "Why not?"

"Because if we're going to go—I'd have to tell Paule."

"Yes, yes! Whatever you need to do. You could do it today. But hurry, Lili!"

Lili made no motion to get up. "How long do you want to stay there?"

"Oh, let's stay the rest of the summer!"

"You think your virgin and her new husband would appreciate having us as neighbors for the whole month of August?"

"But she's moved, Lili." Pierre laughed. "Of course she's moved! She's gone to her husband's village. Hurry, Lili. I'll dress Claude while you go and tell Paule that we're leaving. Do tell her I'm sorry to miss her cousins."

"I couldn't get away for more than a week," Lili said. "I have work to do. It's all right for you, you've just finished a book. But I haven't written anything in over a year."

His face faded, but only for a moment. "We don't have to decide anything now. Let's just go and see. The rocks are beautiful, Lili."

They were. She was happy to admit it now. They'd driven through the night so that they could arrive by daylight, and she was drunk with sleeplessness, the drunkenness mixed with desire, with the excitement of saying good-bye to Paule.

All through the dawn, with the darkness draining slowly out of the sky and the cliffs rising darkly on either side of them so that it was as if they were going down, not up, out of night and into night, she pictured Paule at her small, unsteady table, in the faded pink silk robe she wore sometimes half the day until she decided to get dressed.

"Oh, well," Paule had said, a little coldly, staring at her fingernails as if she had just finished painting them. "I guess you have to go then."

"Yes," Lili said, surprised by Paule's unfriendliness. "Yes we—"

"I'm sure it's lovely," Paule said.

"Oh, I doubt that," said Lili. "It's purely a matter of obligation."

"Familial obligation." Paule laughed. Was it possible that she was mad at Lili, that she wanted her to stay?

"Are you mad at me?" Lili asked cautiously.

"Oh, no," Paule said, meeting her gaze again. "You've just caught me at a bad moment. I'm sorry."

"Oh," Lili said. "Oh, I'm sorry." It had nothing to do with her that Paule was in a bad mood. Of course. No doubt she wasn't even thinking of Lili's departure. "Shall I leave?" Lili asked. "I didn't mean to intrude. Only I couldn't imagine leaving without . . ." Her voice trailed off. Paule looked away again, staring at nothing.

"Without?" Paule asked at last, as if she were forcing herself to remember the thread of the conversation.

"Without saying good-bye to you."

Paule stared at her for a long time. "How important is that to you, saying good-bye to me?"

"It's important," Lili whispered, as if she were in the confessional, and again Paule looked away from her, and Lili did not understand her harshness, the sense of disaster in the room.

"Has something happened?" she asked suddenly, and she imagined that Marcel had been hurt somehow, had gotten into trouble.

"No," Paule said, and her voice was suddenly soft, generous. She looked at Lili again. "I really am sorry. Nothing's happened. I'm just in a rotten mood. Not fit to be around. I hope you have a nice time in Sauxillanges."

"Oh." Lili laughed uncertainly. "I don't expect I shall. Anyway, I just came to say good-bye."

She rose, trying to think of something to say, something to extend the visit, but she felt embarrassed and sad: no doubt Paule had fought with her lover, whoever he was, and what of it? It only mattered to Lili because Lili had spent so much time imagining things about Paule. Her fantasies had nothing to do with the real flesh-and-blood Paule, Paule with her generous heart and her secret lovers, her perpetual fatigue.

Paule rose, too, to kiss Lili good-bye. She pushed herself up from the table and her robe fell open slightly. Without thinking, Lili glanced at the strip of smooth pale skin, the black hair. She saw Paule's hand go for the sash, to tighten it, then stop. When she looked up again, Paule was staring at her, her face expressionless, frozen, like an animal's. Lili met her gaze, unflinching, and in her peripheral vision she saw that Paule had let go of the sash, she wasn't even trying to close the robe anymore.

"Good-bye, then," Lili said.

"Good-bye."

She went to put her hands on Paule's small, round shoulders, the way she always did when they said good-bye, and the silk fabric slipped through Lili's hands. She bent her head and kissed Paule's throat, her shoulder—

"Go," Paule said. "Go if you are going. Go with your husband." Her voice was harsh, then she met Lili's eyes again and she shrugged, laughing softly. "Why should I complain about him now?"

Lili stared at her, petrified. She wanted Paule to do something—kiss her, touch her, anything—but Paule was still, quiet, her eyes locked on Lili's.

"Go," Paule whispered finally. "And come back in a week." She pushed Lili gently toward the door, and the motion made her robe fall open completely now. She made no move to close it. "Go," she whispered again, urgently, and Lili fled into the dark stairwell, into the brilliance of the street. Her stomach was sore and light, the way it had been when she lay in the attic with Claude-François, when she lay all day in bed with Pierre.

From her balcony, Paule leaned out, her robe closed again. "I'd have liked to have gone with you," she called. "Not to see his family. Somewhere else. Pornic? But the ocean gets dull. The Alps—that's where I want to go with you."

Lili waved up at her, running backward along the sidewalk, *Yes you would, you would want to go to the Alps. . . .*

Now, after the sleepless night in the car, with Claude heavy and wet in her lap, her limbs felt vague and rubbery, as if she had been up all night making love.

A line of pink bled onto the horizon, and to the south the ground was swept up into ridges, cliffs: mist hung in the folds of the earth, and low, broad trees grew sideways out of the hills. Everything was green, brown, gray, drenched in the mist, in the sudden rose light. There were no terrifying heights in these mountains, the way there were in the Alps, but the ground seemed to have been rent and molded by some violent hand: between the black peaks, the veiny, muscled hills, such peace, the rich, quiet fields, the overhanging trees.

Pierre had rolled down his window and the damp gray air blew in on them. He was weeping.

How much easier it is to love you now, thanks to Paule, Lili thought, putting her hand on his.

He stopped the car suddenly, in the middle of the road. "I want to wake him," he said, his voice ragged with crying. "I want him to see this."

"Oh, *chéri,* don't expect . . ."

But he was out of the car and opening Lili's door, taking Claude in his arms.

"*Réveille-toi, mon petit,*" Pierre whispered into Claude's head, but Claude was fast asleep, slack in his father's arms. Pierre leaned back against the hood of the car and looked out at the countryside, then he lowered Claude's feet to the ground and held him beneath his arms so that he was standing. Claude opened his eyes, dazed. "*Regarde, petit*— look at the mountains." Claude howled suddenly, violently, and Lili took him from Pierre—he was quite heavy now.

"There, there, *mon petit* Claude, it's all right. You can go back to sleep. All right." Claude gasped, sobbing, and fell back asleep: Pierre was still leaning against the car, his arms limp at his sides, as if Claude's howl confused but did not distress him; all his attention was focused on the hills. The mist was pink and gold, and behind them the sun rose, a clear red pool, its warmth still bearable, though the day would be hot later.

At last he got into the car and drove on. They crossed a stone bridge and there was Sauxillanges, cramped and narrow, everything on top of everything else, like a mound of rubble. The car shook violently on the roughly cobbled road and still Claude didn't waken. She liked the cracked mortar of the houses, the old, unpainted shutters, but a cluster of small children standing at the side of the road, staring at them, frightened her. At last someone who was old enough to know— a handsome, red-faced, red-haired man of thirty or so—emerged from one of the houses, stared, and threw his hands in the air. Pierre stopped the car.

"It's not possible—not possible!" the man cried, shaking Pierre's hand warmly.

"Bruno?" Pierre laughed. "You've grown!" The two men simply laughed for a while, holding each other's hands, the morning sun whitening the facades of the houses.

"My wife and son," Pierre said, and Bruno shook Lili's hand politely, watching her, but said nothing. She was ashamed of her smallness, her city clothes. Bruno had large fleshy ears and the widest thumbs Lili had ever seen.

They hold me responsible for their loss, Lili thought. The whole village does. She lit a cigarette for consolation, and Bruno's eyes widened.

She offered him one, but he shook his head. "*Non, merci,* Madame.

"Well," he said, slapping Pierre on the back, once more hearty, "you'll want to see your sisters. They don't know you're coming today, do they?"

They were stopped four more times, and every time Lili wondered if it was the mother or brother or sister of the girl he'd ruined. But Pierre said nothing to her by way of explanation, driving rapt and moist eyed through the narrow street of his childhood.

Pierre's house was at the far end of the village, the same tall, narrow stone structure as all the others, with the paintless shutters, the mortar turning to dust, but with a garden extending out toward the countryside.

His sisters were standing outside the door, their hands raised slightly, expectantly, like the hands of Jesus, as if a tremor of information had passed silently through the village and they had known Pierre was coming before they had even heard the car, before a child could possibly have had time to run through the back courtyards to tell them. As if, perhaps, they had simply calculated how long it would take for their letter to reach him and then how long for him to pack his suitcase and come down, divining to the minute when he would arrive.

They were huge, black clothed, with thick, wooden crucifixes around their necks. They looked old, like grandmothers, though both of them had blond hair pinned neatly into buns that seemed small and out of place against their massive heads.

When Pierre stepped out of the car, they raised their arms and cried out: a long, sustained, dying note as if they had been holding their breath for twenty-two years and could exhale at last. Pierre walked toward them, dazed, and the crying ceased abruptly. They touched his face, his arms. Their fingers fell everywhere on him, with the light, passionate touch of the blind.

No one spoke while his sisters felt the fabric of his clothes, the thickness of his hair. He stood between them, his arms at his sides, tall and lean and urban, accustomed, no doubt, since infancy to this inspection, these caresses. "*Comme il est devenu maigre . . . ,*" murmured one, *How thin he's grown,* and the other answered, "Look! Look at the circles under his eyes!"

Then the touching grew more feverish. One who had a mole above her upper lip—a beauty mark—held his face between her hands and kissed his eyes, his forehead. The other circled around behind him, huge and dark and yet graceful, and passed her hand along his back, down almost to his buttocks, as if she were feeling the flank of a horse. She stretched up and kissed the back of his neck, murmuring something in patois. And all the while Pierre stood motionless, passive and dazed, in their arms.

"Look how hairy he's grown." The one with the beauty mark laughed, reaching her fat hand down the front of his shirt, and Pierre's cheeks reddened; he backed away slightly, like a child shrinking from his mother. The one with the beauty mark laughed again. "*Mais enfin . . . !* It's just us. . . ." So he surrendered to them, and the one without a beauty mark, who was, Lili thought, a shade less obese, was standing behind him now, running her fingers through his hair.

Lili sat in the car with the door open, holding Claude, who was waking in fits and starts. The sun was warm now, and the smell of his urine was strong in the heat. She was tired and hungry, and she wondered how long it would go on, the fondling and the murmuring. He is still my husband, she thought.

But at last he did turn from them and lead them to the car. They shook Lili's hand cautiously—the one with the mole was Margot; the other was Nanette—and Margot lifted Claude right out of Lili's lap and carried him into the house, speaking gaily to him in patois.

By the fifth day, Lili realized that there would be no variation in their days. In the mornings they worked in the garden in back of the house, all four of them—Lili, Pierre, Margot, Nanette—while Claude crawled in the dirt between the rows of tomatoes, peas, cabbages. Every few minutes Margot or Nanette looked up, laughed, and moved Claude out of the way of some invisible, fragile item. The garden was meticulous, abundant: they weeded minute weeds, the width of hairs, daily inspected every centimeter of each plant, watered each one differently, harvested with the slow, sensual care of a lover. They were famous in the region for this, the fanaticism of their gardening, and at the market their tomatoes, especially, were sought after. *Have you ever seen anything more beautiful, Lili? So red and full. . . .*

Margot and Nanette slid through the garden on their haunches, like two great black low-flying birds, staring at Lili now and then, who knelt miserably, trying to determine which plants were weeds. Every few minutes Lili gave up, sat cross-legged in the dirt, and lit a cigarette. Immediately, she was happy, imagining Paule's robe falling open again and again, the sleep-rich smell of her skin. She could have sat there for hours, thinking of Paule, even with the fat black crows gliding around her, and Pierre with his shirt off, growing brown from the dirt and the sun, absorbed in a way that she had never seen him. But as soon as she finished her cigarette, she felt obliged to search for weeds again. And she couldn't think in a kneeling position: her mind went perfectly blank, and all that came to her, like memories of childhood songs, were the stations of the cross.

She would have taken the train back to Paris after the first day, but Claude was too happy. Only the garden in Saint-Germain made him as happy. He didn't even mind when Margot or Nanette lifted him up and redirected him in his crawling: it made him laugh, his wide, lopsided, moist laugh. All morning he crawled, getting dirtier and dirtier, until Lili finally took off all his clothes and let him crawl naked between the rows of vegetables. Then he was ecstatic, stretching out full length on his belly and squirming against the cool, dark ground. Margot and Nanette looked over and laughed. In this, at least, they were like Lili, letting him do whatever pleased him. Yes, Lili must stay because Claude was happy. Claude was happy, and Pierre, inexplicably, was warm. It wasn't much, it wasn't anything compared to the warmth she imagined with Paule, but, still, it was something.

And yet the days, how alike they were! At eleven o'clock, Margot and Nanette rose from the garden as one and went inside the dark stone house to make lunch. Lili washed Claude in a bucket in the garden, squeezing a rag over his head so that the water streamed down him, tickling him. He laughed and laughed in his lopsided way, trying to catch the water, grabbing instead at the air, at Lili's shirt. I must find a private garden in Paris, she thought, where he can crawl naked all summer long. Where Claude and Paule and I can spend whole days, hidden away.

Lunch was interminable and heavy, filled with incessant gossip and lapses into patois. Pierre said little, sitting between Margot and Nanette and smiling down at them as Margot continued the report she had begun for Pierre the first day: an account of every birth and death and harvest and broken window of the past twenty-two years, events that they must have written about in their weekly missives but that Margot seemed compelled to recount out loud, in minute detail, as if the letters hadn't existed at all, as if nothing of the last twenty-two years were certain except their longing for him. Nanette spoke much less, interrupting only now and then to fill in a detail or to laugh and agree with Margot.

All through lunch on that day when she gave up hoping that any day would be different from the one before, Lili's heart pounded, and she could barely eat the potato-and-cheese casserole. She held Claude on her lap, feeding him with one hand and smoking with the other. She could not even feign interest in Margot's stories. Monsieur Carreaux, the mailman, was either late today or had no mail for them.

But at last the door opened, and Monsieur Carreaux, thin and wiry and grizzled, handed Paule's letter to Margot and apologized for interrupting their lunch. Margot finished the story she was telling Pierre—the neighbor's daughter had died ten years ago giving birth to twins—then she read the envelope slowly, turned it over to see who it was from, and handed it to Lili.

"Mademoiselle Jacob," Margot said in the aggrieved voice she saved for Lili.

"How is she?" Nanette asked, acting by now as if she knew Paule herself, and Lili was forced—as she was every day—to read the letter out loud.

But the letter only described the way the light fell into the street below her apartment at different times of day, what she had eaten for supper the night before—each slender stalk of asparagus—a bolt of fabric she had seen in a shopwindow, the smell of the wind, the sound of her neighbors' quarreling. Only at the end did she even hint at anything, and then it was brief: "Madame Chardonner has grown sarcastic, answering her husband in her small clipped way. It won't be long before he howls and throws something against the wall. You know that I long for you. Paule." Lili, of course, never read the last line aloud.

"What a vivid picture she draws," Margot said. "I feel as if I'm there when you read her letters." She wasn't stupid, Margot; she was simply drunk with devotion to Pierre.

In a mocking, affectionate tone, Nanette added, "They're much more vivid than your letters, Pierrot."

"Well," Margot said, turning to Lili, "will you join us this afternoon?" The afternoon's activity was indoors—pickling or canning or cleaning or mending—some dark, tedious job which Margot always invited Lili to join in.

"I've got to walk Claude," Lili said.

"Every day," said Margot.

"Yes," said Lili, as if it were, in fact, part of some daily cure.

"I'll join you, Lili," Pierre said.

"As you wish," said Margot, her eyes reddening suddenly.

And every part of this conversation was exactly as it had been the previous day.

Pierre put Claude in his wheelchair, and Lili cleared the table, and then the three of them left Margot and Nanette standing sadly in the doorway.

Everywhere along the bumpy, ragged road people stopped Pierre and talked to him. Every conversation was the same: How well his sisters' eggplants were doing, how hot the sun had been. The repairs to the bridge, the new schoolmaster, Heloise Forêt's chickens. No one asked about Paris. It was as if he had spurned them all twenty-two years ago, and they were willing to have him back—they'd never loved another the same way—but they did not want to hear about his other life.

Only one woman, the wife of a farmer who lived at the opposite edge of the village from Pierre's sisters, did not seem hurt that Pierre had left them for so long. She seemed, simply, happy to see him. She had a broad reddish face and thin faded blond hair and could have been anywhere between forty and sixty. She was missing a front tooth and had a habit of flicking her tongue in and out of the gap so quickly that it was impossible to tell if she had developed a growth at the end of her tongue that just fit the hole or if she were simply narrowing her tongue to a point every time.

She sat half inside the dark entryway of her house, sorting and cleaning her milk pails. Her name was Madame Battendier.

She rose quickly when she saw them—she was a heavy woman, but she moved easily and gracefully—and pulled an apricot out of her pocket.

"Voilà, *mon p'tit!*" she cried, holding the apricot between her thumb and forefinger. "A tiny little ball for you." She leaned down and put the fruit in Claude's hand, wrapping her hand around his so that he would hold on to it. Claude smiled crookedly and made a low, soft sound deep in his throat.

"His father's eyes," murmured Madame Battendier, loosening her grip on Claude's hand. The apricot rolled out from between his fingers, into his lap.

"There!" she said, putting it back in his hand, and again it rolled out, and again she put it back. The game made him laugh, low, deep gasps of pleasure, and she laughed with him, feeling his hair between her fingers the way you might feel fabric to judge its quality. At last she took a knife out of her pocket and, so quickly that it seemed like a single motion, cut the apricot into a dozen tiny pieces and slipped one after the other into Claude's mouth. He swallowed them all, gasping with laughter between each swallow, amazed that the ball was so sweet.

"He's got a good heart, this one," Madame Battendier said, sitting down on the ground near his wheelchair so that she was eye level with Claude.

She motioned to two chairs beside the doorway, but Lili and Pierre sat on the ground next to her.

"*Alors,*" she said, looking at Lili. "*Ça vous plaît, notre pays?* You're not too bored here?"

"Oh, it's very beautiful here," Lili said, blushing. "I've never seen mountains like these."

"Yes, it's very beautiful. . . ." Madame Battendier looked across at the hills to the west, the jagged ravine that looked so cool and dark from the village. "It is beautiful. But Paris is beautiful too, isn't it?"

"Yes," said Lili. "Paris is beautiful. But it's man-made."

Madame Battendier nodded slowly. "It's true, isn't it, that the more man-made beauty there is, the less of God's beauty you can see. God's beauty is superior, but as long as man is capable of creating beauty, he should. He should, but the more he does, the more he obscures God's. I went to Paris once and the problem bothered me so much—it was so beautiful, but I couldn't see the shape of the earth— that I had to come right home. And life is hard here. . . ."

"This is the best life there is," Pierre said.

Madame Battendier laughed. "Easy for you to say! Well, I've got to get back to work. We've got forty cows now, Pierre. It's crazy, isn't it? What are we doing with so many cows?"

They pushed themselves up, and Lili and Pierre and Claude continued their walk. They followed the road out of the village into a gentle, sloping meadow, where the Battendiers' cows were grazing, and then around a craggy outcropping of rocks. The stone gleamed in the afternoon light, and the back of Lili's neck was hot. She felt Claude's smooth, silken head, but he was all right; he hated his hat anyway. Then the road curved again, into a ravine leading down to a river. The walls of the ravine were mossy and cool, and the trees here were tall and lush, not like the sideways, bitten trees higher up. They pushed the wheelchair off the road, behind a stand of trees, and sat on the ground. Lili unstrapped Claude from his chair and, holding him on her lap, took off his shirt, his trousers, his soiled diaper. Without a word, Pierre lifted Claude in his arms, and he and Lili scrambled to the river and washed out the diaper, washed off Claude's bottom—they cleaned him so many times a day that they did not think about it anymore— then they went back behind the stand of trees, spread out the diaper to dry, and let him crawl naked on the ground. He peed suddenly and the sight of his own urine made him laugh. He was on his hands and knees, and he looked down at the puddle he was making, and the gasps of laughter were higher and quicker than with Madame Battendier and the apricot. Lili went to lift him so he wouldn't pee on himself, but it was too late. She shrugged, laughing, and the sound of her own laughter reminded her of Paule. Suddenly it was intolerable to be here, even with Claude so happy, with Pierre nearly like a husband to her now. She lit a cigarette and sat down, hugging her knees to her heart, impatient for evening when, feigning drowsiness, she would go up to the bedroom—it had been Pierre's parents' bedroom, and it was large and drafty, smelling of disuse—and she would write to Paule. Her letters were no more explicit than Paule's; she described her days: ". . . the same again today, dear Paule. The same again and again, I shall go mad. Potatoes for lunch instead of rice. A long discussion on the neighbor's chickens. An invitation to help darn Pierre's socks—! I withstood the temptation." But then, composing the closing line, that could take her as much as an hour. What verb to use? "To love"? "To miss"? "To desire"? It excited her to hint as much as possible without saying anything directly, and always there was the fear that she had misunderstood Paule the last morning.

Claude had stopped crawling and seemed to be staring at the smooth, sculpted root of a tree. But he was not staring; he was growing drowsy. She took his coverlet from the bottom of his wheelchair, spread it on the ground, and laid him on it. She curled up behind him and hummed to him until he fell asleep.

Pierre was leaning against a tree, watching them, and when Claude was asleep, he rose, went to Lili, and lifted her off the blanket. He led her to the tree where he had been sitting and sat her on his lap. He began to kiss her and fondle her breasts. He had been doing this every day since they arrived. She did not resist him, but she did not touch him either, sure that if she did he would immediately stop. She looked down at his head burrowed in her breasts and wondered if he had come to this very spot with his virgin, touched her in just this way. The thought didn't anger her. Even the possibility that he was pretending she was the girl didn't upset her. She felt almost nothing at all.

The first time, naturally, she had been shocked. She had gasped as if a total stranger had begun to touch her, but when he kept on, she grew quiet, curious. It was out of the question that she would let herself enjoy what he was doing only to be humiliated later, but she did not pull away. She tried, once, to imagine that he was Paule, but there was no similarity between the two, and she soon gave up. She did not know if Pierre was reliving his youth—and certainly the way he fondled her, never quite consummating the act, suggested that he was—or if he was simply moved to passion by the land itself and must touch something: the ground, the water, his wife, whatever was at hand.

But until Claude woke again, she let him kiss her, let him reach into her brassiere and up her skirt. She watched it all, dispassionately, she thought, though she never stopped him. And she never suggested that they go back to Paris.

When they had been there two and a half weeks, a letter came from Paule that she knew would be more revealing than the others. It was thick, and the writing on the envelope looked rushed. She opened it slowly, inventing what the letter would say. Marcel was sick? Paule's mother had died? She glanced quickly through the pages and shrugged.

"This isn't a letter," she lied. "She's simply giving me information on some books I'd asked her about."

Pierre glanced at her sharply. "Do you—do you need to go home? To work?" She had said, after all, that she'd stay only a week, and she'd not reminded him of that since.

"I don't know," she said, and she was aware, suddenly, of an urge to frighten him a little, to add a little urgency to his desire. Perhaps, thinking it was their last afternoon, he would finally consummate their lovemaking. "I'll have to look over these papers," she said. "This evening. After our walk." She was ashamed of tricking him, and sad, too. How pathetic to be thirty-seven years old and resorting to this, a young girl's deception.

"Why don't you go upstairs and look over the papers now," he said. And she could hear the anguish in his voice, the need to find out right away if they could stay.

"But couldn't you work here?" cried Nanette, and Margot said, "Or let us keep Pierre and Claude, if you must go—"

"Oh no," Lili said, "that would be too much trouble for you." But she rose from the table and went straight upstairs, as Pierre had asked her to do.

The small, cramped handwriting filled her with the ache of desire, but she could not make her eyes slow down enough to make sense of the words. She had to read each sentence two or three times to understand it, and the effort of reading—of keeping her eyes open, focused—was almost painful. "I thought you would be home ten days ago and you are still not here. Every day I expect to see you and it's hard to eat, to sleep. Why can't you leave that miserable little village? Or don't you want to? I am so tired of not speaking the truth . . . of wondering if we really do understand each other. *I am in love with you.* I want you. And I also love you in the simplest, most natural way. If my desire revolts you, tell me and I will leave you alone. We will go on as before. I simply thought, when you came to say good-bye, that you wanted me, too—that you understood what I am—but if not, please spare me any more humiliation. Write to me and don't read the rest of this letter, which is meant for a lover, not a friend."

The letter spoke of Lili's collarbone, of her thin, fragile body, her vicious wit, her innocence.

It described the two of them naked, making love, in such exquisite detail that Lili felt she would go mad. She lay on the bed, drenched in sweat, and she could barely bring herself to look at the pages on the bed beside her. It was like holding André's letter, and how strange that that despair and agony should feel so similar to this desire, as if there were really only one or two feelings in the world and all that mattered was the intensity: extremes of horror and fear and love all had the same symptoms.

❧

"I don't have to go to Paris. Not right away. Shall we go for our walk?"

As soon as the words were out of her mouth, she regretted them. What was his little bit of kissing compared with the love that Paule promised? She was certain that the kissing would end as soon as they returned to Paris. She did not know why the landscape made such a difference to him, and she did not imagine that if they lived here always he would kiss her always; but she had no doubt that the moment they returned to their ordinary lives, he would stop. It gave her no real pleasure, kissing him. His caresses made her think, actually, of a dead bird's flapping. Still, the flapping proved that the bird was alive once. Pierre *had* loved her; he had wanted her above all things. She could not tear herself away from this reminder, this strange little souvenir of their courtship.

They walked farther along the road this time. Pierre sang *Il était un petit navire* at the top of his lungs, but it was hard to tell if singing mattered to Claude or not. His head rolled back and forth against the blue velvet pillow that Lili had attached to the wheelchair, his mouth fixed in its wide lopsided grin, his pale, shattered eyes reflecting light and shade as indifferently as a blind person's. He could do so much more than he'd been able to do as a baby: he recognized people easily now, expressing his pleasure or displeasure with them by his willingness to be held. He recognized the shape of a ball, attracted to roundness wherever he saw it. He knew the difference between being clothed and being naked, between the taste of candied chestnuts and all other food. But only rarely now did his gaze express the wordless knowledge that it seemed to express so often when he was younger. As if his few, rudimentary abilities had cost him his wisdom.

She had not been away from him for more than eight hours since he was born, she could not imagine life without him, and yet, though she loved him more than anything, she didn't notice him the way she used to. It was as if his weakness, his muteness, were her own, and, though she couldn't help but think constantly of the logistical difficulties, her vision of him was dimmed.

So when Pierre stopped singing suddenly—they had paused on the narrow stone bridge crossing the river and were looking down at the green, swift water, the sun full on their backs—and said, "I'm so grateful to you, Lili, for the kind of mother you are," she was ashamed.

What kind of mother was she, who lost sight again and again of her child's beauty, who went whole days simply resenting Claude's misery?

"I don't know any other woman with your capacity for respect."

"Respect?"

"Look at Margot and Nanette. They are wonderful women and they adore Claude, but all their love is fraught with condescension. The whole maternal instinct in them is coupled with the urge to minimalize."

Lili laughed. It was true that however else she failed, she was not condescending. She didn't speak to Claude in a high-pitched, idiot voice.

"I do appreciate that in you, Lili. It's the sort of thing that"—he hesitated and a look of anguish passed over his face—"that makes me glad I married you."

"Oh, Pierre." She put her hand on his and looked away: the green, heavy river absorbed the light, radiated it back as a dull sheen. Her heart felt sore, thick. How heavy was the burden of marriage! One managed to forget the other, to cauterize the wounds, to go on, living side by side, even naked, but without revelation or union. Even those, no doubt, who made love twice a day: there must always be this blindness at the heart of it, this absence of feeling—until, suddenly, something welled up again. She could not say for certain if it was love or grief—like a creature rising out of the mist, mute and disfigured, like this mute child with his wild lopsided grin, his useless legs. Perhaps it was love.

She understood nothing about Pierre. This man who did see her, did recognize her qualities, but could not be her lover in any natural way. Perhaps it wasn't even she who had come to repel him, but something else—? The act itself?

She stared down where the trees hung over the river and the water turned from green to black.

"You are a good father," she said at last, and then she pushed herself off the railing and continued over the bridge.

The road turned left, into another ravine, but they stayed close to the river, pushing Claude's wheelchair over the moss, the rocky ground. They came to a grassy bank, and Lili said, "I want to go in, will you watch him?" and she took off all her clothes and waded into the cold, strong current. She waded up to her waist, clinging to the rocky riverbed with her toes. How delicious it was to stand in the sun and the freezing water, naked, her skin taut—to stand here alone, the sound of water muffling everything else—the possibility of death was so near at hand (how easy to let her legs relax, to be carried off by the current), and yet she felt wildly alive, with the sun on her shoulders, the cold water racing over her legs. She would see Paule soon—in another week or two at the most—she didn't feel at all unfaithful. Even with Pierre's kisses—even if they were to make love—whatever she had or didn't have with Pierre, he was not her lover. *You see, Tante Alice, I'm doing exactly as you instructed. Marriage, Tante Alice, is heavy, bruised. It is more painful than just a duty.*

She did not feel the cold of the water anymore, only the current and the sun on her shoulders, her breasts. She held her arms straight out at her sides to keep her balance, and for an instant, watching the heavy green water wash toward her, through her, she was perfectly blank, peaceful. She was aware only of her own hands, hanging in her peripheral vision, of the green, rushing water.

This time, after Claude had fallen asleep, Pierre did make love to her, a rushed version of the way he'd made love to her before they were married—still, except for the speed, it was exactly the same. She remained passive, detached, careful not to initiate anything herself, and now she saw, when he clutched her shoulders at the end, that what crossed his face was not longing but a kind of horror.

She dressed quickly and they sat together without touching, shy and awkward as strangers.

"You know," he said at last, "if you want to go back to Paris to work, I can stay here with Claude and look after him myself—with Nanette and Margot—it wouldn't be any trouble. You did everything while I was writing."

"Oh," she said. "Oh, that would be nice. Yes, I'd like that." If she stayed now they would be miserable with each other. She could not imagine leaving Claude, but it was more than she could manage to take him back to Paris alone, and it was impossible to stay.

And then I will be alone with Paule. We will be alone together, day and night.

But she did not go straight to Paris after all. In Clermont-Ferrand, instead of taking the northbound train, she waited three hours and took the night train south, to the Alps. Because what she wanted, after all, more than the comfort of anyone's body, was to be alone. She wanted to look at Mont Blanc and the Aiguilles nakedly, without the confusion of God. And she did not want to suffer from Paule's desire yet or think about Pierre's interminable rejection with its brief respite, like a moment of confusion.

The little red local train from Saint-Gervais to Les Houches wound its way precariously through the mountains, as if it were barely attached to the earth, crawling with incredible and terrifying slowness along the thinnest of ledges, poised like a toy above the endless free fall of the gorges. She stared out the window, dazed and sooty from the sleepless night on the train, watched the cool dampness of the morning rise out of the depthless valley, and the drop below caught in her throat, made it hard to breathe, it was so exquisite.

She got off at Viaduc-Sainte-Marie and ate the last stale end of the ham sandwich she had bought in Clermont-Ferrand. Behind the unmanned stone shelter which marked the stop for Viaduc-Sainte-Marie was a mossy cliff with a thin stream running down it. How cold and delicious the water was, in her mouth, on her face; she lifted her bag and began the steep climb toward the path. She remembered exactly how to get to the barn where she and her family had stayed the summer of Mademoiselle Duroc's tuberculosis, how the path curved on and on through the dense trees. Cold, wet cobwebs covered her like a veil, and she heard cowbells in the distance and, always, the rush of water: the mountains melting all summer long, though still the peaks were frozen, would be frozen forever.

By the time she reached the barn she was drenched with sweat, and the morning was full and brilliant. There was no one around for kilometers. Before her the range of Mont Blanc rose blindingly white, impossibly high, vast: she wanted to be up there, in that thin air, that brilliance that would leave you blind for days if you looked at it too long with the naked eye. She remembered stories of young girls wandering alone into the mountains, getting lost in the fog, falling into crevasses. (It was always young girls. Helga's age, she thought, imagining Maurice's wife falling to her death in her wedding dress.) She wanted even to climb the Aiguilles, to test their jagged sharpness. . . . But all around her the meadows were so soft, and the stream in its grove of birch trees rushed down to the little lake where she had bathed as a girl. She had no idea how to contact whoever owned the barn now, assuming the old proprietor was dead, but she remembered a little room off of it that could be entered from the outside, that had always been left open for travelers. It was still there, still open, with the same words carved into the wood: THE TRAVELER'S SHELTER, FOR HE WHO

WANDERS THESE MOUNTAINS WITH GOD AS HIS ONLY COMPANION. She pushed open the door, and there was a thin straw-filled mattress on the floor and two moth-eaten blankets. Mouse droppings were scattered about the floor, and spiderwebs were everywhere, but it was a shelter and it was free. And it was in the middle of this lost, exquisite meadow.

She dragged the mattress and the blankets into the sun to dry the mildew, took off her blouse, and used it to wipe out the mouse droppings and the spiderwebs. Then she propped open the door with her suitcase to air out the room, took off the rest of her clothes, and walked down to the stream. The sun was warm, but the stream was freezing. She sat on a flat rock in the dappled shade of the birch trees and splashed herself over and over with the cold, clean water. Then she lay on her back on the rock and dipped her head in the stream. The water froze her scalp, made her head feel like a hard, cold stone, and she felt her hair being pulled, snagging on something. She lifted her head and laughed out loud at the stunning cold; then she jumped over to the bank and ran, freezing, back to the barn. She squeezed the water from her hair, trembling from the cold, but she felt clean and delicious, with the sun beginning to warm her, the blinding white of the mountains still facing her, mysterious and terrible and gorgeous.

She lay down in the warm grass, naked, to sleep. Someone had brought cows here this summer—there were dried cow pies scattered about but no fresh ones—and any cows who were coming would be here by now, this late in the morning. She was still exhausted from her night on the train and it felt so good to lie here, naked and clean, with her arms spread out, the wind barely moving across her body.

She woke a few hours later, quite warm now, and rose lazily, deliciously, for a bite and a smoke. In Clermont-Ferrand she had bought tins of sardines, chocolate bars, packages of *petits-beurre* and *biscottes*, dried apricots, a Camembert and some *saucisson*. She ate half of a chocolate bar and lit a cigarette, leaning against the rough, warm wall of the barn. The day was utterly still, round and clear and blue around her, and there was nothing she had to do except sit here, naked, sucking on a bit of Suchard, watching her stream of smoke in the sunlight.

She thought of Paule receiving the letter she had posted from Clermont-Ferrand; imagined Paule in her robe, sitting in her dark apartment at the unsteady little table, smoking. It was a short note, the most that Lili could bring herself to say: "You didn't misunderstand me. I will be home soon." It terrified her to say even that much, to have everything in the open, explicit, before they had kissed. There was something barbaric about it. And the strength of Paule's desire, the confidence that allowed her to describe sex, ahead of time, in such specific detail without worrying that the description would burden them, destroy the mystery and the improvisation, were terrifying. It was a side of Paule she had never seen before, not just the frankness but the intensity of her need, this woman who had seemed to have no needs, to be happy just to absorb the world before her. Her need made Lili shudder, sickened her slightly, and excited her beyond belief.

She was not afraid of embracing a female body—that was the part, for all its strangeness, that excited her—but she was afraid of being surrounded by female need, with its desperate quality. She felt as if Paule had shown her a glimpse of something dark and wounded that she would always feel responsible for, guilty about. As men felt guilty. She wondered, feeling the sun warm against her naked body, if Pierre felt this way toward her—this sense of guilt, of unending responsibility, because she wanted him. And suddenly she realized that his surge of interest in her in Sauxillanges had nothing to do with Sauxillanges: he had sensed—though he could not know the reason for it—Lili's sudden independence. It wasn't a state of affairs that could last. As soon as she began to believe in his desire, she began to want more of it, and he couldn't bear that. For a moment, as she sat across from Mont Blanc in the sunlight, smoking, her understanding of him was simple and pure and forgiving. Face-to-face it was impossible to go on forgiving him! But just for now. . . .

She couldn't sustain it. She thought again of Paule's letter, of the discomfort it caused her: it did not make her want Paule less but more; only her desire was complicated now, mixed with an urge to flee, to find a clear, light, masculine freedom.

She put out her cigarette, walked back to the stream, and knelt on the wet bank to drink from it. She imagined Paule, naked, kneeling beside her, and she flushed with longing.

But when she stood up again in the dappled light of the birch trees, the roar of the creek, she felt confused, disoriented. The only thing still clear to her was that she had left Claude because she wanted Paule, wanted solitude, did not want to face Pierre's coldness. She had said good-bye to Claude with a few sweet embraces, *I'll see you soon, chéri;* but what did those words mean to him? He would have woken this morning wanting her, and even if they guessed what he was crying about, they would be unable to explain anything to him. They would talk and talk at him, and he would just keep crying, not even knowing himself what the source of the pain was. She scrambled up the hill to the barn to dress herself. She would go back down to Viaduc-Sainte-Marie and wait for the next train. Because even if he didn't miss her, even if he was just as happy to be with his father, there was no way of finding that out until she went all the way back to Sauxillanges and asked. Pierre didn't even know where she was right now.

She stood in the warm sun, still naked, holding a fresh blouse against her chest, and she thought of the day extending before her if she stayed, the imperceptible changes of light, the stillness, the solitary night. And Claude adored Pierre, could not get enough of him. If Claude was unhappy, Pierre would bring him to Paris tomorrow, and if she went to Paris tomorrow, they would arrive at the same time. But she could have this day, and it would only be one day—one and a half days—that Claude would be without her. She put the blouse down slowly and went back to the front of the barn, where she could sit in the grass and watch the mountains. She felt chastened by the thought of Claude, and she imagined him with her, imagined holding him in her lap in this warm, dry grass.

Then as if the thin mountain air could not sustain her musings, her guilt and desire and confusion, she grew suddenly, mercifully, blank. She could have been twelve years old again, with a twelve-year-old's simple desire for pleasure. There was just the endless blue afternoon surrounding her. Now the light was different from the morning's— richer and darker, though the sky was still brilliant—but she could not say when the change had occurred or how. She considered going for a walk, but she still felt dazed from her sleepless night, and this was the view she craved. . . .

Now and then she smoked a cigarette or rose for a bite of food— she gnawed on the *saucisson*, ate a *biscotte*—or walked a few steps away and peed in the grass, then she sat back down, smelling the old wood behind her, hearing the birds and the creek. Once in a while there was a gust of wind, then nothing.

In her daze, her stillness, her life seemed to fracture and dissolve. She tried to imagine herself in Paris, but she could not. It was hard to feel that anything besides this—this meadow, her naked thighs in the grass, these terrifying mountains—was real.

Then the light deepened and she realized that she was cool and needed to put some clothes on, but she didn't; she didn't even pull her knees up to her chest and wrap her arms around herself. She simply sat with her legs outstretched, watching the goose bumps rise on her flesh, a breeze lift the pale blond hairs on her legs. She opened her legs slightly, to feel the chill more fully.

She was still naked when the snow on the mountains began to turn gold; she was deep in the shadow of the barn now. At first it was just a gold rim, and the crevasses became visible: rose shadows in the white flank; then the whole mountainside was washed with yellow and pink. The light that had changed so slowly all through the long afternoon was changing minute by minute, rose deepening to violet and gray, and still the mountains gave off a warm, gold radiance. But the arc of the sky was pale and the Aiguilles were blackening. It went on and on, the evening bleeding into the mountains until they had turned gray and the sky was a terrible, deep, final shade of blue. She rose and dragged the mattress back into the room, put on some clothes, and when she looked up again, the moon had risen, and the Alps were white again.

She wept. How innocent and cruel she had been the last time she saw this. How simple it was, twenty-five years ago, to stare straight past André at the mountains. To see God! But this was no proof of God; it was only random beauty. In some distant future these mountains would be worn down into low, gentle, inoffensive hills. It was possible, looking at the soft white peaks, to believe in an exquisite and terrible God, until you remembered that not even these would endure—and during the slow, tedious grinding of mountains into hills, what human suffering had time to occur: what selfishness, what misunderstandings, what failures of love?

The night was long and cold, filled with mice scratching, with sudden, changing winds. She woke often and each time the depth of her solitude—there in the darkness, far from anyone—thrilled and scared her, made her crave Paule's body more than ever.

In the morning, the fog was so thick she couldn't even see the trees near the barn. She wanted to stay in her little room, on her mattress on the floor, with the mice, and wait however many days it took for the weather to change again, the mountains to reemerge. But the thought of Claude's anguish, if Pierre brought him home and she wasn't there, made her hurry to get up, put the clothes she had piled on herself during the night back into her suitcase, tie her hair in a knot, pee somewhere in the blind white fog and search for the road. She found it at last, never letting herself lose sight of the barn while she stretched her neck out, peering—

On the small red toy train, she sat with her face pressed to the window and saw nothing but fog. Only for a moment, high above, she saw the top of Mont Blanc emerge and get swallowed up again: the sight of it tore at her, like the face of the long dead.

Thirteen

When she arrived in Paris, the night was balmy and gentle. The grimy smell of the train station, the rush and press of bodies, soothed her: she was home, in the great, oblivious, forgiving city. It was like being young again, to be here alone. Like being a student, she thought, remembering how she had felt when she first met Paule and Marcel in the Luxembourg; and suddenly the enormity of what she was doing— coming here to make love with a woman—struck her, and in the middle of the station, she burst out laughing.

She rushed out the doors and walked quickly across the Pont d'Austerlitz and along the quay up to boulevard Saint-Germain, staring hard at the lights, the dark spires against the horizon, the black, lapping water; for it was important to stay calm, not to give way to hysteria. She imagined Claude sitting on the floor of the living room, his bony legs in a V, his hands flat on the floor in front of him, supporting all the weight of his narrow, hunched back—she pictured his grinning, holy face—and she did not want to see him yet.

And he was not there. The apartment was empty, steeped in a deep, abandoned silence. There wasn't even a letter from Pierre saying whether Claude was happy. The omission stung and relieved her: it was as if they did not exist, as if she lived alone in this huge apartment, with all its rooms.

She opened the windows and let in the mild, summer night. Then she went to the bedroom, closed the curtains, and undressed. But she couldn't decide what to wear next—to Paule's—so she sat on the edge of her and Claude's and Pierre's bed and smoked. The sight of her own body—her empty breasts, the loose, thin flesh of her thighs—made her eyes sting: to be so ugly . . . ! To have only this body to offer. . . .

She forced herself off the bed—because what could she do but offer her body anyway?—and took from the closet the violet silk dress she had worn the day she met Paule. She laid it out on the bed, smoothing the folds in the silk like a girl tending her wedding gown. If only she could go barefoot and did not have to ruin the effect with her shoes—because it was a pretty dress, with the loose, concealing cut of the twenties, and it showed off her collarbone, which Paule had said she liked.

She knew that she was being ridiculous.

She shrugged, left the dress lying on the bed, and went to the bathroom. She did not know what to do there. She was afraid that brushing her hair would only make it worse. She brushed her teeth instead, and she splashed Pierre's lavender cologne under her arms and between her thighs.

The cologne revived her, gave her courage, and she went back to the bedroom, put on a black brassiere Thérèse had given her, slipped the silk dress over her head, fastened a pair of stockings with a pink ribbon from a cake box that was still in the trash—the ribbon didn't work well, but it was better than putting on the old, dingy girdle she normally wore—laced her ugly shoes with the intention of taking them off outside Paule's door, and went outside without any underpants.

Her stockings slipped out of the ribbon and made it difficult to walk, so she hired a cab. She leaned back in the oily leather seat, and she was trembling. And then, suddenly, crossing the river, she felt got up like a prostitute. She wanted to tell the driver to turn around, take her back to rue Guynemer—she would put on her good, strong girdle, her underpants, change into the gray skirt she taught in, the white blouse with the high-buttoned collar—she lit a cigarette instead: after all, she often wore this dress; the only visible difference now was that her stockings sagged. And if Paule were to discover that she wasn't wearing any underpants—by then they would be making love.

It was like thinking about visiting another country. Like when she went to England as a girl. *By tomorrow I will be in London. I will not be here anymore; I will be there.* She will be naked in my arms.

And then she was there, turning onto rue de Parme, and her hand shook so that it was hard to pay the driver.

She stood awhile outside Paule's door after she had removed her shoes. Her heart was pounding, but it was steady, a beating loud and regular and certain, as if she had already taken off her clothes, already begun this affair which would change everything. She breathed in the dusty, cool smell of the landing, breathing slowly, deeply, feeling the heavy pounding all through her limbs. Then she knocked on the door and waited for the sound of Paule's feet on the floorboards.

Paule was wearing the pink silk robe, as if no time had lapsed between this meeting and the last. She stood, holding the door open, staring silently at Lili. Her hair was wet, clinging in small, black curls to her forehead, and there was a raw, naked quality to her face that reminded Lili of André. It made Lili's mouth tremble.

"Come in," Paule said at last, touching Lili's arm, and Lili started; her whole body was trembling, her heart furious and uneven, her teeth chattering absurdly.

"Sh-sh," murmured Paule, and she took Lili's hand and led her to the bed. They sat on the edge of it, chaste as schoolgirls.

"Have a cigarette," Paule said, reaching into Lili's purse and taking out Lili's own cigarettes. "I'll get you a glass of wine."

When she came back, she put her hand on Lili's wrist. "Thank you for your note." Her voice was grave and Lili knew that this was no experiment for Paule, no "adventure," and she was afraid.

"Sh-sh," Paule said again, watching Lili while she smoked. Lili could only meet her eyes for a few seconds at a time. Paule smiled, stroked her fingers along Lili's cheek. "Such soft skin," she murmured. "As soft as a peach." She took the cigarette from Lili and stubbed it out. "Feel how soft your skin is."

Lili obeyed, letting Paule brush her fingers across her own cheek, down into the hollow of her throat. She wanted to weep; it was more terrible than anything she had imagined, to feel Paule's hand on hers this way, to feel her own feverish skin. She did not know what to do, sitting with her feet dangling off the edge of the bed, letting Paule play with her fingers in her slow, greedy way.

"They taste like tobacco." Paule laughed softly, running her tongue along the tips of Lili's fingers. "And like the soot of the train . . . a little like Camembert . . . taste—" And she put Lili's finger into Lili's own mouth.

"I could make love to your hands all night. A different corner of your body every evening until I knew you thoroughly . . . and only then . . ." She took Lili's finger into her mouth, bit it gently—it was intolerable, such slowness: Lili reached with her free hand for the sash of Paule's robe, but Paule pushed her away. "No," she said. "Not until you can stay the night with me."

"I can," Lili said, laughing now. "Of course I can! They're still in Sauxillanges."

"Oh," Paule said. "Oh—!" She laughed, and pressed her cheek to Lili's hand. "I have wanted to kiss you for so long." She pulled Lili toward her, and suddenly there seemed to be so much of Paule, the silk-robed body, the soft, feminine mouth opening on Lili's, tasting of wine and tobacco.

And then—it was the small, forbidden thing you have imagined a thousand times without daring—Lili slipped her hand inside the silk fabric of Paule's robe, how rich and full and tender Paule's breasts were, and pushed the robe off Paule's shoulders: her nipples were even darker than Lili had imagined. Then Lili did weep, overcome by the sight of so much beauty. It was like drowning, always drowning, but this was different from all other desires, darker and wilder. There was something in it that repelled Lili, something she could not name, and that thing was inseparable from the desire itself. Paule lay breathless, letting Lili unfasten the robe, letting it slide off the jet black hair, the pale, smoky curves. Then Lili sat, staring with trembling arms at the fine, downy hair on Paule's thighs, the mound of her belly, so like Lili's own.

"Take off your clothes," Paule whispered, her voice confident, easy. Lili hesitated.

"Take them off so I can see how beautiful you are."

All night they made love, their small, slender hands like four restless, mating birds; and whatever had repelled Lili vanished, washed away by Paule's lovemaking.

How soft Paule's skin was, as velvety and smooth as the inside of a rose. Her mouth was like butter, a pool of silk water, a small, darting fish. And everywhere such fullness, plushness, the impossibly round, tender breasts, round bottom, round calves—and then! The delicate skin of her shoulders, the damp, sweetish smell of her underarm hair. It did not seem real, this body, offered up to Lili without restraint, that she might touch it freely, for as long as she liked, in any way that occurred to her. Even the arches of Paule's feet were like silk: they tasted clean and salty, as if she had just stepped out of the ocean, though she had not left Paris in years.

Except for the sounds from the street—a shop's grate rolling up, the scrape of wooden crates on the pavement—it was impossible to tell, in that darkened apartment, that the night was ending. They had not slept at all except for a few minutes at a time: falling suddenly still in each other's arms, having gone into a deep, senseless blackness—and then returning, refreshed, sleep concentrated into short, dark fragments. Lili was not tired: her head was light, like a shell, and there was a buzzing in her arms. She knelt between Paule's legs, and the ache of desire washed up through her limbs. It was as if she were looking at Paule for the first time, as if she had not looked at her again and again all through the night.

"*Ma belle,* Lili," Paule murmured, pulling Lili down on top of her, cupping her pale, smooth hands around Lili's buttocks. "Take me," and she guided Lili's fingers down to feel how wet she was, and it was unbelievable, how wet, how slick and smooth, yes, like butter, like the smooth rocks on the ocean floor, impossible to stand on, and then—Lili had just begun—Paule took Lili's hands away, sucked on her fingers like an infant, pushed her thighs apart, and Lili could hardly breathe, so deft and sure Paule's hands were, the wet, silken fingers. Lili's body was swollen, aching.

"And yet," Lili said afterward—she thought it was right afterward, her limbs still felt sore, heavy—"what you actually remind me of is the Alps."

But she realized she was speaking to no one: Paule was not in the bed. She rose, disoriented, stepping over the silk lilac-colored dress, the pink silk robe, fragments of pink ribbon from the cake box, and Paule was nowhere. She went to the window and pulled aside the heavy green fabric: it was bright as noon outside. Behind her, on the little square table, Paule had left a note: "Back soon, my darling one, my darling delicious one, I have gone out for food before things close: a pork roast, a leg of lamb, some fish, steak, a roast chicken. . . . I could eat them all, I am ravenous, and I love you."

Lili smiled, read the note again, and made a knot in the curtain so that it would stay open, so the brilliant day would come into Paule's little cave of an apartment. Then she went to the bathroom and drew a bath. Everything felt still, quiet; even the water rushing into the enamel tub, the voices in the street below, seemed part of the stillness, the deep silence of the day.

She lay back in the tub and washed herself with Paule's soap, Paule's washcloth, and she felt, for a moment, that she possessed everything; that to lie for half an hour in this pool of clear water, holding her lover's washcloth, *to feel this peace:* this was everything, the universe.

She heard the door to the apartment open, and she called out, "I'm in the tub!" and Marcel's voice answered, "Who is it? Lili?"

She gasped—but she was simply taking a bath; there could be a dozen reasons. "Oh, Marcel," she said, standing and wrapping a towel around herself. She poked her head around the bathroom door; he was standing in the middle of the apartment, looking around with a confused, suspicious air. "They cut the water off in my apartment." She laughed. "And I was so filthy from the train. I just came up from Sauxillanges last night. . . . That's where Pierre's family is. . . . Did you know we were gone? They're still there, Pierre and Claude, but I had to work . . . and then I came home and there was no water. . . ." She was babbling, but he did not look suspicious anymore: he was smiling, his face flushed, adolescent, his eyes falling again and again to her naked shoulders. But how to explain that she had left her clothes on the floor beside Paule's bed? And he would see, anyway, when she pulled the curtain aside, the devastation of the bed itself. . . .

"I've broken the zipper on my dress," she said. "Throw me one of Paule's dresses from that pile on the chair, will you?"

He picked one made of dotted swiss and held it out to her, stretching his arm so he would not have to come too close to the bathroom door.

The gesture made her smile: he was a beautiful boy, growing into a masculine copy of Paule, with a longer nose and a thicker jaw, as confident and certain as a man, except when it came to sex, and then he was a child still: embarrassed and alien and preoccupied.

She closed the door, dressed, and came out to join him at the table. "Shall we have a cigarette?" she asked, kissing him hello. "Your sister's gone out for food. I'm going to eat lunch here, and then I've got to get started on my work. . . . But tell me, how have you been? And the cousins?"

"The cousins have moved here for good, did Paule tell you?"

"No, we've barely spoken—I've barely seen her. She just went to get food. But how wonderful. Your mother must be so happy."

"Yes, it's a relief."

She smiled again: he was so grown-up. He had been born in France, had never met these cousins before, and yet he spoke with such authority about their troubles.

"Tell me about them," she said. "Are they nice? Are there any your age?"

He didn't answer for a moment. "Why are you using that tone with me?" he asked finally. "As if I were five years old?"

She blushed. He was right, of course. Her whole manner was arti-ficial, condescending—like Paule's—because she had a secret. It was as if they thought that if they could keep him childlike, he could keep brightening their midst and never know a thing.

"I'm sorry," she said. And she added, "It's from being with Pierre's family. I don't know how to be myself anymore." How easy, after all, to invent excuses—to seem, while concealing, to be exposing herself.

Marcel, flattered by her confiding tone, laughed. "They were awful, were they?"

"Oh," she said, rolling her eyes. "Worse than you can imagine."

"Tell me!"

"No." She laughed with him, infected by her own act. "It's too depressing. Tell me about yourself. What have you painted?"

"Well . . ." He rose to get his portfolio, which was leaning against the wall beside the door, and just then Paule flung the door open and Marcel was trapped behind it.

"Lili—" Paule said, her voice already thick with desire, and Lili rose abruptly and cried out, "You've trapped Marcel behind the door!"

Paule flushed violently. "Oh," she said, her voice dry and tight. "What are you doing here, Marcel?"

"I . . ." Marcel hesitated: he dropped in at Paule's all the time. Lili wanted to take him in her arms, to tell him it had nothing to do with him, the awful way they were being. It wasn't his fault, but he should go. He said nothing at all, standing there bewildered and offended.

"I mean," Paule said, trying to soften her tone—it had shocked Lili to hear the edge in Paule's voice—"I thought you'd be outside. It's so beautiful out—outside painting."

He gave his sister a narrow, unforgiving look. "That isn't what you meant," he said at last, his voice remote, and the words hung between them, spare and injured.

"I came to tell you I'd been accepted at the Academy," he said qui-etly, and Paule dropped the parcels of food she was carrying and cov-ered her mouth with her hands. "My God," she murmured, her eyes filled with tears. "My God, my God, my God . . . ," she said, embrac-ing him, whirling him around, laughing. "My God . . ."

"That's wonderful," Lili said, going to him and kissing him on both cheeks, and then Paule asked him to stay for lunch, and they began unpacking the parcels of food Paule had brought—the roast chicken, goose-liver pâté, carrot salad, blue cheese, chèvre, bread, a whole flan, an onion pie, a blueberry tart, a bottle of champagne—

forgetting in their excitement and hunger any awkwardness. Marcel, if he thought it strange that Paule had shopped so extravagantly, said nothing, and the three of them ate greedily, messily, Paule and Lili toasting Marcel's success again and again.

Lili was so happy, happy beyond words, to be sitting with the two of them, a little drunk, with Paule's knee pressed against her thigh: to be eating with these dark, fine-boned, lovely siblings and to feel, almost, like one of them. It was as if, each time they toasted Marcel's acceptance, they were toasting to the night that Lili and Paule had just spent together, as if Marcel were their witness, giving his blessing.

Lili pushed herself away from the table and unbuttoned the side buttons of her dress. "I am so full," she cried. "I'm going to explode!"

"You're not really going to go back to work now, are you?" Marcel asked.

"Oh, I don't know." Lili laughed. "I'm a little drunk for philosophy."

"Let's go for a bicycle ride," Marcel said.

Lili laughed. "I'd be sick if I tried to climb on a bicycle!"

"What we all need now is a nap," Paule said.

"What an odd suggestion for you to make," said Lili, and they all laughed to the point of tears, coughing and choking as if it were the funniest thing anyone had ever said: and everything was laden with meaning, tense and electric and shimmering.

"This is a wonderful day," Lili said, reaching over and squeezing Marcel's hand. "You'll always remember it."

"We'll all remember it," Paule said. "Always. When we are very old, and Marcel is famous, we'll say, 'Do you remember the day Marcel was accepted into the Academy and we ate so much we couldn't move? Do you remember that day? How good it was?'"

In the afternoon, they went to the Bois de Boulogne. Marcel said he wanted to sketch them, and they should let him, because this was his day, after all.

Paule laughed. "He wants to sketch you, Lili. But I've told him you're too fidgety. He'll never get a clear image."

Marcel was blushing. "I want to sketch you both," he murmured.

Lili laughed. "Why not, after all? But a quick sketch. Just long enough for us to finish digesting. Paule will sleep and I'll read the paper, how's that?"

"You need to be touching each other somehow," Marcel said, and now his embarrassment left him: he bent over them and moved them around like props, an arm here, a foot there, oblivious of Paule's half-hearted protests, Lili's exasperated laughter—"I can't hold this position!" He was no longer a boy, distracted and embarrassed by a woman's shoulder: he did not even seem to see them as human beings anymore but simply as limbs, shapes, textures. He pushed Paule's head into Lili's lap, lifted her up again and directed Lili to put her head in Paule's lap instead, separated them, and made them sit side by side—Lili felt she would go mad, it was such torture, this light brushing of their two skins, this boy guiding them over and over into staged embraces he would not let them hold. He settled, at last, on sitting them back to back.

Lili leaned against the warm, slender length of Paule's back, feeling the rims of their shoulder blades meeting, their sun-warmed heads pressed together. In her peripheral vision she could just see Marcel opening his sketch pad.

He shut it again, abruptly. "It's really a position for two nudes," he said. "Sorry."

"Oh, Marcel," Paule said.

"Forget it," he said, shrugging, standing up.

"But what are you going to do?" Paule asked.

"Sketch the tree behind you, maybe."

"He can't bear anything man-made," murmured Paule. "No clothing on his figures, not even a footbridge in his landscapes. Such a romantic . . . ! You really ought, just for practice, to sketch what least appeals to you. A factory, for example."

He rolled his eyes. "Don't lecture, Paule."

"I'm sorry. And this is your day. Maybe Lili will pose nude for you."

"Would you?" Marcel asked. "Just for a few minutes?"

"Oh," Lili said. "Oh, Marcel. I am a middle-aged philosophy professor. You'll have so many models at the Academy—it's just a few months off."

"Not even for a few minutes?" Marcel asked. "A quick sketch?"

"Oh, Marcel." Paule laughed. "Enough! When you are famous people will look at your sketch of this chestnut tree and see two middle-aged nudes sublimated in every stroke and it will be much more interesting than if you actually drew the two women."

Marcel shrugged. "It's probably not a day to draw anyway. My hand isn't steady. I drank too much. I should go and tell Maman that I've been accepted, shouldn't I?"

"Marcel!" Paule exclaimed. "Of course you should! Go right away. We'll come this evening to celebrate."

"Will you come, too, Lili?" Marcel asked, blushing: no longer dispassionate but youthful again, shy, enamored.

"Yes, Marcel," Lili said. "If I can."

Alone again, Lili and Paule looked at each other, said nothing, sitting in the warm, dappled shade of the chestnut tree they had suggested Marcel draw.

Paule sighed heavily. "You are beautiful in that dress. Will you keep it?"

Lili smiled, was silent; then she said, "I used to watch you while you slept. Stare at you. I wanted so much to touch your skin, just for a second, like this. . . ." She brushed her fingers across Paule's throat.

"Don't," Paule murmured thickly.

They could have left, gone back to Paule's apartment, or to Lili's, but it was so still and warm in the forest, and they were filled with such a delicious sense of torpor: what they wanted was to lie in the forest in each other's arms, but someone could find them too easily.

Lili lay down on her side, curled up like a child. Paule lay beside her, facing her, so close they were nearly touching. But they did not touch, staring at each other without speaking for what seemed to Lili like hours.

After a while Lili felt as if she no longer had bones, flesh, veins: she was aware only of the flecks of yellow in Paule's dark eyes—gold threads in dark rock—and of a kind of burning, but she would not have said, *In my heart, my thighs;* it was just burning, there was no body to contain it.

And then—a breeze might have started up—she was once more arms, legs, skin, wearing dotted swiss, her hair falling into her eyes, her throat aching to speak, her lungs to smoke. "I love you so much," she said, propping herself up on her elbows and lighting a cigarette.

"Oh, yes," Paule said emphatically, sitting up and joining her for a smoke. "We do love each other."

"And yet," Lili said, smiling, leaning her head back, feeling the dappled sun on her throat, "I don't know anything about you."

Paule laughed. "'Anything?'"

"Only that you think your poetry is bad, that you are sick to death of teaching, that you believe in God."

"And that I love you."

"Yes, you love me. But the others. I don't know anything about them."

"What others?"

"Lovers . . . even friends . . . who else you spend your time with."

Paule laughed warmly. "There's no one! When would I have the time? I am always with you or with my family or working."

"What did you do before you met me?"

" 'Sucked on country pleasures childishly.' Oh Lili, you think I only sleep and eat, but in fact I work hard. I haven't the time for a lot of friends. And the ones I have—they're all irritated with me for ignoring them. Because of you. I've been an awful friend since the day Marcel and I met you in the Luxembourg. Do you remember Babette Duasé, from Sèvres? I saw her the other day and she asked in such a hurt tone how I'd been . . . and what could I say? That I was still trying to write just one decent poem before I died, that I was in love with a married woman? I haven't the patience for niceties. And then, it was a beautiful day. We met beside a bank thick with impatiens, and I was actually quite happy just looking at them . . . and poor Babette, that would have made her happy, for me to tell her just that, that the flowers at her feet were beautiful, but then she would have suggested we meet for coffee someday, and I would never have done it, so why bother? Why even mention that the flowers are lovely? Why open your mouth at all unless you are willing to give yourself over completely to someone? It's no good, trying to form a dozen partial friendships with people. You see"—she laughed suddenly—"you are all I want, and so I have no secrets from you. . . . I have no mystery. It might be disappointing to you, actually, how simple and absolute my love for you is."

Lili flushed with pleasure. "No, not disappointing but mysterious. It's hard to fathom. And yet you still haven't answered my question, about other lovers. Before me, even."

"Oh, Lili! What kind of inquisition is this? I have had one lover. A sculptress, Jacqueline Vernier. We were lovers for eight years, but I was never entirely comfortable with her. I thought perhaps I wanted a man, that that was the problem, though there were no actual men I wanted. And then when I met you, I knew that the problem was simply that she wasn't the right woman. So I went to her house that night, after we met in the Luxembourg, after Marcel had gone home, and I told her I wouldn't be coming over anymore. I was sad, because I did love her, and I didn't know if you and I would ever be lovers, only that

I wanted you in a way that I had never wanted her. She tried to reason with me, and then she hit me, and then she simply cried and cried and cried. And I did love her."

"After eight years? You left all of a sudden? Without any warning?"

Paule didn't answer.

She is capable of that, Lili thought. Capable of doing anything she wants, without regret. Then she thought: Because of me. She left this woman who loved her before all others because of me. And the thought of how certain Paule's love for her was was more disturbing even than the thought of Paule's selfishness. She closed her eyes, feeling again the faint, incomprehensible recoil she had felt when she first undressed Paule; and again there was the old desire that she had felt with Pierre, to have all questions obliterated by lovemaking.

She pictured the day in the Luxembourg and asked, "How could you have wanted me after I hit Marcel?"

"Oh you were a banshee," Paule said, smiling faintly. "But there's no accounting for tastes."

"And so," Lili asked, "no way to ensure that you will keep loving me either?"

"Oh, Lili. How would I know? You are the only person I've ever loved in this way. . . . I don't know what the course of this sort of love is. It's difficult to imagine not loving you—difficult to imagine myself feeling anything but this, but you ask for such certainty. And it's not certainty I object to—how could I not love you?—it's the severity of your tone. I have just finished telling you how simple and absolute my love for you is, and you want more: an absolute absoluteness, infinity, God."

"Yes," Lili said, lighting a cigarette. "Yes, all right. Enough. If God were absolute enough, I'd believe in him. Forgive me."

"No, Lili. You have the nerve to ask me for guarantees, you who sleep in the arms of a man all night long! I'd give you your guarantees, I'd give you anything you asked for, if I thought you'd be wholly mine." She was flushed, her eyes narrow and furious, and Lili thought, amazed, She is jealous of Pierre, and a wave of desire washed through her—a longing to touch Paule's round, soft shoulders, so intense Lili could hardly stand it.

"My God, Paule, Pierre and I aren't lovers anymore!"

"You're not?" Paule asked, amazed. "You're not lovers?"

"Oh, no—"

"Not at all?"

Lili thought of Sauxillanges. But it was impossible to count that. "No," she said. "Not at all."

"Oh," Paule said, laughing, "I'm so relieved, Lili."

They were silent, then, spent, as if the conversation itself had been an act of love—more tense and violent than their actual lovemaking—and yet, still, leaving them in the end raw and tender and weak. Lili's scalp was damp, her heart beating heavily.

After a while, Lili said, "I should go home now. In case Pierre and Claude have come back. And to work, if they haven't. That's how I got away, by saying I had to work. You go on to Marcel's celebration. Come over afterward."

"And if Pierre is there?"

"We'll go in my study. He's oblivious anyway."

Pierre was not there, but this time there was a note. "My dear Lili, I hope your work is going well. Claude seems to be managing. . . . I'll let you know, of course, if there's any change. Today we canned tomatoes all day. But that sort of thing bores you to death, doesn't it? You would have liked, though, to see Claude squirting himself with tomato juice. Margot had to wash him a second time. Your Pierre."

She stood in the sparsely furnished living room and held the note to her heart, holding herself perfectly still, blank. She saw Claude's red rubber ball, lying by the window, covered with dust. She knelt down on the floor and crawled over to it, wiped it off, and held it in her lap. Maybe he didn't notice her absence at all. He might not. *Do you remember, Claude? I am your mother, who would not put you down for a second when you were a baby.*

She forced herself up and to her study. Everything was dusty, scattered about. She hadn't written anything in so long, and the inkwell looked foreign to her: a souvenir from another country. But she must sit down, wipe off her desk, open the inkwell; yes, that would calm her, a cigarette, the need to formulate an argument, to be logical and clear. Yes, and the confusion of life falls away: *If there is no God, there are no contradictions.*

If there is no God, there are no contradictions—she began to write, and how solid and real and true the motion of her arm moving slowly across the desk. She was, somewhat mindlessly, elaborating on a point she had made in her book—how a belief in God renders meaningless all altruism—but what she was really thinking about was simultaneous and opposite truths: her need for Claude and the relief of being free of him; the hatred and gratitude and unfulfilled longing of her marriage; her desire for Paule. This last was the most paradoxical of all, for longing and revulsion were one and the same. She brushed her hand down the dotted-swiss dress she had borrowed from Paule, across the curve of her belly, and she thought, These are not the hands I used before, this is not the same mouth I taste. She thought how beautiful Paule was, how soft and firm, and she stopped writing and folded her arms tightly across her chest. It was not shame. The fact that Paule was a woman, that she herself appeared to be partly a lesbian, gave her great satisfaction. She thought of the good housewives buying their Sunday provisions and the old men in the Luxembourg sitting in their green chairs like little kings while their food was shopped for and prepared and their bedclothes were folded down, and she wanted to undress Paule in front of all of them and take her in the most extreme ways possible. So it was not shame, embarrassment. It was something else altogether. No one—not Claude-François, not Pierre in the beginning, not even her own mother—had loved her as nakedly as Paule did. It was intolerable. She wanted to throw it up, be rid of it, and she knew that now, having had it once, she would die without it. She had felt, last night, as she knelt above Paule, that she, Lili, was beautiful: that her skin was soft and her eyes full of meaning; she had felt that she was good, that to be alive was good; and she could not bear that Paule had seen her this way: lost, happy, forgiven. She felt as if Paule had both made her and violated her, the way a mother does. And all of this was separate from Paule's small, white teeth, her laughter, her endless sleeping: separate from the things Lili loved. It was not Paule but what she uncovered—such pleasure!—that horrified Lili. And still Lili wanted a man, wanted the surprise and excitement of a man, but not right now, this moment. She missed Paule as if they'd been separated for weeks.

Into each life, she wrote. *Into each true life. Honest life. Into each felt life, comes a problem which cannot. A question which cannot be answered by religion. Which is not answered by religion. Why love is so filled with recoil! There is no rationale—one deduces. For, in fact, the further one looks, if, as Spinoza among others suggests—it can be argued that Spinoza suggests—to know oneself is to know God (naturally, argues Feuerbach, since God is a projection of man!). . . . Quelle horreur! Is it God who mixes love and revulsion this way?*

She sat for hours, her writing circular, chaotic, desperate, and yet she felt that she was approaching something, some new understanding—she barely heard the doorbell. Paule, she thought, with a kind of dread.

"Paule," she said, holding the door open, and she could hear the coolness in her own voice.

"You're working," Paule said resentfully. "I could come back."

"No," Lili said. "No. Give me a minute."

She turned from Paule and went into the bedroom, lay down, and shut her eyes. What was it she had almost understood?

It was lost. When she opened her eyes again, Paule was standing in the doorway, looking down at her.

"Pierre's not here," Lili said.

"Yes," Paule said. "I see."

"Don't be mad at me."

"You've grown cool so quickly."

"I'm afraid of you," Lili said simply. "It makes me hate you."

"Oh," Paule smiled. "Sweet Lili."

She could not explain the fear, even to herself—the dread that she would forget her own flaws, her meanness; that she would grow self-satisfied—and so she resorted to that most familiar of anxieties: "Eventually you'll leave me the way you left Jacqueline."

Paule lay down silently beside her. She pushed Lili's dress up, and Lili accepted the gesture as an answer, a promise of fidelity.

That night their lovemaking was tense, confused, heavy with the desire to be possessed, the dread of it.

Fourteen

There was another letter from Pierre in the middle of the week: he hoped her work was going well, Claude seemed all right, they'd spent the afternoon canning beans. She sat cross-legged on the bed—hers and Pierre's and Claude's—and read the note several times. Paule was asleep beside her, sprawled across the bed. There was still another day, at least, to love and be loved.

"Wake up," she begged, leaning down. "All you do is sleep."

Paule burrowed under the covers.

"Please."

Paule slept another hour and a half. When she awoke, she didn't feel like making love. She wanted to go for a bicycle ride. Lili ran out to the pâtisserie, the *boulangerie,* the *crémerie,* the greengrocery—the line at the butcher shop was too long—and packed a picnic basket of éclairs, flan, *tomme de Savoie,* bread, wild strawberries, a tin of sardines; no doubt she was forgetting something, but she couldn't think what. She ran from thing to thing—an extra sweater, the bicycle pump, a bottle of wine—while Paule bathed slowly, deliciously.

On the way downstairs (At last! It was almost noon!) the concierge's husband—a dark wiry man so ugly he was beautiful—smiled at Paule. Was she living at the Larats now?

"Oh, only for a few days," Lili said. "The water's off in her building. And it's nice to have company when Monsieur Larat is away."

"*Bien sûr.*" The concierge's husband nodded, gazing appreciatively at Paule's breasts, the curve of her waist. He had asked Lili, after the first time he met Paule, if she and her brother were Israelites, and he had said that personally he had nothing against Israelites, he didn't believe in the Trinity himself, and if the Israelites were making a successful go of things, well, that was all to their credit. "Show me the man who isn't greedy," he'd said. "Can you name one? Even the priests want what they can get. It's human nature. If the Israelites are better than the rest of us at satisfying their greed, well—what of it? We ought to study them."

But he did play the flute beautifully. Lili had seen him playing once as his wife was coming out of their apartment, his face twisted and filled with light: an absolute surrender to whatever it was he was practicing beside the kitchen table.

"I thought, for a moment, of having an affair with him," Lili said when they were out in the street.

"Poor Lili," Paule said. "Were you as lonely as all that?"

"Oh," said Lili, breathing in the soft clear air—the city was scrubbed and light, as beautiful as she had ever seen it, "yes. Yes, I suppose I was."

They rode their bicycles an hour out until they saw a path leading into a pine forest, and they rode slowly through the trees.

"Here," said Lili, when they reached a clearing, and like a girl playing house, she knelt and spread out the blanket, the pastries and cheese and bread and wine. She felt excited, the way she always had as a child at the beginning of any game.

"Lili," Paule said, above her. "My God you're beautiful."

"Oh—!" Lili said. She flushed, looked away, forgot what she was doing, laughed. "You're lovely yourself." She began to tremble again, as she had the first night. How much more she knew now than she had then, as if she'd been half asleep all these years—or maybe it was now that she was half asleep, dreaming, *Paule and I were lovers, we were alone in Paris and we were lovers.*

She looked up at Paule, in her soft red summer dress that fell in folds around her calves, her hair like some black glossy fruit, and for a moment, in the broken light of the forest, Paule seemed not like a woman at all but like a play of light.

Paule laughed, knelt down beside Lili, and kissed her cheek. "How easily you catch cold, Lili. How easily frightened you are."

"You're never afraid," Lili said.

"What is there to be afraid of?"

Lili laughed nervously. "I don't know."

"What haven't you already suffered?"

"I don't know," Lili repeated. "I'm less frightened of what I have not suffered than of suffering the same thing again."

"What would be the worst thing to suffer twice?"

"Oh—! My brother's death."

"Well." Paule threw her hands up, sadly. "I don't imagine we'll have another war."

"It wasn't that," Lili said. "He didn't die because of the war. Though, God, I'd shoot myself if we did have another war—" She stopped, her eyes burning, wet, and she let out a small laugh. "I wasn't thinking of what I was saying. That's what he did. He shot himself. It wasn't the Germans. It wasn't even because of the Germans. He shot himself because we didn't love him. The family, I mean. None of us. We couldn't any of us stand him, and so he shot himself. As if he were doing us a favor."

Paule shut her eyes.

"I've never told anyone except Pierre. No one in the family knows."

"You found him?" Paule asked.

"Oh, no. I would have killed myself too, I think, if I'd found him. He did it in the army. But he told me. He sent me a letter."

"Oh, Lili. He must have thought you were his friend."

Lili laughed harshly. "Are you trying to make this palatable?"

"No," Paule said. "No, Lili. I am just trying to understand." She put her hand on Lili's arm, but Lili barely felt it. She was thinking of Pierre, wanting suddenly, more than anything, to be in his arms: who had asked no questions, had simply come up behind her and put his arms around her.

Paule took Lili's face in her hands and kissed her forehead. "Poor Lili," she said. "Poor thing. You never told me."

And it was all right again, the soft hands on her face, the light, maternal kiss.

Paule sat down, stretching her legs in front of her, and put her hand on Lili's. "I've never suffered like that. We didn't even lose anyone in the war. I was afraid, because nothing ever did happen to us— we were in Saint-Rémy and all around us there was so much grief, everyone losing their boys—I kept waiting for something terrible to happen to us, too, but we only had Marcel, who was just a baby. We weren't really part of the town. I had cousins in Russia I didn't remember, a father I'd never known . . . I mean simply that I can't imagine— I want you to understand that I'm ignorant."

Lili was silent. Then she laughed wearily. "How is it you're not an idiot, then?"

Paule shrugged. "I know how exquisite the world is. I've always known that."

"Even as a Jew."

"I've never been bothered about being Jewish."

"Haven't you?"

"Well, anyway, not to my face." Paule laughed. "My mother—she has a terrible sense of it, in her bones, the pain of the Jews. But my life has been so easy."

"I used to believe in God," Lili said.

"I know," said Paule. They did not move, sitting side by side on the thin blanket through which they could feel the faint jabbing of pine needles. The light fell through the trees, a bright branch, and then a dark one: such depth of darkness, dank and wet; such blinding light.

"Before André killed himself."

"Did you stop suddenly then?"

"Nothing was sudden," Lili said. Though hadn't it been? Hadn't she stopped believing the moment she opened André's letter? And yet it seemed to her now that it had been endlessly drawn out, like a terrible, painful numbness. As if her limbs were partially frozen and she was having them slowly sawed off.

"I barely read his letter, I didn't need to, as if I had known my whole life what that letter would say. And then I prayed. I got down on my knees and prayed. For what? His soul? Mine? I am as responsible for his death as if I'd removed his helmet so that the bullet might enter unobstructed. I kept praying. There was no comfort in it. It was just noise, sound. And the sound got louder and louder, I was praying so fervently, my lips moving and moving till they were exhausted, and through all that clatter, the truth came to me anyway: there was no forgiveness anywhere, from anyone. And I had known that too, all along. I had known that we were torturing André and that all our praying and genuflecting—putting stones in my shoes to mortify my senses!—were distractions. So we wouldn't think about what we were doing: the little daily cruelties, the mockery. They attracted us like opium."

"And yet," Paule began.

"And yet?"

"He did write you."

"So?"

"You couldn't have been as cruel as the others."

Lili laughed. "What of it? What if I was a little less cruel? Will I go to heaven? And anyway," she continued softly, "the ones who are a little less cruel—we are the worst of all. We have a conscience. We can see what we're doing and we do it anyway. We go on anyway."

"All right, then," Paule said. "All right. You are irredeemable. Evil. Why do you make love to me so tenderly? Why do you take such good care of Claude? Why bother? Why didn't you simply kill yourself?"

"Oh," Lili said, and she felt peaceful, yes, here it was again, and every time it was like being saved, "at first I thought the only reason I didn't kill myself was because of a simple animal urge to live, to keep going, and that was part of the horror—that I could still have such an urge. And then I began to realize that religion had not been merely a distraction from self-knowledge—that it was, in fact, inseparable from our cruelty to André. They both had the same origin: the desire to be well thought of. In one instance it is the longing for approval from an imagined omnipotence, but, of course, it's hard to maintain a fantasy—the more pious and intelligent you are, the more you speak of a struggle for faith—so you turn to your fellow man for approval, and when does that not involve shunning a third? You must distinguish yourself from everyone else in order to gain approval. Sometimes that leads to very nice, noble behavior. But even then! What's the use of that niceness when you're just doing it to be well thought of? It's all so proud and self-satisfied. Isn't an act of altruism purer when it's done for its own sake and not because of some longed-for reward—in this life or any other?"

"Oh, Lili," Paule murmured.

"And I began to realize," Lili went on, excited now, as if she were giving a lecture, "I began to realize how much cruelty was done in the name of God. The war! The war itself! These little boys, seventeen years old—we were such children!—sent off to be exterminated, and it was all right, because they would go straight to heaven. Imagine! Imagine that!"

"Oh, Lili," Paule said again, her palms flat on her thighs.

"What, Paule? Say it, *chérie*. But what is there to say? What is there?"

"Nothing," Paule said. "I still don't understand why you kept living."

"Because," Lili said, calmer now, "I could still make good of my life. When I saw how much religion was at the heart of evil, I had hope. If I gave up religion—gave it all up, that sweet, stupefying comfort—I might be purified. I might start over, simple and naked and even, possibly, decent."

"And how do you tolerate me, who believes in God more than anything?"

"Oh, you," Lili said, lifting Paule's hand and kissing it. "You're an invert and a pagan. A little savage. If there is an afterlife, you're going straight to hell. You think you're religious, and no doubt you have some strong religious feeling you confuse with God, but you're full of contradictions. Like Thérèse. And isn't it interesting that the nicest people one knows are always the ones who can't begin to live religious lives?"

Paule laughed. "It might suggest that belief is more complicated than you'll admit."

"It suggests nothing of the kind. It suggests only that you and Thérèse both have lazy minds and that, if you followed your thoughts through to their logical conclusions, you'd have to give up your God."

"Or that God isn't a thought."

Lili laughed. "The problem with having an argument with a true believer is that you can never progress beyond the most elementary concepts. And the reason for that isn't the enormity of our difference; it's that the faithful—even if they're Jewish—must keep their minds soft and small if they wish to keep their faith. Like keeping one's eyes deliberately unfocused."

Paule shrugged. "When you ride a horse, you have to keep your eyes slightly out of focus in order to see the whole picture. If you focus too narrowly on one thing, you fall right off."

"Really, Paule. If we're going to compare metaphors, there are as many to convince a person of the importance of clarity and precision as there are to convince him of the ecstasy of dull wittedness."

Paule shrugged again. "Never mind, Lili. But I think . . . a Jew would find you blameless in your brother's death. I don't know about Catholics. Don't they believe that children are incapable of committing mortal sins?"

"Before the age of seven," Lili said.

"Well, then, surely they would feel that you've repented enough. That you are worthy of mercy."

"And they would be wrong," Lili said softly, lying back and staring up through the fractured light.

"Oh, Lili."

For a while they didn't move or speak. Then Paule touched the space between Lili's breasts. She kept her fingers there, still and quiet, and it was terrible for Lili to feel that soft pressure against her heart. "Stop," Lili whispered, but she didn't move Paule's hand away.

"I want . . . ," Paule said, touching Lili's throat now. "I want . . ."

She gave up, but she did not remove her hand. She rose and in the trembling shadows of the trees she pulled off her dress, her underwear, her socks, and threw them in a heap on the pine needles. She stood there a moment, naked, as if she didn't know what to do next, and then she knelt beside Lili and pulled her clothes off, as if she were undressing a child or an invalid. She rolled Lili over, unbuttoned her skirt, lifted her back to take off her blouse, pulled off her underpants. Lili was limp, passive; she felt again the terrible, painful numbness, as if she had been insufficiently etherized, as if she were thawing.

Paule lay beside her, stroking her throat, her collarbone, over and over. "Poor Lili," she said. The shadows of the pine branches fell over their nakedness like fringed shawls. Lili wanted to scream, but it was like a dream now and she couldn't open her mouth.

"You poor, poor thing," Paule repeated. She kept sliding her hand down Lili's throat, the same endless motion. Then she stopped and took Lili in her arms. "Do you want us to put our clothes back on? I'm sorry if I—I thought . . . I had an idea that if I made love to you when you were feeling sad . . ."

Lili found her voice, let out a soft, wounded laugh. "You'd make it better?"

"Oh, no. No. No, I didn't think you'd even want that. I simply thought I'd understand you better. I suppose. . . ." She laughed helplessly. "What an idiotic notion, I guess."

Lili didn't answer. It was like sinking into the dream again. There was no possibility of speaking, moving. She imagined that she was in her mother's arms, in the big bed in Saint-Germain. Then she heard herself say listlessly, "Do whatever you like."

"Oh, Lili." Paule's lips fell on Lili's eyes, her cheeks, her heart. "My darling." The dry, soft kisses landed again and again on Lili's face, like butterflies.

"But you have to breathe," Paule said. "You have to breathe or you'll die." Lili realized that she had been holding her breath for a long time. She inhaled deeply, and for a moment her head cleared: she could see that Paule was making love to her, and she was surprised that she felt nothing, no arousal, only a dim awareness of the weight of Paule's lips, her fingers.

"Not just once," Paule said, almost laughing. "You have to keep breathing." Her hand was cupped over Lili's vulva, as if she were protecting it, and Lili breathed dutifully in, out, in and out, and Paule's hand fluttered in time to her breathing.

André lifted his white, bony arms and held the pistol to his temple—his thin face, his smooth white skin—and then she was choking, spitting, as if she'd swallowed water the wrong way, and a wave of pain washed up through her legs, her belly: she realized she was crying, and Paule lay, with her head on Lili's belly, murmuring, "Oh my darling. My darling. Cry."

When Lili was done, she put her hand on Paule's head and said in a weak, simple voice, "I've cried before, you know. It doesn't take it away."

"I wouldn't have presumed," Paule said, looking up.

They lay back in the deep stillness of the forest, watching the angle of the light slide down through the trees. After a while, they sat up and tore the bread apart with their hands and took bites straight off the *tomme de Savoie*—Lili had forgotten utensils. Paule had a corkscrew, and they drank straight from the bottle of wine. There seemed to be, in both of them, a deep, slow hunger and thirst, so that they filled their mouths with wine before swallowing and sopped up the oil from the sardine tin with their fingers. Lili picked the bread crumbs off her breasts and out from the tiny folds in her belly and ate them, and with each bite, each swallow, the sorrow reverberated through her body.

All around them was the green, dank, acrid smell of the forest: the rotting earth, the sap, the new light pine needles, such an intensity of light and dark that flooded through them, and yet still they kept consuming: the skin of the cheese, the cream from the éclair that had oozed onto the paper.

When there wasn't a crumb left, they lay back on their elbows and digested. Then they curled up on their sides, belly to back.

"I didn't come straight here from Sauxillanges," Lili murmured into the soft nape of Paule's neck.

"No?"

"I went to the Alps for a day first."

"You didn't invite me?"

"I wanted to be alone."

"Ah."

"I was already afraid of you then," Lili said.

"Yes," said Paule.

"Do you know why?" Lili asked.

"I can imagine a number of reasons."

"I was afraid you'd grow dependent on me . . . need something from me that I couldn't give you. The way women do with men."

"Oh," Paule said, laughing softly.

"Does it offend you?" Lili asked.

"Not at all. I am dependent on you. And I want much more from you than you could ever provide."

They stayed until the mosquitoes came out, and then they put all their clothes on and buried their faces in their knees, only looking up to take a puff on their cigarettes. The whining of the bugs was terrible, and they found their way again and again into Lili's and Paule's ears so that they had to keep boxing their heads like madwomen. They told each other that if they just waited a little while longer, the air would cool down and the mosquitoes would stop and the ride home would be so much nicer in the cool of the evening. It was awful and Lili stopped caring at all about riding in the cool of the evening, but she kept batting away the mosquitoes and encouraging Paule. She felt that staying past dusk was important—maybe even sleeping here, in the woods—she could not say why, except that she felt as if they were lost and no one could find them here, and like a child she wanted to extend the game of being hidden as long as possible.

At long last—it went on longer than either of them expected and by the end they were crazed, crouching and jumping and shaking themselves—they realized there was only an occasional mosquito now and, looking up, they saw the moon rising between the trees.

Lili laughed, exhausted, her forearms covered with welts, and she clapped her hands around a lone mosquito and killed it. "That was truly horrible," she said.

"It had better really be exquisite to ride in the cool of the evening," Paule said.

"We could not ride at all," Lili said. "We could sleep here."

"Oh, *chérie*, after this battle, I want a nice dinner, your comfortable bed. I want to bathe my arms in vinegar."

"Such a delicate little thing." Lili laughed. "Don't you want to stay here?"

"No, I want a nice steak and then your big soft bed."

"I hate to go back," Lili said.

"*On reviendra, ma belle,*" Paule said, running her fingers through Lili's hair. "*On reviendra, chérie.*"

❧

180

They rode back side by side when the moon was high and the countryside bathed in light. Now and then they held hands, though it was hard for Lili to keep her balance. They stopped near Sèvres and had a dinner of potatoes and bleeding steaks, and the food was delicious and filling. Then they climbed on their bikes again and rode slowly through the night streets, their stomachs distended, to Lili's.

It was Paule who noticed that the lights were on in Lili's apartment, and she said with a false little laugh, "We must have forgotten to turn them off. What a waste of money!"

Lili stood still, holding her bicycle, staring up at the bars of light that came through the shutters; he hadn't closed the ones in the living room: perhaps he would come out onto the balcony in a moment, look up and down the gaslit street, searching for her.

"Well," Paule said softly. "Good night."

But neither of them made a move to go. They stood sandwiched between their bicycles, on the corner of rue Guynemer and rue de Fleurus, not moving.

Paule brushed her fingers lightly across Lili's throat.

"Oh—!" Lili caught Paule's fingers, squeezed them as hard as she could: she let her bicycle fall clattering to the ground, and she wanted to take Paule in her arms, to hold her, to kiss the velvet skin of her throat—she picked her bicycle back up.

But why not? What did she care if Monsieur Manier, stepping out onto his balcony for a smoke, saw her holding Paule and reported it to his wife? What did she care if Pierre himself chose that moment to lean out the window? And then again, why not simply invite Paule up? They didn't have to leave each other now, play the comedy of star-crossed lovers.

"This is ridiculous," Lili said. "You'll just come upstairs. There's no reason—"

"Oh, Lili," Paule said, letting out a soft laugh. "Lili. You've no idea what you're talking about."

"But why not? I've told you we're not lovers."

Paule's laugh was almost cruel. "Don't be stupid, Lili."

Lili caught her breath, and Paule climbed on her bicycle. But she did not take off. She dropped her foot to the ground and looked down the street. "*Merde*," she murmured. An old couple walked slowly and laboriously toward them. Lili held her breath, listening to her heart, to the shuffling steps of the old couple.

"*Bonsoir*, mesdemoiselles."

"*Bonsoir,* Madame, Monsieur!"

She didn't exhale until they had passed, and then Paule was kissing her, her hand hot and tight around the back of Lili's neck, kissing her violently and then with a tenderness that exploded in Lili's arms, her heart, Paule jumped on her bicycle and was off.

Lili watched her vanish, Paule's sweater catching the night breeze like a sail, and she felt all the misery of a childlike loneliness, of the end of her father's dinner parties, when all the guests had gone and there was just the family: Papa grown sour and Maman wandering wearily through the mess, the children all asleep except Lili, who hid in the stairwell and wanted to leave with the laughing ladies, to be carried off into the night with them.

She went, dazed and saddened, into her apartment.

And there was Claude, riding on Pierre's hip. She had forgotten how hunched he was, how beautiful the violet of his eyes.

"She's here!" Pierre exclaimed; a record was on the gramophone and he was winded from dancing. "She's here, *mon chou!*"

She ran to Claude, gathering his thin, crooked bones in her arms. He let out a single, terrible wail, and then he buried his head in her shoulder. "My darling, oh—did you think I was gone? I was just having dinner with Paule, you know Paule, oh my darling. I'm not gone. Not gone. I'm here, *chéri.* I'm here and you're here. Yes. Both here." She squeezed him, breathing in his soft, sourish skin, her face pressed into the slender stalk of his neck. "My darling, darling, darling, oh *chéri.* . . ." She tried to look into his face, to see his eyes, his translucent skin, but he would not lift his head.

"He was fine until this morning," Pierre said, catching Lili's eye. "And then he was inconsolable."

Lili looked away, kissing Claude's fine, thin hair. "Has he slept at all?"

"On and off," Pierre said.

"I'm sorry," Lili said.

"It was a late dinner," Pierre said.

"Yes," said Lili. "I've been keeping late hours . . . not thinking to eat until ten or so."

"We were here at seven."

"Yes, I went out. For a bicycle ride. I needed to clear my head."

"So your work has been going well?"

"Oh, yes. Yes, Pierre. Thank you for giving me this time. You and your sisters. I ought to write them. It was very kind."

"Well," Pierre said. "I'm glad your work is going well."

"Yes, thank you." She sat on the bed and rocked Claude back and forth, back and forth. She could feel his body soften in her arms, and he let her lift his head, look into his pale, uncomprehending eyes. They were like two small oceans in his head: deep and wild. "*Mon chéri,*" she murmured, kissing his forehead, his loose, uneven mouth. "If you knew how much I love you. How much. We'll play with your ball all day tomorrow. We'll go look at the boats in the fountain." He closed his eyes and butted his head sleepily against her breasts: he held no grudges.

She lay down with him, waiting for him to fall asleep, her own eyes closed: she felt that she could bear this night without Paule only as long as Claude stayed quietly in her arms, did not wriggle out into the middle of the bed, into his night of curved and broken fish motions. In the morning, they would go with Paule to the Bois de Boulogne and they would find a private place where the three of them could lie together until noon. She thought of the soft, taut skin in the hollow of Paule's thigh—the smell of it: warm and humid and washed with lavender water—

"Don't you want to take your clothes off?" Pierre whispered. "Before you fall asleep?"

"Oh. Yes. Yes—!" She sat up, flushed—Claude was fast asleep now—and pulled off her dress, the dotted swiss which Pierre had failed to notice, and the motion of lifting even her bitten arms, of feeling the fabric slide against her ribs, made it difficult to think clearly. She reached for a cigarette and went to sit, in her slip, in the armchair by the window. Pierre sat on the edge of the bed, watching Lili, his hands hanging between his knees, and Paule was on the other side of the Seine, in her green cave. Asleep? Awake?

Lili should say something. "How was the trip up?"

"Fine. A bit of rain near Clermont, but otherwise good weather the whole way."

Lili scratched her arms. "That's good."

"Mosquitoes?"

"Yes."

Pierre stared down at his hands and said nothing.

"And in Sauxillanges?" Lili asked. "The weather stayed fine?"

"Yes." He looked at her again. There was an anxiety in his handsome, sunburned face, as though he needed to confess—what? She was curious, and at the same time she could not bear to sit here, making small talk. . . .

Her stomach was sore and light. Suppose Paule had gone out when Lili went over there tomorrow?

"Yes," Pierre repeated. "It was beautiful the whole time in Sauxillanges."

"Yes," Lili said. "Yes it was, wasn't it?" She would make an excuse to go over there before breakfast, before Paule had even woken.

"Did you like it, Lili? Did you really?"

She might have forgotten something there. She might perfectly well have forgotten a book or something. "Did I—? Oh, yes. Yes, of course! Why not?"

"I thought you hated it, actually."

"Auvergne? It's beautiful. I couldn't live there, of course."

"Couldn't you?" He took her hand in his and the feel of it startled her; it was so big. "Couldn't you?" he repeated.

But what was he talking about? She jerked her hand away.

"Sh-sh, Lili. Hush. Oh, Lili, I don't mean now. I knew you wouldn't consider it now. I meant later, when we're old. When we're ready to retire. Maybe in the summers, too."

She raised her hand. "Hush." She stared at his sun-bleached eyes, his ruddy skin. She had only to say *Paule and I are lovers, we are in love with each other.* He could live wherever he pleased, if that's what he was so anxious about. Paule could help her with Claude, and Pierre—the choice was his: which he had a greater need to see every day, those little rutted streets or his son. She shrugged. She knew perfectly well he would never leave Claude, even for a day, and her eyes stung: because she did love him, after all. He was a good father. A good man.

"Maybe when we're old," she said.

He squeezed her hand briefly. "I'm glad you're willing to consider it. I didn't know if I could even expect that much. It would be a comfort to me to think that someday . . ."

He threw his hand up, gesturing toward the future, and Lili watched his square, calloused fingers cup the air. She thought of him washing her, when they were first lovers, bathing her like an infant; thought of his soapy hand gliding across her skin that day after they'd been out to Saint-Germain, just before she met Paule: over her knees and Claude's feet, over Claude's tiny buttocks, around her loose, empty breasts.

Pierre yawned suddenly, arching his back. "I'm done for," he said. "Shall we go to bed?"

She sighed. She wanted him to stay awake, though she knew it was a stupid wish. All her nerves were straining across the river—that shadowy body, that silky opaque-white skin!—but Pierre still wounded her. She watched him pull off his trousers, his underwear: such strong, thick, hairy legs and his rough, complicated feet; so many more veins and ridges than Paule's had. What was it? What did she care when he fell asleep? Was it simply the old hope that they might love each other again? The old hope for the old way of loving? She could barely remember that way now; it had been so brief, and they'd stayed yoked together for so many years afterward, waiting for it to return. Or she, at least, waited. She had no idea what he did, faced day after day with his own indifference. It didn't seem, in retrospect, that their love had emanated from them; rather, it had descended upon them like grace, and all around them was the evidence—the old, dry, bitter couples who'd waited too long—that it never came twice to the same place, and yet, still. They waited.

But her arms were sore with longing for Paule, her thighs strained, aching, and it seemed so simple just to stand up, to go to Pierre, give him this love; for a moment there did not seem to be any contradiction in going to him swollen with love from Paule: as if it were simply a matter of showing Pierre a gift that Paule had given her. A stone, a piece of silk, the pounding in her ears. *Feel, Pierre, how smooth and worn it is. Hear how loud.* She reached out her hand, caught his, kissed the inside of his wrist: she felt the life drain away, the sudden coldness, like a slap.

She laughed sadly, climbed into bed, and curled into a ball: she thought of Paule's hand fluttering against her vulva, the pale fingers rising and falling against her own soft, swollen flesh, and she thought again how nothing is ever replaced; all things coexist: revulsion and desire, love and the loss of love.

Fifteen

Every day at lunchtime, Paule stood in the doorway of her apartment, waiting for Lili. The sight of Paule, leaning into the door frame, smoking, made Lili stiffen; her whole body grew rigid, alert, as if she were trapped. Yet how languid Paule was, how slow. It didn't seem to matter to her whether they consummated their lovemaking. She might only hold Lili's hand for an hour, stroking each finger, the backs of her palms, her thumbs, and be as grateful, afterward, as if they'd made love.

She didn't want to see Lili except at lunchtime and on Thursday afternoons. She couldn't bear to see Lili *en famille* anymore, to be reminded of the familial bed she slept in every night, the endless small intimacies of her life with Pierre. Lili loved her possessiveness, its severity; she loved to test it, to be a few minutes late and see the anger and the longing that came over Paule.

But it wasn't only possessiveness: Paule was busy. She was visiting churches. Never during a mass, but when she thought one might be almost empty. It was the darkness and the silence that drew her, she said, and the old, solitary women praying at the ends of the pews. "They remind me of you, Lili." Lili laughed. It was a mania, this desire to sit for hours in churches and gaze at old women and statues of a skinny, bleeding God; a mania that made Lili laugh, it was so incongruous with the full, tender flesh, the silk dresses, the mouth always tasting of wine and tobacco.

Still, despite the charm of her church visits and the sweetness of her jealousy, an hour a day and Thursday afternoons weren't enough. Suddenly, in the middle of an evening, Lili would remember an "errand" she had to run. She hired a taxi, ran up to Paule's apartment, hoping Marcel wouldn't be there, and within an hour she was back at rue Guynemer, dressed, calm, a little sleepy, a little too quick to laugh

. . . Pierre guessed nothing. All that fall, while the leaves turned violet, gold, brown, and at last fell off, and Lili pulled on sweaters, coats, wool stockings, she felt as if she were naked, her flesh tense and exposed, and no one noticed a thing.

Rain ran in slow, greasy streams down the windowpanes and Lili could not stop glancing above the girls' heads at the clock. It was a quarter to twelve. The sky was gray, narrow, and Lili stood dutifully before her desk, explaining Kant's theory of the imagination. Her hand moved in great, explanatory arcs, trailing cigarette smoke, and she thought how she wanted to peel off her own skin, to be completely raw, every capillary exposed.

It was fourteen minutes of twelve. *The secret is not even that we are lovers, the secret is my own body—*

". . . which differs from that of Hegel. . . ."

Only I have to go to her every day to retrieve it, my own body—

"Do you see what I mean, mesdemoiselles? It's really quite fascinating. . . ."

—in her body there is no danger, only love—

But by a miracle, it was noon.

The rain had refined itself to a needle-sharp mist and she ran through it, her coat unbuttoned, hurrying toward the *métro*. On rue de Vaugirard, the men waiting for soup had turned up the collars of their jackets and drawn in against themselves. She brushed past them, her cheeks hot, embarrassed of the warmth, the pleasure she would have while they shuffled their way slowly to the front of the line—she didn't stop; she ran hungrily down the stairs to the *métro*.

In the darkness of the stairwell, she could barely make out the shape of Paule's body. There was just the red glow of her cigarette, the smell of her.

They did not speak or touch when Lili reached the landing. She went past Paule into the apartment, straight to the window, and pulled back the dark green curtain. She heard the door click shut behind her and she opened the window, held her hands out into the rain.

Paule laughed softly into the nape of her neck. "You run straight into the cage and try to run out the other side, but there is no other side."

Lili turned to face her. Her breathing was hard and fast. She thought again of the men on rue de Vaugirard. If she did not crave Paule the way she did, she might have stopped. She might have spoken to the men. Paule stood in front of her, calm, patient, half smiling.

"I just love you," Paule said, shrugging.

"It's too dark in here," Lili murmured.

"'All that is asked of us in the end is to accept that we are loved.'"

"Who's that?" Lili scoffed.

"A priest."

"Ah, well! I'm not surprised. 'The poor you will always have with you.'" But still her breathing was hard and painful and still Paule stood unbearably close. Paule unhooked Lili's dress, brushed her hand over Lili's back.

"I have been thinking," Lili began, though she couldn't think with Paule's hand resting so lightly on her back. "Thinking—"

"*Que pensais-tu, ma chérie?*"

"I've grown selfish. It is selfish, this kind of love. I don't care about my students—"

"Well!" Paule laughed, catching Lili's hands in hers. "You can hardly be blamed for that."

"Every day I pass the soup kitchen on rue de Vaugirard and I don't even pause. I simply see the men lined up there as an obstruction in my path."

"Try to see them differently," Paule said simply. She slipped Lili's dress off her shoulders and Lili stepped out of it. Her heart was pounding: she wanted Paule to make love to her quickly, violently, here in the strip of gray light by the window, but Paule's hands moved slowly and lightly down her back.

"On the other hand," Paule said, kneeling before Lili, her lips brushing Lili's hipbone through her slip, her hands resting on the backs of Lili's thighs. "At that moment—that moment alone—everyone else is an obstruction. Still"—now her voice was teasing, playful—"it surprises me that you care that you don't care. You're usually delighted to be thick skinned."

"I've never been callous about people who haven't any food!"

Paule rose, laughed, pulled off her own dress. "That's the Catholic way, isn't it? To love best those who suffer."

"No, Paule," she said helplessly. "I love you best."

"Oh, yes. You do, don't you? But I suffer, too—for you."

"Do you?" Lili asked.

"Yes."

Yes, Lili thought, so then it was all right. But she must hear it again and again, that Paule needed her, suffered for her.

She kissed Paule's wrists, the crook of her elbow, the damp hair under her arms, and she could feel Paule's body surrender to hers, the warm, silk-clad flesh pressed heavily against her own—she slid her hand under Paule's slip, into her underwear, into the incredible, thick, springy hair, and Paule stopped her:

"There isn't time."

"We've got nearly an hour still!"

"I wouldn't be able to go back to school."

"Oh, Paule."

"Let's just hold each other, Lili." She sat down against the wall. "Come," she said, pulling Lili down into her arms, holding her between her legs. Lili sighed audibly, gave up. She leaned back against Paule, rigid and empty armed, her head thrown back against the fine ridge of Paule's collarbone. Now and then Paule brushed her fingers across Lili's breasts, but otherwise they didn't move. Lili breathed heavily, unevenly; then she lit a cigarette and was calmer.

"Why do you do this, Paule?"

"Oh, darling." She buried her face in Lili's neck. "You know, when an hour is enough, I take it. But some days I need more. Is an hour enough for you?"

"'Enough'—what is enough? This is hell."

"Would it be better if we didn't meet?"

Lili gestured violently.

And again they were silent. Lili watched her smoke dissolve in the air; watched Paule's hand cup her breast, the small fingers pressing against her sagging flesh. Every few minutes, Paule kissed Lili's neck, played with her hair. And it was all Lili could do to keep still, to keep her attention focused on her cigarettes. She would go mad. . . . And yet she could feel, in the hot, dry fingers that grazed her throat, the warmth of the thighs pressed around her waist, that Paule was consumed with desire. And her refusal to do more than there was time to do well—a kind of reverential attitude toward the smallest physical detail of sex—was the very thing that made her impossible to resist.

Lili's fingers trembled around her cigarette. She wanted to leave, to turn around to Paule and force her—she did nothing, caught in those strong, slender thighs.

"How hard you are." Lili crushed out her cigarette. "Strong."

"It isn't strength," Paule said miserably. She shrugged, her arms falling helplessly at her sides. "I hate sneaking around, Lili. This—you—are my life. I am not just having an adventure."

"But you're the one who constrains us. We could have made love today!"

"What do you think this is?" Paule cried. "You are callous, Lili. What you call making love—as if only that were love—I couldn't just stop at one-thirty, put my clothes back on, go back to work. There's something so utilitarian about that kind of thing."

They were near tears, their voices suddenly shrill and miserable; they had had this argument so many times, and neither of them understood it.

"It's time to go," Lili said tonelessly. She pushed herself up off the floor and slipped her dress back on. "You'll be late."

"Please, Lili."

"What? What? You blame me because I can tolerate living apart. I don't like it, Paule, but I can tolerate it. And then you spend an hour teasing me, brushing your fingers—"

"You don't just tolerate it, Lili. You like it. You like having a husband."

"Oh, God. I don't like having a husband. I like having a father for Claude. But what if I do, sometimes, like the secrecy? What if it does sometimes excite me? Is that a reason to punish me? To refuse to make love?"

"I'm not punishing you, Lili. I'm doing the best I can. Don't you understand what we have?" She pulled her knees up under her chin. "It isn't just an affair. This is God, Lili." She began to weep, hiding her face in her knees. "You can't just treat it as an affair, grabbing whatever you can, always in a hurry—"

Lili knelt beside her. How young and defenseless she seemed when she talked about God. It was disturbing but impossible to argue with. Yes, Lili thought. I love those who suffer best. She kissed Paule's wet, salty face, her swollen eyes; and she could not say what moved her most, Paule's weeping or the elevation of their love to a religion.

"There isn't a moment of the day when I don't want you," Paule said.

"Sleep with me tonight," Lili said, her heart still; she had asked so many times and been refused. "Even if he is there. Because I am married. There is no way around it. Please, Paule."

Paule was silent. She stared at Lili for a long time without moving, without even seeming to breathe. Then she threw up her hands. "All right. Yes. It isn't going to change, is it? So I might as well come over and hide in the study with you. It isn't your fault, it isn't anyone's fault. You'll stay married until the day you die, won't you? Because he does love Claude, that is the only reason, isn't it, Lili? Isn't it? If it weren't for Claude, you'd leave him and come to live with me. Don't answer, Lili, don't say anything. Yes. Yes, I'll come and we'll sneak around and lie to his face like a pair of ordinary adulteresses. We'll lie again and again, like a couple of kids stealing candy; we'll lie the way our students do—you don't understand this."

"No," Lili murmured.

"Good God, when we make love, Lili, is it like anything you've ever experienced?"

Lili smiled. "It's like the Alps."

"But you still refuse to believe in God."

"Oh, darling, what difference does it make if we call it God or not?"

"I should think it would make a lot of difference to you."

"All right, then, it makes a difference. But suppose, just for now, that I'm willing to concede a God—then, yes, of course, this is God, but what does that have to do with whether you sleep in our apartment or not?"

"Oh," Paule said disgustedly. "To debase it like that—"

"So you won't, after all?"

"I will," Paule said, shrugging. "I can't help it. Maybe even debasing is important. Yes, maybe. The way, in your religion, humility—"

"It isn't my religion!"

"No," Paule said, half smiling. "Of course not."

"But you will come over tonight?"

"Yes. . . ."

They kissed, then, gently, their lips barely touching, their hands and bodies still, aching.

"I've invited Mademoiselle Jacob for dinner," Lili announced to Patsy, the au pair, when she returned home in the evening. Patsy, a bold, pretty, red-haired girl, jumped up from the floor where she had been playing with Claude.

"I go to make a new lipstick, Madame. I will be pretty—like Mademoiselle Jacob. Where is the best place to make lipstick? Perhaps you do not know?" And without waiting for an answer, Patsy vanished, lithe, lovely, impolite.

Claude sat on the living room floor, toppled over, surrounded by bright, fat crayons. He was grinning up sideways at Lili, trying to clap, but he could not sit up and keep both hands in the air at the same time.

"How is my sweet big boy?" Lili asked, sitting beside him and pulling him into her lap. He clapped gaily, and she buried her face in the soft back of his neck.

"My sweet, sweet boy." She glanced at the pieces of paper scattered across the floor. He had covered them all with thick, unsteady lines. This was something new, his ability to grasp a crayon and make a mark, and she saved all of his drawings in a file in her desk. She thought he might someday learn to draw circles, stick figures, houses; that he would learn to talk to her that way, to tell her stories—it wasn't impossible, was it?

"Did you have a good day?" she murmured, rocking him from side to side between her legs.

He laughed unsteadily, eagerly.

"Paule is coming for supper. She's going to spend the night. I'm going to go into her bed for a few hours, then I'll come back into our bed. All right, *chéri?* You know Paule. The dark hair, the soft skin. Oh my cabbage darling, you are the only one I don't love selfishly. That is the truth." She got up on her knees and lifted Claude under his arms, so that he was facing her, his legs dangling to the floor as if he were standing. His little pants came up almost to his chest and his shirt was stained from his lunch. "When I'm with her, I want to die, Claude. I don't give a damn about anybody then." She looked into his soft, purplish eyes and rolled backward onto the floor, pulling him onto her stomach. He laughed, startled, and laid his cheek against hers. She stared past him up at the ceiling. "It's an apt comparison, actually, the one she makes between our love and God. The selfishness, whether you spend all day praying or all day making love. I know this and I am not stopping, I will not stop, I will keep running to her apartment every day at lunch, it is all I want, Claude. All I want. She consoles me with her suffering, oh Claude. Her suffering. Her little suffering. It's better when I think she might not love me; then there is not this awful guilt over my good fortune. Sweet Claude. . . ." She sat up again and held him on her stomach, supporting his back with her knees. He looked away, his face vacant and slack. "Because I expect nothing from you," she whispered, gazing at him. "No answer, and so it's pure." She kissed his forehead, his cheeks, his slack, pale hands, and suddenly, as if he'd simply been lost in thought, he came to and began to laugh again, his ragged, helpless, contagious laugh, and laughing, throwing his head back, he let a warm stream of pee flood out onto Lili's stomach.

Pierre found them in the bathroom and took Claude in his arms. He tickled Claude and Claude laughed again and tried to clap.

Lili took off her dress and her slip and stood before them in her stockings and brassiere, drying herself with a damp cloth. Pierre did not even look at her, and she thought, wearily, Yes, at least without love there is no guilt either.

"I'm going to run out and get a chicken. Paule's coming for supper."

"Is she?" Pierre asked, still without looking at her. He buried his face in Claude's neck, but he couldn't hide the sudden pleasure in his voice, his excitement at the prospect of seeing Paule.

"Yes," Lili said. "Yes, I thought a chicken would be nice. It's hard even for me to ruin a chicken."

Over dinner, over the dry chicken and the badly washed lettuce, Lili could barely speak. Her mouth was as dry as cotton, and her hands were cold.

Paule spoke rapidly, easily, focusing all her attention on Pierre. She would not look at Lili at all. She laughed, showing her small white teeth, her arms upraised, bracelets sliding from her wrists to her elbows: they clinked faintly. "Oh yes, yes!" she was saying. "Yes, I agree!"

Pierre leaned forward across the table, flushed. "Do you know what I—?" He was laughing, too, his fingers outstretched, toward Paule's.

Lili bowed her head. She couldn't make sense of what they were saying. Their voices dissolved in the air. But they were laughing, there was some joke, and she was angry that she hadn't simply enjoyed the moment of feeling loved, that she had had to feel guilty—she cut the chicken into smaller and smaller pieces, her knife scraping against the china. "Voilà, *chéri*," she whispered, offering her fork to Claude, who sat beside her, surrounded by cushions. He was cranky and pulled away from the food.

Paule and Pierre sat across from each other, as if they were having a private dinner, and across from Lili Patsy sat, entranced, not saying a word, trying desperately to understand Paule's and Pierre's jokes. Lili wanted to scold the girl, to send her away.

"Really, Paule . . . !"

"But I swear to you, Pierre, I swear. At least one church a day. It soothes me."

"And what does your good friend Lili think of that?"

"Oh, well, you know. She thinks what everyone thinks. That I've lost my mind."

"But you've no interest in staying for a mass?"

Paule laughed. "I'm not converting—yet! I like the stone, the silence. I like the smell of the little pools of holy water."

"So that's why we never see you! You spend your evenings sniffing basins of holy water. What a fascinating woman you are, Paule."

She would have liked to have reached under the table and put her hand on Paule's thigh, to dig her fingernails into the soft flesh, to interrupt them: *She's a lesbian, Pierre. She's not a bit interested in you. You're making a fool of yourself.*

But Lili was being ridiculous! Of course Paule couldn't look at her; and as for Pierre: as soon as he had fallen asleep, Lili and Paule could make love. Poor man, idiot that he was. He really had no idea. He simply thought that Paule was beautiful and friendly.

But still Lili kept her head bowed. She discovered a slug in her salad and pushed it off to a corner of the plate; if she looked up at his open, radiant face, she would weep. She could not say for certain if he had ever looked at her the way he looked at Paule, even when they were most in love.

Claude did not want to go to bed. The open door, through which Lili could hear the sounds of Pierre's and Paule's laughter, disturbed him. He whimpered, moving restlessly from side to side.

"All right," she whispered. "All right." She closed the door and lay stiffly beside him. She could still hear a murmur from the dining room but nothing else. And still Claude turned from side to side, his eyes wide open. "Please sleep," she whispered. "Please, Claude."

After a while, she heard the front door open and close. "*Chéri,* she's leaving, Paule is leaving, she grew impatient, oh Claude—" Her eyes stung and she sat up and lit a cigarette. "I can't lie down anymore," she said, stroking Claude's forehead. "I just wish you'd go to sleep. I don't understand why you won't. I've got to go on an errand in a few minutes, Claude. You've got to sleep." She was furious, but she kept her voice low and murmuring, and now at last—but Paule was gone, and what excuse would she use for her errand?—Claude's eyes were closed.

She slid quietly off the bed. The front door opened again: it was Paule; she must have simply gone out for a pack of cigarettes.

Lili smiled, coming back into the dining room; it was bright after the dark of the bedroom.

"I've invited Paule to stay the night," Pierre said warmly. He had drunk more wine than usual and his cheeks were flushed. "We'll make up the bed in your study, like we used to do. What do you say, Lili?"

"Yes." Her throat was painfully dry. "Of course."

Lili made the bed in the study briskly, efficiently. She did not look at Paule.

"I feel sorry for him," Paule said finally. "What does he say to the fact that you're no longer lovers?"

Lili straightened herself, laughed. "It's his choice!"

"Is it really?"

"Of course!"

"Of course?" Paule stared at her, her face once more young, defenseless. "You would be lovers with him if you could?"

"Oh I don't mean that—"

"But what do you mean, Lili?" and now her eyes were suddenly hard, dark.

"Oh, Paule. It was so many years ago. I can't even imagine being his lover anymore. But yes, it was his choice. All of a sudden—I don't know what I did, what happened."

"Oh," Paule said. She smiled faintly, held out her hand to Lili. "Come here. . . ." She kissed Lili's hand, pressed her face against it. "Oh my Lili. I so want to know that you are mine absolutely. That you don't want anyone else."

"I—"

"Sh-sh," Paule said. "Hush, Lili. I don't want your assurances. What do your words mean?" She pulled Lili toward her, kissed her throat. "This. This is all there is. The rest—my possessiveness, Pierre's indifference toward you—all of that is nothing. It falls away. . . ." She unhooked the back of Lili's dress, reached her hand inside her slip.

"Pierre," Lili reminded her, pulling away.

"Oh!" Paule said. "This charade! I suppose you wait for him to fall asleep, and then you slip out of his bed and into mine? It's like a bad novel. And what, really, is the point?"

"His pride, I suppose." Lili forced a laugh. "He certainly wouldn't be jealous . . . except of me, for having you."

"Do you think?" Paule asked innocently.

Lili laughed.

"How disgusting," Paule murmured. "I can't bear a man's desire."

"You, who drink in everything?"

"Oh, but to make love to a man! To sculpt one, I'd like that. If I were a sculptress. Jacqueline, my—the one—she did such beautiful studies of men. Oh, but to love—I would as soon make love to a horse."

Lili laughed again. "Why, Paule?"

"The male personality. The arrogance. Even Marcel, whom I adore—he still assumes a certain air of importance."

And, laughing, Lili felt suddenly light-headed, half dazed. In truth, she knew nothing. They were all—she, Pierre, Paule—concerned with their own separate, random lives; she kept trying pointlessly to connect them: it would just exhaust her in the end.

She was full of longing and guilt, and Paule imagined God wherever she went, but they did love each other, like people from opposite ends of the earth, baffled, foreign, unable to speak to each other and yet, still, overcome with desire.

"*Eh bien, ma belle,*" Lili said softly. "He's waiting for us."

"Why do you suppose he stopped wanting you?" Paule asked, still in that same innocent voice. And then, echoing Lili's thoughts, she shrugged and said, "It is all, everything, the whole world—such a mystery to me." She kissed Lili on the mouth. "You who are so delicious."

Lili closed her eyes and gave herself up to Paule, to her soft rich smell, her love, so exquisite and disturbing.

"Everything," Paule said, kissing her again and again. "A mystery. Only this, the taste of your mouth: it's like eating the ripest fig, and it all makes sense to me, why I exist at all." She kissed Lili so slowly and greedily that Lili wanted to weep. "Do you see what I mean, Lili?" She knelt and kissed Lili's trembling body through her dress, leaving small, damp marks on the wool. "I want to make love to you until I am raw with it, dying, I want to turn you inside out and devour you, to know God. . . ."

Sixteen

She's not the way I imagined a . . . person of her religion," Margot said to Pierre the morning before Christmas. Paule had come with them to Sauxillanges, for the winter holidays.

"Of course," Margot added, ingratiatingly, catching sight of Lili, "I should have realized, after all of her nice letters last summer." She was sitting at the kitchen table with Pierre, fondling his hands. Lili stood in the doorway of the vast, damp room and lit a cigarette. Paule and Claude were outside, in the mild December air, exploring the brittle winter fields, and Nanette, red faced and sweating, was absorbed in a mound of bread dough.

"Will she mind . . . ?" Margot asked. "Christmas, I mean?"

"Of course not," Pierre said, pulling his hands away.

"What do her people do, normally, at Christmas?"

Sacrifice children, Lili thought, inhaling on her cigarette; the tobacco burned her throat slightly.

"Mind their own business, I suppose," Pierre said shortly.

Margot reached for his hands again. "Sh-sh," she murmured. "Sh-sh, *mon chou* . . . I just don't want her to be uncomfortable. She's a nice girl. You've grown short tempered up there, in the big city. We've never met anyone of her faith. Sh-sh, *mon chou.*"

Lili watched his shoulders fall, his hands soften in Margot's grasp. They turned into two large, sleepy animals that Margot squeezed and pressed to her cheeks. "Let's go for a walk," Lili said.

"There's so much to do . . . ," Margot protested, and Nanette stopped punching the dough for a moment to look up accusingly, her face drenched and scarlet.

Of course it was terrible to let them labor alone in the kitchen, but it was more terrible to stay and help.

"Claude," Lili said, as if she and Pierre must right away rush to his side, as if Paule couldn't manage him out there in the fields alone.

"Besides," Pierre said, liberating himself from Margot's grip, "Paule doesn't know her way around."

Margot shrugged resentfully and pushed herself up from the table. "We didn't walk him every day last summer, when *Madame* was back in Paris working on her philosophy."

Pierre turned red, but Lili merely smiled, thinking, Yes, that's when Madame spent all day naked with Paule. "Shall we?" she said to Pierre, and Pierre, still red, speechless, mortified that the hostilities were no longer secret, left the room abruptly. But Lili lingered a moment, still smiling at Margot, who smiled back at her, the two of them savoring their hatred for an instant, secure in the knowledge that it was a lifelong bond. *You've no idea,* Lili thought. *Your baby brother, your little cabbage, married a lesbian, and it's a good thing too, or I'd have scratched his eyes out by now. . . .*

But outside, in the gray, gentle air, she thought, But only partly a lesbian. And she wanted to weep, because it embarrassed her to have had such a hateful moment with Margot, because she did not want to be hated.

Pierre was walking across the meadow toward Claude and Paule, who were small and dark in the distance. He waited for her to catch up. She began to say something, but he didn't want to talk, and she didn't persist. She thought again, I am not what he wants, but he does his duty. He would never force me to walk across this meadow alone.

He brightened when they reached Paule and Claude and led them on the path that wound down to the river. Near the spot where he and Lili had made love in August, he parked the wheelchair, lifted Claude out, and held him aloft in the low, soft sky. "This is the best spot to go fishing," he said, looking at Paule, and he spun Claude around and lowered him to the ground. Claude giggled helplessly, and Paule and Pierre laughed with him in the easy, pointless way of lovers. Lili stood perfectly still, staring at the cold gray river, confused about what to do with her hands.

"I've never gone fishing," Paule said, lying down suddenly in the dead grass.

"It requires a lot of patience," Pierre murmured.

Paule leaned up on her elbows. "Describe the fish to me," she said. The sun appeared and for an instant brightened the white flesh of her throat. Pierre said, gazing at her:

"They are unbelievably tender, succulent."

In despair, Lili lay down next to Paule, so close they were almost touching. She closed her eyes and stretched her arms over her head in an attitude of surrender, as if to say, *Now, either of you, please.*

"Perhaps we'll go fishing sometime this week," Pierre went on. "It isn't the sort of thing Lili has any patience for, but you might like it, Paule."

But last August, Pierre, you made love to me here. She pictured them naked in the warm, tall grass, and she let her memory distort the image, make it slower and sweeter than she knew it had been. Then she jumped up and ran down to the river, skirting past Claude, who was crawling contentedly over the stubbled remains of the summer.

On the damp edge of the river, with the water seeping coldly through her shoes, she lit a cigarette and organized her thoughts.

First, it wasn't possible that Paule was unaware of Pierre's desire. Second, it was pathetic that Pierre never did anything but flirt. Third, it was all her—Lili's—fault for begging Paule to join them. Her fault for wanting them both; for letting Paule think that she stayed with Pierre for Claude; her fault for being thin and angular and difficult; Paule's fault for feigning innocence; Pierre's fault, yes, Pierre's in the end, the bastard, she would never forgive him. . . .

Over Christmas Eve supper, in the dank dining room, Margot and Nanette plied Pierre with sausage, bread, stew, cheeses, cakes. "He's grown even thinner," Nanette lamented, interrupting Margot's recapitulation of all the letters she'd sent that fall.

Lili lit a cigarette, thinking, All I can do is tell Paule the truth, that I still love Pierre. How shameful it is that I love him, but there it is.

Paule listened to every word Margot said. She clucked sympathetically; she nodded; she uttered little oh's of surprise and compassion.

Pierre, in his sisters' presence, stared down at his bowl of soup. Even the sound of Paule's laughter, her slender arms gesturing toward the dark ceiling, could not quite rouse him. He was a boy, dutiful, cowed. How different from the man who had stared so frankly at Paule that afternoon, who'd made love to Lili in broad daylight the summer before.

Lili, leaning back in her chair, blowing her smoke away from the table, stared at the crown of his head in fascination. She could not imagine what that gray-blond head contained, after all. *I must confess to you,* she thought, practicing what she would say to Paule, later, when they were alone: *I do still want him. I want him, and yet—it's important that you know this, so that there isn't any falseness between us, because I do love you, Paule. . . .*

Paule laughed. "And all the cows got out?"

"Every one," Margot said. "That man is a perfect idiot. I've always said—"

"But try to eat a little more cheese," Nanette murmured. "Look! Look how thin he is."

Maybe, after all, all I want is an apology. *Yes, Lili, I am so sorry, I was so wrong.* I'm like a parrot, repeating and repeating, *Say you're sorry, Pierre. Say you're sorry.* But silently, just the lips moving, *Say it, Pierre, say it. I would have given up if I hadn't begged Paule to stay with us, if I hadn't had to see how you are when you love, yes, if I'd never been reminded.*

He took the cheese Nanette offered, stuffing his mouth until his cheeks bulged.

As soon as Margot and Nanette went to bed; he would sit up straight again; he would resume his flirtation with Paule. Did he ever awaken in the night and see that Lili was gone? Did he suspect anything? she wondered. He had been such a good lover to her in the beginning, so strong.

Late at night, beneath Nanette's snoring, beneath Claude's poor swimming, Lili and Paule met in the downstairs bedroom. Lili opened the shutters, though there was no glass in the windows, and a cold moon flooded the room, whitening their bodies, raising goose bumps on their flesh.

Naked, she sat on the edge of the bed and stared down at Paule's soft prone body. Beyond the window, frost lay shimmering on the field; she was not afraid of anyone wandering by now, on Christmas Eve: she and Paule might have been alone, at the cold edge of the earth, instead of hiding at the bottom of this dull well of a house with its dark occupied rooms. Her hand hovered above Paule's body but did not alight, and Paule, unmoving, stared up at her, her eyes still, serious, terrifying. This was something new, this inability to touch or be touched. It felt to Lili as if looking itself were almost more than she could bear, as if to gaze at each other naked in this way were more extreme than all their actual lovemaking, and she must hold herself perfectly still.

For weeks, they might simply undress and look. Only, now and then, there was the quick touch of a hand, or a thigh, as soft and terrible as dying.

Paule had led her to this point. It was as if Lili had been tricked to the edge of an abyss; only she wasn't afraid. She wanted more than anything to describe the abyss, bring it back to the world, to startle and transform everyone she knew.

Still, it was possible to get frightened. "You do still want me?" Lili asked.

"Oh—!" Paule said. Her eyes filled with tears. "If I were to let myself so much as hold your hand right now, I would go mad."

Lili, staring at the soft, flattened ivory breasts, the dark eyes, laughed softly, relieved; Paule spoke of their love now only in lunatic, religious terms: it was like staring at the face of God, it would destroy you; the smallest dose was intoxicating, ecstatic. . . .

And then a wave of sorrow washed over Lili, because Paule did not know the whole truth, and suppose she did, and suppose, knowing it, she stopped loving Lili? And then again, Lili thought, there was no difference between her longing for Pierre and Paule's for God. Each was a kind of infidelity and each was hopeless. There was no reason to say anything: they could not understand each other on this point. And yet here, in this cool stone room, what understanding!

How alive Paule was beneath her gaze, the pale flesh tensed, agonized.

Christmas morning, back in her own bed, she awoke to Pierre's hand resting on her shoulder. The feel of his warm, dry skin, his heavy bones, surprised her: he hadn't touched her in months.

"Please, Lili," he whispered. "Come to church this once. Just this once."

She laughed dully. "Take Paule," she said, a shade too loudly. "She's the one who's interested in that sort of thing."

"It would mean so much, Lili," he said, ignoring her suggestion, his hand still on her shoulder.

She sat up sharply in bed and hissed, "You promised, Pierre. I didn't want to come here, but you promised. You said I could come as I am, I wouldn't have to play at Christmas."

"You went to mass for your brother's wedding."

"That isn't the point. The point is you promised."

"Lili, I'm begging you."

"I said you could take Paule."

"Please, Lili, it will seem so odd, Christmas morning, and you're not in church."

"Take Paule."

"I'm serious, Lili. Please."

"Oh, Pierre. What right do you have to ask me for anything?"

Later, in the narrow, silent house, Lili and Paule waited out the mass by smoking in the parlor. Lili lay with her head in Paule's lap, blowing smoke rings.

"I hope you appreciate it," Paule said. "My being here."

Lili didn't answer.

"It may prove more than I can bear. It's one thing to spend the night with you—but this family vacation. These poor old miserable sisters, sick with love for Pierre, and you so unashamedly disdainful of them. . . . And who am I in it all? The spinster Jew."

Lili sat up, blushing. "I am so sorry . . . I never think . . ."

"Oh, well. I could have refused to come. But a week without you—! And then, to tell the truth, I was interested in attending the village mass."

"Well, Lord, why didn't you, you might as—"

"I wasn't invited."

"Oh," Lili said. Then she began to laugh. "Don't you see, Paule, how idiotic the whole thing is? Pierre begging me to come for the sake of appearances, and you unable to go? That is exactly where the concept of God leads in the end, to the most repulsive forms of convention, it's inevitable—"

"Please, Lili. Please please please be quiet." She leaned over and kissed Lili, without the tense, breath-held stillness of the last weeks and months, with abandon, with a kind of ravenousness. In the dark, dead parlor, with the church bells going on and on and on at the other end of the village, she ground out their cigarettes and fell on Lili hungrily. She dug her fingers into Lili's flesh and Lili cried out in pain, startled, delighted, surrendering immediately to this new, rough lovemaking. Paule stopped a moment, then ran her finger lightly down the center of Lili's stomach, and Lili felt as if her skin were being torn open, like the skin of a peach, a fig, and she felt again that she was good after all. She was shuddering, she couldn't stop, and when she did stop it was a long time before she realized it, before the world resumed its separate, discrete parts: arm and window and floor and thigh.

Paule was holding her tightly, murmuring in a voice of despair, "This is all I know. Just this. You. You are my prayer. I don't understand anything else—"

"Oh, *chérie*," Lili said sleepily. "Is there anything else to understand?" But just then she heard Margot's voice, and she began clumsily to pull her clothes back on, her fingers trembling: she was as terrified as a schoolgirl. Paule didn't move. "Darling," Lili whispered. "Darling, hurry—"

"Why?" Paule asked, shrugging. "They aren't ashamed of their prayers."

"But Paule," Lili began, half laughing, confused, afraid of Paule's expression: there was a remoteness to it, a violence Lili had never seen.

And at that moment, Margot and Nanette and Pierre and Claude entered the parlor. Lili ran to them, gushing explanations; it was like a dream, how easily she invented it all, the terrible fever, Paule was burning up, *Thank heavens Lili had stayed back from mass, she'd had a sense, but Paule was all right now, she had these sudden fevers, it was important to undress her.* . . . And as in a dream, the others accepted it, backing away, *Thank heavens you were here,* but if only they would vanish; she wanted to weep, for there was something wrong with Paule, lying there naked on the floor.

Seventeen

All the rest of that winter, Paule spoke of nothing but God. To look at the cold, lowering sky was to look at his face; to eat an oyster was to partake of his flesh. If the heat went out in her building, it had to do with him; if she tore at a hangnail. . . . It was a three-part God she was preoccupied with, the Son especially. She spoke of Jesus in the same tone in which she spoke of Marcel: with admiration, affection, and slight condescension. It was not unlike the way Margot and Nanette spoke of Pierre. *How thin he is, look—!*

She went to mass; she read the lives of the saints. And Lili tolerated it—indulged it, even—because it was so like a schoolgirlish phase. Religion was, in fact, at that moment, all the rage. Girl Guides were everywhere, with their tiresome sincerity, their disapproval of their irreligious elders. It would pass, Lili told herself, the tide of Girl Guides and Paule's fanaticism.

But she was afraid, and it was fear that forced her to be lighthearted. As if, if she could keep laughing at Paule's fervor, she might keep her from going mad from it. The memory of Paule, naked on the floor of the parlor in Sauxillanges, stuck in her throat like a bone. And all the dreary second half of winter she pretended it wasn't there, like someone at a dinner party smiling mutely and nodding.

Nowhere, Paule insisted, did she see God more clearly than in Lili's body. In the darkness of her apartment, with the icy January rain rattling the windows, Paule knelt in front of Lili and traced her fingers down Lili's bare skin, as lightly and reverently as a blind woman. Lili shivered from being undressed, from trying to delay the moment when she would collapse to her knees. Paule let her hands fall to her sides and stared up at Lili, and now, with those black eyes fixed on her, invading Lili's privacy more terribly than her hands were capable of, Lili could not hold back. Her orgasm was relentless, unbearable;

she was exhausted and Paule was stroking her arms, consoling, murmuring. . . .

It was time to go back to class. It was always time to go. To get up, get dressed, behave as if nothing were out of the ordinary.

In a daze, Lili found her clothes, her heart heavy with the prospect of the long, lonely afternoon ahead. "What is it you do to me?" Lili wondered, putting her blouse on inside out. "I am sicker with love than I was at the beginning."

"God asks everything of us in the end," Paule said, lighting a cigarette. "Nothing can be held back."

Lili looked down at her—Paule was sitting naked on the floor with her chin to her knees; Lili would be late again for school—and laughed. "If the nuns could hear you! If they could see you."

It seemed to Lili as if the winter itself were part of her love for Paule: the narrow days with lights burning at noon, the no-smell of the frozen air, and then, suddenly, the hissing, blue flame rising over a grill of chestnuts and the incredible sweet-burnt smell. It was the same as the difference between her hours with Paule and all the rest of her life: Pierre's coolness and the horror of Claude's trapped life stretching out before her; he would never learn to draw or speak; she felt sometimes as if he lived inside the earth, and there was a hole in the ground, with a grate covering it, through which she could see him, tickle him, hand him bits of food. . . . And then, Paule, the light burning in the middle of the dark day; crazed, yes, but full of love, she would stare unblinking at Lili, racked with desire, and in that desire all failure, loss, cruelty, were absolved.

And if it were spring, Lili thought, hurrying toward Paule's apartment at lunchtime—where, in fact, no lights burned at all, and the curtains would be pulled shut—I would think that every budding leaf was like her; I am completely unoriginal in love.

Paule was leaning against the door frame, a shadow in the darkness, smoking. She was wearing some sweet, cheap perfume that, to Lili's surprise, excited her.

"I want us to pray," Paule said, closing the door behind her.

Lili laughed.

"Please, Lili."

Lili laughed again, uneasily. "To whom should I pray, and about what?"

Paule stared at her. "Don't, then," she said, almost sulkily. "But I'm going to."

Lili sat down wearily at the kitchen table and lit a cigarette. Paule knelt beside her, her hands clasped.

"What?" Lili murmured. "What is it you're praying for?"

Paule didn't answer, her eyes closed, her knuckles almost white. Lili was restless, uncomfortable. She watched Paule's eyes moving behind her eyelids, as if Paule were dreaming: rapid, darting movements. Paule's mouth fell open slightly, and Lili, focused on the dark lips, the white teeth, saw Paule grow more surrendered, more ecstatic even than when she made love. She remembered her own childhood prayers—that morning in the Alps!—remembered, suddenly, the oddly banal voice she had heard from time to time. *God spoke to me today,* she had written in her diary, when she was nine. It was a voice at once ordinary and astonishing: simple, brief, almost ridiculous except for the silence it left behind, the absolute stillness.

But what could she do? That voice was gone. She was like someone who learns to play the violin too young and who forever after tenses at the sound—she leaned over and kissed the back of Paule's neck, and Paule gave in instantly, helplessly. But their lovemaking was confused, frenetic, and afterward they lay on their backs on the bare floor, hearts pounding as if they had both suddenly awoken from disturbing dreams.

A week later, Lili invented an excuse to go to Paule's house in the evening. They needed to be alone for longer than an hour, without the threat of Pierre waking and finding them. They needed to talk. Paule, Lili had decided, needed to calm her nerves.

It was a clear, cold night, the sky hard and beautiful, and Lili walked from the Gare Saint-Lazare to rue de Parme. She clambered over the heaps of dingy, frozen snow, and the air stung her lungs, and she was happy because she had named the problem—Paule's nerves— and now they would find a solution.

In the distance she could hear the voices of demonstrators on the place de la Concorde. They had been protesting for days, Fascists mostly, but now a few Communists too, apparently, and Lili thought that perhaps Daladier, seeing that the left was unhappy too, would do something. Perhaps the soup lines would begin to vanish and the Fascists to crawl back from wherever they had come, for all things were possible, suddenly; yes, one had only to name a problem, and solutions began to arise.

As if she could distinguish the shouts of the small band of Communists from those of all the other protesters, she smiled at them across the city, felt the explosion of their voices all through her limbs, *all things are possible,* all things would burst into flame and be reborn: of course Paule was overwrought; it was natural, at the edge of the abyss, to be frightened, but soon they would fall over into that dark, clear void, and the fear and the nervousness and the crazed praying would dissolve. Paule would not lie naked on the floor of anyone's parlor again; they would be strong, stronger than this world: yes, soon they would burst through the veil of the universe and be free; it was the other side of madness, but it was nerves that made you mad, made you humiliate yourself before the enemy. She began to run and stumbled over a mound of snow. She laughed aloud at her own clumsiness and, looking up, caught sight of herself in the mirrored panels outside a confectioner's shop: her red, cold cheeks, her hair tumbling out of her scarf. How beautiful her reflection was, like the face of a stranger.

Paule wanted to talk, too. She talked and talked and barely gave Lili a chance to answer. She sat at the kitchen table, and she did not smoke. Her voice was calm, even, softer than Lili had ever known it, and her hands lay folded in her lap. She was wearing the red silk dress, but instead of her fine silk stockings and her black silk shawl, she had on wool socks and a sweater the color of mustard that clashed with the red silk.

"I can't see you anymore, you must realize that. It's impossible to serve two gods. I thought for so long that the road to the spiritual lay through the physical, but that has simply made me crazy. . . . If I could see you without wanting to make love to you—but I can't. I'm always tempted. I tried to make a religion out of my temptation! Oh, Lili, it's such a relief to give up. I feel so calm now. I very nearly lost my mind, didn't I? And then last night, I understood everything. There is only one way, the path of the solitary and the ascetic. The world is a veil of suffering. Isn't it, Lili? Isn't it?" She didn't wait for an answer, her hands paralyzed in her lap. "I wonder now why you didn't stop me, seeing me so torn and confused. But that's the nature of desire: it makes a person selfish, I say this without ill will, only it strikes me that you might have let me destroy myself, so great was—is?—is it still?—your desire. It's not you I blame, Lili. It's the very nature of longing. And I think how Jesus himself struggled with his body, how he suffered *in* his body, and—"

Lili was no longer listening. There was a moment when she realized that her affair with Paule was over, a moment in which she foresaw her own confusion, the scenes and arguments and battles between them which would change nothing, and it was like the instant in a dream when you realize that you have been poisoned: it will be a long dream, full of incomprehensible scene changes and surges of panic, idiotic tangents; but all of that is simply a coda; you have already been poisoned and everything is already too late—and then she had stopped listening. She was sitting across from Paule, her eyes fixed on the doorway leading back into the hall. She felt nothing. The soft, even, droning voice simply went on and on, uninterruptible, and the cold air seeped in around the windows, past the thick green curtains. Now and then she glanced at Paule, to see if Paule looked ready to shut up yet, but Paule sat up straight in her red silk and her mustard-colored wool, indefatigable.

Lili couldn't move. She couldn't even summon up the energy to light a cigarette. Before her, blurry now in the foreground, for Lili's eyes were so sharply focused on the door, Paule's mouth was like a small red bruise in her small dark head. On and on it went, the mouth, articulating, defining: "And I . . . I . . . JesusJesusJesus . . . I know, because I . . . I . . . Christ . . ."

Lili could not feel her own skin or her legs. The cold air and the cold soft voice enveloped her like ether. . . .

And then, a bright yellow bird, the sound of her own voice—it startled her to hear herself speak—"If you're going to be a Catholic, you're going to have to shut up. Being a Catholic isn't something you talk about. It's a mystery, dark and illogical. At this point, you sound, frankly, like a Protestant."

The small red bruise of a mouth clamped shut and the small pale face blossomed red, wounded, and then, suddenly, the door blew open: and there was Marcel, with blood streaming down his face.

It took a moment to understand what had happened. She watched Paule leap up and run to him, her hands no longer paralyzed, but flying around like two tense birds. Paule's voice was urgent, high pitched, and Lili, staring at those hands, felt her own heart dissolve, for Paule was alive, after all. "Marcel, what happened to you? What did you do? Did you go to that demonstration, Marcel?" Paule was shrieking, and Lili almost laughed, so great was her relief, her love for this lovely, erratic woman. She went to Marcel and calmly took his face in her hands, brushing Paule aside for the moment, for she must take charge, be strong, someone must save Paule from herself, and that one was Lili.

There was a cut across his forehead and across his lip, but obviously he was fine or he wouldn't have made it here, all the way from the place de la Concorde. Lili led Marcel to the kitchen table quietly, calmly; she forced him into a chair, went to the sink and washed out a rag, calmly washed off his face. In the background, Paule was hysterical. "A doctor," she was insisting. "A doctor! I don't know his number. In rue Bonaparte—"

"I don't need a doctor!" Marcel said harshly.

Lili took an egg from the garde-manger, cracked it into a cup, and laid the shells neatly on the counter. She interposed herself between Paule and Marcel and plastered pieces of the egg's slippery, translucent membrane to Marcel's forehead, to seal the cuts. Then she lit two cigarettes and put one in Marcel's mouth. He looked up at her gratefully, his eyes swimming with love.

"You're lucky it missed your eye," Lili said gently. "Whatever it was."

"But what was it?" Paule asked furiously. "Marcel—!"

"I don't know." He shrugged. "A rock, I suppose."

"The Croix de Feu?" Lili asked, her voice still gentle, soothing. She loved this moment, Marcel's and Paule's need for her, her own superior Red Cross skills. "Was it the Croix de Feu?"

"The Fascists!" Paule hissed, her eyes full of tears, and she began to squeeze Marcel's hands, to stroke his arms over and over.

"Your pupils are fine," Lili said. "Still, we should wake you every hour or so."

"A doctor," Paule began again. "There's a doctor in rue Bonaparte!"

Marcel smiled, calmer now. "Lili is all the doctor I need."

Lili blushed. "We should put you to bed," she said. "Come." And she led Marcel to Paule's bed, as if it were her own bed: as if he were their son, and they, his parents, would sleep on the floor.

Paule hovered around the bed: she would find the doctor, she would go herself into rue Bonaparte.

"Sh-sh, Paule," Lili said, and she touched Paule's arm. "He really is all right."

At her touch, Paule met Lili's eyes for the first time. "Of course," she said. "Oh, of course. . . ." Her voice was suddenly calm again, softened. "I get so"—she laughed gently—"distraught." She sat down on the edge of the bed and took Marcel's hand in hers. "Oh, Marcel, you frightened me. My sweet darling. . . ." Then she looked up at Lili and said, her voice still gentle, easy, "Please go now, Lili. I did mean what I said. Please." She indicated the door with her head, and then, without waiting for Lili to leave, she turned back to Marcel and began fingering his hair. Marcel frowned, confused, then gave up understanding—didn't Paule and Lili always speak nonsensically around him?—and shut his eyes. Lili stood frozen, like a child who, treated cruelly, is only surprised at first. Then, mercifully, she felt nothing again, neither her arms nor her legs nor her heart, and when Paule asked her again to leave, she did, and it was like floating, to be back out in the street, her limbs thick and soft, the pale, distant voices raging on the horizon.

She gave the girls a surprise test the next day; what else could she do, with her heart beating so fast and the clock moving so slowly? It would never be lunchtime, and if she didn't hurry it might be too late, she must hurry to Paule's, hurry, for it must still be possible to talk, cajole, seduce. . . .

The demonstration of the day before had been declared a victory for the right. She'd read the news dully, at the newsstand on boulevard Raspail, her feet soaked through by the cold slush—the day had begun gray and damp, the beginning of a warm spell, though she was cold to the bone—then she folded up the newspaper and walked to school. And before she was even halfway to the lycée, her heart began to race, for perhaps all wasn't lost, people wouldn't tolerate the right for long, Paule would give up her asceticism, and there was still the noon hour, a well of freedom in the long day.

Lunch was an unpleasant scene of begging; of calm, gentle refusal.

And in the evening—*Patsy, I have to go out again tonight, you will help Pierre with Claude won't you? Oui, Madame, bien sûr*—an exact reenactment of lunch. Until Lili remembered Jacqueline Vernier. *She tried to reason with me, and then she hit me, and then she simply cried and cried. And I did love her. . . .*

"This is what you do," Lili said, her voice suddenly sharp. "You discard."

Paule stood in front of her, her arms at her sides, pale, still in the mustard-colored sweater, as if homeliness and fanaticism were one.

"No," Paule said. "This is different."

"Different." Lili gave a soft, contemptuous laugh. She was no longer crying at all. She wanted to claw at Paule's face, to mutilate her for her wastefulness. "How is it different?" she asked. "You lived with

Jacqueline Vernier for eight years and then you saw me once and left her. You loved me for six months and then you saw God and that was the end of me. It seems the great difference between me and Jacqueline Vernier is that you loved her longer. And for whom will you discard God, I wonder? A man?" Her voice was cooler even than Paule's had been, and the more violent her fantasies, the stiller and calmer she grew.

Paule stared at her with a look of innocence, of martyrdom almost. "It's different because I still want you. I didn't want Jacqueline anymore. I'm not sure I ever fully wanted her."

"Ah," Lili said. "You still want me." She laughed again, but she did not feel calm anymore: her arms and legs were trembling. "Let's see," she began, pulling off her dress. "Let's see how much you want me—" Her fingers shook and she knew that this was terrible, that it was not Paule but she who was mad, but she could not stop, this was all that mattered, to be desired. Paule was lying, she didn't want Lili anymore, she didn't want her at all, she was like Pierre: repelled. By Lili's ugliness, her sharp bones, her temper, her desire most of all her desire—who wouldn't be? She grabbed Paule's hand and made her touch her breast.

"Stop it!" At last, a little life in Paule. "Stop it, Lili. I don't want you when you're like this, I don't—"

"Oh," Lili said, completely naked. "Oh. Say it again." Her voice was the voice of the beloved now, drinking in the lover's endearments, *Say it, say it again, please,* if Paule would only say it once more, a few more times, then Lili could rest. "Please, Paule. Tell me—"

"But I don't. I don't want you when you're like—"

"Don't qualify," Lili whispered. "Please. Just say, 'I don't want you.'"

"But I do want you—"

She grabbed Paule's head, the dark, slick curls, and shook her again and again. She wanted to push her to the edge of the room and shake her head against the wall, but she refrained, and the refraining was both terrible and delicious. She stared into Paule's wide, dark, terrified eyes, shaking her, yes, over and over, until, aghast, she let go. Her fingers were stiff, trembling.

They did not move, then, staring at each other, and Lili could see that Paule's mouth was trembling, her fingers, her arms, and she was horrified by the stiffness in her own fingers, what had happened to her? She wanted to hold Paule and beg her forgiveness, *I am so sorry, sorry, I lost my mind, I don't even know what you said now that angered me so I don't want to think about it I came to talk to you about your nerves and look at me I hurt you, I didn't mean to.*

"Perhaps," Lili began, her voice gentle, barely audible, "If you took a vacation. I could go with you. You seem so tired these days. Anxious. All this talk of religion. Perhaps if we went to the ocean."

"What?" Paule's voice was as small as a child's, her mouth still trembling.

"The ocean," Lili repeated. "If we could get away for a bit. I've been worried, frankly. Your nerves—"

"My nerves?"

"I'm sorry," Lili said softly, gesturing toward Paule's hair. "I went off my head, I've been so worried about you—"

"Oh, Lili." Paule was no longer afraid; Lili could see that. "I think you should go now. You really don't understand. I am at peace. My 'nerves' . . . all of that is taken care of. There are waves of longing, but even they are receding. Soon I'll be able to see you without any discomfort. I suppose that sounds awful; but, Lili, it's so much better. Not to be possessed by one's lust, to be possessed only by God. Even saying this, asking for it, makes it so."

"The ocean," Lili insisted weakly. "A few days outside the city."

Paule laughed, a light, easy laugh. "Poor Lili," she murmured.

Lili raised her arm to slap her; stopped. Paule had not even winced. Lili dressed hastily and went toward the door. "Sister Paule," she said, her voice heavy with disgust. "Pray to her when you are moved by the smell of a rose or discover that your thighs are wet. Pray to her for numbness, for a monstrous transcendence of the flesh. There's nothing worse than a convert, Paule. A little Jewish convert."

In the stairwell, Paule's voice fell down to her, filled with sadness now. "I'm sorry I laughed."

And in the doorway of her own apartment, Pierre stood, waiting for her, holding Claude in his arms.

He turned away abruptly. "Patsy!" he called out. "Patsy—" Claude began to wail. "Take him, Patsy—good God what happened to you, Lili?"

She had scratched her face until she could feel the warm soft blood on her fingers, her arms, the blood as soft as rose petals; vomit dried on the side of her chin; it hurt only a little, her fingernails against her cheeks, her eyes; only the vomit drove her home, finally, to get cleaned up.

"Good God, Lili." And he carried her into the bathroom. Yes, she thought, this is your job, the bather. "What happened to you? Did someone—?" He was peeling her clothes off slowly, carefully.

"People were celebrating," she said. "The fall of Daladier. Someone flung out an empty bottle."

"Oh the bastards," Pierre said. "The bastards."

How well he did his work, touching her lightly with the wash-cloth, letting the water stream gently over her shoulders, her knees. He was at his best, more focused even than when he flirted with Paule.

"It's awful, isn't it?" she said. "This new cabinet—"

"They'll regret it," Pierre said bitterly. "The very ones who protested. They'll see."

"Thank you, Pierre." She rose from the tub and reached for a towel.

"Wait a minute," he said. He dabbed some Mercurochrome on her forehead, her cheek. "You'll be all right," he decided. "What bastards."

Of course he knew that she was lying. It was obvious that she hadn't been hit by a bottle; even Patsy could see that. She didn't know why he was willing to go along with her lie. Out of indifference? Or because he knew that she and Paule were lovers and was too polite to interfere? She couldn't guess.

"Thank you," she said again, touching his arm. "They should have made you a medic in the war."

Eighteen

But Claude, seeing her, began to wail again.

"It's nothing, darling." She took him from Patsy, who stared, wide eyed, at Lili's face. "*Maman a un bobo . . . c'est tout . . . Maman a un petit bobo. . . .*"

But he would not be consoled. Tears and spit ran down his face, and he could hardly breathe.

"*Ça va, mon chou. Ça va . . .* sh-sh." She bounced him up and down, but he only shrieked more loudly. He had never cried like this before, and she could not distract him: he did not want his crayons, his rubber ball; he did not want to dance to a record on the gramophone. He refused to go to Pierre or Patsy. He did not want a bath. At last, taking him into her study, she unfastened her robe and offered him her breast. He stopped shrieking, startled, and she realized that if the sound had lasted a minute longer she would have begun shrieking in return. He whimpered slightly and then he began to suck on her breast, a big boy, six years old, his feet dangling to her calves. She stared down at his blond, silky head, his awkward body, and she was ashamed, because he was too big. Then she closed her eyes and gave up. It was like crying herself to sleep, nursing him, feeling her heart fill her breasts, which were already the breasts of an old woman, which had not given milk in years.

She awoke with a start, her ribs sore from the weight of Claude's head, and she lifted him off her and put him on the sofa. The smell of Paule's perfume in the upholstery was heavy and sweet and suffocating.

She did not go back to the bedroom, and Pierre did not come to check on them. His discretion knows no bounds, she thought, sadly, and then she thought again of Jacqueline Vernier, of how gratefully, triumphantly, even, Lili had welcomed the passion and devotion—the adoration!—that poor Mademoiselle Vernier had cried and begged and hit for. She went to the toilet and vomited. She vomited until she was retching air, until it seemed her stomach was being torn out of her. Then she carried Claude into the bedroom where Pierre lay, fast asleep and slack jawed, on his back. She lay down beside them, her stomach still clenching like a fist, around nothing. She lay rigid, wide eyed, until the dark began to fade, and Pierre, at last, to waken.

She did not go to school the next day. She lay all day in bed, with the shutters open and the light burning, waiting for the hours to accumulate and pass; but the day was endless, gray and flat and cold. Pierre came home at lunch and felt her forehead. Should he call the doctor? Would she take some bouillon? *No, nothing, go back to school, please. It is just a little indigestion, please.*

What she felt, lying on her back, with her eyes fixed on the damp, white walls, the armoire, the gray stone across the street, was that her heart was swollen, like something diseased, and the only cure was to put leeches to it. Or she must keep very still, she must not even move the muscles in her face, because the slightest movement would rupture her heart; but if she did not move, if she froze, eventually—what? Then what?

There had been that moment when she had known absolutely that the affair was over and because of that she might go mad, but she did not have the heart to scheme: *How I will win her back, how I will change myself for her.*

All I can do, she thought, is to hold myself perfectly still.

At some point in that endless, damp day, Patsy knocked on the door and brought her a package. It was a box full of Paule's clothes: her silk dresses and stockings and shawls and bracelets and necklaces and lace underthings. Lili laughed, the clothes spread out across the bed, thinking, bitterly, The first time tragedy, the second time farce. She had not looked at the chest in which she kept Claude-François's helmet and jacket in years. She opened the note that had come with the clothes, the handwriting as brutally familiar as her own body:

> *I am sorry to cause you such pain. If there were another way— but I cannot give up the possibility of salvation, even to ease your pain. How mad and selfish this must sound to one without faith!*

I know now that to receive God I must empty myself of everything: the hope of fame, of human love; my preoccupation with beauty.

I burned all my poems tonight. And you will forgive me, I hope, when I tell you that it was infinitely more painful to do that than to turn my back on you.

For years I thought that I could fool God: if I loved the things of this world well enough, I imagined, I would be spared the necessity of giving them up. And so I immersed myself in all that was sensual, temporary: the taste of food, the sound of words, the feel of a woman's body. I did not eat a crust of bread without drowning in the taste of it. . . . And perhaps I chose to love women rather than men, to write poetry rather than prose, simply because they are more extreme. I might have been perfectly content as a novelist married to a man, but I wanted words concentrated, flesh fattened and curved. I wanted steak almost raw, cheese past ripeness, fruit that was bursting. It became a religion for me, the path of the sensual.

When I met you, it wasn't simply your beauty that attracted me (the very things you think are so ugly: your uneven features, your exaggerated gestures)—it was your hunger—I smelled it the way a dog smells fear—without understanding it—I knew, even when I did not know if you wanted me, that you were the hungriest person I'd ever met, and I lusted after you the way I lusted after all things awful and extreme. I still lust after it, and that's why I can't see you. But to say more about that is pointless, destructive.

I came to see that in relishing the physical world, I was not getting closer to God, I was simply feasting on myself: my appetites, my "sensibilities," my hope for fame. And the more I devoured myself, the bigger I became. And so there is no answer for it but asceticism. Silence.

The agony of burning my poems is the greatest I have ever known. I felt as if I were being tortured, and it was all I could do not to scream, to give up, to kill myself. But, yes, to go on and on like this is a waste of time.

And, in truth, at the heart of any pain I feel is such peace, Lili. There is a kind of ecstasy, trembling and clear and beyond words. All I have to do now is be still, and silent, and I know that if I am patient, God will be revealed to me, whoever God is.

Paule

She said nothing about the box of clothes. "I was going to give my clothes to the poor," Lili said aloud, in a mimicking voice. "But you are poor, after all, in spirit. I thought, If a person must turn her face from God, why not at least let her have the feel of silk against her skin?"

Then she lay back against the pillows and read the letter over and over. *I still lust, still lust.* Lili began to laugh, softly, miserably: Paule was mad, madder than anyone. . . .

Unless she was not mad. Unless she was perfectly sane and this was all a ploy to make Lili leave her alone—to feign some idiotic religious experience and throw in, like a bone to a dog, *I still lust.* . . .

No, Lili thought. She is completely out of her mind.

And it was a great consolation.

Yes, insane. She is insane.

Suddenly Lili felt hopeful. She sat up, reached for her cigarettes. She would eat a big lunch; she would bundle up Claude and take him for a walk. If Paule was insane, Lili must do something. But Paule had always been crazy, and no one had ever done anything. She had left Jacqueline Vernier, burned her poems, spurned Lili—but who would know the difference? On the surface, she was simply a pretty spinster, an uninspired teacher.

And then it came to Lili that it was a lie: Paule wasn't genuinely ascetic; she cared only about more and more extreme experiences. Because that's what all of this was, the search for God, the renunciation: it was only a way of pushing the known borders of the world as far back as she could. She was pursuing God—a Christian God!—the way another person might take to opium or swim across the English Channel. The object made no difference, as long as it was desperate enough. . . . Lili simply hadn't satisfied. In the end, she'd been too ordinary, too content simply to love and be loved.

She imagined that if she looked through Paule's apartment, she would find proof that Paule, far from being too tempted by Lili, had simply grown bored. If she could search every corner of that dark, tiny cave, lay her hands on all of Paule's belongings . . .

She felt through the pile of clothes on the bed and dressed feverishly, pulling on an ivory-colored slip, the best stockings, the string of pearls. She slipped the dark red dress over her arms. It all smelled of Paule, and for a moment she weakened; then she lit a cigarette. She went to look at herself in the mirror inside the armoire: her face was orange with Mercurochrome, covered with scratches around her temples and cheekbones.

She sat back down on the bed and finished her cigarette. She was ashamed. She thought: I am thirty-seven years old and I am acting like an eighteen-year-old. I have a son, students, a decent husband. And I scratch my face like a madwoman.

"Well," she murmured. "What of it? What if I am mad?" Speaking aloud was strange, different from the way it had been when she was a little girl and she talked aloud constantly. In those days she imagined an audience—Jesus, the Holy Ghost, Claude-François, Sister Thomas—and she prattled away without embarrassment. But now there was no one, and the sound of her voice caught in her throat. It defined her solitude, the way an echo defines a tunnel, a crevasse.

There was a terrible pleasure in it, like the pleasure of scratching her face, and she forced herself on: "I'm going to go now. I'm going to go and search through Paule's apartment. Take a souvenir, perhaps." Then she just said words, nonsense: "Lili Lili Lili loved a girl and couldn't keep her oh yes, hello. Hello? Paris calling. Have you a teleph—" But she shut herself up when she reached the street.

On the *métro*, people cast secret, sidelong glances at her face; and Paule's concierge, an angry, mustached woman who had never approved of Lili, smiled faintly at the sight of her scratches, but let her in.

It was the first time Lili had been alone in Paule's apartment since their first day, when she'd taken a bath and Marcel had found her. She stood in the middle of the room, letting her eyes adjust to the dark, smelling the dust, the perfumes, the cold tobacco; the faint mustiness of Paule's disorganized, unwashed life. It wasn't the room of an ascetic. But Paule might wash the walls, throw her ashtrays, her bottles of wine, her bars of chocolate, out into the street. She might shave her head and buy a rosary. Only now, still, the air in the room was heavy, dusty, echoing with desire. It shocked Lili to realize, suddenly, how separate Paule's life was from her: a summer shoe lay on its side in the middle of the floor, the cracked, glossy insole catching a thread of light from behind the curtain. As if Paule had run out for a package of cigarettes, wearing her summer shoes into the cold as she might have worn a pair of slippers, run back up the stairs, torn open the package, flung off her shoes. . . .

"And you think that's the way to God?" Lili said aloud, venomously. If she could not possess Paule, she might, still, criticize her. "Running out in the middle of the night for a smoke? What do you know about God? I'll tell you about God. He won't save you. He won't even try." She laughed now, desperately. "He won't lift a finger. He'll just sit there and watch you, omnipotent, omniscient, bored, perhaps. Yes, who wouldn't be bored, century after long century, watching people bloody their own heads against the stones? No doubt he's not even watching anymore. That's why it's so hard to tell if he exists or not—he isn't paying attention!—you'd have to agree: if he exists, he's a bastard. Forgive me for refusing to accept such a thing!" She was standing, breathing heavily, her arms tense at her sides; she was drunk with the pleasure of speaking aloud: it *was* now, like imagining that Paule was hiding somewhere in the room; like imagining the Holy Ghost. . . .

"Yes, forgive me." She laughed. "After such a passionate love affair—mine with him—why talk about you and me? It would have distressed me to think I'd given my heart to a bastard. Why believe such a thing? Why interpret silence as cruelty? If I go into an empty room, I don't imagine there are people there refusing to greet me. I understand that the room is empty.

"I poured such love on him! I lit the candles, I put rocks in my shoes, I prayed, I wept, I fasted. You can't imagine. I was such a little girl. Small even then for my age. I sang all the time because the only person to mock me for singing off-key was André, and who could take him seriously? The rest of the family was tone deaf. I sang to my dolls, I sang in church, I sang as I did my various pointless self-imposed tasks: my book straightening and my hankie folding. Oh, I was a tidy child, you can't imagine! Small and serious and devoted to God. I thought I'd be a nun, so I dug my fingernails into my palms to punish myself for the slight sorrow I felt at the prospect of cutting my hair. I wasn't even grief stricken about it, just a little sad, but everything, every vanity, no matter how small, had to be burned away. *Because I loved him.* I believed that he was pure love, pure light; who wouldn't be drawn to that? Who wouldn't sacrifice everything for that brilliance?

"And André? What was André? A sulking, awkward boy. Hardly a blinding light. Was I to blame for slamming the door in his face when he interrupted me at prayer? There I was, small and serious and tidy, saying the rosary in my bedroom, and there he was, a big boy. He stood in the door and tried to get me to play with him. So I shut the door. What else could I do? Through the closed door he taunted me, and I sang my prayers at the top of my lungs to drown him out; I didn't know I was tone deaf.

"And to tell you the truth, it was a relief, now and then, to be cruel. You'll find that out. The self-sacrifice exhausts you.

"And yet I loved God. There were times when the entire world seemed full of light. And my heart was so full I wept. A little girl, in a tidy white dress. I was so grateful to be alive, so astonished by the simple fact of trees. The sky. How was it possible to be so fortunate? I can't tell you what I felt, my heart swelling—every moment, every *thing* so unbearably alive.

"And there was André, whining about a pebble in his sock. A big boy, embarrassing the whole family.

"We had to kill him, what else could we do? You'll see. Everything that isn't God must be singed at the root. Lust, vanity, the complaints of a miserable boy.

"And I did so want him. I gave my childhood to him. . . . There was a kind of love. . . . The excitement I felt . . . the thrill. . . .

"But surely that wasn't God. Teasing me—a child!—giving me a taste, and letting André suffer. Surely it wasn't God favoring me!

"Surely there isn't a God. And you—look at you! With your little religious clichés. You know nothing, Paule—"

She stopped, trembling, sweat rolling down her sides, and dizzy, as if she'd been spinning. She sat on the floor, near the summer shoe, and lit a cigarette. She remembered the excitement of childhood—all things new, radiant—the thrill of being alive; it would never be like that again. And that, too, was something she'd never realized, the way she'd never realized that Paule had a life apart from hers. She sat with her knees to her chin, drawing the smoke into her empty heart, amazed.

But it was impossible that anyone could be so stupid—to have imagined the things she did!

She forced herself up and out of the apartment. "Enough," she whispered, and she did not glance back at the summer shoe, the dark, green, perfumed apartment, the doorway.

"Would you like to take the afternoon off, Patsy? I'm feeling better now."

Claude, letting his crayon slip out of his hand, reached for Lili but did not wail today at the sight of her orange face.

"Thank you, Madame. I go to make? Buy? A dress. Paris have fashion. Is? You say?"

Lili nodded, sank to the floor, and pulled Claude into her arms. He was content to give up drawing. They lay together on the carpet all through the end of the darkening afternoon, and she could feel her heart against his small, hot, twisted back. It seemed to her that beyond the warmth of their two bodies pressed together, this knot of limbs and flesh, there was nothing: no sounds, no smells, an empty, devastated city.

She kissed his silk head at last and hummed to him. How peaceful he was, how forgiving!

Nineteen

In the weeks that followed, she taught her classes; she read the news; she ate, bathed, shopped, spoke to Pierre, to Patsy; she was efficient, brisk even; she felt nothing at all except a kind of absence, as if the nerves in her face and hands had been damaged. She did not try to visit Paule. The friendship had simply ended, abruptly and absolutely. It was as if the entire city had grown silent: as if, for all the endless chatter of her days—the lectures she gave her students and the instructions she gave Patsy, the bits of trivia she used to ward off the women in line at the butcher's and the pâtissier's and the greengrocer's—there was, in fact, no sound at all.

At lunch, regardless of the weather, she sat in the garden of the Musée Rodin, and stared at the statue of Ugolin and his children. She was surprised to realize how completely she had stopped noticing statues. For years after the war, before she had begun going to the list of the dead, she had paid attention to every statue on every street corner, in every garden. It was their very silence, their immobility, that had moved her. Century after century, they stood or sat or lay on their backs and watched: the great battles and the private, inconsequential suicides; a dog scratching; an impatient conversation about whether to buy liver or sausage; the boundless cruelty of children; a couple making love; the life-or-death anxiety of a student rushing late to class—all this and more: they watched the progress of social convention, the grave seriousness of fashion, and, behind its fashionable exterior, a city of mute and terrified hearts. They allowed themselves to be casually urinated on. And it was not only that they watched, permitting everything; it was that they themselves stood utterly revealed. They were so often naked, and, naked or clothed, their faces, their arms and legs and twisted torsos, expressed such pain, joy; such confusion, loss, ecstasy, horror. Of course, there were also the dull little queens in the Luxembourg, the guardians of propriety, but they were a minority.

And here, holding her umbrella in the garden of the Musée Rodin, her cigarette splashed with rain, her bottom wet from the bench, she had half a mind to wade in the little fountain where Ugolin, covered with bird droppings, struggled on with his children, oblivious of the rain. Not to touch him. She had no desire to touch him or the stone children clinging to his body. She simply wanted to look more closely into his face. As if she might then understand his patience, his nakedness, his lack of scorn. But she had learned years ago, climbing onto the pedestal of the woman on the corner of boulevard Saint-Michel and rue Auguste Conte—that woman who lay huge and naked on her back, her bare feet, her bare, parted legs, visible to the endless stream of passersby—that to look closely was useless. For the woman had no face, after all. No face to speak of. And if Lili waded through the fountain toward Ugolin, his anguish would dissolve, would reveal itself to be simply a play of light and stone.

And so Lili sat, lunch after lunch after lunch, in the winter silence of the garden, with her cigarettes and now and then a pastry, gazing at Ugolin from her bench; and she did not know whether to be consoled by his stillness, his endurance, or whether to despair at the illusion that even a stone can project.

And then one Sunday—it was the end of March, raw and windy, and the daffodils were out in the Luxembourg, the fountain choppy like a small ocean—Pierre asked her, after lunch, why they hadn't seen Paule in such a long time.

"She's sick," Lili said. She was standing in front of the window, drinking her coffee. Pierre and Claude were playing with the red rubber ball.

"Sick?" Pierre said, his voice filled with concern. How?"

"Oh—" She turned around and saw him, his eager, worried face. "Actually," she said, her voice cool and even, "that isn't true. She doesn't want to come over anymore."

"Why . . . ?" He looked stricken, like a child, but he had new gray hairs every day.

"Because," she continued, in her cool, iron voice, "it makes her uncomfortable. To be stared at. Longed for. By a married man. Whose wife is her friend."

Pierre let the ball roll pointlessly out of his hand. "Is that what she said—?"

Lili laughed furiously. Claude began to whimper, but she didn't stop.

"Lili, I don't—"

She kept laughing.

"I don't know what you're talking about." He was flushed and, from across the room, she could see his heart beating rapidly beneath his shirt.

"The ball," she said. "Are you playing ball with him, or aren't you?"

He began to play ball again, dutifully, but Claude kept whimpering.

"Oh, forget it," Lili said suddenly. "Forget I said anything." She walked past them, out of the room. She went to her study, locked the door, and wept. It was the first time she had wept since the day she'd scratched her face raw, and there was no comfort in it. She felt cast out, like a child no other children will play with: raw and ugly and stupid. *It's your own fault, André, going off and sulking. A big boy!* But it isn't his fault. It makes no difference what he might do. We'll hate him in any case.

And then, another day—it was only a week or two later, and Lili had opened all the windows so that the apartment was cool and clear—Marcel appeared at the door.

She stood in the doorway, not letting him in, her heart pounding in her throat, pounding so loud in her ears that it hurt to listen to it, so loud her eyes stung. But why shouldn't he come to visit?

"May I speak with you?" he said softly, gently.

But she only stared at him.

"Please," he said.

"Please," she repeated stupidly.

"If I might talk to you. Alone."

She laughed then, inappropriately. "Of course," she murmured. "Alone. Of course."

But in the study, he sat on the sofa and stared at his hands. He said nothing, after all. She stood with her back to the door and listened to her blood, to the sound of the gramophone coming from the living room, where Pierre was swinging Claude around by his arms. Then she collected herself and offered him a cigarette. His fingers, holding the matches, were long and slender and muscular.

"I asked Paule why you don't come over anymore," he blurted out, finally, and the blood rushed to his cheeks.

"And?" Lili said, a strange calm coming over her; she felt suddenly maternal, as if it were her job to console Marcel.

"Well—!" He threw up his hands. "You can imagine. She didn't tell me a thing."

"Oh," Lili said. She sat down at the desk now, businesslike, efficient. As if he had come for some document, some business.

"You know she doesn't smoke now? She's given up meat?" he asked, outraged.

Lili suppressed a smile. "Does she sleep on nails?"

"Don't you care what happens to her?" Marcel cried.

"Oh, Marcel," she said, weakening. "What would you have me do?"

Marcel didn't answer, and she added, with hope, her heart beating quickly again now, "Does she seem sick to you? Do you think she's—"

Marcel shrugged. "No. She seems perfectly fine. The truth is it makes sense, this business of her being an ascetic. Her poetry is much better now—"

"She's writing?"

"Oh, yes. All the time."

"I thought she'd given it up, along with meat and tobacco."

He shrugged again. "Maybe briefly. I don't know. Anyway, that wouldn't last. You don't simply stop writing poetry."

"No," Lili said, her eyes wide and frozen. "Of course not. Why did you come here?"

"Because I don't understand why—why you aren't—"

"Well," she said, forcing herself to stay calm, he was just a child, "she and I no longer understand each other."

"You were lovers, weren't you?"

They were both silent, mortified, as if he'd shocked himself as much as her.

"I should slap you," she said at last, gently. "For being so impudent."

"The way you looked at each other," he continued, emboldened now.

"That's enough, Marcel."

"But you won't deny it."

"Of course I'll deny it!" She laughed, outraged. "I'll do anything I please. How old are you, Marcel?"

"Nineteen."

"Oh, *chéri*." She took his hand. He was such a strange, handsome boy. Frail in a way she never quite understood. "Why are you troubling yourself over this? What business is it of yours?"

"I thought you might talk to her."

"You yourself say that she seems fine." But now her heart was beating too quickly again: it was the smell of him, the way his mouth moved, like Paule's.

"I miss you," he said, and it took a moment for her to hear the words, as if he were far away. He rose and took her hands and kissed them, pressing her palms to his face, and she did not stop him, her heart beating so fast, the room spinning, everything in the wrong place.

"Good Lord—!"

She pulled away and he stared at her, his lips dark and moist and trembling.

"Did you take the rest of her cigarettes, too?"

He said nothing, staring silently at her, as if his physical presence alone should be enough to seduce her. And he was beautiful, with his dark, shiny hair, his dusky skin, red mouth. He was beautiful, and he longed, apparently, for an older woman, one who had made love to his sister and who—in fairness to herself, Lili—respected him, made him laugh, gave him cigarettes; longed for a body that he thought, no doubt, more interesting than the bodies of the young girls his age. It did not make her feel beautiful to be desired by him— his was not like Paule's desire—but, still, after all, why not say yes? If he did not find her so ugly. Why not make love with him, and with his friends, if he had any; with his friends' friends? Why not lie naked every Sunday in the dark, so that whoever came to her would not even have to see her, if, as was likely, they did not share his strange tastes?

"You're very kind," she said, stroking his soft, glossy hair. "I was Paule's lover. That's the difficulty. I will always be her lover, though she has no use for me."

"That's absurd—"

"Yes, who would have thought? I'm like someone who believes in God."

"You're as crazy as she is," he said sadly.

"I think," she said, "that we are all stark raving mad." Then she said, "Go now please." Because her heart was starting to race again and she wanted more than anything to taste his soft red mouth.

❦

226

Then again the days grew pale, silent, stiff. She regained the peaceful lack of feeling she had had before Pierre and Marcel shocked her with their questions, *Why aren't you friends—?* On Sundays, she went to Saint-Germain. Helga was learning a few words of French. Thérèse's bastard children were big and strong. Papa dozed and Maman was growing tired again, as in the old days. And poor Mademoiselle Duroc, with her sagging, dull face. She had begun to murmur to herself, in the way of old people, and Papa—as if she were some charity case Maman had dragged in off the street—would look up suddenly, impatiently. "What? What is it? What is she muttering about?" They swarmed in on Lili, pressing against her, Maurice with his Fascist goading, Thérèse with her fat, promiscuous beauty. She couldn't get them off her; it was the way it had been in the old days, before she met Pierre—that is why one takes lovers, as a buffer against one's family—and yet, the more they swarmed, the colder she grew. It was not comfortable to be so blank, so stiff, but it was not the same as pain.

The first Sunday in April, they took their coffee into the garden. Thérèse's boys ran noisily on their fat little legs, falling onto the cool, damp earth, and Thérèse, carrying her daughter—an immaculately dressed girl whose white shoes shone unnaturally in the spring light—followed after them clucking, scolding.

"They are beautiful children," Papa said. He was standing beside Lili, staring through the open living room door out into the garden.

"Yes," Lili said. She shifted Claude's weight in her arms. He had fallen asleep in the car, and his warm, damp face was buried in her neck. She looked out at Thérèse playing with her children, at the chestnut tree ready to burst into bloom, the rosebushes, the irises, the damp green film on the garden wall, and it all seemed cheap and trivial, like a postcard. And like the family, the garden crowded in on her, but it had no depth, no smell, no texture. But here were Pierre and Jean-Louis, needing to get past her, with the dining room chairs held high in their arms. They were talking rapidly about Daladier, Spain, the specter of fascism—hurrying through their remarks like two schoolgirls who must fill each other in on the latest gossip as quickly as possible before they're interrupted—because it wasn't worth talking about politics once Maurice arrived. Since his party was in power, he wouldn't let himself be dismissed or ignored. He went on and on, not giving anyone else a chance to speak. The only solution was not to bring up the subject at all. As soon as he arrived, Pierre and Jean-Louis stopped talking and buried themselves in their newspapers.

"Beautiful children," Papa murmured again, and then, turning suddenly to Lili and Claude, as if he had just realized they were there, his eyes welled up with tears. "Well," he said in an odd, brusque tone. "Well!" Then he tousled Claude's hair and hurried off to his spot beneath the chestnut tree, where he promptly closed his eyes and let his chin fall forward on his chest. It occurred to Lili that he wasn't sleeping this time, that he had simply closed his eyes in embarrassment. She closed her eyes, too. Her heart felt big and heavy and misplaced. Then nothing. She was only tired from holding Claude so long. She must sit down. Of course, that was the solution.

It seemed she had been sitting for a long time, that Thérèse's children had been playing for hours, that Jean-Louis and Pierre were simply repeating themselves (what was the point of talking about war anyway?)—but it could only have been a few minutes: Maurice was never late; still, the branches of the chestnut tree were almost touching her, there was no room here—and then, as if the whole tense, crowded garden burst apart, there was a sudden, terrible yapping. She looked up and saw two tiny dogs with long hair and perfectly flat faces and behind them, puffed up like a pair of penguins in their Sunday best, Maurice and his German child-bride. Yvonne, in her glistening white shoes, began to scream, and Claude woke up, whimpering. Maurice glared at Helga.

"Make them shut up," he ordered, and Helga ran plumply across the garden, gathered the dogs into her pale arms, grabbed two petits fours from the box of pastries on the garden table, and dropped them into the dogs' mouths.

Everyone stared, aghast.

"I am so hungry," Helga said, shrugging her plump, white shoulders.

"They are hungry," Maurice said furiously. "'Ils ont faim,' pas 'j'ai faim.'"

"Ils ont faim," Helga said dutifully; and Maurice, as if he had done all a man could be asked to do, sat down, heaving, and studied the box of pastries before selecting a miniature coffee éclair for himself.

"You have dogs," Maman said weakly. Yvonne had stopped screaming, but Claude was still whimpering, disoriented from his nap.

Helga blushed. Then she said in the injured voice of a child, "They are my children. Everyone have children."

"What she means to say," Maurice said, "is that they're going to have children. They're a male and a female. Pekingese. Incredibly expen-

228

sive. I offered her a doll instead, but she was set on the dogs. She can't conjugate worth a damn."

"No," Helga said. She was still holding the dogs on her lap. "They are my children."

"Of course they are," Maman said, patting her arm. Maman hated dogs, but she would encourage anyone who opposed Maurice. "Of course they are, Helga. They're beautiful."

Lili began to tremble with suppressed laughter. Paule and I were lovers. Now I will tell them. *We were lovers and what I love in her is the very thing that made her leave me: her fanatical devotion, to a tomato, to sex, to God even, even that.* . . . Then once more she was calm, blank, a little tired. She could not hear them anymore. They were merely color, fabric, a flutter of hands. Nothing mattered except time, accumulating and passing.

She almost failed to notice when Maurice held out a box of chocolates for Claude. He did this every Sunday now; it was an aberration—a box for Claude, not for any of the other children; and every Sunday Lili held her breath, waiting for the moment to pass: the terrible, awkward way Maurice nudged Claude with the glossy white box, *Oh Maurice, my darling.* How horrible his tenderness, Thérèse's lovely laughter, Papa's sudden, tear-filled eyes. I have to leave right away, she thought, and she began to push herself up from the chair. Yes, leave, for it is not their love I want, I cannot bear their love—but just then Papa woke, turned to her, and offered her the house.

"This house?" she asked, confused, and Pierre and Jean-Louis lowered their newspapers in unison.

"We're moving to Caen," Papa announced. "Your mother and I, and my secretary. You'll move into this house, Lili, and you will pay Jean-Louis and Maurice twenty thousand francs each a month in rent. That's all. That's your inheritance. I was born in Caen and I'd like to die there. You'll need the garden, Lili, for your boy. See that you take good care of it." Then he shrugged slightly, closed his eyes, and went back to sleep.

There was a moment's stunned silence, and then Jean-Louis, Pierre, and Maurice began to speak in loud, important voices to one another. Thérèse listened to them politely, but the other women couldn't have been less interested: Mademoiselle Duroc, as if she had heard nothing, burrowed furiously into her knitting; Maman muttered wearily about packing; Helga threw pastry after pastry into the air.

Lili was trembling. To move from Paris? Into this house! Tears rolled down her cheeks, but she did not make any sound and no one noticed. She thought she was laughing, but she could not be sure, and the garden walls swarmed in on her, as if to say, *Come back, you must live it all again, again and again, here, in this house—*

She trembled more and more violently, so that she had to clamp her teeth down to keep them from chattering: in despair, she realized that the next time Marcel came to her, she would invite him into her study; she would not wait for him to ask. What else could she do? He would understand that she was giving him permission to make love to her. He might, realizing that he had triumphed, hold off for a moment, fingering the objects on her desk: her bottle of ink, her dusty papers, her cigarettes. He would keep his eyes lowered. Then, suddenly, he would look up and stare her full in the face. It would happen quickly, violently—he was so young!—but quick or slow, it made no difference; what mattered was his desire. It would save her awhile from this house, these people. Yes, what else could she do?

She imagined, in despair, the black hair, the pale, dusky skin, the slender bones—and felt herself come alive again, felt the numbness of her hands and face begin to thaw. How painful it was! She could feel the weight of his head against her collarbone, the dry feverishness of his skin—how passionately she wanted Paule.

You are the hungriest person I know, Lili.

But either a person is starving or dead!

Yes, she would sleep with him. Sooner or later, she would not be able to resist it. The way a man, dying of thirst, at last drinks salt water.

And then, afterward, after all, she might as well move back here, into this terrible house, this beautiful walled garden; because it would ruin everything to make love with Marcel, to hold someone in her arms who was so like Paule, but not . . . , to make love in the ordinary way of lovers. Yes, she was like a man who knows the salt water will kill him but who cannot bear his dry throat any longer.

All afternoon, while the men discussed a deal there was, in fact, nothing to say anything about, Lili planned her meeting with Marcel: the red silk dress, the sofa, his dark hair in her hands. Then they would leave Paris, she and Claude and Pierre.

There was no one to give herself to, after all. There was only the family, with its eternal, elastic arms.

"No more!" Helga was saying. "All gone!" She picked up the empty box that had held the pastries and showed it to the two Pekingese. "No more!" she cried again, and she picked the dogs up one after the other and kissed each on the mouth. The sun was going down and the men had retreated behind their newspapers again; Claude, circling around and around the garden on his hands and knees, was growing tired; the other children, who were not yet old enough to mock him, were busy collecting pebbles. Lili's stomach hurt, her throat was tight, as if she had already made love with Marcel, already ruined everything. She glanced at Claude—his slow, determined gestures, his slack, lovely face—and back at Helga. She felt a sudden kinship with Maurice's beautiful, illiterate bride and tried to meet her eyes, to smile at her. Helga ignored Lili. With no principles to distract her, she had long since outstripped Lili. If it took a pair of dogs to love her, what did she care? As long as there was love.

Lili kept staring, watching Helga's red hair in the afternoon light, her young, fat arms. For an instant, her gaze fixed on Helga's red, darting tongue as it flicked the dog's black nose, Lili sensed that there was no shame in being hungry. Perhaps, after all, she would refuse this house. She might even refuse Marcel. What could she do, after all, but obey her heart, as foolishly as Helga had? She and Helga were derelicts, beggars, starved for a love that was absolute, all consuming, and, still gazing at Helga, she saw that there was grace in being derelict, grace in the act of begging.

She was still thinking of Helga a few weeks later at the butcher's, when, arriving just before noon, she found the butcher all alone. He was smiling, gazing down myopically over his large, bloodstained belly, holding in his palm the wax paper with the slices of ham.

She didn't look at the ham but gazed right back at him. "Thank you."

He kept holding out his hand, waiting for her to look, his smile fading.

"Oh," she said, embarrassed, and she glanced down at the parcel finally. "Yes. Yes, just that much."

He turned from her, tying the parcel closed with a single gesture, handing it back to her.

"But you know," she said, for not even his wife was in the shop at that moment, "three hundred grams or five hundred, I don't really care. It's that you are the one who slices it that matters to me." Her cheeks burned with shame: she could not imagine why she had said that, what horrible impulse had come over her.

But the butcher simply lowered his voice. "In that case, Madame, if you would take a kilo. You are so thin." He was looking at her again, his wide, red face full of forgiveness, wise with the pain of hunger and slaughter.

"Thank you," she said, on the verge of tears, and she turned to leave before she realized that she must return the parcel to him and let him open it and take the ham back off its hook and slice it again—all of which would take several minutes, during which she must stand, exposed, patient: she felt the thrill and horror she had felt all those times in Paule's dark, green apartment when she stood for what seemed like hours, naked, feeling Paule's light, warm fingers brush down across her skin—and then she did begin to weep, but the butcher simply went about his business, slicing and wrapping, kind, gentle, unperturbed by her excesses. Then he untied his apron, for it was past closing time and his wife was waiting; for it is not enough to ask and to receive: everything, even the butcher's kindness, must be relinquished.

PART TWO

Twenty

Nothing happened the way she expected; and then again, she had foreseen it all: only from the wrong side.

There was the war. The butcher stood motionless behind his bare windows, with a few lone entrails, a single tongue, a half a chuck roast. Germans requisitioned three apartment buildings on rue Guynemer, and Lili and Pierre fled to Saint-Germain, where there were hardly any Germans and Claude could crawl in the garden in peace. Paule and Marcel—who never returned to visit her in her apartment in Paris—were arrested on the eleventh of March 1944.

And then, in June, she stood outside her parents' house in Caen and watched the house explode, over and over again. It went down slowly, gracefully, like a wounded animal.

No, it was dark, and she could not have seen a thing. She lay on the ground, her arms wrapped around Maurice. His heart beat against hers, and they were alone. Around them the town exploded and burned—how loud death was, how sudden!

The house was made of stones, and the stones collapsed, and beneath the stones were Thérèse, Maman, Papa, Mademoiselle Duroc.

The rest of the family was safely in Saint-Germain. Lili and Maurice and Thérèse had come to Caen in honor of Maman and Papa's fiftieth wedding anniversary.

In the little toolshed, Lili held Maurice as tightly as a lover. Their bowels had exploded in the dark, a smell terrible and shameful and confused, somehow, with Maurice's heart—wild, like some great furious bird trapped beneath his flesh.

Mademoiselle Duroc said it was absurd to come to Caen for Maman and Papa's wedding anniversary. The Allies were bombing all the trains. Imagine! Traveling all that distance in the middle of the war!

"It's a special occasion," Lili had said, staring right at her.

They lunched in the garden. They had heard bombs during the night, but the morning was calm.

The garden was twice as big as the one in Saint-Germain, flooded with light from the south and east. Papa had planted strawberries, daisies, peonies. There were pink and yellow roses, daylilies, impatiens. And of course, now, a chicken coop, a few rows of tomatoes, peas, cabbages, eggplants.

They ate a whole chicken, a *clafoutis,* a tomato salad. Thérèse had found butter somewhere; Lili had gotten hold of a packet of sugar. Lili ate with relish. Once more she thought of nothing but food, the way she had during the first war. Of food and of Paule, about whom she must not think, she must put Paule out of her mind, what was the use of thinking about her? It was a perpetual fluttering in her throat, an unbearable tightness around her heart. In January, Lili had gone to her for the last time to ask her to move to Saint-Germain. Paule had smiled a terrible, condescending smile. It was not painful for her to see Lili anymore—she was past all that. She was busy hiding other Jews, busy preparing for her baptism. Lili left, furious, resisting the urge to slap her. That was six months ago. She must be dead now. It was not possible that she was alive.

"Lili?" Thérèse asked. "Aren't you hungry?"

She's more and more eccentric, they said, when they thought she wasn't paying attention. *The war's gone to her brain.*

She looked at the half-eaten slice of *clafoutis* on her plate. She had craved it all through the chicken and the tomato salad: craved its sweet, milky denseness. It sickened her now, the yellow custard. She thought of food constantly, but it was impossible to eat. It was the final insult, Paule's willingness to die. But surely she was dead by now! Surely they had given up torturing her!

She looked over at Maurice, stuffing himself. On the train ride, he had made polite small talk with a German officer who offered Lili a ready-made cigarette.

"Maurice has taken up smoking," Lili said suddenly.

"Lili?" Thérèse asked.

"At least when the cigarette is offered him by a German."

"Oh, get off it," Maurice said, spitting out a cherry pit. "An officer on the train very nicely offered Lili a cigarette and she refused it, so I took it."

"Since when have you been so concerned with manners?" Lili asked.

"Children . . . !" Maman said.

"Well," Mademoiselle Duroc said. "I agree with Maurice. If they're going to do something nice for you for a change, you might as well accept it graciously."

"Nice! Nice—?"

"Sh-sh, Lili," Thérèse murmured. "It isn't worth it. . . ."

"It certainly isn't," Maman said wearily. "We're all likely to be dead soon anyway."

After the lunch celebrating their marriage, Maman and Papa went inside the cool stone house, into separate bedrooms, and rested. Thérèse and Mademoiselle Duroc cleared off the table. Lili sat before the remains of the *clafoutis,* trembling. Maurice sat on the other side of the table from her and glared hatefully out over the garden. If she spoke, she would burst into tears. But Paule must be dead by now!

And then the sound of planes, and how swiftly, like deer, Lili and Maurice ran into the toolshed, as if that would save them, and it did— not the shed itself, of course, but the chance location of their bodies.

When it was light again, they stood side by side in the doorway of the toolshed. They were not touching now, and there was between them the embarrassment of strangers who have made love impulsively. The light was glaring, brilliant, the light of dreams. She could not understand why they could see so far, all the way to the neighborhood of Saint-Gilles. She kept staring, away from the house, out across the dark landscape. Then she heard it, and her neck snapped around violently. Maurice was sobbing. She heard it again, and she ran across the garden, around the small, dry lake where the picnic table had been— near the cherry tree the ground was slippery, covered with the dark burst fruit that had been shaken from the branches—she kept running, and she heard Maurice behind her, stumbling to keep up. They might run for hours, years, across the ruins of a garden that was not one acre but the world. It would make no difference. However close the mound of stones, however quickly they moved, they would never reach him: it was Papa, woken from his nap, crying beneath the weight of the house.

Maman and Thérèse and that poor servant, Mademoiselle Duroc, died instantly or held their tongues; but Papa moaned for hours. He did not say anything, and if he heard them calling to him through the stones, he didn't answer. He simply cried.

They pulled at the stones all afternoon.

When they looked up at last to catch their breath—they were black with dirt, their hands bloody, their thighs smeared with their own excrement—the sun was going down: they saw it sinking through the heavy atmosphere, orange and swollen, saw the unchecked flames of the town, the airplanes on the horizon, and, so beautiful in the blood-red light of the setting sun, the red tulips, the white anemones.

Papa was still crying faintly.

In the street beyond, people ran in the direction of the church, and beyond that still, there was the sound of bombs.

Then, suddenly, toward dusk, such absolute silence. Papa had died, finally. She squatted for a moment at the edge of the enormous mound of rubble, her arms hanging over her knees, her head bowed. Then she forced herself up and continued pulling at the impossible weight of the stones. Out of the corner of her eye, she could see Maurice: fat, straining, filthy. His arms were wrapped around a jagged rock, his chest pressed against its sharpest edge. He was perfectly focused, absorbed, as if he could not hear this new silence, as if it were still possible to save them.

They worked until the sky was black. Then they made their way through the desolate streets to the river, stripped off their clothes, and washed in the freezing water. They put their wet clothes back on and walked back through the same charred and littered streets toward l'Abbaye-aux-Dames. They did not speak, but now and then they stumbled, exhausted, into each other, and there was a terrible comfort in the feel of Maurice's body, his wet, heavy arm brushing against hers.

For two and a half weeks, they lifted stones and found nothing. At night they slept in the basement of l'Abbaye-aux-Dames with the other survivors. On the third day, they were able to give a letter for Pierre and Helga and Jean-Louis to Monsieur Bouts, who was fleeing north. They heard nothing in return.

On the morning of the eighteenth day, they found Thérèse and Mademoiselle Duroc. It was impossible to look at Thérèse, at her dirty, blue summer dress; but at the sight of Mademoiselle Duroc, Lili burst into tears.

She was still clutching the corner of a plate she'd been washing, but she was so soft, so rotten, they had to lift her slowly to keep her in one piece. Monsieur Degènes, from down the street, had already carried Thérèse to the communal grave beyond the church. Maurice had shouted for Monsieur Degènes as soon as they came upon Thérèse's body; then he and Lili looked away while Monsieur Degènes took care of her. It was terrible not to be able to look at her, not to be able to touch. But they would have gone mad. Thérèse was just a baby, after all: they could almost imagine she had never been born.

At night, now, Lili and Maurice slept in each other's arms, sandwiched between Monsieur Degènes and Babette Laruelle. But during the day they barely spoke at all.

When they found Papa, they did not turn away; they did not call out to anyone. Papa lay beneath a pile of rocks, his open mouth dark and silenced. His head and half his chest had been protected by the angle of a beam. Stone by stone they cleared him off; they touched his old, fat body. How fragile he was, after all; how delicate!

They found Maman's hand by accident, half lying under a rock. They thought they'd find the rest of her attached to it, but when they lifted the rock, there was just a swarm of ants.

That was all. The rest Lili didn't remember: how they buried Papa, what day they gave up looking for the rest of Maman.

Only this: that old, brown hand with its arthritic knobs, its black stump of a wrist, wrapped in a piece of silk torn from her slip, carried all the way back to Saint-Germain. She held it tightly, the whole long, hot way home. The war rained down all around them, the Germans furious and terrified, the Americans loud, pleased with themselves. Lili and Maurice walked, with the other refugees, through Mezidon, Lisieux, Evreux, sleeping in the grass at night, eating the tomatoes that grew everywhere. She barely noticed a thing, holding Maman's hand carefully in hers. Maurice must have realized, must have smelled, but he said nothing. They were still silent with each other, and now, moving away from Caen, they did not sleep so closely together at night.

They reached Saint-Germain one evening toward the end of July. They paused outside Maurice's apartment building and looked at each other for a while, then Maurice turned to go inside. Her eyes stung, seeing him walk away: they had so little in common, after all.

She let herself into the garden of the old house through the side gate. Pierre was standing in front of the lit window of the master bedroom in just his trousers, staring out into the darkness. Had he heard something? Or was he simply pausing on his way to bed? How casually he stood! She crouched in the shadow of the chestnut tree and watched him. The breadth of his chest, his grace, shocked her, as if she'd not noticed his beauty a thousand times before. Impossible to imagine he was not someone's lover; to imagine that, if she ran upstairs to him, he would not take her in his arms, relieved beyond words to find her alive, and kiss her eyes, her mouth, her throat. She fell to her knees and scratched in the dirt with her calloused, scabby hands. She could feel that he was still in the window, looking out. Never had she wanted him so badly. She kept her head bowed, pulling at the grass.

She was so tired, so sore; now and then she fell asleep in the midst of digging—a sudden, dark sleep—then her head snapped forward and she woke up and kept digging. At last the hole was deep enough for Maman's hand, and she curled in a ball over the little grave and slept.

When she awoke, Pierre was squatting beside her, his head in his hands, weeping. She reached up to slap him, claw at his skin, something; but he caught her hand and held it firmly in his, then he reached under her to lift her up. She swiped at him again and stood up on her own, glaring at him. She did not want this no-lover's pity.

"Lili—!"

But she hit him again and again, watching her hand fall against his face, his neck, his arms; he just stood there, dry eyed now, perfectly still. Then he reached for her, to stop her, and again she slapped him off.

"OK, then. OK, Lili. What do you want?"

"Don't touch me. Don't talk to me. Don't touch me!"

"OK, then. OK." He turned to go back into the house, his shoulders bowed but his stride loose, easy.

"Is Claude still asleep?" she asked.

He turned to her and nodded. Then he asked, "Did any of our letters get through? The ones Jean-Louis and I wrote?"

"If you think we had time for the mail!"

She slept with Claude after that, curled up with his big, adolescent body in his narrow bed. For the first month, she slept better than she ever had in her life—nine, ten, eleven hours without waking, an absolute darkness. Then she began to dream:

There was Mademoiselle Duroc, smartly dressed, carrying a bag of food. *But where are you going?* Lili asked.

Oh, my street is fine, Mademoiselle answered. *We were lucky.*

Is Thérèse with you?

Naturally, she's doing the dishes.

And Maman?

Poor thing, she's practically blind.
But she was always blind!

She awoke sharply, knocking her head against the stone floor of the church; and that, too, was a dream: it was impossible to get out. Maman held Lili in her warm, soft arms, but there was nowhere for Maman to put her hands. How foolish Lili had been to bury her in two separate places! She must go back to Caen, but if she went back they would make her sleep in the church again, and there was hardly any tobacco there. Everyone was praying, and Monsieur Payen, who'd lost his entire family, was talking to the priest about conversion. Surely this is why he'd been spared, he said, to satisfy his dead wife's wishes that he'd become a Catholic. But that had really happened. It wasn't a dream:

She watched the house explode, but the house was a horse, a big horse, like in the Trojan War, and the knees buckled first. . . .

Mademoiselle Duroc did not want anyone except Papa to look over the top of the towel while she undressed.

She rose at last, felt her way downstairs in the dark, and put on her coat and shoes. Outside, she walked quickly, staring at her small black shoes against the night-damp cobblestones and the white hem of her nightgown beneath her coat.

Up and down the streets she went, one after the other, covering the entire town. The moon was out, and a fine mist rose off the streets—it was a pretty night, a pretty night in this old, pretty, solid town. There had been no Germans at all for the last three months, no curfews. A burst of laughter came from an open window above her, and, looking up, she saw a white curtain swell in the breeze, the shape of a woman throwing her arms up in laughter. Lili dug her hands into her pockets and kept walking, more and more quickly now, almost running. She came to the park at the edge of town and sat down on one of the benches outside the gates. She tried to roll a cigarette, but her hands were trembling and the tobacco kept spilling everywhere and it was too dark to find it. A few benches down, a girl was arguing playfully with her lover. They were laughing and whispering, and every now and then the girl made a sound of mock outrage.

"Excuse me," Lili said.

The two kept kissing, laughing secretly.

Lili cleared her throat. "Excuse me," she tried, more loudly.

The lovers stopped and stared at her.

"Excuse me, could you roll this cigarette for me?"

There was a moment's silence, and then the man laughed. "Well, why not?" He rolled it deftly and handed it to her. The man was handsome, and the girl was homely, and Lili wanted to squeeze their hands in gratitude.

"Take some tobacco—please," Lili said, but they had already begun kissing again.

She walked away, smoking, back into the center of town, listening to the sound of her shoes on the stones. She passed Maurice's apartment building, stopped, went back to it. She thought how kind the young lovers had been to her, how fortunate she had been in this war, how fortunate, always, and she felt as if she would go mad. She went upstairs and knocked on Maurice's door. She hadn't seen him in a month, not since they'd returned from Caen. She saw a lot of Jean-Louis, and Thérèse's children but not Maurice. He opened the door in his robe, groggy, saw her, and looked away.

She said nothing for a while, standing in his doorway, touching the hem of his sleeve.

Then she said, "I thought you might come to tea sometime. You and Helga. The way we used to do. On Sundays. I thought I'd invite Jean-Louis and the children, too."

"Well, yes," he said, clearing his throat. "We've got to keep on. It's important to keep going."

Then suddenly she thought of Paule, and she turned and hurried downstairs, out onto the street. She walked as quickly as she could, all over town; she did not even realize she was in her own street until Pierre called her.

He was sitting in the doorway, in his pajamas.

"Where did you go, Lili—?"

"I invited Maurice to tea."

"OK, Lili. Good, I—"

She glared at him harshly, though he had suffered too—in the first war. What terrible things had happened to him then? What terrible knowledge that she had never forgiven him for, all these years?

But she had spent any kindness she had on Maurice.

"Good, Lili, good. I'm glad you—"

"Shut up, Pierre."

She went to cross over him, to go inside, but he caught her leg; he held her fast, not speaking, then he reached up and lifted her under her arms. He carried her upstairs, and then it was as if she were above them both, looking down. She wondered hopefully if he would hurt her. But he didn't. He lay her on the bed and sat next to her, holding her down. "Stop," he whispered. "Stop it."

She turned her head away from him.

For a long time, they did not move. The room grew light again, and at last, toward dawn, he sank down and fell asleep. She lay wide awake, feeling the hard, enclosing torture of his body half lying across hers. That strong, still-youthful body that would hold her but not make love to her. Why? Everything about him was strong, masculine, but he had no desire. It was an absence as secret and invisible as the absence of God. How idiotic she had been to hope for either! And yet, as she fell asleep, her train of thought dissolving into—what? the bleeding pulp of cherries, a spade hanging pointlessly in the toolshed, Paule's soft, white throat—she thought she was lying in her mother's arms, for this was her mother's bed, and that was the moonlit shadow of the balcony against the far wall. So it was all right; the pounding in her heart was only a dream. In the morning Maman, smelling of overripe peaches, would kiss her awake; she would peel the skin off Lili's hot chocolate.

PART THREE

Twenty-one

Lili awoke, and the air was pale and shimmering as mother-of-pearl. She was eighty-three, but she did not feel old, at this still hour, sitting in the garden of her childhood. She closed her eyes for a moment, and when she opened them, the sky was flushed, rose, scarlet, tangerine; a gold light slanted through the chestnut tree. Still, the garden wall was cold and gray. Lili had accidentally fallen asleep here, on a white plastic lawn chair. (Where had it come from? She could not remember buying such a flimsy thing.) She was knee deep in the long, weed-choked grass, and her feet were soaked with dew, but she did not want to move yet. How beautiful the garden was, in all its dereliction—the stubborn roses, the mossy, leaf-filled birdbath, the wild dandelions—how impossible to describe, with the gold light slanting in, farther and farther now, almost reaching the wall, filling the garden like water.

In the distance she could hear the sound of trucks on the highway. They never stopped. She'd heard that there were enormous hotels on the sides of the roads with hundreds of bare, tiny rooms—a concrete honeycomb—where people who drove all through the day and night stopped for an hour or two of sleep. The thought repelled Lili.

Oh but here, in the garden, how beautiful—! She reached into the pocket of her nightgown and shook out a cigarette. And how delicious, still, after all these years, the first taste of nicotine in the morning. It was 1982 now, July. Was that right? It had to be, or she wouldn't be eighty-three. Sometimes, confused, she said '72, as if it could possibly matter, and whatever young person she was speaking to—it had to be a young person; there were no old people left—had a suddenly pained look on her face, as if Lili had accidentally farted, pained and yet tolerant; how tolerant Thérèse's children were; they should be, con-

247

sidering they were all bastards, and it was that tolerant, pained look that clued her in. Was it the date she'd gotten wrong? Someone's name? Her sweater inside out? Honestly, to care about those things.

Of course, Papa would weep to see the mess she'd made of the garden. At the thought of her father, she grew suddenly still. She bowed her head. Her naked calves hung in the grass and she felt like a child, ashamed. Her father was dead now. Her father and her mother and baby Thérèse. Even poor Mademoiselle Duroc had died. But she mustn't forget Maurice. She and Maurice had lived, the way rats live, no matter what. . . .

She exhaled. The crisis was past, whatever it had been, the terrible thought—there were so many!—banished. Now and then she had great control over her mind, she thought, throwing her head back, letting the soft, damp air wash over her face. How delicious, how terribly delicious it all was. The air, the half-dead roses.

She was perfectly aware that she'd just been thinking about D day. That was not what caused the crisis. One could certainly think of D day; one could hardly help thinking of it. It was the way you thought about it that was important.

And—now she must hold herself even stiller, because this was the most terrible truth she knew, and to know it was to know the world to be as fragile as the thinnest film of ice—the dying roses were beautiful, the air delicious.

She did miss Paris. But there had hardly been any Germans here in Saint-Germain, only the occasional soldier invited to tea by Madame Maurice Ravaudet, her own sister-in-law, the little German ex–chorus girl, it turned out—yes, she'd been a chorus girl after all; once she learned to speak French, she spoke of nothing else. You would have thought she'd been a ballerina. But during most of the war, Lili barely spoke to Maurice and Helga. So she didn't much have to worry about the German soldiers. And it was less than an hour to Paris nowadays on the RER, so swift, and you were at Etoile; she could go whenever she pleased.

She dropped her cigarette into the long, damp grass, rose, and stretched her thin, veiny arms above her head. "I'm monstrous," she said aloud, lightheartedly, observing the condition of her skin. Only she knew when she was being lighthearted: her voice had grown as deep and graveled as a man's; everyone always thought she was angry when she spoke. If they only knew. Angry! She'd been angry when she was young, when her voice was smooth. No, this, this was something other than anger.

The garden was almost warm now. All the orange, crimson, pink, had faded and left behind a clear blue summer sky. But the light in the garden was still gold; tiny waves played across its surface. Was it a dream she'd woken from that had led her down to the garden before dawn, to sit here, old and nearly naked, in a plastic lawn chair? (From where? Where would she have bought such a thing?) Ah, no, it was the phone call the evening before. That's what had made her restless. She had a date that afternoon, at the Convent of the Holy Cross, with Paule. Paule was alive. She was alive and today, this very afternoon, in a few hours, Lili would see her. Touch her. They would kiss on the cheek, at least, wouldn't they? Yes, Lili would see Paule. They were the only ones who had lived so long—too long, perhaps, but, still, they were the only ones, and today . . .

She lived in a convent, of course. A nun. Sister Francis! Bald as an egg. Lili hadn't seen her in thirty years, not since right after the war. Paule had left the things of this world—the ties, the affections—all of it discarded, tossed away.

Paule was a nun and Pierre was dead and Claude was dead. Maman, Papa, Thérèse, Mademoiselle Duroc, Maurice, Jean-Louis—the list went on and on. Lili had held off as long as she could. She fell to her knees in the still-wet grass, in her faded, flowered nightgown, and covered her face with her hands. Her weeping was dry, silent. She simply shook, hiding her face. It was uncontrollable, but she had almost made it to breakfast today without doing it.

Breakfast was a cup of instant coffee in which she soaked a *biscotte*. She adored all these new, quick foods. The bins of frozen meals at Felix Potin. How pretty they were, in their small, cold, flat boxes. The food wasn't pretty when you actually took it out of the box and heated it up, but she loved the meals anyway. She felt as if they had been invented just for her. No one else she knew even went over to that aisle in Felix Potin. They were so horrified, as if it were a moral outrage: oh children. If they only knew! To speak of a perfectly good meal as a moral offense!

They were so ignorant, Thérèse's grandchildren. And yet she loved them. Differently from the way she loved their parents—Yvonne, Bernard, Nicolas—she adored them. She wanted—still!—to gaze and gaze at those three, to stroke their limbs, to touch their rough, middle-aged faces. Yvonne was insufferable, Bernard a criminal, Nicolas lazy and charming, but they were all that was left of Thérèse: Nicolas's warm laugh; the way Yvonne threw her hands in the air; the look of innocence Bernard had when you asked him to explain his criminal behavior. They, of course, knew about hunger. But their children! So ignorant, so bright! It was difficult to feel that they were even the same species as she. They knew nothing. Nothing at all. They were completely tabula rasa. And yet, now and then, when they came to visit her (dutifully: she was so old) she saw that they were still Thérèse's, after all.

Catherine came to lunch on Sunday. She was Yvonne's youngest, a girl of eighteen, as lovely and voluptuous as Thérèse had been but as studious and lacking in social graces as Lili herself. She was Lili's favorite. She took a bite of the salad Lili had made and spat it out. "You must have confused the bottle of dish-washing soap with the bottle of salad oil." That was all, a simple statement, no embarrassment. Quite openly, Catherine wiped her tongue with her napkin. Yvonne, no doubt, would have forced herself to eat the entire soapy salad without making a face. Then she would have suggested hiring a governess. Catherine simply gave a little laugh and picked greedily at the caramelized bits of sauce that stuck to the bottom of the plastic tray in which Lili had cooked the frozen *canard à l'orange.*

"I can't imagine being old," Catherine said innocently.

"No," Lili agreed. "You can't."

"Do you think we would have been friends if we'd been born at the same time?"

Lili thought for a while. "Hard to say."

"Oh!" Catherine's eyes filled with tears. "I always like to imagine we would have been."

Years ago—Catherine was barely three (was it Catherine?)—she walked over to Claude and put her head in his lap. He moaned in his wheelchair, a full-grown, pale-headed man, his gorgeous red lips hanging open. Catherine stared right up at him, her face perfectly round and open. "Will he talk when he's a little bigger?" she asked of her mother, who gasped in horror.

Lili shrugged, rose from her chair in the kitchen, and rummaged in the drawer. She wanted a bit of chocolate. Something dark and barely sweet after the reviving bitterness of her Nescafé.

The other grandchildren weren't nearly as interesting as Catherine. They were all successful, nicely dressed, and hadn't an original idea among them. They were complacent, condescending. Still, she loved them. She wished to warn them—and also, yes, to unsettle them. She wished to cry out when she saw them, *The hunger, you can't imagine—the hunger!* Actually, she did cry out the words from time to time. And then, she could feel it, it was as if their blood slowed down, as if they left their bodies—*There she goes again*—but it must be told! The gnawing! And it hadn't been the first time. That was the nightmare. To be hungry again so soon after the first war. Impossible ever to feel safe again! As soon as she felt safe, she began to hear the air-raid sirens, to feel a pit of hunger in her stomach, like a stone.

She let the chocolate sit on her tongue, relishing the way it dissolved all through her mouth. Nothing like the host. No flavor at all in those little wafers, Paule.

What time was her date that afternoon? Five? Not that it really mattered. Paule would certainly wait for her if she was late, welcome her tactfully if she was early.

Lili laughed sadly. Not a word in thirty years! She had written Paule once, an unanswered letter. And now this, a date in the afternoon. It couldn't possibly live up to Lili's expectations; couldn't possibly be any kind of answer to her years of anger and longing. Lili had been so nervous yesterday making the call. And then how brief their conversation had been, as if they saw each other every day, each of them hurrying to get off the phone, *Yes, I can meet you. Tomorrow at five, then?* Six? Noon? *Yes, good-bye.*

Lili, standing in the entryway, holding the telephone and the *écouteur,* had wanted to phone her back. *I thought you were dead. For weeks, I couldn't speak, my tongue was so heavy and dry. Not a word. Eighteen months I thought you were dead and at the end of it I was speechless, my tongue had grown fat, like something poisoned.*

But what was the use? She had said it all before, years ago.

At the end of the war, she went to the train station every day to look for Paule. Trainloads of them came back, inhuman, miserable. She couldn't understand what had happened to their faces. She stood in the cluster of women outside the Gare d'Orsay—every day the same ones came, looking for their husbands, sons, brothers. The police put up a barrier so that the women would not rush forward and crush the prisoners; the women leaned out over it, squeezing past each other, calling, "Did you know Louis Terrasse?" "Is Stephane Grouls alive?"

"Victor Pecker? Pecker?"

Different groups of prisoners were scheduled to arrive on different days, at different stations. She went from station to station but always ended up at the Gare d'Orsay. Even if there were no women and children on that day's schedule, perhaps Marcel would appear or someone who knew Marcel or Paule.

Hour after hour she stood, caught between those anxious, red-faced women, waiting for the prisoners. They always came later than expected, too weak sometimes to walk. Everyone spoke of typhus and typhoid fever, of prisoners getting sick on the slightest bit of solid food. Elsewhere in Paris, people celebrated. In Saint-Germain, Pierre waited for her with Claude, as he had waited all through the long month of June, when she was in Caen, digging through the debris of the house. This was the end of the war for her: a wild, sleepless search for bodies.

She watched the prisoners, the dark of their faces, so many pools of shadow. They were like blind men, except they did not use walking sticks or dogs. She did not understand; every day she called out, "Paule Jacob? Marcel Jacob? Jacob?" half expecting to see Paule emerge from a line of starving men, in her red dress, plump and beautiful.

But beneath the singleness of her purpose, her preoccupation with a red silk dress, she felt a mounting panic until at last she forgot why she was there. She saw only the ravaged bodies of men passing before her. She opened her mouth, knowing there was something she was supposed to call out—a word, a name—and nothing came. Her tongue lay swollen and useless in her mouth. It made no difference. All along, her cries had been lost in the cries of the other women.

One afternoon, a small group of Jewish women arrived at the Gare d'Orsay. They looked like the men—hairless, blind seeming, fleshless—except they walked a little differently, their necks craning forward, their shoulders curved around what was left of their breasts. Out of the line, one came toward Lili, shaking. Lili put her hand on the woman's shoulder; she had no idea who the woman was. She had been going to the different stations for weeks, completely mute now, oblivious of her original purpose. It was a kind of daily pilgrimage, something to use up the time, though she had forgotten why it needed to be used up.

"He's dead." Over and over the woman repeated it: *He's dead, Lili.* Then Lili remembered:

Marcel, Paule.

Lili lifted Paule like a child and carried her away from the station.

Someone shouted after her, "You can't do that! She may have typhoid. . . ."

Lili ran, stumbling beneath the weight of those ravaged bones. Paule's arms dangled at her sides, her head hung limply on its fragile stalk. She had seemed light for a moment, a tiny skeleton, but she was more than Lili could carry. Still, Lili made it across the Quai Anatole France, down the steps to the river. She sat on a bench on the quay, beneath the Pont Royal, holding Paule on her lap. Paule did not even look at Lili, her face as blank and terrifying as a dead woman's. But she was breathing steadily. It was the faintest stream of air, dark and rank, like rust, like old spinach. Lili sat perfectly still, breathing in her terrible breath and the damp stone smell of the quay. She didn't know what to do now. She didn't know how to get Paule home.

In the end, a little boy came by, and she offered him two francs if he would telephone Pierre. She was weeping with fear by the time she saw the boy, but he was a good boy—still in shorts—he didn't pocket the money she gave him for the call.

Lili and Pierre gave her their own bed. They put pillows beneath her knees, beneath her arms. They washed her with a warm rag and rubbed salad oil and cologne into her skin. They made a thick, watery gruel for her and fed it to her with a baby's spoon. Claude sat in the corner, in his wheelchair, his mouth agape. His lavender eyes were shot with pain: For Paule? Lili wondered. For himself, to be so ignored?

Lili could speak again—her tongue had shrunk back to its normal size—but she had nothing to say. She and Pierre moved silently together, washing, stroking, mixing the gruel. She was glad Pierre was with her, grateful beyond words for the way he took care; it was, she thought, almost as if they were starting over, as if they had a new child.

On the fourth day, Paule raised herself up on her elbows.

"Careful!" Pierre said, rushing to her.

"I want some chicken," Paule said, in a low, urgent voice. It was the first time she had spoken since the train station, and it shocked them to hear words coming from her deadened face. "Chicken," she said again.

"You can't, *chérie,*" Lili said, sitting on the edge of the bed, resting her hand lightly on Paule's knee. "You have to get strong first—"

"Chicken," Paule repeated. "I want some butter, some chicken, I want a roast chicken."

"Lili's right," Pierre said, sitting on the other side of Paule. "The doctor said—"

"A roast chicken and some new potatoes. Crispy skin, butter."

"Oh, *chérie,*" Lili said. "I am so sorry. Soon. Soon we'll make you everything you—"

"Roasted new potatoes, butter. A roast chicken. Listen to me! A leg of lamb. A pork roast. I'll settle for a roast pork. As long as there is plenty of butter. And bread. A lot of bread. Oranges, apples, strawberries, tomatoes, asparagus, a blueberry tart, a pork roast. What do you have in this house?" She moved to get out of bed and Pierre touched her. She was so weak, she couldn't resist him, and she lay back down, her eyes and limbs twisting suddenly with pain. Claude began to moan.

"Hush," Lili said. "Hush, please."

Paule lay on her side, broken, muttering her list of food. She was no longer talking to them; she was simply chanting, *Bread, butter, chicken, lamb, pork, potatoes, chocolate. . . .*

Claude would not stop moaning.

"Take him out of here!" Lili whispered hoarsely. "Paule. Paule, *chérie,* soon—"

In the end, Lili put cotton in her ears. She kept Claude downstairs and only went to see Paule for an hour at a time. They had to lock Paule in her room, or she would have tried to crawl down the stairs to the kitchen. Pierre could sit with her all afternoon, stroking her hand, listening to her. He didn't mind; he was braver than Lili. Paule looked at Lili with hatred, muttering at her, but Lili closed her eyes, and then it was only a faint sound through the cotton, like the rasping wings of a cricket.

How excitedly Lili and Pierre prepared her first meal. A pale slice of chicken, some boiled rice, a few spoonfuls of custard. They used their finest china and decorated the plate with parsley. Lili's heart pounded as she brought Paule the food. *See?* she wanted to say. *We are not so awful.* But Paule was oblivious of the parsley, the fine china, the couple who had so lovingly arranged the meager portions on her plate. She ate with her hands, all in a rush, silent for the first time in weeks. She was still skeletal, unrecognizable. Her hair grew and immediately fell out: little clumps of black down on the pillow. Her eyes expressed hatred or nothing. And yet Lili began to see, in the structure of her bones, a suggestion of the old, lovely friend. It was as if she were looking at the fossil remains of something and divining, in the spidery pattern, a voice, motions, smells. . . .

At night, Lili and Pierre slept in Claude's room, on a mattress on the floor. The room adjoined their usual room, and through the half-opened door they could hear Paule lying silently in their bed, exhausted from her daylong monologue, her obsession with a rack of lamb, a chocolate cake, a calf's tongue. They held hands beneath the covers, listening to that terrible, spent silence and to the rasping sound of Claude's breath: he was an adolescent now, almost as tall as a man. In Lili's absence—when she was in Caen, when she was searching the Paris train stations—he had grown hairier, thicker, though he was still pale, and he had developed asthma. He wanted to crawl all the time now, and, if they needed him to sit still, they were forced to strap him into his wheelchair.

They did not speak during the night, Lili and Pierre, but they held hands tightly until they fell asleep. Paule was no longer the woman Lili had secretly been lovers with, a woman Pierre had found charming and desirable; she was, simply, someone they were bringing back to life. She could have been anyone. What mattered was saving her. They, who— it seemed to them—had never saved anyone.

If only they could succeed! All things would be possible.

At last Paule could eat normally. Lili spent hours in the kitchen, perfecting recipes. Paule did not mutter anymore; the hatred began to fade out of her eyes. Lili stroked Paule's bald head, her thin arms.

"You're beginning to look like yourself again," Lili murmured. "The steak isn't too well done, is it? You'll stay with us always now— we'll make you an apartment in the attic."

Paule grew docile, polite. She thanked them for everything, again and again, like an overtrained child.

"Would you like a cigarette?" Lili asked. "There's that nice, round window in the attic. You can see all the roofs of the town—"

"Thank you," Paule murmured, her head bowed. "You are so kind."

"You'll stay right here with us."

Of course, things would never be the way they had been between Lili and Paule. Paule had suffered too much for that. (Oh, and Paule's asceticism in the last years before the war, her turning away—what was that but a kind of premonition?) Still, they could be a family: she and Pierre and Paule and Claude. A quiet life in Saint-Germain, like the one her parents had had. Now and then one of them could go into Paris alone and remember the old days, but together they would never speak of the past.

In the spring, when the tangle of forsythia and the pale daffodils began to bloom, Paule was well enough to get out of bed.

She sat in the garden, wrapped in a blanket, and she looked straight at Lili and smiled, as if she were just now recognizing her. She had a bit of hair, black and fine as a baby's, and when she smiled—her back teeth torn out—she was beautiful again. It was a more austere, more remote beauty than before, but it was still her beauty. It was difficult to look at her, wrapped in an old pink blanket with satin edges, her black hair catching the light; painful beyond words to realize who she was, after all.

"Oh, Lili," Paule said, her voice warm and rich. She shook her head laughingly. "Lili Ravaudet. I had such a crush on you."

Lili closed her eyes.

"I've decided to enter a convent, you know."

Lili pushed herself up from the metal stool in the kitchen and opened another drawer to see if she could find some chocolate. Except for the one with the silverware in it, all the kitchen drawers were crammed with notes, receipts, pens, matches, loose cigarettes. Often, if she was diligent enough and searched all of them, she could find several half-eaten chocolate bars. Enough to make a meal.

No luck this time. She opened the little side door that gave out onto the garden and stood in the doorway with her eyes closed, feeling the warm summer morning on her face. She'd have to leave by one-thirty to catch the three o'clock train to Etampes. Yes, they must have agreed on five o'clock, otherwise why would she have the three o'clock train so firmly in her mind?

She wondered, leaning against the door frame, her eyes still closed, if Paule, too, had lapses of memory. Though it was best not to wonder too much about the condition of Paule's mind, now that Paule was a nun. Best not to grieve the loss. Lili had grieved enough. You couldn't even blame the Germans this time; in retrospect, you could see that Paule had been heading for the convent all along.

Sooner or later the Church swallowed everyone Lili knew. Even Pierre had had his little conversion in the end. A country full of atheists, and Lili was surrounded by the devout! Claude alone had remained pure to the last.

Oh, well. Through the fragile skin of her eyelids, she watched the sun shatter and explode. She smelled the night's dampness rising in waves out of the earth. It'll be a hot day, she thought, turning back into the house to take a bath.

But just then she heard the front door open and the sound of her niece's voice, full of false cheer:

"Tatie! Tatie? Hoo-hoo! It's me! Yvonne!"

"You might knock," Lili murmured, going toward the front door.

"Tatie!" Yvonne exclaimed. She stood in the doorway, her arms open, a brilliant, determined smile on her face. She was a coarser version of Thérèse, with loose, slightly graying curls and strong forearms. "Tatie!" she repeated. "How are you, Tatie?"

"Well," Lili shrugged, "I'm irritated, at the moment, by your presence."

"Irritated?" Yvonne repeated, full of concern, as if it were a medical condition.

"Sh-sh," Lili said. "Just keep still for a moment. I want to look at you. There, that's better." She ran her fingers along Yvonne's arm. "You're just so loud, first thing in the morning." She reached up and kissed Yvonne. "Now. What brings you here?"

"Tatie—! Tatie, I always come by in the morning—"

"A joke!" Lili said, laughing easily, naturally, though she had, in fact, forgotten to expect Yvonne today. "Of course you come every morning."

"Your nightgown is all wet at the bottom," Yvonne said accusingly.

"I was out in the garden. Come see how beautiful it is right now."

Yvonne sighed, but she followed Lili, through the dining room and the living room, out through the French doors.

"Have you ever seen anything more beautiful?" Lili asked, gesturing toward the dandelions and the roses, the hopeless tangle of living and dead ivy on the garden wall.

"It's rather a mess," Yvonne said sadly. Then she said, "That chair. Where did you get that chair?"

It came to Lili, suddenly: she had bought it last week at the quincaillerie. It was the price that had attracted her—twenty francs, less than the price of a meal—and the chair's incredible lightness: she had carried it home all by herself.

"It's an antique" she said. "It's been in the family for generations."

"Tatie?" Yvonne said. Her voice was soft, panicked. "Tatie? It's plastic—"

"I was trying to fool you," Lili said, feigning despair. Now she was having fun. "If you must know, I stole it."

"Now you are teasing me," Yvonne said. "Aren't you, Tatie?"

"I've always felt that you were too well behaved," said Lili. "You need to relax, have some fun."

"I'm past that now, don't you think?" She threw her hands in the air, and they seemed to brush Lili's throat, the gesture was so exactly like Thérèse's.

"Don't insult me with your pretense at old age," Lili said wryly, coming back to the present. "Why are you so curious about my chair?"

Yvonne blushed.

"Are you thinking of refurnishing your apartment? Because if you are, I highly recommend this line of furniture. It's lightweight," Lili said, picking the chair up by the arm.

"Oh!" Yvonne gasped and took the chair from Lili before she realized that neither one of them needed to hold it at all. She set it down carefully. Then she blurted it out, the truth, the terrible weight on her heart—the same confession she made every morning—"We worry about you, Tatie. The frozen food, all these new plastic—plastic things. What if you were to fall? You're all alone here. And those frozen dinners—"

"Poor Yvonne," Lili murmured. "Have you a lover?"

"Oh, Tatie. Tatie, your mind wanders. It's the truth. It has to be said. Suppose you were to fall?"

"I don't think," Lili said, her voice cold now, even, "there's a connection between a wandering mind and a broken hip."

"But your mind does wander," Yvonne whispered, her eyes suddenly swimming with tears.

"And so will yours, when you have amassed as much intellectual territory as I have. Right now, *chérie,* your mind has about half an acre to explore. Naturally it doesn't wander. It can only pace. And no matter where you are in that little half-acre plot, you can always see the entire layout of your property—"

"It's got to be said," Yvonne went on shrilly, her lip trembling. "All we're suggesting is a woman to come once a day—"

"Oh, hush," Lili said, softening all of a sudden. "Why is it that they always make you do the dirty work? You're too serious, I've always said it. You need to have some fun, Yvonne."

"Tatie, please."

"Why didn't your rake of a brother, Bernard, come to talk to me about a governess?"

"It isn't a governess, Tatie. Tatie, I'm afraid you'll fall."

"Hush, Yvonne. I've got to die eventually. It can't be avoided. Not for any of us—"

Yvonne began to weep freely.

"Hush. It's nothing. Sooner or later, I'll be completely incapacitated, and then you can do whatever you like with me." It wasn't a happy prospect, but she had to give Yvonne some hope. Yvonne had been longing for power since before she could speak, when she must have looked up from her white kid shoes and her lace socks to see that Bernard and Nicolas could roll in the dirt without the slightest reproach, while she, Yvonne, must play quietly all day long.

"For now, though," Lili said, "you'll have to leave. I have an appointment to make."

"An appointment?" Yvonne asked hopefully. "With the doctor?"

"A specialist in geriatrics."

"Really, Tatie? Really?"

"I'm afraid not, *chérie*. I'm actually going to a furniture show. A warehouse full of plastics."

"Please tell the truth, Tatie."

Lili shrugged. "A convent, then. I'm going to a convent."

"Oh, Tatie."

"That's the trouble," Lili said, squeezing Yvonne's thick fingers, that square hand that was capable, in a single, unconscious, inherited gesture, of such lightness. "We must speak, the same way we must breathe and eat and defecate, but to what purpose? Impossible to understand one another! A person finally tells the truth, and the others think he has lost his mind. I really am going to a convent. I don't imagine I'll say much once I'm there. I've already said all I have to say to the nun I'm visiting. But I can't resist going." She shrugged, laughing. "So why try to? What does it serve, in the end, Yvonne, to hold back?"

Yvonne sighed heavily, convinced of Lili's madness. "I have to leave now, Tatie. I have to go to work. Do you need anything? Any groceries? I could send Catherine over in the afternoon."

"Sweet Catherine," Lili murmured.

"Anything? A baguette?" There was the slightest edge of impatience in her voice.

"Sh-sh," Lili said. "I'm sure they have bread at the convent."

Twenty-two

She made her way upstairs, past the room where Paule had lain after Auschwitz: the door and door frame with the pair of small, round holes, like matching scars—all that remained of the latch Pierre had screwed in to keep Paule from opening the door.

It was the room where Lili and Pierre had slept together, night after night, cupped together like spoons, after everyone else had died or left, and where, in another life altogether, she'd rested in Maman's mournful, fat, rich-smelling arms.

It shocked her to have gotten no farther than this: her childhood house. She had only stayed on after the war to keep the garden—for Claude—and then to keep it for herself. But the garden was attached to this house. Impossible to have the wild roses without the lost passion, the hidden sadness of childhood; without the ceaseless sound of Paule begging for food.

She threw her hands up in despair, went into the bathroom, and turned on the hot water. The pipes shook violently, making terrible, anguished sounds, then gushed forth. She slipped off her damp grass-stained nightgown and sat on the edge of the tub, waiting for it to fill, surveying the wreckage of her body. From the breasts down, she was just fold after fold of soft skin. As thin as old silk, as dead leaves, as powder. No pubic hair at all. But her shoulders were strong and bony and elegant. Her neck, from a distance, looked smooth. Her hair, however—! All the color was gone, the heft, the texture. Short gray tufts covered her head like wild grass. Still, at times, she liked herself. She was leaning forward, peering into the mirror on the back of the door, and behind her she could feel the rising steam of her bath. If she looked only at her nose and her eyes, she was pleased. Even her hair had a certain derelict beauty, like the garden.

Oh, Pierre, I am not so ugly.

Though as for her mouth, the less said the better.

She put her hand into the bathwater, gasped, and turned the cold on full strength.

At last, having adjusted the temperature to her liking—just under scalding, so that her scalp could sweat—she leaned back in the deep, clear water and lit a cigarette. Pierre never liked the water as hot as she did, in the early days, when they bathed together. Later, when they were already old, after Claude died, when Pierre spoke three or four words a week, he got into the habit of filling up the bath for her, as hot as she liked it, and then, when she had soaked awhile, he would come in and—still without uttering a word!—wash her back. Oh, but in the early days, how she suffered in the tepid water for the pleasure of his company, in the big bathtub in the hotel in Pornic!

They went to Pornic again, finally, after the war, after Paule left for the convent. Claude was eighteen—long limbed and hunched, his body covered with pale, soft hair. He sat in the sand for hours with his legs splayed in front of him, gazing at the great crashing waves. Lili, in a brand-new bathing suit, walked back and forth at the edge of the water, smoking. To her amazement, her nakedness embarrassed her. That she was still capable of embarrassment, after the war, was astonishing. It revolted her to be so trivial, and it made her happy. That's how everything was, now. There was no single emotion, no point of rest, no peace.

Pierre sat up in the dry sand next to Claude, digging a moat around a castle. After a while, Lili walked up to them. She put her wet hand on Claude's forehead, and he let out a deep, clumsy laugh.

"Do you know, I'd actually forgotten about your sand castles. Isn't that remarkable? If you'd asked me what we did on our honeymoon, I wouldn't have thought to mention your sand castles. Be sure he keeps his hat on, will you? Do you remember how I loathed the sun? It doesn't bother me at all now, I like this stupid feeling. We did have a good time, didn't we, Pierre?"

"Yes, Lili." He was intent on deepening his moat. He took Claude's hand and made him feel the cool, dissolving river he was creating. Claude laughed again, a low, loose, generous sound.

"Anyway," Lili said. "I had a good time. The oysters. The crepes. Do you remember you made me sing?"

"Did I?"

"Yes, you did."

He looked up from the moat and shaded his eyes with a sandy hand. They were still so raw, so awkward, these attempts at ordinary conversation. It seemed to her that the last unembarrassed words they'd spoken to each other were right before D day. But that wasn't true. The last unembarrassed words had been here, in 1929, on their honeymoon.

"Poor Lili," Pierre said at last, glancing back down at his castle. His hair was gray, but still his shoulders were broad and straight, and still the arc of his chest was as hard and beautiful as a shield. "You remember so much. It's better to forget."

"Forget!" she cried, in despair. "Forget! What is the point of living if you're just going to forget it all?" She was squatting beside him, her toes curled into the sand. "Forget!" she cried again, and a young couple down near the water's edge stared up at her rudely.

It was impossible not to scream at him. He seemed so close since the war, so near to the point of baring his soul to her—the way his mouth quivered sometimes, in the middle of talking about nothing, and his eyes swam with tears—and she was like a hunter stalking him, sometimes quietly, putting a little extra effort into her cooking, smiling at him, patting his hand, and then leaping, pouncing, wild with impatience; he evaded her every time. And yet how close she got. At night, now, with Claude in a bed of his own, Pierre sometimes reached for her in his sleep, the way he'd done in the early days. The first time, she gasped, and then she began to laugh nervously, fearfully, laughing until tears rolled down her cheeks. He didn't wake up. And soon—how easily she was seduced!— she accepted it. She even began to look forward to it. It wasn't much—he reached suddenly for her breasts, kissed them, and fell back to snoring; or he fumbled desperately with the hem of her nightgown, trying to push it up and, having accomplished that, lay flat on his back again, in the deepest of dreams—but, she told herself, it was more than anything that had happened between them in years. And he had never reached for Claude. It was not just a body he sought. He seemed to know, in his sleep, that it was she, to know the gestures of love.

A shadow of marriage, a reflection. Still, it was something.

"Forget?" she cried, over and over, squatting there on the beach at l'Anse aux Lapins. "How can you forget?"

Claude, unfazed, stared expressionlessly out to sea.

Pierre's moat was as deep as his elbow. "Sh-sh," he said without looking up at her. "There are people—"

"I know there are people," she said loudly, staring at the young couple. "We've already made eye contact. The people are not the problem. Your memory is."

"Oh, Lili. Why?"

"Because, Pierre, it's all we have." She leaned her face close to his. "What else in the world do we have?" She was speaking normally now, having frightened the young man and woman into the water.

Pierre shrugged. "I don't know, Lili. Surely there's something else besides those awful memories."

"Like what, for example? What? God?" She laughed and did not wait for him to answer. "What else do we possess besides our awful memories? Though actually"—she paused—"what I was speaking of just now was not an awful memory. What I was speaking of just now was our honeymoon. But perhaps, for you, that isn't such a pleasant memory. I thought we had a nice time. But maybe—"

"Oh, Lili. I had a nice time. But what we have—what we possess— is the present."

"Oh!" She laughed bitterly. Then she sat down in the sand and buried her face in her knees. She felt, suddenly, exhausted.

"You think too much, poor Lili. You think, and you worry."

"And you?" she said, looking sideways at him. "What do you do?"

He shrugged. "I teach my classes. I'm a good citizen."

"A life of good citizenship? *Quelle horreur!* I detest that kind of asceticism—or whatever it is."

"Yes, you do, don't you? We're an odd pair that way, aren't we?"

She smiled, despite everything. He had called them a pair, after all. And they were now. They were practically all alone. Just the two of them and Claude. Like orphans. How tired they were, and nervous. But the Germans were all gone. One had to focus on that. You could walk the streets at any hour, buy whatever you pleased; yes, yes, you could do anything. . . .

She burst into tears.

"Hush," Pierre said. "Sh-sh." And then, more brusquely, "You've got to stop thinking about it all, Lili. . . ."

She forced herself to stop crying. She remembered him crouched over her in the garden when she returned from Caen, his face drenched with tears. *Yes, Pierre, I do love you*—and she wanted to fall on him, to cover him with kisses, to embrace him under the hot, clear sky, but she must not do that. Bastard, she thought.

"It would be easier to focus on the present if there were anything in the present," she said quietly. She turned to Claude, took off his hat, and ran her fingers through his fine, wheat-colored hair. He did not move, his eyes fixed on the cold green water. They had parked his wheelchair at the end of the dirt path, and Pierre had carried him down the stone steps and into the sand. That was how Pierre stayed so strong, his muscles adjusting year by year to Claude's weight.

It frightened Lili, how relieved she was by Claude's near paralysis. At home, he crawled everywhere, up and down the stairs, out into the garden, knocking into things, tearing up the flower beds. You never knew where you'd find him, what he would have destroyed. And he was so big, like Pierre. She yelled at him, beside herself, and then she wept.

Only Madame Perichet could always manage him. Madame Perichet was a thick-boned Protestant in her sixties, with hair and a mustache the color of iron. She disapproved of Lili—her cooking, her clothes, her love of cigarettes—but she was fiercely loyal to Claude. They had hired her when they moved to Saint-Germain, when it was obvious that Claude was too big for the au pair girls, and right away Madame Perichet let them know how little she thought of au pairs. She, Madame Perichet, would let them know what was what. She put Claude on a strict schedule: a sponge bath at seven (she didn't believe in total immersion), café au lait at seven-thirty, crawling at eight, a nap at nine, prayer for his soul at ten. . . . She was abnormally strong and could carry Claude up and down the stairs over her shoulder, could force him to lie down while she changed his clothes. She let him draw from two until three and sang to him from three until three-thirty. She had a startlingly sweet soprano.

Claude adored her.

"I don't think much of the ocean," she had said when Lili told her they were going to Pornic. "The mountains are more instructive. I won't come along."

"No, no of course not," Lili stammered. "It's high time you had some vacation—"

"Hah! Vacation! It's no vacation when you come home to a child who's been spoiled in your absence. You'll have to keep him on his schedule. Now, if you were going to Grenoble, I might join you."

Lili stared at her for a moment, considering her offer. But to go only to the foot of the Alps—! And with Madame Perichet! She wanted the mountains only if she could be alone in them. She shook her head. "I'm afraid . . . I'm afraid I'm not much of a mountain person," she said.

"Well!" Madame Perichet said, offended. "I just hope you don't completely ruin him."

"I'll do my best not to," Lili murmured, terrified of two weeks with Claude without help.

But as it turned out, Claude simply sat, mesmerized. Even at night, in the hotel room, as if the image of the waves stayed with him, he was calm. Of course, there was the awful possibility that it could rain, and they'd have to stay inside all day, but the sky had been perfectly blue every day so far.

Oh we had a wonderful time, Lili imagined herself saying to Madame Perichet. *A true vacation.*

Let Madame Perichet figure out for herself how Lili had "managed" Claude. Schedules!

He's a sea person, that's clear, Lili would say.

She brushed Claude's hair behind his ears and put his hat back on.

"Anyway," she said, looking at Pierre again. "You did make me sing. On our honeymoon. I remember it."

"Then I must have," he said. He sighed. He put a spade in Claude's hand, but Claude wasn't interested. He just wanted to stare. "Maybe," Pierre said, "we should have gone straight to Sauxillanges instead of coming here for two weeks. Sauxillanges doesn't upset you so."

"Oh!" Lili said. "I'm not spending a minute more than I have to with your cow sisters. Besides," she went on, " I do have disturbing memories of Sauxillanges. I have your memories. A young, fresh girl, the prettiest in the village, ruined and abandoned by Pierre Larat."

"For God's sake, Lili. What's gotten into you today?"

"Oh, who knows. Sometimes I feel like everything's been tossed up and some things fell back in odd places. I start thinking about a question I answered poorly for my *bac.* A minor slipup I haven't thought about in years, and suddenly I am obsessed with it. I want to go back to the examining board and tell them that of course I understood what Spinoza—"

"Poor Lili." Pierre laughed. "Go in the water and cool your head."

She laughed with him, sadly. Then she rose and walked down to the foamy waves. Far out in the water, she could see the cheerful heads of the young man and his wife. Yes, she thought, I will cool my head in the water. I'll do whatever he tells me. Then he will love me.

That was an old, pointless thought. Too late now.

The water stung her skin, her scalp, buoyed her up—

Oh, to embrace—

She ran out of the sea, streaming, up to the castle, to Claude with his set, purple eyes, and Pierre, beside him, scooping and scooping—

"Bring him down!" she said, out of breath.

Pierre paused in his digging, looked at her, at Claude. "Into the water?"

She nodded, excitedly.

"I wonder—"

"Oh, stop worrying about Madame Perichet. The old horse isn't even here now." Pierre was even more afraid of Madame Perichet than Lili was; if he'd heard what Madame Perichet had said about Claude's schedule, he would have felt bound to obey her. "Come on!" Lili said.

"It's awfully cold," Pierre began, halfheartedly. Then he laughed. "Oh, why not, after all?" He lifted Claude, his whole body straining— *Viens, mon vieux*—carrying him unsteadily into the waves, the deep water, into Lili's arms.

Claude laughed, a deep, reckless laugh, his large body slipping against Lili's arms. She laughed, too, amazed that she could carry him after all. "*Mon chéri,*" she cried, kissing Claude's cool, salty cheeks, his shoulders. She was standing on the points of her toes, struggling with the ocean floor, off balance, but she did not want to let go of him. How good it was to hold his whole, huge, helpless body in her thin arms, to lift him up—she kissed his shoulders again, his throat, where the water collected in a thumb-sized pool; she kissed his cheeks over and over. She was turning and turning on the treacherous floor, laughing. "My sweet darling Claude, my boy. . . ." And he laughed again, too, his wet, shiny mouth wide open—he swallowed part of a wave, coughed, smiled.

"Such a fish you are," she murmured, and they stayed in the water, bouncing weightlessly from side to side until she saw that his lips were blue and realized that she was on the point of dropping him. "Pierre!" she called, and he ran to them through the heavy water, laughing, embracing them both for a moment before carrying Claude back up to shore.

The next day, suddenly, Claude began to push at his bathing trunks. "Oh." Lili laughed. "Not here. You can't get undressed here, *mon chéri,*" for there were several other people on the beach today: an old woman beneath an umbrella, two little girls, the young couple from the day before. The sky was hot and glaring, fish colored, and it was hard to keep one's temper. "Darling, not today."

Pierre looked up from his castle but said nothing.

And still Claude fumbled with the top of his bathing trunks, trying to push them down.

"No, no, *chéri.* It isn't private. You're a big boy—a man—now. Please, Pierre."

"*Ah, mon vieux,*" Pierre said, rallying to the cause. He offered Claude a spade, a ball, but Claude wanted only one thing: to be naked. He was beginning to whimper now, trying desperately to get his shorts off. The young couple was staring again.

"That's enough now," Lili said in a sharp, quiet voice. She put her hand on Claude's to stop him, and Claude flung her aside, his arms strong and graceless. She toppled slightly in the sand, hurt, and struck him back.

He stopped. He stared at her, his mouth hanging open, and then he began to wail, over and over and over, a sound flat and terrible like a siren. But Pierre was carrying him away, stumbling in the sand, into the water where Claude would become as light as a child again, as easy.

Lili curled up into a ball in the hot sand, her eyes shut tight. Beyond her, she heard the two little girls flock to their grandmother.

"Why is that man crying?"

"Was he crippled in the war?"

"Hush, children."

She lay in that dead, hot, white light, her eyes squeezed so tightly that she saw small gold explosions, and for the first time since before the war she let herself think of how Paule had been in the beginning: the pale, slender arms, the incredibly soft body. *I was a decent person then*, she thought.

The bath had grown tepid, so she drained out half of it and filled it up again with scalding water. Every time, the hot water faucet wheezed and gasped, as if it objected, not in the tiresome, condescending way of a young person—*It's much too hot, Tatie. I'm sure it's not good for you*—but in the tired way of the old: *Why, Lili? Why? Aren't you hot enough? What about your heart? You might die.*

"If I'm lucky," Lili murmured. She sank back down into the hot water. *If I am ever that lucky.*

But, in truth, if she wanted to die, all she had to do was walk to the highway and let one of the all-night trucks hit her. She was small and wasted now; it wouldn't take much—and she didn't want to die. That was her great secret. She loved to speak of dying; it was like imagining a soft bed, an exquisite meal. But she wasn't ready for it. She hadn't wanted to die after André committed suicide, and she didn't want to die now. It was a lifelong struggle not to be ashamed of this—this desire to keep going—but there it was: despite all the horror.

She slid under the water again, holding her breath, and washed the small, gray tufts of her hair. She wanted to look good today. As good as possible; she wasn't an idiot. She did not expect that Paule, seeing her, would feel a sudden resurgence of desire.

She stood up, the water slaking off her, and reached for a towel. There was so little left of her, a handful of bones; this is what caught in her throat, made her ribs ache: the sight of her own body, vanishing.

She would wear her favorite clothes. She would dress up, as if she were going to a party.

"Oh, Paule," she whispered, into the steamy bathroom.

I will wear your old clothes, as I have for so many years now. Someone has to keep you alive. I have done my best. I am a poor choice for the job—this job of smelling and tasting—but I have done my best.

She'd said nothing when Paule told her she was joining a convent. What was there to say?

It hadn't taken long for Paule to leave the house: all she needed was a toothbrush and a change of underwear, a picnic for the train ride.

She remembered the way Pierre looked at Paule the day she left. It was a look of longing, the look of someone who has always wanted to go abroad and who stands on the shore while the boat pulls inexorably away. Lili saw the look, but she didn't understand it.

"Thank you," Paule said, bowing her head, taking Pierre's hands in hers. "It is so little to say. . . . There is nothing I can say."

She kissed the top of Claude's head, bent down, and looked into his purple eyes. She stared at him for a long time, and then she kissed him again. "Little child of light," she murmured.

Lili stared at her silently. Pierre would accompany Paule to the train station; Lili didn't want to go. They kept staring at each other, Lili and Paule, and after a while Pierre said, "We'll miss your train, Paule," and Paule said, "Yes," and she opened the front door and went out into the warm, sunlit street, and that was all. Lili closed the door and wheeled Claude quickly out the other side of the house, into the garden.

Once, a few years later, in a moment of weakness, Lili wrote to Paule and made the mistake of mailing the letter. Naturally, there was no answer.

And then yesterday, on the telephone:

"It's me—Lili. I didn't know if you were allowed to receive calls."

"Yes, of course. Oh, Lili—"

"That's Vatican Two, I suppose, the right to receive phone calls."

Paule laughed: a soft, old woman's laugh. "Well, the modern world. . . ."

"Are you allowed to receive visitors?"

"Oh, Lili. Lili, I would love to see you."

"Well, then, tomorrow at five?"

"Yes, good."

"How are you?" Lili asked suddenly.

"Very well, Lili. A bit tired. . . . Life is such a gift, don't you think?"
Lili laughed.

"You saved my life," Paule said, her voice faint over the phone.
"You and Pierre."

"We should have put you in an asylum."

Paule laughed. "You and Pierre and God. . . . Through God . . ."

"I don't know which is worse," Lili said, "electroshock therapy or
a convent. . . . I don't know of anything sadder than this eternal longing for God. Anyway. You're all I have left, such as you are. I'll see you
at five then."

"Yes, good-bye."

A gift, Lili thought, standing in a puddle in the bathroom, wrapped in
a towel. She was going to take a two-hour train ride to spend an hour
with someone who would tell her that life is a gift, and then she had a
two-hour train ride back. She could even bear the thought. . . . After
all, what else did she have to do with her time? Listen to Yvonne? She
could only read for so long nowadays. Yes, she could almost bear it if
it weren't for the fact that, having spent a lifetime studying philosophy,
she still managed to be thrown off course by this idiot, soft-brained
Jew-nun. All night, sitting in the garden, she'd worried about whether
or not life was a gift until at last, in despair, she'd fallen asleep.

It was hardly a new problem, much less one that posed a serious
intellectual challenge: If life is a gift (from what? whom?) does that
imply freedom or a lifelong debt of gratitude that can never be fully
repaid? How disquieting Paule still was with her simplistic little propo-
sitions. The work of the intellectual Paule dismissed, laughing. And Lili
was left behind, pondering the most sophomoric of questions: Gratitude or freedom? Freedom or gratitude? What kind of gift? The Marshall Plan?

A gift—what is that? André, lifting his helmet? He was wise to commit suicide; he would have died anyway, so close to the front. Regiment
after regiment blown apart, almost as systematic as what came later.

Oh, yes, she would wear her best dress. Perhaps it was, after all, cause for shame, her will to live, the pleasure she took in the feel of old silk. What of it, then? She'd be shameful.

"*. . . et Jean, d'un coeur vaillant, l'a rebâti, plus beau qu'avant*," she sang loudly, suddenly, in her old, toneless voice. "*Là-haut, sur la montagne, l'était un vieux chalet*—"

She went into the bedroom, toward the old armoire where her dresses hung. The shadow of the balcony fell against the white wall. How still the room was, how lovely with the light falling in. She never closed the shutters on the garden side of the house. Even her mother had not closed those shutters. Another life altogether, in her mother's fat, brown arms; she remembered the shadow of the balcony from the beginning of time: the slender, scrolled mark, like the stroke of a watercolor. Oh, that body. The softness of it, the smell of coffee and sweat. The window in Paris where she had sat, morning after morning, nursing Claude, watching her cigarette smoke curve away and dissolve, as watery as a shadow. That was all, in the end: memories of light. And the dead years, when she did not notice the light at all. A lot of those, mostly those. *Do you believe in the life to come? Mine was always that.* She sat in the theater with Pierre one night in the fifties, watching the play, and Hamm said that—or was it Clov?—and she began to cry, and Pierre said, "Hush, Lili, really, what you see in Beckett . . ." Did Claude remember anything, one day to the next? In the last years, crawling around the house, breaking all the vases, did he remember the window in Paris? The taste of her milk? She hadn't guessed a thing at first; he was so perfectly formed. Oh, the red lips, the violet eyes. *Whom I loved above all others and whom I neglected again and again*—yes, neglect, to forget to love, to simply feed and wash and put to bed—alternating between seeing him as an obstruction and, then, such love. Such love no one can imagine, not even Paule; *my own mute, retarded heart sprung forth. . . .*

He was almost blue when he died at twenty-one: a pale milky blue, like glazed porcelain. Sitting day after day in his wheelchair, he'd lost all interest in crawling, in breaking things. He grew weaker and weaker until at last he could not even sit up, and they moved his bed into their room and watched him. Madame Perichet gave notice; Lili would always be grateful to her for that. Claude lay on his back with his eyes wide open and his mouth, for once, closed; his expression serene, almost intelligent. He was breathing quietly, and part of her expected him to speak—she had never given up, thinking he might learn to draw, might burst out suddenly into a normal, sensible laugh—

while with the other part she realized that she had never expected anything, that even when he was in her womb she did not imagine having a child who would speak to her. Still, she sat on the edge of the bed, staring down into his gold-and-gray-flecked eyes, squeezing his hand, waiting for him to tell her things. . . . That her love had buoyed him, carried him through his mute, crippled life. Yes, that he had felt surrounded by her love, that he forgave her her moments of impatience.

The doctor came and went, uselessly.

At last Pierre lifted him into their own bed, and they curled up on either side of him. He wouldn't eat, not even chocolate.

"Do you suppose he'd enjoy a bath?" Pierre asked.

"His rubber ball?" asked Lili. But neither of them moved, afraid he'd die the moment they left.

Pierre sang to him—*Il était un petit navire, il était un petit navire*—and Lili sat up suddenly, stroked Claude's hair, his arms, his fingers. They were like children with him. He was doing something neither of them had managed to do yet: he was dying. He was the first person Lili had known to die a natural death. Then she began to kiss him, over and over, like someone who is about to be separated from her lover. She fell asleep at last, with her head on his chest, listening to his heart beat grow fainter and fainter and fainter.

They never considered anything but cremation. They did not even discuss it, except to say, "Do you know whom to call? How it's done?"

The man from the morgue took care of everything; they themselves were helpless.

And at Pornic, the next day, when Pierre opened the small, flimsy box from the morgue, she put her hand in the ashes, expecting something powdery and soft, like at the bottom of a fireplace, but there were teeth, bits of bone, hair, and she understood, suddenly, how it is that wild animals eat their young, to take them back—she flung the ashes into the bitter January sea. There was no wind, and the finer ones fell through the air like dust motes.

Afterward she and Pierre sat in the wild sage grass till dusk. They sat with their legs drawn up, a couple in late middle age, speaking of nothing. The evening was pale and cold, white as ash.

Twenty-three

We should have divorced after that," Lili murmured, with her eyes closed, reaching into the silky coolness of the armoire. "We should have divorced sometime." She let the dresses slip against her arms, reached up and stroked the various pleats, folds, tears. Her eyes were still shut and she felt the clothes with the pleasure of the blind. All the dresses were old and frayed—they were the ones Thérèse and Paule had given her long ago—Lili pulled one out at random and looked at it: it was sleeveless, covered with yellow chrysanthemums, cut low in the neck and narrow at the waist. A silk summer party dress with only a stain or two near the hem. The perfect thing for a convent.

"Yes," she went on, slipping the dress over her old arms. "We should have divorced."

Except, of course, that after Claude died they had only each other for consolation. *What a relief,* everyone said. *The poor creature.* As if he'd been a sick dog. Yes, everyone said it: the doctor, the grocer, the director of the lycée, Helga, Maurice, even Jean-Louis. Jean-Louis sat at the garden table, next to Helga—because those Sunday teas went on forever! One moment of kindness in the middle of the night, and Lili had them coming every Sunday at two o'clock for the next thirty years. Yvonne and Bernard and Nicolas, poor orphaned bastards, stopped coming the minute they could, not because they didn't love Lili—they did!—but because they loathed Maurice and Helga; so it was just the two unhappy couples and Jean-Louis and Claude, until Claude died. Yes, he sat there, Jean-Louis, in the dark widower's suit he wore every day after D day, and he patted Lili's hand and said softly, "I know it must be a relief to you." Lili just stared. Pierre looked away quickly— even Jean-Louis, his one friend, had failed to understand—and Lili thought: We will never be free of each other. I thought it was the need to take care of him that kept us together, but apparently it was more than that. Because now it is the need to mourn him.

Relief! Of course it was a relief! That went without saying. Most deaths are a relief.

But if that were all, how simple! She could buy a pistol and shoot them all.

They left his room the way it was, with his rubber ball lying on his pillow and his bright, colorful markings in the frames Lili had put them in. Sometimes, in the evenings, they sat silently together in Claude's room, one on Claude's bed and the other in Claude's wheelchair. It was a habit so secret, so intimate, that they never once spoke of it.

And the rest of the time they were as ill suited as ever: she complained, he ignored her, and during the night sometimes he reached for her.

A year and a half after Claude's death, Pierre changed completely. It was summer—a strange, pale, hot summer—and he spent every day in the upstairs study, writing until one or two in the morning. On Sundays he said a brief hello to Jean-Louis, barely greeted Helga and Maurice, and returned to the study. He ate little and spoke less. He did not tell Lili what he was working on, but she supposed it was a sequel to his study of Auvergne. His passion for his work inspired her, reminded her that she, too, still had a book's worth of ideas, and she began to go into Paris herself now and then to work at the National Library. She couldn't believe how good it felt to use her mind this way again and how good it felt at night, when she had fallen asleep, to be woken by Pierre's brief, fumbling desire. She enjoyed his abortive caresses as much as if they were the only kind she had ever known. His groping was brusque now, almost violent, and it made her stomach hurt a little, the lack of tenderness, but still, she told herself, it was desire, and they were both working so hard: she could imagine that they were like students, impatient, excited, on the brink of discovery. The verge of consummation.

Then he began to carry his meals into the study; he forgot to wash. One night he didn't come to bed at all. She slept badly, waking every few hours, too hot beneath the covers—she hadn't slept alone in years—but it was all right. Of course! It was inevitable. It was impossible to discover anything without first getting lost. Naturally he was forgetting to eat, to sleep. She should follow his example, be less concerned with her own rest and meals and hygiene.

He lost the slight paunch he had developed, and his face grew lean and ascetic looking. He slept less and less, and her nights were restless, waiting for him to come in, though he had given up reaching for her. But the harder he worked, after all, the sooner he would be done. Often he did not even address her when they passed in the hall.

One day he was downstairs in the WC, and she saw that he had left the door to the study open. It smelled of old food and sweat. There were piles of papers scattered everywhere, plates with crusts of bread and cheese, rotting sardines, spoiled pears. She went in and glanced at one of the papers: it was a letter. *Dear dear Mariette, I couldn't come back, after the war, but I have never forgotten your goodness, I have never forgotten your white, silky skin, your exquisite breasts.* She began shaking, rifling through all the papers. They were all drafts of letters to Mariette or—she almost laughed out loud—psalms that he had written out. *Be merciful unto me, O God, be merciful unto me.* The letters to Mariette were exactly the same, with only the tiniest variations: *Your exquisite breasts, your so exquisite breasts, your breasts, which I found so exquisite. . . .*

She went downstairs. He was still in the bathroom, and she stood outside the door. It was hard to breathe: she could hear him rustling things.

"Lili!" he said, throwing open the door, as if he were surprised to realize that she lived there.

"I'm going out," she whispered, though she hadn't informed him of her daily schedule in weeks.

"Out?" he said, too loudly. "What's so great about out?"

"Groceries."

He laughed, then, long and pointlessly.

When he was done, she said, "Well, I'm going out, then." It was as if the words were being torn from the flesh of her throat. She wanted to hit him, over and over and over, until he was swollen and purple, the way he was in her dreams, when she beat him for not loving her.

"Wait," he said softly. "Wait," and he touched her wrist. He went into the kitchen and she was so relieved. She had made a mistake. Everything would be all right. She had misunderstood—the letters, everything.

He returned with the kitchen scissors, went behind her, and cut the chignon from her head.

"Good God, Pierre—!" She reached up to grab the scissors, but he pulled away from her, laughing.

"Going out? Without your hair?"

Oh, Pierre, I had no idea you'd gone crazy. . . .

"Eh Lili? Without your hair?"

"Pierre, you need to sleep—"

"Idiot!" He laughed, his face red and splotchy. Her mind grew perfectly clear, and she felt nothing: she must go to the post office and call an ambulance. How stupid she had been not to see it before, that it was coming to this. She must act as if everything were all right, she must go to the post office. . . .

He waved the scissors, and her heart contracted. But he only undressed: he took off his pants, his shirt, his socks, and cut them to pieces.

He could not move quickly enough, and he swore, struggling with the scissors.

When he was done, he pushed the clothes aside with his foot. "Jesus had nothing," he said. "Nothing."

She nodded. "I'm going out—"

"Without your hair?" he asked, but his voice was calm now, concerned. "Without your hair?"

"Oh"—she shrugged—"my hair. I can't very well stay in till it grows back." She opened the front door. "It's awfully hot," she commented, looking up at the pale, glaring sky.

"Lili!" he called after her, and suddenly his voice was desperate, as if he knew what she was going to do.

She turned back to him, full of longing, her hair short and bristly on her neck. "Pierre—" but he ran out past her into the street, naked except for his scissors. His skin was pale and his penis had shrunk to nothing.

"Jesus!" he shouted, running down the street. "Christ the Lord!" And a policeman arrived, caught him, and then another, and an ambulance.

"Leave him alone!" she said, but her voice was weak and empty. And it was like the war again, his eyes, the excitement of an arrest, the onlookers' stares.

At the asylum they gave him electroshock treatments and taught him to sew buttons onto a piece of fabric. She visited him morning and evening, her heart always tight at first and then just dull and heavy. They sat in the visitors' lounge, a room with windows that opened and shut, looking out on a graveled yard. He would not speak to her except, at the end of the first week, to ask for his papers. She brought them, the psalms and the letters to Mariette, but the doctors only let him write for an hour a day.

Once, after she had asked him to no avail how he had slept, did he want a newspaper, should she see if they could take a walk outside—inside it was so hot—she said, "I always knew you were still in love with her."

He answered her for the first time in seventeen days: "The Lamb of God takes away the sins of the world. You have only to repent, Lili."

"For God's sake!" she said, and that afternoon she did not visit him.

But the next morning he was alone in the little visitors' lounge—the attendant had vanished, and none of the other patients ever came out anyway—and he asked her how she was, had she slept well, after all it was so hot. . . .

"I slept terribly. What do you think?"

"You could sleep here," he offered, and there was something in his voice—and in his eyes, also—that let her know he was himself again. He was not dreaming anymore, and yet he was himself disoriented, softened, out of step. To her horror, she realized he was the way he'd been when she first met him, when he told her that it was not to get her into bed that he was following her. It was almost unbearable to see him this way: to be reminded. As unbearable as all things that thaw and melt and come to life, that deceive you, in that fragile, shuddering moment of transformation, into thinking you might possess them: how alive they seem, how generous, like the dark forest dissolving back to green.

It was intolerable. She gestured sharply with her hand. "Here? Here? What do you think? Two little cots side by side, in an asylum?"

"Well," he said, and he actually blushed, "I miss you."

"Miss me? Me? What about Mariette?"

"Oh, Mariette," he said dismissively.

"Yes, Mariette," she said, and only her fear of the asylum doctors kept her from screaming at Pierre; he was torturing her: not sick at all anymore, just softened.

"I barely know Mariette."

"Good God you're a brilliant man. To have come up with a little gem of knowledge like that, all on your own."

"I really lost my mind, didn't I?"

"You certainly did."

"I feel better now."

"Oh!" She laughed harshly—she couldn't help it. "Ready to return to a life of good citizenship?"

"Perhaps," he said innocently.

"What is the matter with you?"

"Oh, Lili. Don't you ever just want to touch the hand of God?"

She stared at him: above all, she must not scream.

"But, of course, we can't. That's why we are human beings."

"Tell me," she said, lighting a cigarette with trembling hands. "What does this have to do with celibacy?"

She saw him flinch, draw back. He looked away and said, "Still, I wish it were possible. Just for a moment. To touch his hand. How it must burn!"

"No doubt," she said dryly, calming down again. "Would you like a divorce?"

"A divorce?"

"Yes. Now that Claude is gone, there's no need for us to stay together. You can pursue God, and I can—live my life. Maybe you could join the monastery adjoining Paule's convent. There must be one next door, don't you think? The boys' school and the girls' school?"

"I can't join a monastery if I'm divorced."

"Oh, dear."

"Why do you want a divorce?"

"Well! We've almost nothing in common."

"But I like you a lot."

"Do you? Do you like me, Pierre?"

"Yes—"

"Oh, Pierre. What do you take me for?"

He went on innocently, as if he could not hear the anguish in her voice: "You're a remarkable woman, Lili. Brilliant, funny, defiant. I like all that. And then we've been through a lot together."

"We haven't made love in twenty years."

And again he flinched, drawing away.

He had gained weight in the hospital: his face was puffy from overfeeding. He sat on the edge of his chair in his gray pajamas, his hands dangling between his knees. He looked suddenly helpless, disturbed—perhaps he wasn't well yet. Perhaps she was out of her mind to expect anything of him—and then again, he looked like the most ordinary man in the world.

"Do you want to leave me?" he asked softly.

"Don't you want me to?"

"You're the best friend I have, Lili."

"You have your sisters," she said.

"You're my friend."

She sighed, defeated. "Well," she said, "it's always been some consolation to me that you might be mad. I suppose it's time to take you home now."

"Oh! I don't know if they'll let me."

"Oh, Pierre. I'm sure they've electrocuted you enough by now. You're certainly behaving again."

There was a brief struggle with the authorities and then they were on the steps of the asylum, in the harsh sun.

"I like your haircut," Pierre said, casually, on the walk home.

"You did it," Lili said, with a soft, small laugh.

"Did I?"

"I felt so sad for you. So afraid—"

"No need to be afraid of the dark," Pierre said in an odd, singsong voice.

"Well," Lili said, unnerved by his tone, "you had the Holy Ghost with you. I was all alone."

"Christ is always with us," Pierre said, solemnly, and Lili burst out laughing and crying.

"Oh, God," she said, taking his hand. "If I had known, when I was little, how much our lives are composed of madness!"

"Like the light," he said. "Always shifting."

"Please, Pierre. Try to avoid clichés."

"Why so unfriendly?"

"I'm always unfriendly," she said, protectively. "This is nothing new."

"Yes, why?"

"I still want you."

"That's no reason to be unfriendly."

"Hah!" she said, letting go of his hand. But they had reached the house, and she could feel, as they entered the hot, dusty vestibule, the silence and weight of their marriage descending upon them again.

"Hah!" she said again now, thirty years later, admiring herself in her chrysanthemum-covered sundress. "I should have left. Should have freed him from the asylum and then fled myself. Walked the streets, become a prostitute. Anything. Anything to lie naked under a man's body again. A woman's. Just a few more times before I grew too old. . . ." She gestured helplessly at her reflection. She had not lost her desire. She had stayed with Pierre in the hope that he might want her again. But after the asylum, if he reached for her in his sleep at all, his hands were as weak as if he were underwater.

Look at me, she thought, still staring at her reflection. In the pool of shadow, she was a bouquet of chrysanthemums, floating in a dark mirror. She moved into the light, became veins, bones, gray hair, dust, though she dragged a piece of beautiful yellow silk; what did she care if it hung off her now as it would have hung off a child, almost reaching the floor? Look at me, all alone. In the end, you weren't even a companion.

But Paule. The reason for all this commotion: the bath, the need to dress, her unsteady hands. "Well," she said aloud. "Paule." Her stomach tightened around the name, and she sat down at the vanity in front of the mirror. (She remembered, briefly, her mother sitting here, powdering her arms and throat. Had she hoped till the end that Papa would want her again? Or did she settle finally for fantasies of killing Mademoiselle?) Yes, Paule.

Lili put her head in her hands. She tried to imagine them, in some small, meagerly furnished sitting room at the convent: herself, in this lovely, nearly transparent dress, and Paule in a habit. One of those new midcalf ones with an abbreviated wimple? It was unimaginable.

Unimaginable, too, why Lili was going there.

Oh, because I am old and alone, she thought, and I have not given up. I didn't give up on Pierre and I have not given up on Paule.

She pictured herself sitting knee to knee with Paule, their heads bent close together, like schoolgirls.

But they were old women now, and Paule, no doubt, was perfectly calm. A nun didn't worry about her clothes.

Lili shrugged, lifted a long strand of blue glass beads from the clutter on the vanity table, slipped it over her head, and tied a knot in it. She turned to the side and saw that, if she lifted her arms and leaned forward (an unlikely gesture), a person could see her breasts. Ah well, it wouldn't kill anyone to see an old woman's breasts. What else, then? Lipstick? Rouge? Time she put in her teeth; those would help the most. She reached her thumb and forefinger into a jar of water, pulled out a set of craftily stained artificial teeth, put them in her mouth, winced, and was amazed, as always, by the transformation in her face. It was a face again. She put on pale pink rouge and rose-colored lipstick and was satisfied. Then she took her teeth back out, and all the colors folded in on one another, but what a relief—her eyes swam with tears—to stop the pinching; she could put them in again right before the train.

Why? What did she think? That she could impress Paule with pink cheeks? A woman who believed in God?

"If I believed in him, I'd have chosen him, too," Lili said, acidly.

But it was no use. Her hands stopped trembling only to start again. She might have been fifteen.

She pushed herself up from the vanity and went to stand on the balcony overlooking the tangled, sun-drenched garden. The light was no longer fragile, various; and beneath her, the wild roses shone in the full sun. It was not true that she had completely neglected the garden. Look at the roses, the dandelions.

Yes, she was old. Alone. She had stayed with Pierre because everyone else was relieved by Claude's death; because she hoped he might want her again; because, however patchily, he screened her from the others.

They came for tea when Pierre was in the asylum; they came when he was released. Sunday after Sunday, forever and forever and forever.

Two o'clock sharp, Maurice swung open the garden gate and began criticizing her.

"Good God, Lili, look at this! Will you look at it? A person can't even imagine anymore where the flagstones might have been. The irises, the marigolds! What do you do all day?" Then he would laugh. "Oh, oh, I see. It's deliberate. Your own private anarchy. Yes, yes, an anarchy behind stone walls . . . very good, Lili. How your husband can tolerate it, I don't know. But then, he tolerates you!"

He never said: *Papa would weep. . . . He worked so hard to trim his hedges, to weed his flower beds. Till the last, Lili, you will remember, he kept a meticulous garden. . . .* He never said anything like that.

But he came to the garden gate, every single Sunday, with his aging child-bride and her Pekingese; he came and called out, "We're still invited, I assume?" and then: "Look at this! Will you look at it? We'll have to go around."

Every Sunday the Pekingese tore ahead of him, yapping through the tall grass, and Helga, like a peach that has wrinkled without turning brown, ran after them, breathless, laughing. "*Mein liebchen . . . mein petits chiens . . . liebling!*" Outraged and defeated, Maurice followed, walking gingerly over the grass his family had flattened for him.

The dogs' mouths were already coated with pastry cream by the time Jean-Louis arrived, in his black widower's suit, carrying an armload of flowers for Lili as if, Lili thought, she were Thérèse's grave. And Lili, turning to kiss Jean-Louis, to thank him, to reassure Helga— *Of course there are more éclairs on the kitchen table, help yourself—* stood beneath the bedroom window and shouted up: "Are you getting up or aren't you? Everyone's here, it's past two! Well, are you moving?

Pierre? Have you died yet?" Pierre appeared at last at the little balcony, groggy, disheveled. He nodded, touched his forehead in greeting, and lumbered downstairs to take his place beneath the chestnut tree.

And now, as if she were following him, as if she might catch him— still!—Lili pushed herself away from the balcony railing and went downstairs, through the dark of the stairwell and on outside, into the light again, among the thick weeds and the butterflies, the lazy, droning bees. She dragged the lovely plastic chair out of the full sun and into the shade of the chestnut tree and lowered herself onto its burning surface. She was all alone. Pierre had vanished forever.

She remembered one Sunday, the Sunday after the Russians had stormed Prague, Pierre was hidden behind the newspaper, and Maurice was yelling at her. She stood on the far side of the garden, plucking dead leaves from the roses. Her heart beat painfully with the news of Prague, but Maurice would not let her be. "What do you think, Lili, eh? What do you have to say for your friends now?"

Jean-Louis, who had lost all interest in world events after the war, sat daydreaming, playing with the brim of his hat. They were a kind of memorial service for him, these Sunday afternoons. Maurice could have brayed like a donkey and Jean-Louis would not have flinched, so lost was he in his memories of Thérèse, his unwavering grief.

Helga, cheerful and oblivious, laughed as one of the Pekingese licked her cleavage.

"The Czechoslovakians!" Maurice cried out, leaning forward in his chair like a bulldog. "The Czechoslovakians, Lili! Killing their dogs! Helga! What do you think of that? Dog killing!"

Helga gave a sharp, startled cry and held the Pekingese more tightly. "What are you—? What is he—?"

Lili gestured impatiently with the rusty shears she was holding. "I have never been pro-Soviet, Maurice."

"But in the name of God you've got to choose, Lili. It's the United States or the Soviets."

"After all," Helga said brightly, in the way she had of interjecting nonsensical comments into any conversation, like a madwoman, "the Americans and the English kill everyone. They are the ones."

Jean-Louis moaned slightly; it was barely audible, the kind of sound dogs make in their dreams. There was a moment's stunned silence: even Pierre, behind his newspaper, seemed to freeze. Helga laughed nervously. "It is so hot. I like to go to the beach. Oh! I am fat. I look terrible in those bikinis. You remember I am a dancer? Such beautiful legs. You remember, Jean-Louis?"

"Leave the man alone!" Maurice snapped, to no avail: he could humiliate his wife but not stop her.

"Well, what? I am a dancer. You remember, Jean-Louis?"

"Yes," Jean-Louis murmured, softly. "I remember."

"We dance, Jean-Louis?" Helga offered, cheerfully.

"What?" He looked up, startled.

"For God's sake leave him alone!" Maurice hissed.

"Oh, you," Helga said gaily. "You are no fun. But Jean-Louis, he is dancer! He dances with me, yes?"

"That's enough!" Maurice cried.

But Helga, ignoring him, carefully put the Pekingese in the grass and stood. Lili glared at Pierre, stunned that he ignored it all, that he did not even try to help Jean-Louis—Helga was wearing a bright pink dress with a gathered waist and sleeves and a low ruffled collar. She looked like a baby doll, the kind with lace-trimmed socks and eyes that really open and close, except suddenly you noticed the huge, helpless breasts, the sagging skin, the gold-capped teeth. A rumor had circulated during the war that she had had an affair with one of her German soldiers.

But suddenly, in a voice so naked and innocent it was unbearable, she asked Jean-Louis again, "You invite me to dance?" And Jean-Louis—out of despair?—jumped to his feet, at attention.

"We have no music, I'm afraid," he said.

Lili glanced sharply again at Pierre. He might offer to dance in Jean-Louis's stead, anything. . . .

Maurice was scarlet, trembling; Lili had never seen him so furious.

"I sing?" Helga offered sweetly.

And she did, a German lullaby, filling the garden with her voice, pure and high; the terrible German consonants ringing out softly like commands, like mockery. They danced around and around, and it was like a dream in which the wrong people are paired and from which you awaken laughing. . . . How trim and erect he was, how soft and cheap and worn she was, though she sang with all the authority of her race. Lili was afraid Jean-Louis would faint.

But they had stopped.

Jean-Louis bowed slightly, and Helga, pink with excitement, curtsied, gave him her hand to kiss, looked around for a moment as if she expected applause.

Maurice was on the verge of tears, his hands white in their grip of the armrests.

"He was your friend, for God's sake!" Lili yelled that night, as she and Pierre got ready for bed. "You might have helped him—*you* could have offered to dance with her. You don't even talk to him anymore. You sleep, read, sleep—that's all you do. Why don't you die? What's the difference?"

Pierre sighed, pulled off his shirt, his trousers—all the hair on his body was white, and his chest had begun to sag, but his shoulders were still straight, his legs strong—he said nothing.

"Doesn't your friendship mean anything? For Jean-Louis to have to listen to her talk about the bombings without her even realizing what she's saying—and then to have to dance with her—you might have helped him."

He sat on the edge of the bed, lifted the covers, swung his legs up onto the bed, lay down, and turned away from her.

"Answer me in the name of God! Why don't you die? It would be more efficient."

He reached out and turned off his lamp.

"But why?" she cried, sitting bolt upright, her cigarette glowing in the dark: it was the same, night after night, day after day: the unanswered monologue.

Except that that night, in the end, he did speak. She had been quiet for hours, smoking, waiting to grow tired, and all that time he had not moved at all. Then, suddenly, he raised his head. "There's nothing I can do for him. Nor he for me. We are still friends."

"Oh," Lili murmured, feeling the smooth hot plastic under her hands. "Yes, friends." Jean-Louis died a few weeks later—he was crossing the street and he simply fell down in the middle of the road and never got up again—and Pierre grew, if such a thing were possible, even quieter, stiller, more turned in on himself.

Lili put her hand to her heart, feeling the ache of longing for Pierre that she had never successfully rooted out, and she thought how her forty-year anger with Pierre had, at least, been something to hold on to—not a screen, not that after all, rather a stone in her palm. But the garden gate swung open. Was it two already? She had forgotten the pastries! No. Everyone was dead; it wasn't even Sunday. It was the doctor. A short, bald man with a black bag.

"Madame Larat," he said softly from the edge of the garden, giving a slight bow.

"What do you want?" Lili asked, irritated.

"Your niece sent me," Doctor Ropion said, picking his way through the tall grass. She watched him approach, lifting his leg as nervously as a colt, trying, apparently, not to get even a drop of dew on his fine gray trousers.

Her heart tightened. "What do you want?" she repeated, but her voice was small and frightened. Suppose he'd come to take her away? She pushed herself up but did not go near him, and the plastic chair toppled over lightly behind her. "What—?"

"You're looking well," he said, still in that soft, consoling voice, and, having reached her now, he righted the chair and offered her his hand in one single sinister motion.

She let him have her hand, because it was important not to betray one's suspicions. How could she escape? Through the house, swiftly, out onto the street—? Such a short man, in such fine trousers, he couldn't catch her, could he?

"Please, Madame, sit—"

But she stood quite still, her eyes locked on his.

"Your niece is concerned about you being here all alone."

She had to strain to hear him: it was as if he were whispering, the sound of his voice drowning in the rush of her blood—if he touched her again, she would run.

"If you would consider . . ."

She must stay calm. Breathe.

"Since your husband's death . . ."

And she burst out laughing. Relief washed over her, and fury: he didn't want to take her away, he only wanted to needle her. "Pierre's death? Is that why you've come? I can assure you it hasn't made any difference in my life. He was nearly catatonic as it was. Really, Doctor, the one I needed condolences for was Claude."

Doctor Ropion was silent, and she could see that she had said something wrong.

"Well, what?" she asked impatiently. If he wasn't trying to lock her up, she didn't have to be polite.

"Your niece and, I confess, I, too, feel that a live-in nurse—"

Oh. Pierre had been dead for years. If only this man would leave her alone! A decade Pierre had been dead—at least. No one offered her condolences anymore. But why she had agreed to bury him in Sauxillanges she couldn't say. That awful train ride with the coffin and then his hysterical sisters. All day long muttering behind Lili's back because she wasn't dressed in mourning—*O mes chéries,* Pierre never cared much about my wardrobe—but they were dead now, too, oh merciful God, and she could go to Sauxillanges and scratch in the ground until she unearthed his bones, carry them back up here in a parcel in her lap, white as the ocean litter she imagined them, and when she died, they could burn her bones with his and send them out to Claude. . . .

"Someone very discreet, you understand. A safety measure only."

"Oh, for God's sake. What is it exactly that you're worried about, Doctor?"

He took a deep breath, bowed his head, and she noticed several rows of tiny, shimmering beads of sweat stretched out across his pate, like a veil. "I'm afraid, Madame Larat, that you're no longer young—"

"Really?" she murmured, and, heartened by the possibility of reclaiming Pierre's bones, she pulled off her dress and stood before him, naked except for her stockings. "Sh-sh, sh-sh," she said, for the doctor was suddenly frightened. "It's nothing. A few wrinkles. You can't lock me up for undressing on my own property, behind a stone wall. Now listen, Monsieur—Docteur—have you got a stethoscope in your bag? A little rubber hammer? Because what I'd really like to know is how much longer I've got to endure."

Doctor Ropion was as still and silent as a rabbit in the middle of a road. Then, like a rabbit, he twitched. "Please," he whispered. "Dress yourself."

"My heart," she insisted. "I want you to listen to it."

"I can do that through your dress." He tried to speak normally, but his voice squeaked on "dress."

"Oh, all right." She picked the dress up off the ground and put it back on. "Now," she said. "Listen."

Dutifully, he bowed his sweat-veiled head, unclasped his black bag, and pulled out a stethoscope. In truth, his obedience startled her, and she supposed he must have been a student of hers toward the end, when the classes were mixed. She was tempted to ask him, but her former students were always so hurt when she didn't remember them precisely, what seat they sat in, their scores on the *bachot.*

He put the stethoscope to her flat chest and listened intently, so that she had an urge to pat his head, wipe away the film of sweat. Poor boy. Had she failed him once along the way? And now he must report another failure: *I couldn't get your aunt to talk sense.*

He looked up at her with his sad, pale eyes: "You're in good health, Madame. You have the heart of a sixteen-year-old." He shrugged, and, in a voice filled with despair, he murmured to himself, "There's nothing I can do. I haven't the nerve. I should have been an engineer."

She watched him go, unable to speak, to move. The heart of a sixteen-year-old? What was she to do with such a thing? Pierre's bones would turn to powder by the time she died.

Oh, and what did she think? That burning together, dissolving into the ocean, they would connect at last?

Twenty-four

But it was time to go to the convent. Almost time. She didn't need to rush. She had always been early for everything, and what had her earliness served? She was still here, beneath the window of the bedroom in which she had been born. Everyone else had left, and still, she was here.

It was Maurice who found Lili and Pierre after Pierre had died. He died on a Sunday, a death as simple and easy as Jean-Louis's. He was sitting in his chair, so it didn't show from behind, and Lili, returning from the pâtissier with a box of éclairs, began scolding him, urging him to wake up, Maurice and Helga would be there any minute. She went around in front of him and saw the muteness of his face; still scolding him, she knelt and buried her head in his lap. She pressed her fingers into his thighs and tried to keep speaking, to defend herself, to explain—something—trying to call out, as if, if she were loud enough, he might still hear her. But she could not make any sound at all. She could feel his knees against her heart, and then the Pekingese arrived, and Maurice pulled her up, away, as if he knew, had always known, that Pierre did not like to be touched.

And then, naturally—no one would abandon a widow, no one would do her the favor—Maurice and Helga kept coming on Sundays; it was a form of torture. With Pierre gone—Not gone, Lili thought, dead—with Pierre dead, since he'd died, she'd been stripped naked. They came, Maurice and Helga and the Pekingese, and it was as if Lili were sitting in the garden—or in the living room when it was cold—without a stitch of clothing on. Stark naked she had to bring the dogs their pastries; she had to endure Maurice's rage. She wanted to weep, but her eyes simply grew brighter, drier, colder.

One Sunday, at one-thirty, she left the house and went to Paris.

The Luxembourg was full of Japanese taking photographs, and outside the gates cars honked and screeched without mercy, but the windows of her old apartment on rue Madame were exactly as she and Pierre had left them—slender and grimy above the glimmering bank of cars below. She stood on the sidewalk and wept silently. How they had loved each other in those two small rooms, before they moved to rue Guynemer—he had wept at the sight of her. How they had loved.

She wanted to ring the bell, to ask if she might look around, but what would she find? The walls repainted, a television set, a young couple in blue jeans comfortably interlaced on the floor?

Oh, Pierre. How long ago we were.

She glanced in the direction of the butcher shop, her vision watery and confused. There was no solace there: a new, shiny scale, an incomprehensible assortment of animals—rabbits, venison, all kinds of things—a brusque, red-armed woman. She did not know where the old butcher and his wife had fled.

She was still quietly weeping when she went home at five and found Maurice and Helga and the dogs, sitting in the garden, waiting for her.

"What in God's name happened to you, Lili?"

She stared at Maurice, her eyes dry as stones again. "Oh, Maurice. Maurice. Maurice and Helga. You're still here. After all this time. Still here. In the garden. Maurice. I needed to be alone—"

Only now she was alone. After five years (yes, it had only been five years since Pierre died, not ten, not yet), exactly two months ago—who could accuse her of being confused now?—Maurice died.

Helga had stood in Maurice's hospital room, disheveled, flushed, wearing a red coat.

"What about me?" she cried.

Maurice did not even look at her. All his attention—the thin thread of consciousness that was left him—was focused on Lili, who sat on the edge of his bed, holding his hand.

"What about me?" Helga insisted.

"Come here," Lili whispered, and she gave Maurice's hand to Helga, but Maurice shut his eyes immediately.

That's how they were in her family: no pity. Only love or disgust.

And here she was in the garden, with her heart. Left alone, as she had longed to be, she could think seriously, clearly. She stiffened: she did not necessarily want to think too clearly. And anyway, she must go to the station—!

No, no, there was plenty of time. No point in being early.

The condition of her heart was like the nightmare in which you find yourself still in grammar school. You awake in a sweat, and it is such a relief: you have not failed anything, you have passed your *bachot*, you have been to Sèvres, you are *agrégée*, you will never again have to stand in a little blue apron beside your desk, reciting *La cigale, ayant chanté toot l'été*. . . . But she, Lili, might as well recite it over and over. What else had she to do with the expanse of years before her?

She lit a cigarette.

She ought to think about it . . . the thing she did not want to think about, the thing—the argument—she had avoided all day. She might, being all alone, come to some sort of understanding.

Yesterday she had seen Helga to the train station. That had been a distraction. At first, after Maurice's funeral, Helga kept coming on Sunday, like a windup toy that can't stop. The first time, Lili was horrified. It had never occurred to her that Helga would come alone. Lili didn't have her teeth in; she hadn't bought a single pastry. She had been sitting in the kitchen, trying to force herself to eat something, but she had no appetite since Maurice's death; she felt lost and heartbroken.

"I haven't any pastries," she murmured, aghast, the words slurring against her bare, swollen gums.

"That is all right," Helga said. "We are too sad to eat."

Lili stared at her. *You are sad? How could you possibly be sad?* The possibility that Helga had loved Maurice was unbearable. She kept staring at Helga, rudely, as people stare in horrified fascination at those who endure more than they. Then she went upstairs to get her teeth.

All afternoon, Helga sat and sang a lullaby to her lone, last Pekingese. She had stopped breeding them: she could not bear their inevitable deaths. She was wiser, Lili thought, than any of them had realized. At exactly five o'clock, Helga left.

She did this every Sunday for two months until yesterday. Yesterday, she spoke:

"Who is Mademoiselle Duroc?"

"My father's mistress."

"Achh, really? A mistress?"

"Yes."

"I don't think Maurice has a mistress."

"No?"

"He will be too tired. He never leave me alone, why would he had a mistress?"

"Did you love Maurice?"

"He is so mean. Why love him? You are lucky. Pierre leave you alone. I see that."

" 'Left,' " Lili corrected. "Pierre left me alone."

"Achh, I hate the French."

Lili laughed softly.

"Well, Lili. I go back to Germany. I take the night train. First class! He did not send me first class first time, from Germany, when I am so young. But now, he does not know it, he sends me first class! *Wagonslits!* I have my packed bags."

"You're leaving?" Lili said, and to her amazement, her eyes welled up with tears. She remembered, suddenly, Mademoiselle Duroc's dead body.

"I have no friends here," Helga said, shrugging.

"Oh," Lili said. "I—"

"You will take me in the taxi?" Helga asked. "You will take me to the station?"

"Of course," Lili murmured sadly. "Of course."

They went to Helga's apartment for her suitcase, and a young Moroccan was there, packing the hideous but valuable statuettes and figurines that Maurice had devoted his life to collecting. "He send them later," Helga explained, all business and efficiency.

But at the Gare de l'Est, Helga hung back from the train like a young girl afraid to travel alone.

"I go, Lili," Helga said. "I go now. You have nieces and nephews. They never like me. I go now. I find my soldier. He will remember me, you think?"

Lili stared at her.

"You think, Lili? You think he will remember me?"

"Well," Lili said at last. "I never had a good feeling about the German army."

"Never anything happen that was incorrect," Helga insisted. "Only words, looks."

"He could be dead," Lili warned.

"Yes." Helga sighed. "Probably. It is a dream. And I am fat. Still, I go. I go now, Lili." She kissed Lili—the press of a soft, powdered cheek, heavy with perfume—and she lifted herself and the last Pekingese into the train, and Lili followed as far as the second step, watching her make her way down the corridor, fat, resplendent, dressed in an orange silk traveling suit, her hair still red, glossy: disappearing from Lili's life like some great, exotic butterfly.

Lili bought herself a cup of coffee at the Gare de l'Est and sat for a long time in the crowded café, watching the travelers: young people sprawled on the station floor, resting against their knapsacks; old women with sweatered dogs; bands of *colonies de vacances,* bright with kerchiefs and terrible, forced cheer. She thought of going back to Maurice's apartment and making conversation with the young Moroccan. And then she rose, went to the pay phone, and called the convent.

Well, really, now it was almost time to go. In the middle of the day the RER didn't run as frequently. Only suddenly she was nervous: she wanted to go back in the house once more, to look at herself in the mirror.

It was dark and lonely inside; the light no longer spilled in from the garden, and she had to wait for her eyes to adjust. Then, slowly, she saw the yellow chrysanthemums emerge from the gloom, the round, yellow blossoms swim up from the bottom of the watery mirror.

Oh, Lili. Good-bye.

But she was going to board a train, not throw herself under it. Still, good-bye. *Good-bye, Lili.*

Oh! It was thinking all morning about the dead and departed that made her talk to herself this way. "You're not leaving anyone," she muttered. She could see herself clearly in the mirror now: the blue glass beads, the rouge, the fallen mouth. This, she thought. This body, this face. All I have to offer. But was she out of her mind? What did she want? To embrace Paule in the convent visiting room? *I'm a bit tired, Lili.* Well, naturally. One ought to be exhausted by now.

And yet Lili wasn't. That was the difficulty. She shouldn't go to the convent; she'd never had a soothing effect on anyone; that wasn't her gift. But she couldn't resist. She was all ready, in her dress with the yellow flowers.

She did keep feeling, though, that she must first say good-bye to herself. The way she had felt as a child, when she went off to school. *I will be gone for a long time; I won't be back until this evening.* She felt a sudden need to check that the stove was off, to close the shutters, lock all the doors. Instead, she checked in her purse to make sure she had plenty of money; she touched her reflection—*Good-bye*—the way she would do as a girl. Then she went to the French doors and stood on one foot, staring into the blinding light.

Oh, Lili. Lili. What? What is it?

The old quarrel was finally beginning; she could feel it pulling at her, tiresome and irresistible.

I don't want her to make love to me.

Don't you?

Not right away.

Well, she's not going to make love to you at all.

Lili sighed, watching the light slant to the west, begin its hot, slow descent. . . .

I want her to forgive me first.

Forgive you? She left you, remember that.

I want her to fall to her knees and forgive me.

Oh, Lili, you're beyond forgiveness.

What did I do?

You know what you did, if we're talking about that, and there's no forgiveness for that.

She bowed her head. It was always the same. Every day, she replayed the scenes, how she had fed Paule, how she had held Claude in the water, how Pierre had refused her offer of divorce—it changed nothing: André held his pistol to his head—the metal cold and heavy, she imagined—and then? Could he feel the explosion for an instant before he died? Did his brain, torn apart, suddenly begin to see the world differently?

I killed him, she thought. That is all there is. What of it that I loved, was loved for a while in return? I killed André.

She stepped back out into the tall, warm grass and finished her cigarette. Then she stood straight in her silk dress, in the summer air, like a girl waiting—hoping—for punishment. Her memories of love, of disappointment, were all a distraction, an attempt to alter the fact that she had killed André. She was beyond redemption. She stood as straight as she could, feeling the summer breeze through the silk of her dress. *I cannot be saved.* Still, she waited hopefully, without defiance or fear, longing for the release of punishment.

And then—there was no decorum in the order of her feelings—she was overcome with desire for Paule. She wanted to be smooth skinned again, both of them, and ravenous. She wanted Paule to wait for her in a pink silk robe. Even if we are not young, she thought. I still want her.

She hid her face in her hands. There was so little time left, even with her relentless heart. She must stay focused, clearheaded. André was the only thing left worth thinking about. Nothing else mattered, not the convent, not her desire, not whether Helga had found her Nazi lover.

Please, she thought, and she knelt down shamelessly in the tall grass. *I am so sorry.*

You would do it again. It's not repentance if you would do it again.

I would be kind. If André came to me right now, I would embrace him.

You wouldn't recoil in your heart?

She lit a cigarette.

I don't know. I might recoil.

She tried to imagine André, his ears, his red, splotchy cheeks. The other boys were mocking him, and his arms were raised in front of his face.

She dropped her cigarette and lay down in the grass, curled up in a ball. It was time to go now. Even someone who was habitually late would say that it was time to go. She watched the moment pass, as still and bright as any other.

Well? Wouldn't you recoil from André?

Yes.

Her heart was like something waterlogged, swollen and foul.

I have missed my train; she will be waiting for me, and I will not come.

It signified nothing that Paule, after Auschwitz, had forgiven God. Easy enough to imagine him grieving and impotent, helpless in the face of man's free will. What would be significant, what might possibly help her case, would be to find someone who had forgiven a German. Just one Jew, one German.

She hugged her knees to her mouth, hidden away in the rough, tangled grass.

Years ago, in that other lifetime, when she was old enough at last to go to church in the afternoons, it had seemed for a moment as if Christ were not in pain; as if he would lift off and fly. . . .

She laughed softly, inconsolably, feeling again the old longing for God.

Then she grew still again, silent.

Of course she believed in God. She simply didn't like him. Why should she? He didn't like her. She had tried to please him, but she had gone about it all wrong. Obviously, if she had wanted to satisfy God, she should have loved André. He himself wouldn't lift a finger for André, but if Lili had truly wanted to please. . . .

Well, she thought. I failed.

You did worse than fail, Lili. You killed a boy.

Yes, I killed a boy. I killed André.

Still she did not move, lying with her knees to her mouth, waiting for hell.

The thought of herself as a young girl, cruel and tidy, driving André mad, was unbearable. It was like being skinned alive.

Then she sat up.

I will try to repent, she thought. She rose and straightened her dress: there were grass stains at the knees.

I will repent, though I've missed the train.

Now? At eighty-three? You will repent for what you did as a child?

Well? What of it? I will pretend that I am a child and I will find it in my heart to love him.

He'll still be dead.

For God's sake, he'd be dead by now anyway. I am speaking of repentance, not reparation. Let the Germans make reparations.

She tried to picture herself as a little girl again. This time it was not so bad. Her heart was pounding, and she thought she might be sick, but she could bear it. She pictured André, his arms covering his face. She went to him—a little girl in a white frock—and pulled one arm away from his face.

She couldn't do it; she was no more capable of loving him now, at eighty-three, than she'd been at seven. She reached into her purse for a cigarette. What could she do? Idiotic to believe in God, to try to win his love! Look what it made her do! She'd missed her train. Impossible though Paule was, she didn't deserve to be brushed aside. Better to forget God and get on with life. A person could still do good, even with an unforgivable past! She looked at the timetable in her purse: there was another train, at four. She could see Paule after vespers then, if Paule didn't go straight to bed. Or tomorrow. But she must phone and say she'd missed her train.

I was thinking about God, you understand, and it paralyzed me.

God? Oh, Lili—God? Have you had second thoughts?

She laughed. "Never. I have been steadfast in my revulsion."

She had no desire to tell Paule the truth: how, in loving her, Lili had begun to love God again. Slowly, questionably, she had been being led to faith. It hadn't been the same with Pierre. For all her desire, her own peculiar steadfastness, it wasn't God. But Paule. Even after she left Lili, when Lili was so blank, so miserable—still, Lili could so easily have surrendered. Until, as if in fact the universe were a rational place in which events happened in order to instruct, Hitler came down the Champs-Elysées. . . . *You were waiting for God? God? Oh, Lili!*

Sooner or later you were brought to your knees for having hoped for order in the universe. If only it were possible to remember that! Not to have to keep being humiliated, again and again.

Even a dog learned to anticipate being beaten, did not leap up, over and over, hoping. . . .

Oh, well. She smelled the ivy on the other side of the garden, turning the wall to dust, and the rich, dusty, sweet roses.

Once again, this time without meaning to, she pictured herself as a girl in a white frock. How tired she suddenly was! So tired for her first confession. The dress scratched her knees, and she wanted to take it off, to go for a swim, though she didn't know how to swim. To drown, as a body drowns in love. Was it her first confession or her First Communion? *This is my body, eat it in memory of me.* . . .

No, it was neither; she would have been wearing a long dress for her First Communion, a bridal gown. This was the ordinary little white frock, and she was walking down the street with André while the other boys taunted him, and she held his hand, though her heart was a cold, smooth stone.

Eat this in memory of me. Flesh of my flesh, bone of my bones, this is my body, this is what I have to give to you. That is the mystery, not that I became flesh but that I said, "Take, eat: this is my body which is broken for you."

That is what they didn't know, Pierre and Paule. The one Paule loved, for whom she renounced everything, that God was, if not flesh, if not mortal, completely superfluous. The whole point of his tediously invoked martyrdom was not renunciation; it was communion. *My body, which is broken for you.* . . . What would you do? Pull back slightly? *No, no Jesus. I can't. Not now.* . . .

The butcher on rue de Fleurus had known; had loved the moment when death and life come together; when the slaughtered animal gives you strength to endure; when you take him into your mouth; *In that case, Madame, if you would take a kilo*. That beautiful, myopic man, Monsieur Antonna, standing at last before the puny remains of his bounty like a man forced to drop his pants in the street.

But what of André, who had wanted to carry her in his arms like a baby? What if I hold him, kiss him, though my heart is closed? Though I have no charity.

I might suckle André, a little boy. *This is my body*, I have never held it back from anyone.

She began to pull the loose, silk dress down over her shoulders.

She hesitated, imagining herself pulling André's arm away from his face. Yes, after all, he was just a child. Ugly and clumsy but, still, a child. Could she suckle him? Impossible. He was four years older than she. She pulled her dress back up hastily. She did not want him to see her naked and make fun of her.

I can't, I don't have the strength.

For consolation, again, she thought of Claude, whom she had loved, who had loved her. She went to sit in the plastic chair and imagined she held him in her arms. His pale head rested on her arm, and his eyelids fluttered over his violet eyes; nothing but a distraction: she had killed André. And yet there had been, in the early years with Claude, a kind of innocence. She did not remember how, but she remembered that, holding him in her arms, she had not felt evil. And again, when Paule made love to her.

If she was going to phone the convent and still catch the four o'clock train, she would have to hurry.

She did not move, staring at her garden. She had driven André insane, and yet, still, she was certain that she had been innocent. At certain times, in certain situations. In her mother's arms, in Paule's, in Maurice's when they lay together in the basement of the church in Caen. In every embrace she had been innocent. She was certain of that.

Twenty-five

A novice was waiting on the train platform, holding up a sign with Lili's name on it. The sign made Lili's heart race, as if she were being called up for an exam. She had slept on the train, and the possibility struck her that this was a dream, this young, slight, blond girl with her sign, MADAME P. LARAT. But that was ridiculous: even in dreams, if you were late, you simply failed. No one pursued you with signs.

"That's me—I'm Madame P. Larat!" Lili called out anxiously. She could not shake the terror and bewilderment of waking from an afternoon nap. It was still light out, the sky as bright and blue as midday.

"Madame Larat." The novice smiled, tucking the sign under her arm and shaking Lili's hand. Tendrils of pale hair had escaped from her wimple and they moved slightly in the summer breeze. She looked about seventeen, as pretty and smooth as a debutante.

"Where is Mademoiselle Jacob?"

"Sister Francis is waiting for you in the dormitory, Madame," the girl said, still smiling.

"But I thought we would go and have a drink somewhere." Lili didn't know why she said this, only that she was afraid of going into the convent; it was somehow connected to the terror of napping. The girl kept smiling, as if, in fact, this were her first dance and she was frozen with hope and anxiety. Lili smiled back, at a loss. The yellow silk brushed against her old bare legs, and the world seemed momentarily fresh and young and ripe.

Why had Lili come here? Clearly she was expected: the girl had a sign. Lili's heart started to race; everything began to fall apart, to dissolve into spots, as if she were fainting—she must pull herself together, try to make sense of things despite the frightening blue sky: Who was this little girl in a novice's habit? Who was Sister Francis?

She remembered then that she had come to visit Paule, who was a nun, who was waiting for her in her bedroom, and she thought that her heart must be beating for love. She imagined Paule, sitting on the edge of the convent bed, in a pink silk robe, with her bags packed, waiting for Lili. They would go back together to Saint-Germain, and they would spend their old age in the deep bed on the second floor. It made no difference that they were no longer smooth and supple; all that mattered was that they should be naked.

And then the pieces fell together—the thirty years of silence, the phone call from the station, that unoriginal choice, *Francis,* and she thought, Paule is dying. She looked back sharply toward the train, which had not yet left; she would board it again, slide down into the leather seat, let it take her to the end of the line. She was ashamed to have taken her heart and the blue sky and the word "bedroom" all to mean love—what did it ever mean but death, now, when a person waited for you in her bedroom?

"Dying, is she?" Lili asked. Her hands were trembling, but she would not weep, not for Paule, whose life had been nothing but a farewell—who had invited Lili so Lili could watch her leave, one last time.

"Well, is she?" Lili asked shortly. The novice was frowning, and the train was sighing, shuddering: at any moment it would heave into motion.

The girl stared straight at Lili with round, blue eyes. "Sister Francis did say to tell you that she was dying, but—"

"She might have told me over the phone. She might have saved me the trip. *Merde,*" Lili swore, her hand fluttering toward the train: it was moving slowly away. She could catch it if she ran. She sat down on a cement bench instead and lit a cigarette. Her heart ached, and her throat, and she wondered if she might be coming down with the flu. She had never expected that Paule would die. It was the most obvious possibility in the world, but it had never crossed Lili's mind—Paule had survived the war, after all. She had, for a while, genuinely loved the world. Loved it to excess, with her taste, smell. *See how ripe the tomato is, how the oyster catches light, can you believe it, Lili?*

The beauty of this world, the smells, the sounds, I will renounce them all, you wait and see. Oh, then why not expect her to die? Go in peace, Lili thought. Go, sweet silky Paule with your full, apricot bottom, your insatiable appetite; your cigarettes and wine and *Smell, Lili, taste, this world.* Oh, this world.

Lili felt weak, and she began to weep, shamefully, helplessly. The little nun sat down beside her and touched her back. Instantly, Lili's eyes were dry and glittering. "Look at you," she said sharply. "Fourteen or fifteen if you're a day. Why are you becoming a nun? What makes you think you can make this sort of decision at your age?"

The girl looked down bashfully.

"Well?" Lili insisted. "Why?" She felt that she might slap the girl—how, in any state of delirium, could Paule have imagined that Lili would want to attend another death? Besides, she hadn't been delirious on the phone. She'd been perfectly clear: *I'm a bit tired.* Perhaps, after all, Lili would throw herself under the next train and vanish down the tracks as lightly as a thistle. "Well?" she repeated.

"I always wanted—" the girl murmured.

"Oh, spare me," Lili said. She did want to commit some violence, but, hearty as she was, even this girl could hold her down; she must weigh less than thirty-nine kilos by now. She threw her cigarette casually onto the tracks and arched her head back to feel the day's last breath of heat on her throat; but the ends of her fingers were still shaking. "So, Paule is dying, finally. I should have thought of that."

"Sister Francis says she's dying," the girl repeated, hiding her eyes again.

"Well? Is she? Or has she gone mad again? Is she simply hallucinating her death?" Lili felt hopeful again, eager.

"She isn't mad," the girl said, hastily. "But God alone knows the hour of our death."

Lili glared at her. Paule was dying. She was in her bed, leaving this world. She would never again try to convince Lili of God's presence; never, with her earnest, half-crazed intensity, try to form a new religion out of her desires.

She had already died once, and now she was dying again, and she had invited Lili to watch. Why? She had no pity; she never had.

Lili still glared at the little nun, and the little nun looked back at her timidly. What was it she had said? That God alone knew the hour of our death? "Good Lord," Lili murmured. "You don't look stupid."

Why, for that matter, had the convent allowed Lili to come? Did they think she was young?

Did they think she had not seen enough of this sort of thing?

The nun was blushing. "Would you like to see Sister Francis, Madame?" she asked. "I've brought a car."

Lili sighed. "Do you have any thoughts? Of your own, I mean. Ever. Do you ever have any thoughts?"

The girl smiled frankly at Lili, the way she'd done at first, before she'd had to deliver her message of death. "I'm in love with Christ," she said proudly. She might as easily have said "Jean," or "Michel," or "Bertrand." But, after all, Lili had believed in God, too, when she was the novice's age, with Claude-François kissing her in his urgent way, his teeth pressed into her lips—so what did it matter? The little nun could always defect, tear off her wimple, and lift her skirts, and there was no point in Lili pointing this out to her now, no point in showing the way to salvation if you wouldn't be there to greet the person as she arrived. Taste, Lili, smell, but I'll be leaving now, I'm going to shave my head. . . .

"Well," Lili said. "See that he treats you well."

The girl laughed, a light, musical laugh, full of small, perfect teeth.

And what is it to me? Lili thought, following her to the car. Another death?

Paule was dying beneath her crucifix, with a view of the hills.

"The little girl who brought me here is not convinced you're dying," Lili said. She stood in the doorway, looking across the small room at Paule in her bed. Lili had not said hello, and she did not now go to Paule; she simply stood, staring at the hair that had stayed nearly black, at the closed eyes, the barely parted lips. Paule, if she heard Lili, did not open her eyes, did not lift her flabby, pale arms from the coverlet. The Auschwitz tattoo was still on her forearm. It surprised Lili that that of all things should have remained intact, but what shocked her, what was unbearable, was Paule's beauty. It was not the beauty of her youth—that soft, Oriental face, her round firmness, like an apricot's—this was something different. She was starving to death, the mother superior had said when she greeted Lili—she was a tall, broad, flat-faced woman, and she held Lili's hand and asked her to keep her visit short, because Sister Francis was tired, and the convent closed its doors at eight—but Paule looked nothing like she had after the war. Her face rose out of what was left of her flesh, a smooth skull, the skin taut and innocent. Her cheekbones were higher than Lili had realized, her nose finer. Lili took a few steps into the room, but she kept an arm's length between herself and the bed. Paule's youthful charm, she saw, had been purely decorative: this was the true Paule, this sculpted bareness. Lili's longing for her was suddenly more terrible than it had ever been, even in the days when, without touching at all, they would weep with desire, with pleasure. It was the purest face of death Lili had ever seen, for it knew itself, and it knew itself without struggle: it was like the tops of the Alps, those smooth, white expanses that would blind and kill you, all the while remaining still, frozen, undisturbed.

At any moment, the little novice would come back to drive Lili wherever she wanted to go—the train station, a hotel, a bar—but Lili kept moving closer and closer to Paule's face, her hands restless at her sides.

Paule opened her eyes, the irises as black and clear as a moonless sky, then closed them again.

But had Paule recognized Lili? Had she thought anything? It made no difference. She was dying. Soon she would be gone, erased as utterly as all the other dead. It wasn't a thing you could speak of. Lili rang the bell for the proprietor of the town's only hotel and waited; her fingernails dug into the skin of her palms.

The proprietor—a man in a soiled white apron over a distended belly—shuffled slowly down the stairs and over to the desk.

"I need a room—for several days," Lili said anxiously. She felt as if the length of time the proprietor allowed her would be the same as the length of time Paule had left. "It could be six weeks," she added. "I'm waiting for someone to die. You never know."

The proprietor studied his reservations without moving, without even seeming to breathe. He reached for his keys at last and silently handed her one, his eyes never leaving the register.

"Breakfast at seven," he called out, sadly, as she rounded the corner to the stairs.

She did not sleep. She lay wide eyed in the dark, thinking of how she had imagined that she and Paule were together in staying alive. She was wrong, fooled; that's what happened to her in life. *Yes, I renounce the flesh.* Though they starved and tortured me, it wasn't enough; it is never enough. *I will renounce this world, my love, you, my Lili, who, faithful and stupid to the last, will attend my death.*

All night Lili lay, running the rough, frayed silk of Paule's yellow dress through her fingers.

In the morning, Paule could swallow again, and Lili sat on the edge of her bed and gave her some broth. Paule was propped up with pillows, and though she didn't open her eyes, she opened her mouth like a bird and swallowed.

"Lili," she said, her eyes shut fast. "That's you, isn't it?"

Lili did not answer. She did not want to talk; she simply wanted to feed Paule, to slip the spoon over and over into her open mouth. Already she was afraid of the evening, when the nuns would tell her to leave.

Who could have dreamed such a face? So bright and terrible, Lili shook with desire for it.

The mother superior came to take Paule's temperature. She did not leave right away when she was done but stood in the doorway, watching Lili. Was she jealous? Lili wondered. Had she dreamed of nursing Paule herself? She hovered, watching them. Lili turned to her at last, annoyed, and the mother superior's face was drenched with tears.

"Oh," Lili said. "Oh, I—" but the mother superior turned and strode quickly, heavily, away.

"Did you say something to her?" Paule murmured. The dark, incredible eyes opened again and fell shut. "Something unkind, Lili?"

Lili was silent. Her hands still trembled with the desire to touch Paule's face, to feel every curve and ridge and hollow.

In the afternoon, Paule opened her eyes and stared at Lili. Her gaze was at once startled and peaceful, and Lili leaned forward, eager, dreading the moment when Paule's lids would slip back over the bright black irises.

"Lili," Paule said. "Lili." And then: "You've been here all day, haven't you?"

"Yes." It was the yes of a lover, *Yes, yes*.

"Were you here yesterday?"

"Yes."

"But you were late."

"I was thinking about God."

Paule's eyes fell shut, and her mouth hung open darkly. But still, how beautiful her smooth, bare, sculpted face! Lili could not resist now: she reached and touched Paule's forehead. Paule didn't move, and Lili kept stroking, over and over.

The nuns came and went, though the mother superior did not reappear. They brought bowls of broth in which Paule showed no interest now, lying motionless, her breath catching on the phlegm in the back of her throat. They asked Lili to leave the room so that they could check Paule. Each time they left disappointed: Paule did not move her bowels; she did not urinate.

"Oh!" Paule said, suddenly, toward dusk. "God! Well . . . if that's what kept you."

Lili laughed softly, her old man's laugh. Paule opened her eyes and looked around the room, as if she'd misplaced something or wasn't sure where she was.

"Have you abandoned your faith?" Lili asked, and it made her voice tremble, to have such an ordinary bit of conversation.

"Well, faith," Paule said, as clearly now as if she weren't dying at all, as if she were merely resting. Then she was silent for a long time. "I haven't seen God in years," she said at last.

"How long?" Lili asked softly, leaning over the bed.

"Years," Paule answered, and fell asleep.

When she awoke, she was clear, focused. "Please feed me," she said, and Lili went for a cup of broth. When she returned with it, Paule asked, "Please kiss me."

Lili put the broth on the nightstand and leaned over Paule's body. She kissed her forehead, her cheeks: over and over, small, butterfly kisses. Then she fed her. When Paule was finished, Lili sat on the edge of the bed and stroked her forehead.

"Talk to me," Paule said.

"I think—" Lili began.

"You always thought a lot."

Lili laughed. "What I think—"

"Tell me," Paule said, and she reached for Lili's hand and held it tightly in hers.

"Renunciation," Lili said. "That was your mistake. Why you lost sight of God."

"And you?" Paule asked, closing her eyes again. "What was your mistake, then?"

Lili laughed again, the old man's laugh. "I still want everything. . . ."

"It's how you've kept your youth."

They sat quietly. Paule was kneading Lili's hand, clutching it with all her strength.

"Kiss me again," she said, and Lili took Paule's head in her hands and covered it with small, light kisses.

A nun came and found them like that, stood in the doorway a moment, and left. Who could deny them anything, at such extremity of old age? This is all I want, Lili thought; nothing remained for her in the world but the comfort of embracing.

And forgiveness? Lili thought. The thing I long for? For my crime?

Paule, tell me—as a Catholic: Will I go to hell for André's death?

Oh Lili you have already been. There may be a little extra punishment, for how unforgiving you've been, but it won't be much, a few Hail Marys, a rap on the knuckles.

Even that I cannot bear.

Sh-sh, Lili, you can bear everything.

Tell me, Paule, as a nun. Tell me. Will I?

Everything will be forgiven, Lili. Everyone. You, your father, Pierre, me, all of us. We will all be forgiven. That is the mystery.

What about hell?

Oh, hell. I've already been.

Will the Germans be forgiven?

If they repent.

That's always the catch.

Oh, you. Lili. Lili you are already forgiven.

What do you know? A little Jew. A lesbian.

Already forgiven, Lili, hush.

A Jew.

Oh, Lili. Paule laughed so softly it was barely a breath, and her laughter, whatever caused it—some odd dream of death—woke Lili: her head snapped forward and she came to with a start, astonished that she had slept, or dreamed without sleeping, it was impossible to tell anymore.

It was almost eight, and Lili was afraid. She did not want to go back to the hotel, to sleep alone while Paule died. She went to the mother superior's office, but the mother superior was nowhere to be seen. Lili bowed her head and spoke to Sister Ignatius instead. Mademoiselle Jacob had been like a sister to her, Lili explained. She understood that in becoming Sister Francis, Mademoiselle Jacob had left behind the things of this world, but she, Madame Larat, had no one else.

Sister Ignatius, pale and cool, stared down at the mother superior's desk where she had settled herself, her long translucent fingers fanned out across its surface. "Stay with her, my child, if it comforts you." Lili resisted the impulse to roll her eyes. She bowed her head again and thanked Sister Ignatius profusely.

In the night, while Lili held Paule's head in her lap, Paule said, "You're a delicate lady."

Lili laughed softly, but Paule continued: "I'm not ready to say good-bye yet."

"Oh!" Lili said, and she lit a cigarette.

"Would you marry Pierre again?" Paule asked, suddenly.

What a thing to ask! And at this late hour.

Lili paused. "He was a good father," she said, finally. "A good citizen. But he couldn't kill, and he couldn't make love."

Paule closed her eyes.

After a while, she murmured, "Please. Please, Lili."

"What? What is it? Are you hungry?" Lili leaned down toward her, down in toward her small, rank-smelling mouth. "Do you want me to feed you? You can have anything—chocolate, wine, my breasts—they had such sweet milk in the old days. . . ."

But Paule was asleep. Lili sat back up, still murmuring: "Yes, it was sweet and warm. I would give you anything. My breasts, my heart, everything.

"And with that?" she sang—the same four notes she had sung over and over to Claude. "With that?" Then she grew silent, staring down at the naked, innocent face, her fingers brushing Paule's forehead, a thousand times, good-bye.

Suddenly, Paule grabbed Lili's hand and began to suck on her finger like a baby, and Lili knew that the end was near. She smelled the foul, bitter odor of a dying woman's feces, and she pulled back the covers and lifted Paule's nightgown—how loose and wasted her pale body was!—she rolled Paule over on her side as she had done so many times for Claude and wiped Paule's flattened bottom with a damp cloth: there was so little there, it was like wiping an infant's bottom, except that it was hard to hold her up, and Paule mumbled unhappily, and it was not yellow and sweet as it is with a baby, it was black and rotten.

Then Lili lay next to her in the narrow bed and held her and kissed the side of her head. How old they were, Lili thought, old beyond words. But what a pleasure to hold her body against Paule's, to feel her thin bones embrace Paule's soft and empty flesh. Then she fell asleep, with Paule sucking her finger.

In her dreams she heard the rattling, last inhalation of breath, and she awoke, but she was not afraid; there was no last thing she needed to say: all that mattered was that she should keep holding Paule. She fell asleep again, when she could tell that Paule had died, and when she awoke, Paule's forehead was cool and hard. Lili had not noticed its hardness when it was warm. Her hands and face were cold, too, but she did not look dead, lying there on her back with her eyes almost closed, her lips barely parted. She looked as if she were about to open her eyes and take everything in in her peaceful, startled way. The sky was beginning to fade, and soon the nuns would rise and see that Paule was dead and there would be a terrible flurry and commotion. That was the thing Lili dreaded: to be separated too quickly from Paule's body. She rose and sat in the chair next to the bed and traced her fingers along Paule's throat, her collarbone, her empty breasts. Paule's heart was still warm, and Lili covered it with her hand.

She would have lifted Paule if she could, carried her to the bathroom at the end of the hall, and bathed her, like a good Jew, but she did not have the strength. She sat instead, her hand over Paule's heart, gazing at her bare, innocent face. Then she leaned over to kiss Paule, and for a long time she didn't move, her lips resting on Paule's, the warmth draining away beneath her hand. She hadn't known this before: that something remains after heart and brain and lungs have given up—heat, light, a kind of radiance—it vanished, and vanished again, and then again, a fading swift and prolonged as the end of a summer day.

Lili sat up and watched as she had watched the light change on the Alps so many years ago.

She could not say when Paule turned cold and blank, only that at last she had—so blank she looked half vicious. And then it was all right, all over; the nuns could do as they pleased. She woke the novice on her way out, and that was all: she did not even go back in to look one last time at the body.

She walked to the station—it was a good four kilometers, and the sky was thick and foggy—and sat to wait on the cold cement bench where she had spoken to the novice two days before. She was still and quiet and peaceful, smoking while the sun rose across the hills, and the horizon turned from gray to violet to rose to blinding white (as the Alps that night had turned in reverse from white to rose to gray), and then her cigarette fell out of her hand, and, fast asleep but with her eyes wide open, she watched the train pull in, watched the few sleepy passengers who had joined her on the platform get on, watched the doors close—"But that's my train!" she called out, running after it—slow and stiff despite her heart, her yellow silk dress flapping against her calves.

She slid breathlessly into the leather seat and stared out at the old, gentle countryside, waiting for her heart to subside. When she reached Paris, she would board the next train for Saint-Gervais. She would go to the mountains in her yellow dress and she would die there like someone from a primitive tribe. No, not that. She wanted to see the Alps again but not to die, not yet, when cigarettes were still so soothing, and her garden at this time of day, of year, was so beautiful with the morning light filling it like water; when the taste of chocolate still filled her kitchen drawers. She could feel Paule's smooth, innocent head against her lips and Paule's pale, loose limbs in her hands as if she had lifted her, carried her down the dormitory hall into a warm bath. The water slipped through her fingers; it fell across Paule's throat, her chest, and Lili slipped her arm under Paule's waist and held her, suspended, for in the water Paule was as light as a child, as easy; perhaps that was why Pierre always bathed Lili: she became easier in the water; God knew she wasn't easy out of it.

Poor Pierre. I was a difficult wife. But in the bath so light, so smooth, as slippery as a girl.

She was bathing Paule, squeezing the sponge over her head, and the water ran down her face, into the hollow of her throat, between her breasts, her legs; she was dead, but how light she was in Lili's arms, in the water, dead and clean and pure. Death was the only pure thing. Lili *had* loved André; but she was not dead, not pure, not yet.

LILI

Abigail de Witt

ABIGAIL DE WITT ON HER INSPIRATION FOR LILI

When I was growing up, my family traveled back and forth between North Carolina and France every year. My mother, a French physicist, taught at the University of North Carolina and in the summer ran a physics institute in the Alps. It was the early '60s, and when my sisters and I arrived in Paris every June—stumbling out of a Whisper jumbo jet full of air hostesses in pillbox hats, and into the gray, wet dawn—it seemed we were entering another universe. Forty years ago, France was poorer, still stunned by two world wars, and its culture was old and uniform: all families ate the same meals, all schools followed the same curriculum, all children wore navy blue.

From September to May, I wore flip-flops and orange-flowered bell-bottoms; I ate peanut butter and jelly twice a day. In the taxi from the Paris airport to my grandfather's apartment, I looked out at the beautiful, narrow streets, the dark shop grates being rolled up, and longed for bright, hot sidewalks and the looseness of American voices.

My grandfather was horrified by us; our clothes were garish and our French mangled. In his darkly furnished drawing room with its dozens of porcelain figurines, he greeted us with dismay. So brightly colored, so sleepy, so apt to confuse our articles, we were a disappointment to many of our relatives.

But I had a great aunt, a tiny, fierce, chain-smoking woman who taught history and had a severely retarded son; she adored us and we her. She ate canned food and she never corrected our grammar. Before we arrived, she would search everywhere for ketchup so that we would have something familiar to eat and the first time she saw my orange-flowered bell-bottoms, she exclaimed with delight, "A gypsy!"

She was frightening, too, her voice so rough from smoking that she often sounded angry, her arguments with her husband loud enough for all to hear. And like all old people, she seemed unfathomable. I could not imagine what in the world she might think about, or if she felt the things I did: loneliness, excitement, longing.

Still, I was fascinated by her, and I never ceased trying to imagine her emotional life. Lili is a fictional character, but she is the result of those years of fascination, of the desire to know another as I know myself.

DISCUSSION QUESTIONS

1. How does the novel's opening scene introduce the main themes of the book?
2. In what ways is Lili's childhood epiphany ("then it came to her for the first time that she was alive") a religious experience? In what ways is it not?
3. Discuss the role of hunger in the novel. In what ways are hunger and faith repeatedly linked?
4. Why do you think Pierre could not talk about his fiancée?
5. When Lili decides to have Claude sleep between her and Pierre, she notices that the child serves as a barrier against Pierre. Find and discuss other passages in which De Witt gives metaphorical significance to the physical aspects of domestic life.
6. Compare Lili's two experiences at Mont Blanc: the childhood sunrise and the evening many years later.
7. During one of the nights when she and Paule lie together naked but cannot touch each other, Lili thinks how "there was no difference between her [own] longing for Pierre and Paule's for God. Each was a kind of infidelity and each was hopeless." What does she mean by that?
8. What is so significant to Lili about the butcher?
9. What do you make of the fact that Lili is abandoned by everyone except her family, those "eternal, elastic arms" she so desperately wants to escape?
10. Why does Lili stay with Pierre?
11. What is the difference between Paule's faith and Lili's? How does that difference play itself out in the novel's ending, with Paule

admitting that "I haven't seen God in years" and Lili buoyed by a sense of rejuvenation?

12. After the deaths of Claude-François and André, Lili obsessively visits Claude-François's memorial. It is André's death, however, that proves harder for her to deal with. Why?

13. At one point, Lili, speaking to Claude, describes her love for him as "pure" because "I expect nothing from you . . . no answer." What does she mean by this? What is the significance of purity for her?

14. In a similar vein, discuss the novel's last paragraph in light of the Colette epigraph.

MORE NORTON BOOKS WITH READING GROUP GUIDES INCLUDED

Kerri Sakamoto, *The Electrical Field*

May Sarton, *Journal of a Solitude**

Gustaf Sobin, *The Fly-Truffler*

Ted Solotaroff, *Truth Comes in Blows*

Jean Christopher Spaugh, *Something Blue*

Mark Strand and Eavan Boland, *The Making of a Poem**

Barry Unsworth, *Morality Play*

Barry Unsworth, *Losing Nelson*

*Available on the Norton Web site:
www.wwnorton.com

1993 Preface

When I wrote *Bobby Fischer's Outrageous Chess Moves* in 1985, Fischer was recognized as the game's greatest player though he hadn't competed in thirteen years. The feeling was that he might never play again. Since then, two of his prized records have fallen. Garry Kasparov surpassed his highest F.I.D.E. rating and Judit Polgar became the youngest grandmaster of all time. Other stars have emerged, too, such as England's Nigel Short; America's Gata Kamsky; India's Viswanathan Anand; Russia's Vassily Ivanchuk; and Kasparov's protégé Vladimir Kramnik, also of Russia.

Then last fall, like the phoenix rising from its own ashes, Bobby Fischer announced he was going to play for the first time in twenty years! And so he did, picking up where he left off in Iceland in 1972, defeating his old rival Boris Spassky (this time in Yugoslavia). The excitement of seeing Fischer grapple again led me to read through this book which had been out of print for several years. As I played through the 101 tactical gems contained here, I was struck by their creativity, logic, and simple beauty. I also realized that many of the paradigms of contemporary chess originated with Fischer. Instruction, truth, humor, pleasure: It's all here. See for yourself.

—*Bruce Pandolfini*

About This Book

This book contains 101 of Bobby Fischer's most brilliant, creative, daring, surprising, ingenious, eye-opening, revolutionary—or in one word—*outrageous* moves! They have been selected from all his recorded games, most of them played under tournament or match conditions.

For each of these situations, the setting and Fischer's opponent are designated at the top of the page, along with the impending move number. There follows on each page an outrageous move that occurred at a critical turning point in the game—a move that made all the difference. A diagram shows the position just before Fischer made his decisive play.

The reader is encouraged to guess Fischer's move on the basis of the accompanying clue. The solution for each is supplied at the bottom of the page, and in all cases the reasons for the move are explained in both words and algebraic notation, the contemporary standard. At the top right of each page, you'll find a shaded number that indicates the degree of difficulty, with 5 being the most difficult.

You can solve these positions by looking at the diagrams or by setting them up on your own board. They provide a detailed insight into the mind of a very great chessplayer, and as a source of entertainment, they're *outrageous* fun!

About Bobby Fischer

Robert James "Bobby" Fischer, generally acknowledged as the greatest chessplayer of all time, emerged on earth in Chicago, Illinois, March 9, 1943. His family later moved to Brooklyn, New York, where in 1949 he was introduced to the game by his eleven-year-old sister Joan, using the directions that came with the set.

Less than two years later, Bobby's mother sent a postcard to the *Brooklyn Eagle* newspaper inquiring about places to play chess. The card was answered by journalist Herman Helms, who alerted Mrs. Fischer to a chess exhibition planned for Brooklyn's Grand Army Plaza Library on January 17, 1951. Bobby played and lost that day to master Max Pavey, but he gained a chess teacher: Carmine Nigro, president of the Brooklyn Chess Club. Thereafter, Bobby played at the Brooklyn club Friday evenings and at Mr. Nigro's home on weekends. Sometimes his mentor even took the talented junior to Washington Square Park in Greenwich Village, where they played all day long.

Bobby participated in his first tournament, the 1955 U.S. Amateur, in upstate New York (receiving a minus score), and later that year joined the fiercely competitive Manhattan Chess Club. The Manhattan has "the strongest players of any club in the country," he wrote in his first book, *Bobby Fischer's Games of Chess* (Simon and Schuster, 1958). Starting off with players of average strength, he quickly moved up to the "B" group and then to the "A." And in the spring of 1956 came his first real tournament success, when he tied for first in the Manhattan Chess Club's "A" Reserve section.

This was the launching pad for his meteoric rise. Bobby then won the 1956 U.S. Junior Championship in Philadelphia, tied for 4th in the U.S. Open in Oklahoma City, and for 8th in Montreal's First Canadian Open (actually stronger than its

U.S. counterpart). His most memorable accomplishment in 1956 may well have been in the Rosenwald Trophy Tournament held at New York City's Manhattan and Marshall chess clubs, where thirteen-year-old Bobby finished in 8th place overall. But it was his truly inspired game against International Master Donald Byrne that received worldwide praise and was dubbed "the game of the century." The winning moves were perhaps the most insightful ever played by a youngster.

Even greater success lay ahead for the youthful whirlwind in 1957. He won the U.S. Junior Championship, the U.S. Junior Speed Championship, a match against Philippine Junior Champ Rodolfo Cardoso, and the New Jersey State Open. But the crown jewel came at year's end when, playing in his first Invitational U.S. Championship, Bobby overtook the famous Samuel Reshevsky and won first prize. At fourteen, Bobby Fischer had become the youngest U.S. Champion ever.

Subsequent achievements include:

- Becoming the youngest grandmaster in history at age fifteen in 1958.
- Going undefeated and capturing first prize in the 1962 Stockholm Interzonal Tournament.
- Winning the U.S. Championship all eight times he played, including an 11-0 blitz of the 1963-64 field, the first and only time it's ever been done.
- Demolishing ex-world champion Tigran Petrosian 3-1 (2 wins, 2 draws) in the 1970 USSR vs the Rest-of-the-World Match.
- Overwhelming the field by an unprecedented 5½ points in the 1970 World Speed Championship in Yugoslavia.
- Winning the 1970 Interzonal Tournament in Palma de Mallorca by 3½ points over his nearest rival.
- Destroying consecutively three top grandmasters in the 1971 Candidates Matches: Russia's Mark Taimanov 6-0; Denmark's Bent Larsen 6-0 (the first two such shutouts ever); and the Soviet Union's Petrosian 6½-2½ winning the final four games.
- Defeating in 1972 at Reykjavik, Iceland, his long-time

nemesis, Russia's Boris Spassky, in the greatest chess match of all time, to become America's first and only World Champion.

Bobby's hiatuses from competitive chess from 1964 to 1970 stemmed from various disagreements with chess organizers over rules, conditions, and prizes. His triumph in the 1970 USSR vs the Rest-of-the-World Match signaled his return, climaxed by his incredible 1972 victory over Spassky. In 1975, when he disputed the World Chess Federation's championship rules for a match against the Soviet player Anatoli Karpov, he declined to compete and Karpov was given the title without ever having faced Fischer across the board.

Still, much of the world continued to regard Fischer as the undethroned chess champ, a unique circumstance in that he eschewed tournament and match play thereafter. In fact, when he chose to play MIT's Greenblatt Computer chess program in 1978 (which he beat three times to none), he made no attempt to publicize the encounter and even tried to keep it private. This, of course, was impossible, for Fischer had achieved the status of folk hero.

Beyond the endless puzzlement and speculation about Fischer's future intentions in chess, there is one certainty: his games will live forever. There are one hundred and one of his virtuoso tactics in this book. They are a thing of beauty and sufficient reason for reading on.

Bobby Fischer vs Bent Larsen

DENVER, 1971
5TH MATCH GAME
WHITE'S 43RD MOVE

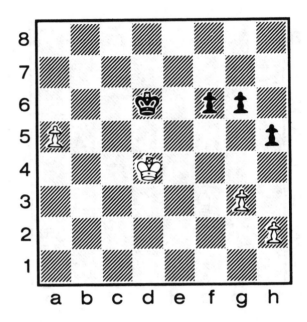

CLUE: Both sides have equal material, but Fischer's outside passed pawn, along with his more centralized King, makes all the difference.

SOLUTION: Fischer played **1. a6!**, trying to decoy Black's King from the Kingside. After **1 . . . Kc6 2. a7 Kb7 3. Kd5 h4,** Larsen is hoping that White accepts doubled h-pawns by **4. gxh4.** Instead, **4. Ke6** and Larsen resigned. His remaining pawns must fall to Fischer's marauding King. **(1-0)**

Bobby Fischer vs William Addison

CLEVELAND, 1957
U.S. OPEN
WHITE'S 29TH MOVE

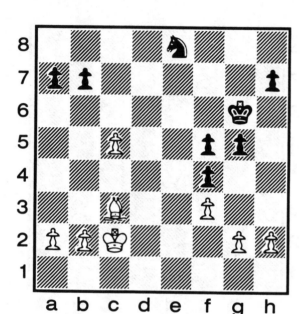

CLUE: In effect, Fischer has an extra c-pawn, for Black's Kingside majority is crippled by White's three pawns. Another advantage: White has a powerful Bishop against an inferior Knight, allowing Fischer to reduce the position to bare essentials.

SOLUTION: Fischer played **1. Be5!**, corraling the Knight so that it can't move without being captured. On either 1 . . . Ng7 or 1 . . . Nf6, White swaps the Bishop for the Knight and arrives at a winning King and pawn endgame, where his Queenside pawn majority decides. The game concluded: **1 . . . Kh5 2. Kd3 g4 3. b4 a6 4. a4 gxf3 5. gxf3 Kh4 6. b5 axb5 7. a5! Kh3 8. c6**, and Black resigned, for after 8 . . . bxc6 the a-pawn moves up the board unhampered while Black's Knight sits by helplessly. **(1-0)**

Bobby Fischer vs Luis Sanchez

SANTIAGO, 1959
WHITE'S 53RD MOVE

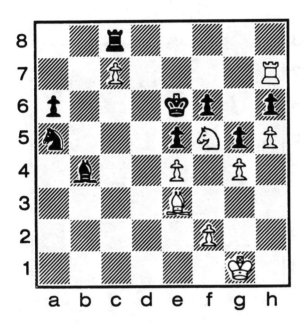

CLUE: White's assets include a far-advanced passed pawn and harmoniously working pieces. Black's are disorganized. Add to Black's woes that his Bishop is tied up defending against Re7 mate—the crux of the problem.

SOLUTION: White scored with **1. Bd2!** Fischer's Bishop cannot be captured because of his mate threat at e7. Defending Black's Bishop with 1 . . . Nc6 fails to 2. Bxb4, and if Sanchez recaptures he's again mated at e7. Finally, if he saves his Bishop by moving it off the a5-e1 diagonal, he hangs his Knight at a5. Black resigned. **(1-0)**

Bobby Fischer vs Joaquim Durao

HAVANA, 1966
17TH OLYMPIAD
WHITE'S 33RD MOVE

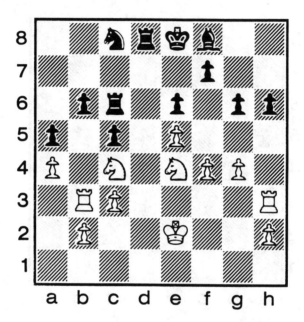

CLUE: Black hasn't lost anything yet, though four of his five pieces are in defensive positions along the back rank. This bodes ill, and Fischer capitalized at once.

SOLUTION: Fischer converted his spatial edge into winning a pawn by **1. Nxa5!**, when 1 . . . bxa5 allows 2. Nf6+ Ke7 3. Rb7+ and mate in two moves (Black can temporarily save his King by discarding both Rooks). Black declined the sacrifice with **1 . . . Rc7**, accepting a pawn-down endgame, which he soon abandoned. **(1-0)**

Bobby Fischer vs Tigran Petrosian

BLED, YUGOSLAVIA 1961
ALEKHINE MEMORIAL TOURNAMENT
WHITE'S 36TH MOVE

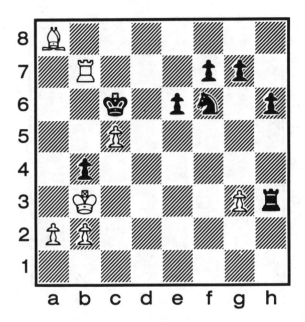

CLUE: Black's King has just played to c6, blundering into a potential discovered attack from the Bishop. White has merely to move his Rook and it's check, but where? Fischer uncorks the answer.

SOLUTION: Actually, White didn't start with a Rook move at all. Fischer first played the preparatory **1. Kc4!**, defending his c-pawn and constructing a mating net. Black resigned, unable to stop a subsequent Ra7 discovered mate. Fischer's outrageous King move brought the house down. **(1-0)**

GAME 6

Paul Keres vs Bobby Fischer

BLED, 1959
CANDIDATES TOURNAMENT
BLACK'S 53RD MOVE

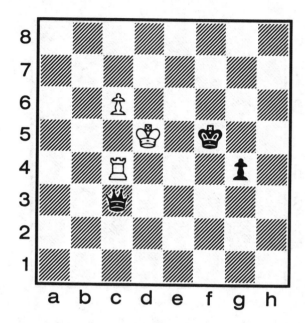

CLUE: Keres has just played his Rook to c4, attacking Black's Queen, but blocking the last escape square for his own King. Fischer quickly knew what to do.

SOLUTION: The curtain was drawn with **1 . . . Qe5 mate**. This uncommon mating pattern is sometimes referred to as a swallow's-tail mate because the pieces are arranged somewhat like a bird in flight, with the c6 and c4 squares as the bird's wings. It was scandalous that Fischer actually thus checkmated one of the world's great grandmasters! **(0-1)**

Bobby Fischer vs Arthur Bisguier

POUGHKEEPSIE, 1963
NEW YORK STATE OPEN
WHITE'S 27TH MOVE

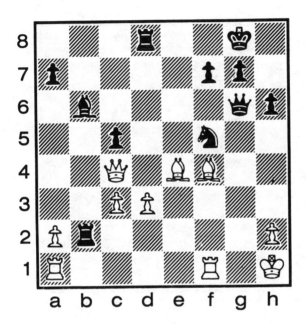

CLUE: With a Rook on the 7th rank and a Queen and Knight menacing White's Kingside, Black appears to have a dangerous position. But Fischer's centralized Bishops, poised for both defense and attack, save the day.

SOLUTION: "Knightfall" overtook Black after **1. Be5!**, when there was no way to avert the loss of the horseman pinned to his Queen by the Bishop at e4. The game concluded: **1 . . . Re8** (one move too late to guard e5) **2. Rxf5 Rxe5 3. Rxe5**, and Black resigned. **(1-0)**

Bobby Fischer vs E. Osbun

DAVIS, CALIFORNIA, 1964
SIMULTANEOUS EXHIBITION, WITH CLOCKS
WHITE'S 44TH MOVE

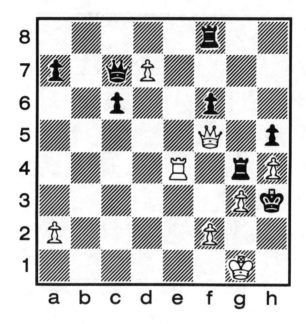

CLUE: Black has just shielded his King from White's Queen by interposing his Rook at g4. Black's reliance on this faulty defense is as "iffy" as the geological crack along the California coast, site of the matchup. It would have taken an eight-point earthquake on the Richter scale to stop Fischer's imminent mate.

SOLUTION: Fischer presciently exchanged Rooks **1. Rxg4!** **hxg4** and then surprisingly retreated his Queen **2. Qd3!**, threatening 3. Qf1 mate. With no reasonable way to extricate his King, Black gave up. **(1-0)**

Bobby Fischer vs Enrique Mecking

PALMA DE MALLORCA, SPAIN, 1970
INTERZONAL TOURNAMENT
WHITE'S 19TH MOVE

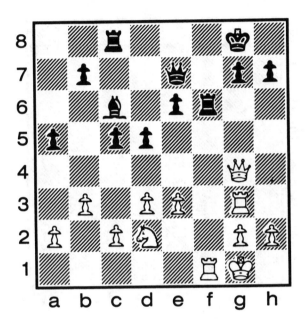

CLUE: White's Rooks and Queen loom down on Black, though all targets seem beyond White's scope. Bobby proved otherwise and won a pawn. How? Time will reveal all.

SOLUTION: After **1. Qxg7 + !** Qxg7, with Black's Queen pinned, White had the time for a mercenary *zwischenzug* (a German word for "in-between move") **2. Rxf6**, knowing Mecking's Queen couldn't escape capture anyway. A pawn to the good, Fischer nursed his advantage to win in 42 moves. **(1-0)**

Paul Keres vs Bobby Fischer

BLED, 1959
CANDIDATES TOURNAMENT
BLACK'S 24TH MOVE

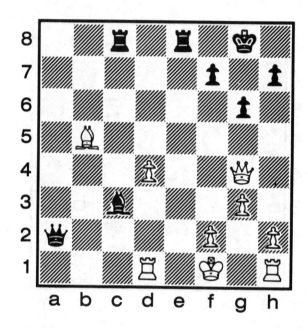

CLUE: White's Bishop at b5 attacks Black's Rook at e8. But Fischer's defense shows who the real attacker is.

SOLUTION: Fischer turned the tables with **1 . . . Qd5!**, attacking White's Bishop (b5) and Rook (h1) simultaneously. The play continued: **2. Bxe8 Qxh1+ 3. Ke2 Rxe8+** (collecting his piece with check) **4. Kd3** (threatening Black's Queen and Bishop) **4 . . . Be1**, and Fischer remained a piece ahead, provoking White's resignation. **(0-1)**

Bobby Fischer vs Pal Benko

CURACAO, 1962
CANDIDATES TOURNAMENT
WHITE'S 31ST MOVE

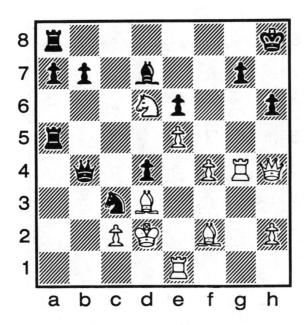

CLUE: White has two Bishops to Black's one. On the other side of the ledger are Black's pieces poised at the White King. It's White's turn, however, and Black could be mated before he can realize his attack.

SOLUTION: Fischer suddenly terminated Benko with **1. Qxh6 + !**. Mate next move follows by either 1 . . . gxh6 2. Nf7 or 1 . . . Kg8 2. Qxg7. **(1-0)**

Armando Acevedo vs Bobby Fischer

SIEGEN, WEST GERMANY, 1970
19TH OLYMPIAD
BLACK'S 47TH MOVE

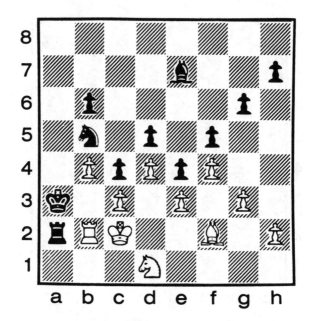

CLUE: White has an obstructed Bishop, a blocked Rook, and a lame Knight. His King isn't so safe either, but how can Fischer administer the death blow when everything is so impeded?

SOLUTION: The quickest road is **1. . . Nxc3!**, when 2. Nxc3? loses the Rook (2 . . . Rxb2+) and 2. Rxa2+ allows Black to extricate his Knight (2 . . . Nxa2). White tried **2. Kxc3** and resigned after the Knight-threatening **2. . .Ra1**. Neither 3. Kc2 Rxd1 4. Kxd1 Kxb2 nor 3. Rd2 Rc1+ 4. Rc2 Rxd1 offers any real resistance. **(0-1)**

Bobby Fischer vs Istvan Bilek

NEW YORK—HAVANA (BY TELETYPE), 1965
CAPABLANCA MEMORIAL TOURNAMENT
WHITE'S 35TH MOVE

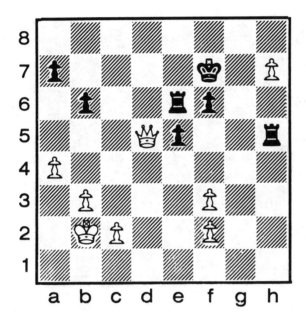

CLUE: It's a classic matchup: A Queen versus two Rooks. The Rooks are effective when they work in unison, but the Queen dominates when the Rooks are not coordinated and there are plenty of targets. Pawns can hinder, and pawns can help, as happens here.

SOLUTION: The humbling move was **1. f4!**, threatening the pinned Rook by 2. f5, when 2 . . . Rxf5 allows White's h-pawn to Queen. Note that another pin (along the 5th rank) prevents Black from playing 1 . . . exf4, which then hangs the Rook at h5 to White's Queen. Of course 1 . . . Rxh7 fails directly to 2. f5, winning the Rook at e6 outright. So the game continued: **1 . . . f5** (to prevent White's menacing advance) **2. fxe5 Rxh7 3. Qd7+ Re7 4. Qxf5+** (giving White connected passed pawns on the e- and f-files) **4 . . . Ke8 5. f4 Kd8 6. e6**, and Black resigned. The marching pawns would only cost him more material. **(1-0)**

Bobby Fischer vs Julio Bolbochan

STOCKHOLM, 1962
INTERZONAL TOURNAMENT
WHITE'S 35TH MOVE

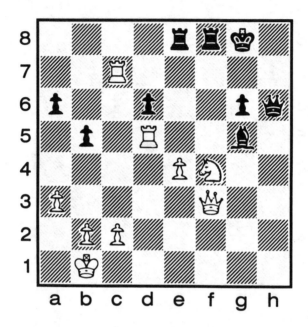

CLUE: It looks bad for White's Knight—pinned, attacked three times, and defended only once. Can the pin be broken?

SOLUTION: Yes. White's shift **1. Qb3!** not only undid the pin, but also set up a winning tactic—a discovered check along the a2-g8 diagonal by moving the Rook at d5. Black bit with **1 . . . Rxf4**. But after **2. Re5 +** (somewhat stronger than 2. Rxg5 +) **2 . . . Kf8** (to guard the Rook at e8) **3. Rxe8 +**, Black resigned. The try 3 . . . Kxe8 allows mate after 4. Qe6 + Kf8 5. Qc8 +. **(1-0)**

Bobby Fischer vs James Sherwin

NEW YORK, 1962-63
U.S. CHAMPIONSHIP
WHITE'S 26TH MOVE

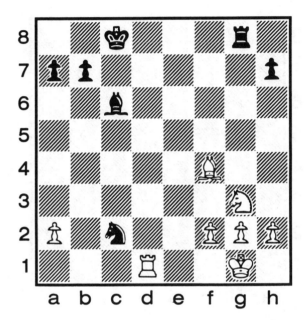

CLUE: If you focus on Black's Bishop and Rook, you might think they provide sufficient counterplay for being down a pawn. They will both ultimately converge on the square g2, where lies Fischer's moment of truth.

SOLUTION: Fischer played the subtly double-edged **1. Nf5!**. It certainly exposes the g-pawn, though it also threatens more seriously 2. Ne7 mate. With Black's Rook vulnerable to the Knight fork at e7, he tried **1 . . . Rxg2 +**, but after **2. Kf1 b6 3. Ne7 + Kb7 4. Nxc6**, he couldn't take the Knight at c6 and at the same time save his Rook. Black played one more move **4 . . . Rg4** and resigned, for White can save his pieces by checking at d8 with his Knight and then moving his Bishop. **(1-0)**

Bobby Fischer vs Pal Benko

CURACAO, 1962
CANDIDATES TOURNAMENT
WHITE'S 31ST MOVE

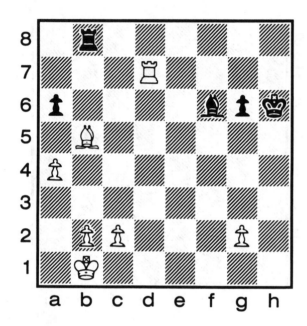

CLUE: Black is two pawns down, but with the Bishops operating on different colored squares, Fischer's opponent does have some drawing possibilities. Fischer calculated a powerful simplifying move.

SOLUTION: The most economical solution is **1. Rd6!**, hitting both the Bishop at f6 and the a-pawn. If Black moves his Bishop to safety, then White wins the a-pawn (2. Rxa6) and obtains a cluster of three Queenside pawns. The game concluded: **1 . . . Bxb2** (a desperate tactic, indirectly exchanging his Bishop for White's, capturing as much enemy material as he can in the process) **2. Kxb2 axb5 3. a5!** (producing a serious passed pawn) **3 . . . Ra8 4. a6 Kh5 5. Kb3 g5 6. Kb4 Kg4 7. Kxb5 Kg3 8. Rd7 g4 9. a7**, and Black resigned. On 9 . . . Kxg2, White follows through with 10. Kb6 and 11. Kb7, winning the Rook. **(1-0)**

Bobby Fischer vs William Addison

PALMA DE MALLORCA, 1970
INTERZONAL TOURNAMENT
WHITE'S 21ST MOVE

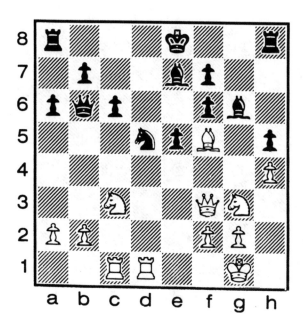

CLUE: White is fully developed and Black's King is still in the center. It won't be there for long, unless White drives home his initiative.

SOLUTION: Fischer controlled matters with **1. Rxd5!**, an exchange sacrifice. After the obligatory **1 . . . cxd5 2. Nxd5**, White threatens Nc7, forking King and Rook. Addison avoided 2 . . . Qd8 for fear of 3. Bxg6 fxg6 4. Nc7+, when 4 . . . Kf7 is answered by 5. Qb3+, soon taking Black to the cleaners. The game continued: **2 . . . Qxb2 3. Rb1 Qxa2 4. Rxb7** and Black resigned. He had to cope with numerous threats, such as 5. Bxg6 fxg6 6. Nxf6+ Bxf6 7. Qxf6 leading to mate. **(1-0)**

Bobby Fischer vs Max Euwe

LEIPZIG, 1960
14TH OLYMPIAD
WHITE'S 36TH MOVE

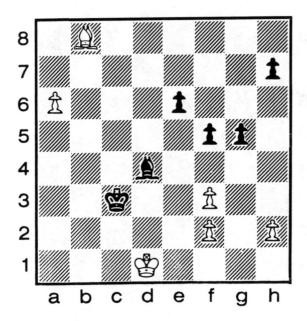

CLUE: White has a lusty passed pawn, but Black has some drawing chances if he can sacrifice his Bishop for the dangerous a-pawn. Fischer dispels the opportunity.

SOLUTION: The end came immediately with **1. Be5!**. This pinned the opposing Bishop and prevented it from guarding the a7 square. Thus, if 1 . . . Bxe5, then 2. a7 makes a new Queen. And if Black does anything else, White trades Bishops and pushes through his a-pawn. The great Dr. Euwe resigned. **(1-0)**

Svetozar Gligoric vs Bobby Fischer

PALMA DE MALLORCA, 1970
INTERZONAL TOURNAMENT
BLACK'S 29TH MOVE

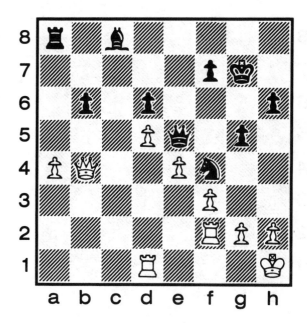

CLUE: Black has a Bishop and Knight in exchange for White's Rook and pawn. White's last move **Rf1-f2** enabled Fischer to exploit to the fullest his slight material edge.

SOLUTION: Fischer instantly saw that **1 . . . Nd3!**, forking the Queen and Rook, worked, for White's Rook at d1 couldn't leave the back rank to capture the Knight (2. Rxd3 allows 2 . . . Qa1+ and mate shortly). Gligoric fought on, only to resign after **2. Qxb6 Nxf2+ 3. Qxf2 Rxa4 4. Kg1 Ra1 5. Qe1 Ra2 6. Qg3 Qb2 7. h4 Ra1. (0-1)**

Donato Rivera vs Bobby Fischer

VARNA, BULGARIA, 1962
15TH OLYMPIAD
BLACK'S 14TH MOVE

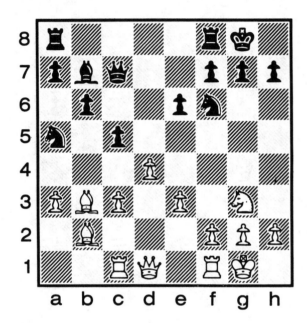

CLUE: White's last move, **1. Ra1-c1**, looked hunky-dory but was a mistake. Black now wins a decisive amount of material by shifting from a rank, to a diagonal, to a file.

SOLUTION: Fischer found **1 . . . Qc6!**, threatening diagonal mate at g2. This forced White to waste a move warding off the threat **2. f3**, which allowed **2 . . . Qb5**, skewering White's Bishops along the b-file. White tried one more move **3. Ba4**, and resigned after **3 . . . Qxb2**. **(0-1)**

Mark Taimanov vs Bobby Fischer

VANCOUVER, 1971
CANDIDATES MATCH 5th GAME
BLACK'S 46TH MOVE

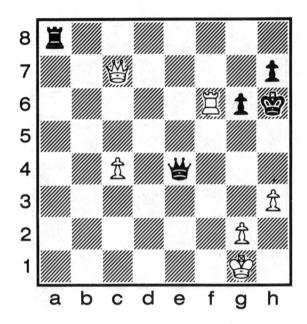

CLUE: What a blunder! How can a top grandmaster be provoked into playing a losing move like **Rf1xf6??**, throwing away an otherwise drawn position? Careful—it could happen to you!

SOLUTION: White was punished for his mistake by Fischer's **1 . . . Qd4+**, a Rook and King Fork. White conceded, for 2. Rf2 Ra1 + wins the Rook. And yet another grandmaster bites the dust! **(0-1)**

Bent Larsen vs Bobby Fischer

DENVER, 1971
CANDIDATES MATCH 2ND GAME
BLACK'S 37TH MOVE

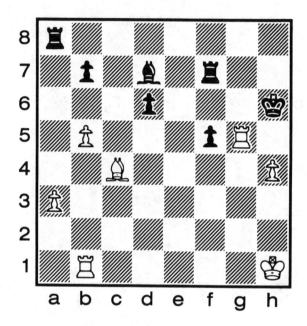

CLUE: White's threat: to capture the Rook at f7 with the Bishop. Is there a powerful countermove for Black's Rook in Fischer's bag of wizardry?

SOLUTION: Yes, there is: for the Rook at a8! Fischer took the offensive with **1 . . . Ra4!!**, when 2. Bxf7 Rxh4 + (shifting from one flank to the other) 3. Kg2 Kxg5 leaves Black a pawn ahead. Rather than accepting his state, Larsen compounded his problems with **2. Rc1?**, which dropped another pawn after **2 . . . Bxb5!**, for the pin along the 4th rank still exists. Fischer won the ensuing endgame with his usual immaculate technique. **(0-1)**

Bobby Fischer vs Jorge Rubinetti

BUENOS AIRES, 1970
WHITE'S 23RD MOVE

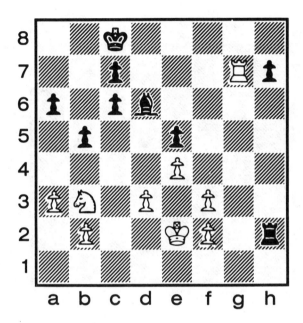

CLUE: It's a strange position. One Black pawn restrains four White ones. Can Fischer solve the mystery of this "Southern Cross" configuration?

SOLUTION: Since White's f-pawns are doubled anyway, he cleverly throws one away to free the others by **1. f4!**. After taking the pawn **1 ... exf4**, Black was in severe trouble: **2. d4 Kd8 3. Na5 c5 4. e5 Bf8** (4 ... Be7 loses a piece to 5. Nc6 +) **5. Nc6+ Ke8 6. Rxc7.** Rubinetti resigned. If he had continued 6 ... cxd4, White pushes 7. e6, threatening the unstoppable 8. Rc8. **(1-0)**

Tigran Petrosian vs Bobby Fischer

BUENOS AIRES, 1971
CANDIDATES MATCH 6TH GAME
BLACK'S 59TH MOVE

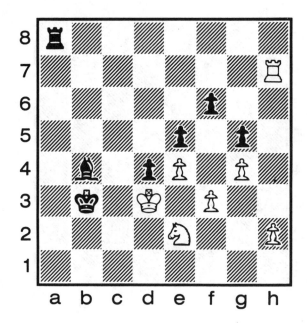

CLUE: A familiar story: Fischer has a Bishop against a Knight and a better-placed King. Throw in a menacing d-pawn and an aggressive Rook, and the White King is soon surrounded.

SOLUTION: Fischer's rapier-like **1 . . . Ra1!** threatens to envelop White's King (2 . . . Rd1 mate). With no recourse, White sacrificed his Knight **2. Nxd4+ exd4 3. Kxd4**, but after **3 . . . Rd1+** (so White's King can't meander to d5 and then e6) **4. Ke3 Bc5+ 5. Ke2 Rh1 6. h4** (on 6 . . . Rxh4 7. Rxh4 gxh4, White hopes to draw because Black's Bishop doesn't guard the h-pawn's Queening square h1) **6 . . . Kc4 7. h5 Rh2+ 8. Ke1 Kd3**, White resigned. If he had played 9. Kf1 (to avoid the back-rank mate) then 9 . . . Rf2+ eats more material. **(0-1)**

Bobby Fischer vs MIT's Greenblatt Computer Program

CAMBRIDGE, MASSACHUSETTS, 1978
WHITE'S 19TH MOVE

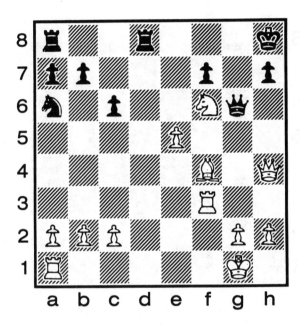

CLUE: When the chess community first heard about this stunt they questioned that it was really Fischer playing (since he hadn't publicly competed since 1972). But how could he resist the opportunity to ruthlessly pull the plug on an upstart robot?

SOLUTION: Fischer essayed the quietly powerful **1. Rc1!**. By guarding his c-pawn instead of moving it, White took away two important squares for Black's Queen to flee to along the c2-h7 diagonal. The computer never resigns, so after **1 . . . Kg7 2. Rg3 Rh8**, Fischer knocked its binary lights out with **3. Qh6** mate. Yes, 3. Bh6 is also mate. **(1-0)**

Bobby Fischer vs Tigran Petrosian

BUENOS AIRES, 1971
CANDIDATES MATCH 1ST GAME
WHITE'S 38TH MOVE

CLUE: If you're in a pawn race, better get off on the right foot. This race is not to the strong, but to the more centralized.

SOLUTION: Fischer stepped correctly with **1. Re4!**, so that 1 . . . Rxg2+ **2. Kh3** leaves two Black pieces attacked and clumsily placed. So Petrosian tried **1. . . Nxg2 2. Kg3** (note the Knight now has no safe move) **2 . . . Ra5 3. Ne5!** (a game-ending centralization). Since his pieces are unable to beat the h-pawn to the finish line, Black resigned. **(1-0)**

Bobby Fischer vs Milan Matulovic

HERCEG NOVI, YUGOSLAVIA, 1970
WORLD 5-MINUTE CHAMPIONSHIP
WHITE'S 31ST MOVE

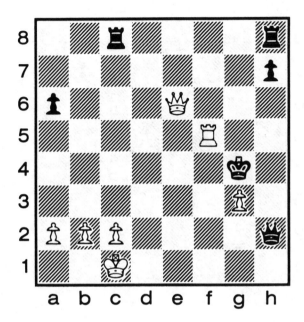

CLUE: Quick! This was a speed game, so answer the question fast. How can Fischer mate in three moves at most? Whew!

SOLUTION: Fischer expedited matters with **1. Rf4 + !**, and if 1 ... Kg5 (or 1 ... Kh5) then 2. Qg4 + Kh6 3. Rf6 mate. But Black found a more rapid way to lose, capturing the g-pawn with his King and allowing **2. Qg4 mate**. Not quite the Fool's Mate, but ... **(1-0)**

Bobby Fischer vs Eugenio German

STOCKHOLM, 1962
INTERZONAL TOURNAMENT
WHITE'S 26TH MOVE

CLUE: White's Kingside offensive has beaten Black's Queenside *Putsch* to the punch, but the knockout will require some fancy footwork.

SOLUTION: Fischer set up his one-two combination with **1. Bg5!**, threatening 2. Rxd8 and 3. fxg7 +, winning the Queen. Black tried to shield himself with **1 . . . Rd4**, but **2. fxg7 + Kxg7 3. Bf6 + Kg8** (3 . . . Bxf6 4. exf6 + uncovers a winning attack on Black's Queen) **4. Qh4** (threatening 5. Qg5 mate) **4 . . . Rxd1 + 5. Nxd1** (5. Rxd1?? permits the sucker punch 5 . . . Qxe5!, when 6. Bxe5 is met by 6 . . . Bxh4, regaining the Queen) and German resigned. If Black captures on f6 (5 . . . Bxf6), White threatens the Queen and mate with 6. exf6. **(1-0)**

Samuel Reshevsky vs Bobby Fischer

NEW YORK, 1963-64
U.S. CHAMPIONSHIP
BLACK'S 47TH MOVE

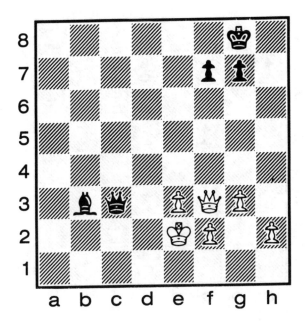

CLUE: White has two pawns against a Bishop, and he can give a few needling Queen checks, if he gets a free turn. That never happened.

SOLUTION: White expired after **1 . . . Qc4 +!**. It's mate after 2. Kd2 Qc2+ 3. Ke1 Qc1 + 4. Ke2 Qd1. **(0-1)**

Bobby Fischer vs William Hook

SIEGEN, 1970
19TH OLYMPIAD
WHITE'S 28TH MOVE

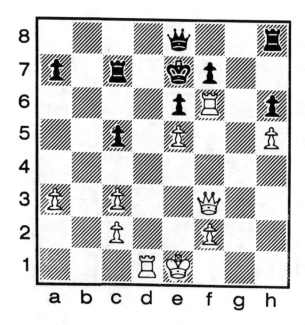

CLUE: White seems to have an inevitable mating attack, even against Black's well-defended pieces, if he can occupy a certain square.

SOLUTION: The clearing sacrifice **1. Rxe6 + !** threatens mate next move, in that either 1 . . . Kxe6 or 1 . . . fxe6 is answered by 2. Qf6 mate. 1 . . . Kf8 only leads to severe loss of material and certain loss of the game. **(1-0)**

Bobby Fischer vs Pal Benko

Bled, 1959
CANDIDATES TOURNAMENT
WHITE'S 39TH MOVE

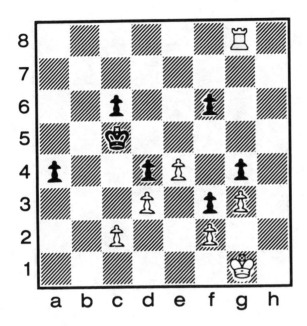

CLUE: White's a Rook ahead but Black's a-pawn may easily threaten to Queen, winning back the Rook. Fischer eviscerated it at once.

SOLUTION: The cutoff **1. Rb8!** stops the enemy King in its tracks. White now wins by moving his own King over to the Queenside. And if Black advances 1 . . . a3, then 2. Rb3 a2 3. Ra3 guts the a-pawn, so Benko resigned. **(1-0)**

Wolfgang Uhlmann vs Bobby Fischer

PALMA DE MALLORCA, 1970
INTERZONAL TOURNAMENT
BLACK'S 12TH MOVE

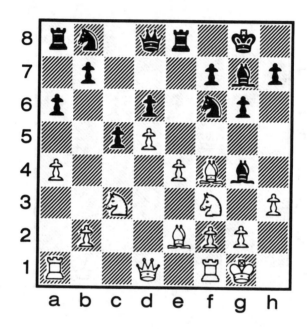

CLUE: Black's Bishop is attacked. Should he retreat it or capture the Knight on f3? Either one is hackneyed, right?

SOLUTION: Why reply in stereotypical fashion, capturing on f3 or retreating, when you can instead pilfer a pawn? Fischer played 1 . . . **Nxe4!**, plucking a hapless foot soldier. As the analysis shows: 2. hxg4 Bxc3 3. bxc3 Nxc3 4. Qd2 Nxe2+ 5. Kh1 Nxf4 6. Qxf4 leaves Black two pawns ahead, and 2. Nxe4 Rxe4 3. hxg4 Rxf4 leaves Black a pawn ahead. Fischer, a master at bypassing quotidian play in favor of unearthing a hidden resource, won in 34 moves. **(0-1)**

Bobby Fischer vs Pal Benko

BLED, 1959
CANDIDATES TOURNAMENT
WHITE'S 18TH MOVE

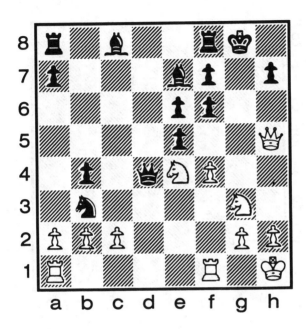

CLUE: Black's Knight has just captured White's Bishop (**Nxb3**). Standard principle suggests capturing toward the center (axb3) instead of away from the center (cxb3). So what else is new?

SOLUTION: If you followed the rule of thumb, you'd capture toward the center, that is, if you didn't have the stronger **1. Qh6!**, preparing 2. Nh5 and 3. Qg7 mate. Black answered **1 . . . exf4** (trying to clear the Queen's diagonal to g7), and the game went on: **2. Nh5 f5** (guarding against Qg7 mate) **3. Rad1** (still not taking on b3 so that he can gain a tempo by attacking the Queen) **3 . . . Qe5** (keeping sentinel over g7 and preparing to sacrifice itself on f6) **4. Nef6+ Bxf6 5. Nxf6+ Qxf6 6. Qxf6 Nc5 7. Qg5+ Kh8 8. Qe7! Ba6 9. Qxc5 Bxf1 10. Rxf1** and Black gave up. (1-0)

Bobby Fischer vs Wolfgang Unzicker

SIEGEN, 1970
19TH OLYMPIAD
WHITE'S 36TH MOVE

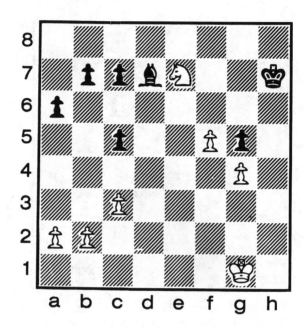

CLUE: White is practically a pawn ahead because of Black's doubled c-pawns. Though a Bishop is ordinarily a shade stronger than a Knight, White's steed can do some fancy prances to win and hold on to material.

SOLUTION: Fischer wins a pawn with **1. Nd5!**, zeroing in on the c-pawn and also threatening the fork 2. Nf6+. Play continued: **1 . . . Bc6 2. Nxc7 Bf3 3. Ne8!** (saving the g-pawn in that 3 . . . Bxg4 loses the Bishop to another fork, 4. Nf6+) **3 . . . Kh6 4. Nf6 Kg7 5. Kf2** (a useful in-between move bringing the King closer to the g-pawn) **5 . . . Bd1 6. Nd7 c4** (taking the g-pawn loses to 7. f6+ Kg8 8. f7+! Kxf7 9. Ne5+, winning the Bishop) **7. Kg3** and Black resigned. **(1-0)**

Victor Korchnoi vs Bobby Fischer

CURACAO, 1962
CANDIDATES TOURNAMENT
BLACK'S 32ND MOVE

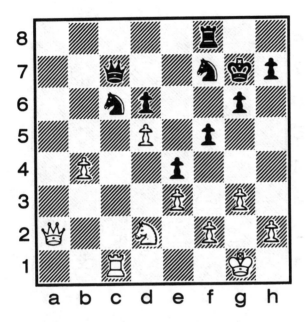

CLUE: White has one less piece than Black, but Black's Knight at c6 is pinned to its Queen by White's Rook at c1 and subject to capture next move. But what's pinned can be unpinned, as Fischer demonstrated.

SOLUTION: The salvation was **1 . . . Qa7!**, breaking the pin with a gain of time. White loses his Queen if he captures the Knight. And if he tries 2. Qb2 +, Black saves both the Knight and King with 2 . . . Nce5. Korchnoi elected to trade Queens but eventually resigned the futile ending on the 44th move. **(0-1)**

Manuel Aaron vs Bobby Fischer

STOCKHOLM, 1962
INTERZONAL TOURNAMENT
BLACK'S 29TH MOVE

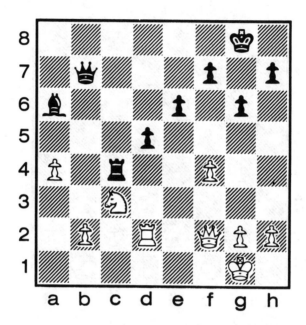

CLUE: White saw no access to his revered King. But Fischer delights in creating his own entree.

SOLUTION: Fischer's open-sesame was a simple capture **1 ... Rxc3!**. If White takes back, he unlocks the b-file and Black checks **2 ... Qb1 +**, leading to mate, the f1 square being attacked by Black's Bishop. White resigned. **(0-1)**

Bobby Fischer vs Ismet Ibrahimoglu

SIEGEN, 1970
19TH OLYMPIAD
WHITE'S 37TH MOVE

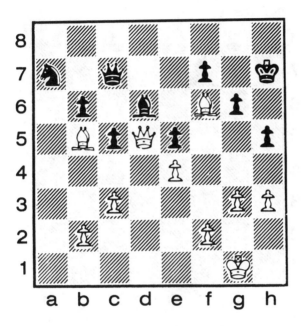

CLUE: White clearly has a spatial advantage, with two Bishops and a centralized Queen. Still, it's vague how to convert the intangible into the material.

SOLUTION: The powerful invasion **1. Be8!** immediately points out the strength of White's Bishop pair. Black had to answer **1 . . . Kg8**, defending the f-pawn, and White then exploited Black's overloaded pieces with **2. Bxf7+ Qxf7 3. Qxd6**. A pawn down, about to lose another, Black resigned. **(1-0)**

Bobby Fischer vs Eleazar Jimenez

HAVANA, 1966
17TH OLYMPIAD
WHITE'S 29TH MOVE

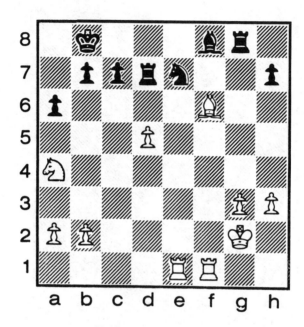

CLUE: White's 1. Nc5 move appears strong, but Black can play 1 . . . Rxd5. Make some room and you have Fischer's ploy.

SOLUTION: Eureka! The clearing sacrifice **1. d6!**, is just what the doctor ordered. After **1 . . . cxd6 2. Bxe7 Bxe7** (2 . . . Rxe7 loses to 3. Rxf8 + Rxf8 4. Rxe7) **3. Rf7**, Black resigned. Fischer must win material. If 3 . . . Re8, then 4. Nb6 Rc7 5. Nd5, taking advantage of the square made vacant by **1. d6!** (this push also drew away the protection for the square b6). **(1-0)**

Arinbjorn Gudmundsson vs Bobby Fischer

REYKJAVIK, ICELAND, 1960
BLACK'S 26TH MOVE

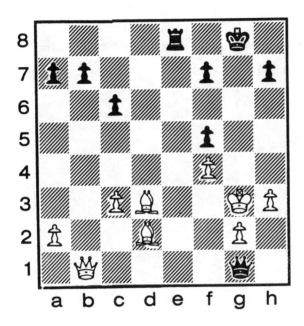

CLUE: White enjoys a slight material advantage (two Bishops against a Rook and pawn), but his King is highly susceptible to attack. Decision: Should Black exchange Queens or try to continue his offensive?

SOLUTION: The attack doesn't lead anywhere, whereas the Queen exchange **1 . . . Qxb1! 2. Bxb1** wins one of the two Bishops after **2 . . . Re2!**. White resigned, for 3. Bc1 allows the skewer 3 . . . Re1. **(0-1)**

Bobby Fischer vs Klaus Darga

WEST BERLIN, 1960
EXHIBITION GAME
WHITE'S 27TH MOVE

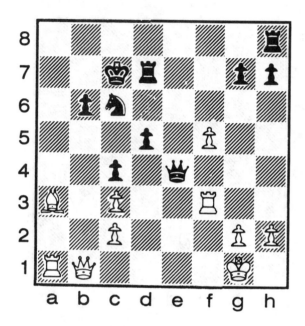

CLUE: White's warfare on the Queenside seems to have reached a standstill. With a Bishop powerfully posted at a3, what could be wrong?

SOLUTION: Nothing's wrong, but the Bishop posted at f4 would be more right. Fischer played **1. Bc1!** (he's not retreating, just advancing backward). The game continued: **1 . . . Qe1+ 2. Rf1 Qxc3 3. Bf4+ Kb7 4. Qb5!**, threatening the heart-stopping **5. Qa6**, a criss-cross mate (the controlled diagonals a6-c8 and b8-f4 cross). Black resigned, for neither 5 . . . Nb8 (6. Bxb8 threatening 7. Qxd7) nor 5 . . . Ra8 (6. Rxa8 Kxa8 7. Qxc6+) offers any real fight. **(1-0)**

Bobby Fischer vs Efim Geller

BLED, 1961
ALEKHINE MEMORIAL TOURNAMENT
WHITE'S 20TH MOVE

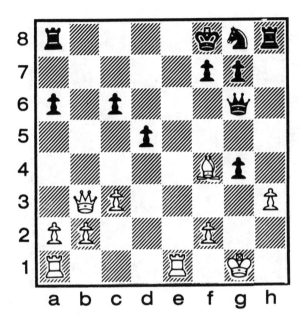

CLUE: This is a sharp position, with Black and White flailing away at each other's King. But it's White's turn, and he's ready for the execution.

SOLUTION: Fischer played the crunching **1. Qb7!**, directly threatening the Rook. Black can't answer 1 ... Re8 because of 2. Rxe8+ Kxe8 3. Re1+ winning Black's Queen or mating. The actual game went: **1 ... gxh3+** (a free pawn captured with discovered check) **2. Bg3 Rd8 3. Qb4+**, and Geller abdicated his King in light of 3 ... Ne7 4. Qxe7+ Kg8 5. Qxd8+. **(1-0)**

Bogdan Sliwa vs Bobby Fischer

WARSAW, 1962
USA VS POLAND MATCH
BLACK'S 34TH MOVE

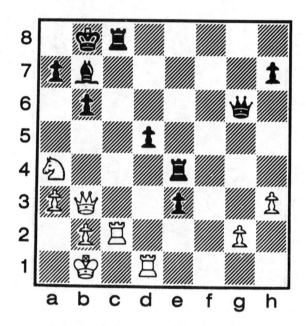

CLUE: White's pieces are prettily lined up along the a4-d1 diagonal—an ornamental, if inexorable, way to go.

SOLUTION: The lovely composition falls apart at the b1-g6 diagonal, which enables Fischer to win a piece by **1 . . . Rxc2!**. If White recaptures 2. Kxc2, Black discovers mate (2 . . . Rc4) thanks to the double check. And if White takes back 2. Qxc2, Black wins the Knight by 2 . . . Rxa4, when White's pinned Queen can't move off the b1-g6 line to capture Bobby's Rook. **(0-1)**

Georg Tringov vs Bobby Fischer

HAVANA—NEW YORK (BY TELETYPE), 1965
CAPABLANCA MEMORIAL TOURNAMENT
BLACK'S 20TH MOVE

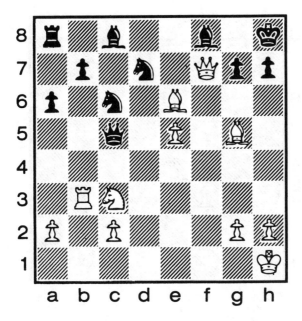

CLUE: White could mate next move at g8. Black's got to stop the mate and hold on to his extra material.

SOLUTION: Fischer consolidated the position with **1 . . . Nf6!**, guarding g8. Now 2. exf6 is met by 2 . . . Bxe6 3. Qxe6 (or 3. fxg7 + Bxg7 4. Qxe6, continuing as in the given variation) 3 . . . Qxg5, with Black keeping his additional piece and breaking White's attack. The game actually concluded: **2. Bxc8 Nxe5! 3. Qe6 Neg4!**, and White resigned in view of the threats to capture on c8 and to deliver mate by 4 . . . Nf2 + 5. Kg1 Nh3 + + 6. Kh1 Qg1 mate. **(0-1)**

Bobby Fischer vs Paul Keres

CURACAO, 1962
CANDIDATES TOURNAMENT
WHITE'S 27TH MOVE

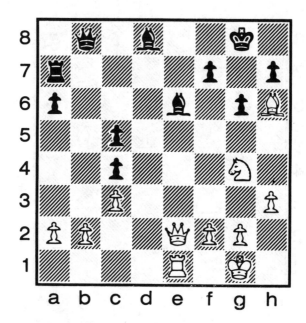

CLUE: White's pieces are the aggressors, though to no material gain yet. But Black is hard-pressed to defend weak pawns on the Queenside and weak squares on the Kingside, and his back row is shaky. Something's got to give.

SOLUTION: The crisp **1. Qxc4!** wins a pawn and Black can't take the Queen because of the mate along the back rank (1 . . . Bxc4 2. Re8 mate). Nor can Black go in for 1 . . . Qxb2 2. Rxe6! fxe6 3. Qxe6+, when 3 . . . Rf7 4. Qe8+ Rf8 5. Qxf8 is mate. Keres continued **1 . . . Qd6** and lost in 41 moves. **(1-0)**

Bobby Fischer vs Bent Larsen

PORTOROZ, YUGOSLAVIA, 1958
INTERZONAL TOURNAMENT
WHITE'S 22ND MOVE

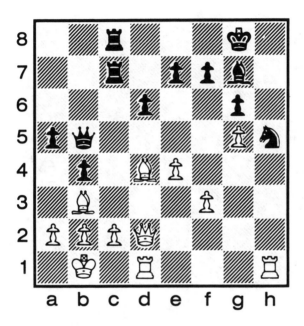

CLUE: White's Bishops, peering onto Black's Kingside, signal the end. Open the lines and mate.

SOLUTION: Fischer's final attack began with **1. Rxh5!**. After **1 . . . gxh5 2. g6** (sniping at the pinned f-pawn) **2 . . . e5 3. gxf7+ Kf8 4. Be3 d5 5. exd5** (5. Bxd5 weakens the c-pawn) **5 . . . Rxf7 6. d6** (attacking the Rook at f7) **6 . . . Rf6 7. Bg5 Qb7** (if 7 . . . Rg6, then 8. Be7+ Ke8 9. d7+ is crushing) **8. Bxf6 Bxf6 9. d7 Rd8 10. Qd6+**, Black resigned. If 10 . . . Be7, then 11. Qh6 is mate. And if 10 . . . Kg7, then 11. Rg1+ wins the Bishop at f6. **(1-0)**

Bobby Fischer vs Lhamsuren Miagmasuren

SOUSSE, TUNISIA, 1967
INTERZONAL TOURNAMENT
WHITE'S 29TH MOVE

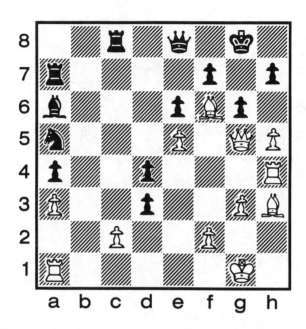

CLUE: White obviously has a powerful Kingside attack, but Black may be able to hold the position (1. Qh6, for example, is answered by 1 . . . Qf8, offering to trade Queens, dissipating White's assault). Fischer played a move so subtle that Black gave it little attention.

SOLUTION: Bobby repositioned his light-square Bishop by the devilishly obscure **1. Bg2!!**. Black should now have played 1 . . . Bb7, neutralizing White's King's Bishop, but he missed the point. Instead he continued **1 . . . dxc2** and lost after **2. Qh6 Qf8 3. Qxh7 + !**. Black resigned, for 3 . . . Kxh7 4. hxg6 + + Kxg6 5. Be4 is mate. The point of **1. Bg2!!**: to be able to check from e4, mating Black in the above variation.
(1-0)

Bobby Fischer vs Svetozar Gligoric

BLED, 1959
CANDIDATES TOURNAMENT
WHITE'S 26TH MOVE

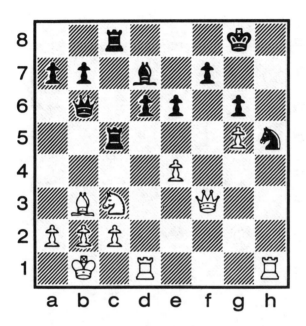

CLUE: Black seems to have his defenses in order, but a startling line-opener discombobulates any presumption of security.

SOLUTION: A familiar Fischer sacrifice **1. Rxh5!**, is the decisive breakthrough. In *My 60 Memorable Games,* Fischer says, "I've made this sacrifice so often, I feel like applying for a patent." The game continued: **1 . . . gxh5 2. Qxh5 Be8 3. Qh6!** (making sure the King can't run away) **3 . . . Rxc3** (hoping to create counterplay against White's King) **4. bxc3 Rxc3 5. g6!** (inflicting further weaknesses) **5 . . . fxg6 6. Rh1 Qd4 7. Qh7+** and Black resigns (7 . . . Kf8 8. Rf1+ forces mate). **(1-0)**

Bobby Fischer vs Mark Taimanov

VANCOUVER, 1971
CANDIDATES MATCH 4TH GAME
WHITE'S 62ND MOVE

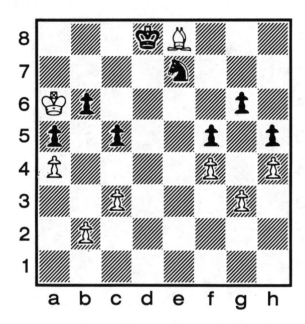

CLUE: If White moves his Bishop along the a4-e8 diagonal or plays it to f7, Black will have the time to defend his b-pawn. But why be mundane when you can rise to empyreal heights?

SOLUTION: Fischer boldly sacrificed his Bishop to get a mass of connected, dangerously advancing pawns **1. Bxg6!**. After 1 **. . . Nxg6 2. Kxb6 Kd7 3. Kxc5 Ne7 4. b4** (here they come!) **4 . . . axb4 5. cxb4 Nc8 6. a5 Nd6 7. b5 Ne4+ 8. Kb6 Kc8 9. Kc6 Kb8 10. b6**, Black resigned, for neither his King nor his Knight can contend with the parading pawns. **(1-0)**

Samuel Reshevsky vs Bobby Fischer

PALMA DE MALLORCA, 1970
INTERZONAL TOURNAMENT
BLACK'S 30TH MOVE

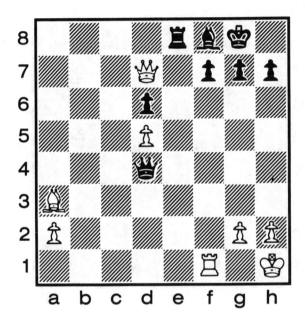

CLUE: White is intimidating Black's d-pawn, Rook, and King (particularly the f7 square). A single move by Black disposes of all three threats and compels White's resignation!

SOLUTION: Fischer dimmed White's hopes with **1 . . . Qf2!**, threatening 2 . . . Qxf1 mate. White gave up because 2. Rxf2 loses immediately to 2 . . . Re1 +, and there is no way to defend the Rook adequately. If 2. Qb5, for example, then 2 . . . Re1 wins. And if instead 2. Rg1, Black plays 2 . . . Re1 and the case is closed. **(0-1)**

Miguel Cuellar vs Bobby Fischer

SOUSSE, 1967
INTERZONAL TOURNAMENT
BLACK'S 30TH MOVE

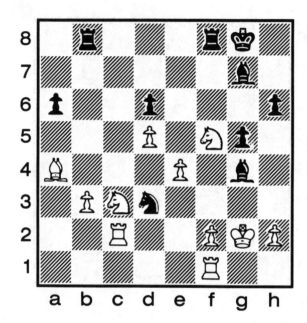

CLUE: White's got one more pawn than Black, but Fischer's got the attack and the neatest, simplest combination that anyone could imagine.

SOLUTION: The jump **1 . . . Nf4 + !** wins. If 2. Kh1, then 2 . . . Bf3 + 3. Kg1 Nh3 mate. If 2. Kg1 instead, then 2 . . . Bxf5 3. exf5 Bxc3, and White can't recapture because of 4 . . . Ne2 +, winning the Rook. The game therefore continued: **2. Kg3 Bxf5 3. exf5 Bxc3**, and as before, recapturing on c3 loses a Rook to Ne2 +. A piece ahead, Fischer had no trouble winning the ending. **(0-1)**

Edmar Mednis vs Bobby Fischer

NEW YORK, 1958-59
U.S. CHAMPIONSHIP
BLACK'S 37TH MOVE

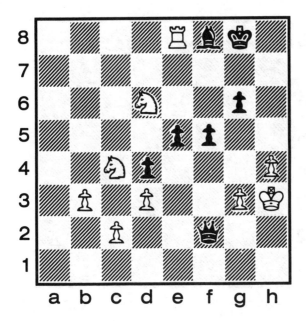

CLUE: In a materially imbalanced situation, Fischer relies on the single most powerful piece on the board.

SOLUTION: Fischer forced resignation with **1 . . . Qg1!**, threatening 2 . . . Qh1 mate. If White tries 2. g4, hoping to give his King breathing room, Black mates anyway with 2 . . . fxg4 mate. **(0-1)**

Ben Greenwald vs Bobby Fischer

POUGHKEEPSIE, 1963
NEW YORK STATE OPEN
BLACK'S 23RD MOVE

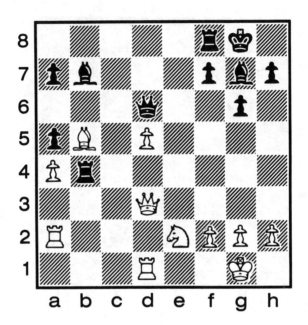

CLUE: It seems like an even game, with Fischer's two Bishops facing off against a Bishop and Knight. When nobody's going anywhere, it helps to get rid of wood.

SOLUTION: The reductive move was **1 . . . Qxd5!**. After White temporarily won a piece **2. Qxd5 Bxd5 3. Rxd5**, Black regained equality with **3 . . . Rb1 + 4. Nc1 Rxc1 + 5. Bf1 Re8** (threatening 6 . . . Re-e1) **6. f4 Re-e1 7. Rf2**. The final point was **7 . . . Bf8!**, for to cope with the impending 8 . . . Bc5, White would have had to surrender at least a Rook for a Bishop. **(0-1)**

Bobby Fischer vs Efim Geller

CURACAO, 1962
CANDIDATES TOURNAMENT
WHITE'S 43RD MOVE

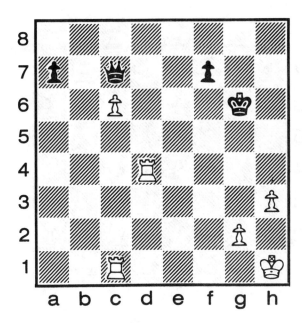

CLUE: Yet another chapter in the continuing saga of two Rooks versus a Queen. Here the Rooks are hungrier, supporting a mouth-watering c-pawn and leaning toward winning more material. How did Fischer consummate his play?

SOLUTION: The best move is **1. Ra4 !**, threatening the simple capture 2. Rxa7, when 2 . . . Qxa7 allows 3. c7 and 4. c8, making a new Queen. Nor does 1 . . . a5 save the pawn because of 2. Rxa5 anyhow. If Black then recaptures, White's c-pawn again Queens. Geller resigned. **(1-0)**

Jimmy Thomason vs Bobby Fischer

LINCOLN, NEBRASKA, 1955
U.S. JUNIOR CHAMPIONSHIP
BLACK'S 21ST MOVE

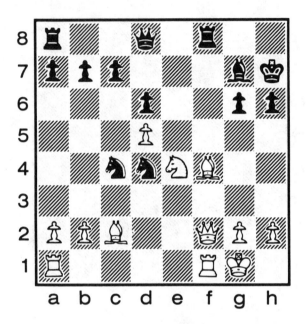

CLUE: White's f4-Bishop is pinned, but attacking it with the g-pawn runs into a discovered check (Nxg5). The answer's so simple even a twelve-year-old can see it.

SOLUTION: It helps if the twelve-year-old is Bobby Fischer. The direct **1 . . . Rxf4! 2. Qxf4 Ne2+ 3. Kh1 Nxf4** convinced White to resign. **(0-1)**

Raul Sanguinetti vs Bobby Fischer

PORTOROZ, 1958
INTERZONAL TOURNAMENT
BLACK'S 21ST MOVE

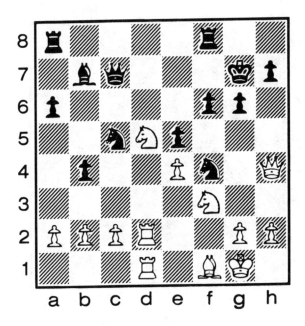

CLUE: It looks rather promising for White: doubled Rooks on the d-file, a menacing Knight at d5, and Kingside attacking chances. Too bad his Rooks have feet of clay.

SOLUTION: The direct 1 . . . **Bxd5! 2. exd5 Ne4** plunders at least a Rook for a Knight, for the Rook at d2 can't move to a safe square. Fischer later converted this material gain into victory. **(0-1)**

Lajos Portisch vs Bobby Fischer

SANTA MONICA, CALIFORNIA, 1966
PIATIGORSKY CUP TOURNAMENT
BLACK'S 28TH MOVE

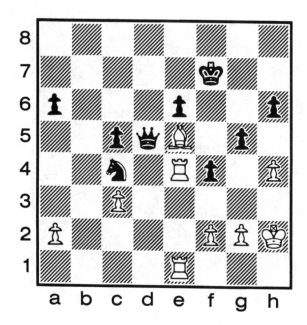

CLUE: Here comes another asymmetrical position: Fischer's Queen and Knight versus his opponent's two Rooks and Bishop. How does Bobby blitz the enemy forces?

SOLUTION: Fischer won the exchange (a Rook for a Knight) by **1 . . . Ne3!**. This cut the communication between the two Rooks. After **2. R1xe3 fxe3 3. Rxe3 Qxa2**, Fischer won in a few moves. **(0-1)**

Bobby Fischer vs Herman Pilnik

SANTIAGO, 1959
WHITE'S 33RD MOVE

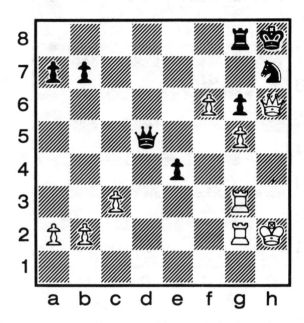

CLUE: Fischer could try to go about this steadfastly, but rather than deal with Black's defensive annoyances, he goes for broke.

SOLUTION: It's a blistering mate in two moves starting with **1. Qxh7 + !**. If 1 . . . Kxh7 then 2. Rh3 is mate. **(1-0)**

Ya'akov Bernstein vs Bobby Fischer

NETANYA, ISRAEL, 1968
BLACK'S 25TH MOVE

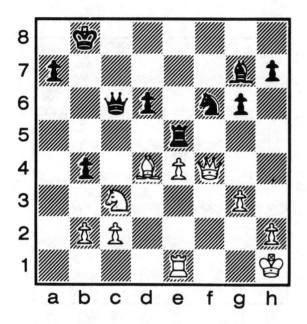

CLUE: A couple of pieces are hanging for both sides. The right move can save Black's and win White's.

SOLUTION: Fischer wins material with **1 . . . Rf5!**, when White's e-pawn is pinned to its King by Black's Queen and therefore can't capture the Rook at f5. White resigned, for after saving his attacked Queen, Black can safely capture White's Knight on c3. **(0-1)**

Izhak Aloni vs Bobby Fischer

VINKOVCI, YUGOSLAVIA, 1968
BLACK'S 44TH MOVE

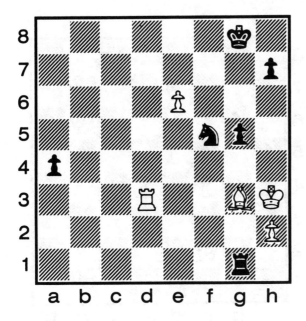

CLUE: White has a Bishop scrimmaging with a Knight and a far-advanced pawn. He also has his King off to the side of the board, about to fall off the edge.

SOLUTION: Black did White in with **1 . . . h5!**, threatening 2 . . . g4 mate. Against this there is no satisfactory defense. **(0-1)**

Boris Spassky vs Bobby Fischer

REYKJAVIK, 1972
WORLD CHESS CHAMPIONSHIP, 5TH MATCH GAME
BLACK'S 27TH MOVE

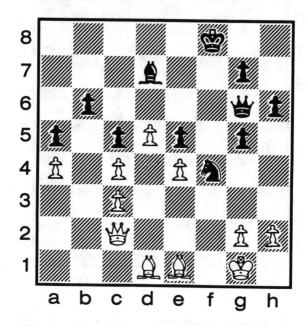

CLUE: They say Fischer played this move in a split second and that Spassky was jolted out of his seat!

SOLUTION: Spassky resigned after **1 . . . Bxa4!**, a punishing capture that can't be accepted. If 2. Qxa4, then 2 . . . Qxe4 threatens mate at both e1 and g2. After 2 . . . Qxe4 in this line, White could try 3. Kf2, but that loses to 3 . . . Nd3+ 4. Kg3 Qh4+ 5. Kf3 Qf4+ 6. Ke2 Nc1 mate! **(0-1)**

Bobby Fischer vs Oscar Panno

BUENOS AIRES, 1970
WHITE'S 28TH MOVE

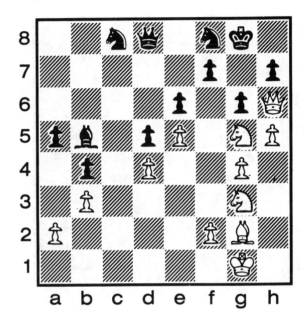

CLUE: White has an extremely aggressive position, but he still needs more ammo before this can be declared over.

SOLUTION: Fischer's remarkable salvo was **1. Be4!!**, transferring the Bishop immediately to a critical diagonal. At e4 the Bishop is immune from capture because 1 . . . dxe4 permits 2. N3xe4, menacing 3. Nf6+ and subsequent mate. Black tried the following defense: **1 . . . Qe7 2. Nxh7** (threatening 3. Nf6+) **2 . . . Nxh7 3. hxg6 fxg6 4. Bxg6 Ng5 5. Nh5** (again threatening Nf6+) **5 . . . Nf3+ 6. Kg2 Nh4+ 7. Kg3 Nxg6 8. Nf6+!** (Black's Knight at g6 can't trot away) **8 . . . Kf7 9. Qh7+** and mate next move (on 9 . . . Kf8 White mates by 10. Qg8). **(1-0)**

Robert Byrne vs Bobby Fischer

NEW YORK, 1963-64
U.S. CHAMPIONSHIP
BLACK'S 21ST MOVE

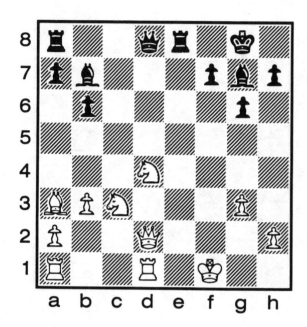

CLUE: What position could be more futile than this? Fischer is a piece behind and grandmasters in the analysis room are claiming he should resign. Outrageously, he didn't.

SOLUTION: Fischer played the incredibly quiet **1 . . . Qd7!**, so quiet that top players were still saying Fischer should give it up. To his credit, it was Byrne who resigned instead! Just look: if White tries 2. Qf2, for example, then Fischer would have crowned the brilliancy with 2 . . . Qh3+ 3. Kg1 Re1+!! (deflecting the Rook at d1) 4. Rxe1 Bxd4, and Black is going to mate at g2 no matter how White plays. **(0-1)**

Bobby Fischer vs Reuben Shocron

MAR DEL PLATA, ARGENTINA, 1959
WHITE'S 40TH MOVE

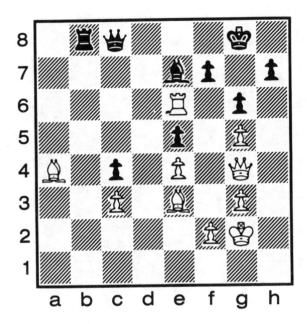

CLUE: Black's Queen pins White's Rook to its Queen, and the rook has no safe move—for now. Fischer concludes the game astonishingly.

SOLUTION: Fischer winds up a piece ahead after the stupefying **1. Bd7!**. If he doesn't take the Bishop and moves his Queen away, then White in turn can move his Rook to safety. And if Black takes at d7, then 2. Rxg6 + discovers an attack on Black's Queen. Shocron capitulated. **(1-0)**

Bobby Fischer vs Pal Benko

NEW YORK, 1965-66
U.S. CHAMPIONSHIP
WHITE'S 37TH MOVE

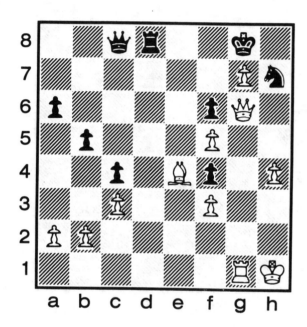

CLUE: White seems to be doing quite well, but how can he force an immediate outcome?

SOLUTION: By disrupting the defense. Benko resigned after the demolishing **1. Qe8 + !**. He realized that 1 . . . Rxe8 (moving off the d-file) allows 2. Bd5 +, after which Black would have to lose his Queen and Rook to temporarily halt the mating attack. **(1-0)**

Bobby Fischer vs Pal Benko

NEW YORK, 1963-64
U.S. CHAMPIONSHIP
WHITE'S 19TH MOVE

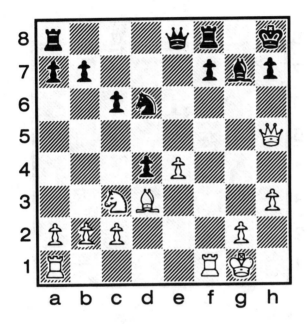

CLUE: White wants to play 1. e5, threatening 2. Qxh7 mate, but Black could defend on the brink with 1 . . . f5. Black must be so prevented.

SOLUTION: To dam up Black's f-pawn, Fischer gave away his Rook **1. Rf6!!**, an ingenious obstruction sacrifice. Black tried to flee with his King by **1 . . . Kg8** (seeing that 1 . . . Bxf6 loses to 2. e5 and 3. Qxh7 mate), but after **2. e5 h6 3. Ne2!** (taking the time-out to save his Knight) Black's position is as holey as Swiss cheese. If 3 . . . Nb5 (to counter 4. Rxd6), White wins with 4. Qf5, threatening mate at h7. And if 3 . . . Bxf6, then 4. Qxh6 leads to mate. Benko therefore resigned after 3. Ne2. **(1-0)**

Miguel Cuellar vs Bobby Fischer

STOCKHOLM, 1962
INTERZONAL TOURNAMENT
BLACK'S 36TH MOVE

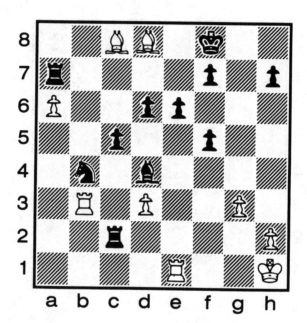

CLUE: If White had a couple of free moves and played Bb7 and Bb6, he'd trap Black's Rook at a7. He never got the chance.

SOLUTION: Fischer skewered the Bishops with **1 . . . Ra8!**, winning a piece. Inertia may explain White's playing another move **2. Bb6**, but he resigned after **2 . . . Rxc8**. (0-1)

Bobby Fischer vs Victor Ciocaltea

VARNA, 1962
15TH OLYMPIAD
WHITE'S 15TH MOVE

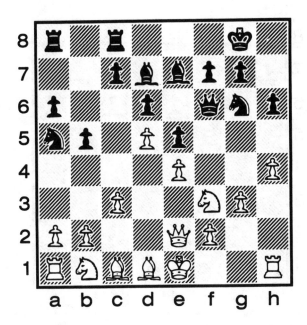

CLUE: It's late in the opening and nothing's been traded. In fact, the position is so log-jammed, it's hard to find any productive move, though not for Fischer.

SOLUTION: Bobby didn't miss that **1. Bg5!** actually traps the Queen. Even though Black can take the Bishop with his h-pawn 1 . . . hxg5, White's recapture 2. hxg5 gives an unanswerable pawn attack. Perhaps in shock, Ciocaltea played on a bit and then gave up. **(1-0)**

Laszlo Szabo vs Bobby Fischer

LEIPZIG, 1960
14TH OLYMPIAD
BLACK'S 21ST MOVE

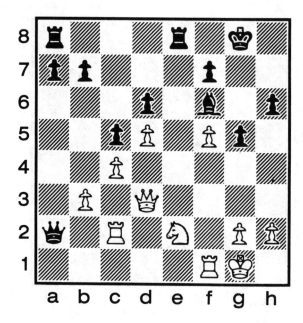

CLUE: Normally, an attack on a Queen from a Rook is sufficient to drive the stronger piece away. But Black here has an unimagined table-turner that leaves White helpless.

SOLUTION: The pulverizing intrusion **1 . . . Re3!** gives Fischer the upper hand. After **2. Qxe3** (2. Rxa2 Rxd3 saddles White with a difficult game) **2 . . . Qxc2 3. Kh1 a5 4. h4 a4**, Szabo resigned. As Fischer describes it, White's pawns now fall "like ripe apples." **(0-1)**

Wolfgang Unzicker vs Bobby Fischer

VARNA, 1962
15TH OLYMPIAD
BLACK'S 26TH MOVE

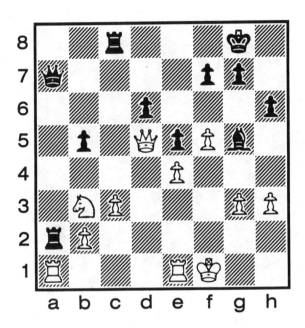

CLUE: White's King is exposed at f1, but still eludes attack. Black's Queen bears down along the a7-g1 diagonal and his Bishop is also strategically posted, but where's the support?

SOLUTION: From the Rooks: **1 . . . Rxc3!**, and if 2. bxc3, Black mates by 2 . . . Qf2, now that the 2nd rank has been ripped open. Meanwhile, 2. Rxa2 permits 2 . . . Rf3 +, with devastating consequences. For example, 3. Ke2 Rf2 + 4. Kd3 Qxa2, 5. Ra1 Qxb2 and White's future looks bleak; or 3. Kg2 Qf2 + 4. Kh1 Rxg3, with mate to follow. **(0-1)**

Bobby Fischer vs Mark Taimanov

VANCOUVER, 1971
CANDIDATES MATCH 2ND GAME
WHITE'S 85TH MOVE

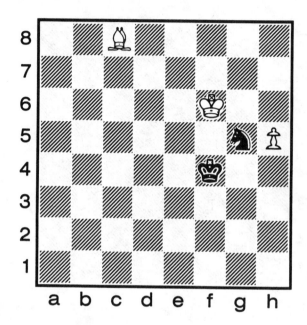

CLUE: Black hopes to sacrifice his Knight for White's pawn, leaving Fischer without enough mating force (a mere Bishop and King can't ever do it). The Knight could also give some pesky checks, if Fischer isn't careful.

SOLUTION: Fischer left Taimanov without a useful move with **1. Bf5!**, stopping potential checks at e4 and h7. Black went through the motions until his game stood still after **1 . . . Nf3** (the only plausible move he has) **2. h6 Ng5** (preparing to surrender the Knight if the pawn advances) **3. Kg6 Nf3** (again there is no other suitable move) **4. h7 Ne5+** (4 . . . Nh4+ doesn't help stop the pawn either) **5. Kf6**. Finding no way to prevent the pawn from Queening, Black resigned. **(1-0)**

Bobby Fischer vs Byela Soos

SKOPJE, YUGOSLAVIA, 1967
WHITE'S 39TH MOVE

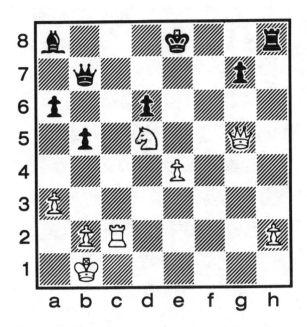

CLUE: White has several winning tries here, but only one of them forces instant mate.

SOLUTION: 1. Rc8 + !. If Black answers 1 . . . Qxc8, then 2. Qe7 is mate. Or if he plays 1 . . . Kd7 instead, then mate is 2. Qf5. And if the King runs in the other direction with 1 . . . Kf7, then 2. Qf5 still mates. **(1-0)**

Bobby Fischer vs Svetozar Gligoric

ROVINJ/ZAGREB, 1970
WHITE'S 35TH MOVE

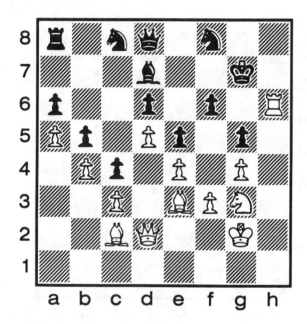

CLUE: White's Rook, in the heart of Black's camp, doesn't need to retreat just because it's attacked. This is the key to undermining the linchpin.

SOLUTION: Fischer played **1. Rxf6!**, and his opponent re-signed. If Black captures the Rook with his King, 1 . . . Kxf6, then 2. Bxg5+ skewers the opposing Queen. And if he takes on f6 with his Queen 1 . . . Qxf6, then 2. Nh5+ forks the enemy King and Queen. Of course, if Black doesn't capture the Rook, it's apparent that 2. Bxg5 is crushing. **(1-0)**

Bobby Fischer vs Alberic O'Kelly

BUENOS AIRES, 1970
WHITE'S 35TH MOVE

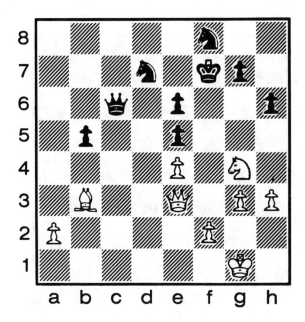

CLUE: Isolated doubled e-pawns can be strong (when they guard key central squares) or weak (when they fall victim to enemy piece attacks). Black seems to have everything defended until suddenly . . .

SOLUTION: White wins a pawn with **1. Nxe5 + ! Nxe5 2. Qf4 +**, forking Black's King and Knight at e5. **(1-0)**

Tigran Petrosian vs Bobby Fischer

BELGRADE, 1970
USSR VS THE REST-OF-THE-WORLD MATCH
BLACK'S 66TH MOVE

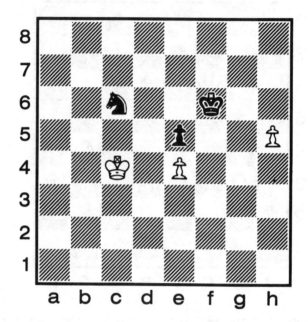

CLUE: Black can go for White's h-pawn with his King (1 . . . Kg5), but only at the cost of his e-pawn (2. Kd5, forcing the Knight to abandon its support). Sometimes the best offense is a solid defense.

SOLUTION: The send-off came with **1 . . . Nd4!**, anticipating 2. Kd5, which now is squashed by 2 . . . Nf3, defending the e-pawn from a secure haven. Fischer then collects the h-pawn with his King and heads back to team up with the Knight to win White's remaining pawn. **(0-1)**

Rene Letelier vs Bobby Fischer

LEIPZIG, 1960
14TH OLYMPIAD
BLACK'S 23RD MOVE

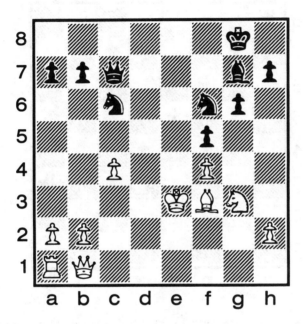

CLUE: White's King is airy but can get back to safety if given the time. That's not Fischer's way.

SOLUTION: The enemy King is immediately hounded by **1 . . . Qxf4 + !!**, an outrageously meteoric Queen sacrifice that can't be accepted (2. Kxf4) because of 2 . . . Bh6 mate. In the teeth of this furious onslaught (2. Kf2 Ng4+ 3. Kg2 Ne3+ 4. Kf2 Nd4), White resigned. **(0-1)**

Dr. Emil Nikolic vs Bobby Fischer

VINKOVCI, 1968
BLACK'S 31ST MOVE

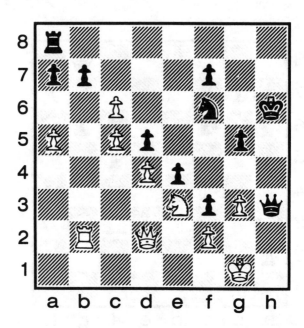

CLUE: Fischer mates at g2 with his Queen if White's Knight didn't command e3. He also mates at h1 if his Rook can occupy the h-file. And if he can guard h2 with another piece, his Queen mates by checking at h2 and then h1. One Black piece hinders these possibilities.

SOLUTION: The King! Thus **1 . . . Kg6!** actualizes all of Black's mating threats. One idea White now must stop—and can't— is 2 . . . Ng4, supporting the Queen's entry at h2, when 3. Nxg4 is prohibited because of 3 . . . Qg2 mate. Nikolic resigned. **(0-1)**

Bobby Fischer vs Dragojub Minic

VINKOVCI, 1968
WHITE'S 20TH MOVE

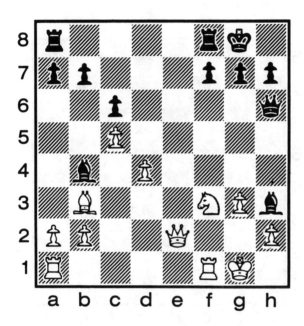

CLUE: White has latent pressure against the f7 square, but now his Rook at f1 is attacked by the Bishop at h3. Should he salvage the Rook?

SOLUTION: Sacrificing the Rook for the Bishop at h3 makes unarguable sense. A deadly massing of White's forces occurs after **1. Ne5!!**, allowing **1 . . . Bxf1 2. Rxf1**, with a robust attack, especially against f7. Then Black tried **2 . . . Bd2** (to trade Queens by 3 . . . Qe3 +), but gave up after **3. Rf3 Ra-d8 4. Nxf7 Rxf7 5. Qe7!** (threatening 6. Qxf7 + as well as 6. Qxd8 +). **(1-0)**

Bobby Fischer vs Boris Spassky

REYKJAVIK, 1972
WORLD CHESS CHAMPIONSHIP MATCH 6TH GAME
WHITE'S 38TH MOVE

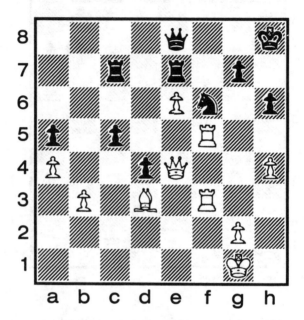

CLUE: Piece for piece, Fischer has a mobility advantage across the board. Black is also very weak on the light squares and White's e-pawn is a real menace to Black's community. The problem is getting through the clutter.

SOLUTION: Fischer elbowed through the maze with **1. Rxf6!**. After **1 . . . gxf6 2. Rxf6 Kg8 3. Bc4** (immobilizing the Rook at e7 because of the lurking discovery), **Kh8 4. Qf4**, Black resigned a hopeless position. **(1-0)**

Teodor Ghitescu vs Bobby Fischer

LEIPZIG, 1960
14TH OLYMPIAD
BLACK'S 14TH MOVE

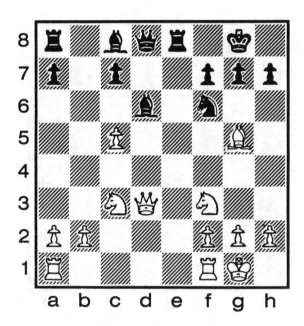

CLUE: White has just played an incredibly bad move, **1. d4xc5**, perhaps thinking it led to an exchange of Queens. Of course, blunders can lead to discoveries (as with Christopher Columbus and America).

SOLUTION: Instead of exchanging Queens, Black wins White's by **1 . . . Bxh2 + !** and 2 . . . Qxd3. A chagrined Ghitescu resigned. **(0-1)**

William Lombardy vs Bobby Fischer

NEW YORK, 1960-61
U.S. CHAMPIONSHIP
BLACK'S 30TH MOVE

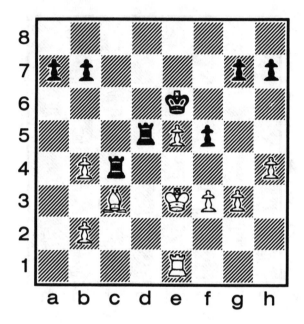

CLUE: Black is an exchange ahead (he has a Rook against a Bishop) but White has a protectable passed pawn. Not for long.

SOLUTION: Simplification is the key. After **1 . . . Rxc3 + !** (removing the e-pawn's guard) **2. bxc3 Rxe5+ 3. Kd2 Rxe1 4. Kxe1,** Fischer won the King-and-pawn ending. **(0-1)**

Bobby Fischer vs Moises Stekel

SANTIAGO, 1959
WHITE'S 35TH MOVE

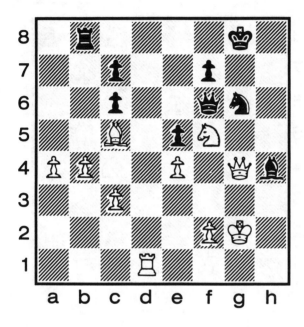

CLUE: Black flails away at defending a particular square, but it's all illusion.

SOLUTION: The telling move is **1. Be7!**, thieving a Bishop in broad daylight. Since Black's Knight is pinned and unable to guard e7, Black resigned. **(1-0)**

Bobby Fischer vs Jacek Bednarsky

HAVANA, 1966
17TH OLYMPIAD
WHITE'S 21ST MOVE

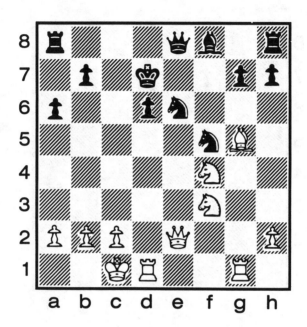

CLUE: Black's King is exposed and his pieces scattered. It's too much to hope that White doesn't have an outrageously crushing move.

SOLUTION: Like a bolt of lightning, the razing fork **1. Qe4!** attacks both Black's b-pawn and Knight at f5. After defending the Knight by **1 . . . g6**, Fischer expropriated his booty with **2. Nxe6.** Since if Qxe6 3. Qxb7 +, Black took note and resigned. **(1-0)**

Bent Larsen vs Bobby Fischer

DENVER, 1971
CANDIDATES MATCH 4TH GAME
BLACK'S 31ST MOVE

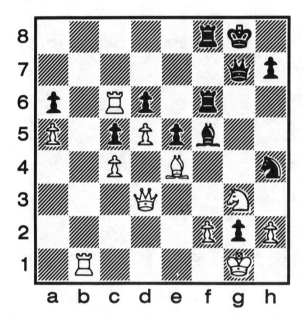

CLUE: They're fighting on two fronts, with White swarming the Queenside and Black storming the Kingside. Who's ahead doesn't matter, for an unexpected yet simple maneuver clinches matters.

SOLUTION: The elementary exchange **1 . . . Bxe4!** does the job. Since White's 2. Nxe4 loses his Queen after 2 . . . Nf3 + 3. Qxf3 Rxf3, he continued **2. Qxe4,** allowing **2 . . . Nf3 + 3. Kxg2 Nd2,** which forked Larsen's Queen and Rook. With White's f-pawn also threatened, it was time to surrender. **(0-1)**

Bobby Fischer vs Samuel Schweber

BUENOS AIRES, 1970
WHITE'S 23RD MOVE

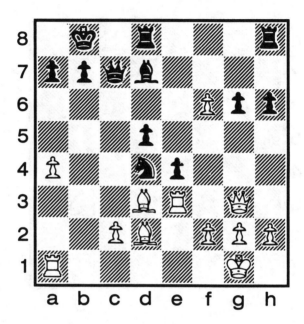

CLUE: This is a peculiar position. If White moves his attacked Bishop at d3, Black could opt to take the c-pawn with his Knight, forking the two Rooks. But White has a profound surprise in store for his wily opponent.

SOLUTION: Fischer struck with **1. Rxe4!!**, when 1 . . . dxe4 is answered by the pinning **2. Bf4**. Even so, Black thought he could first exchange Queens and then take the Rook. But after **1 . . . Qxg3**, Bobby blew his mind again with **2. Rxd4!!**, and Black's Queen amazingly has no exit! For example, if 2 . . . Qc7, then 3. Bf4 pins and regains the Queen. The game continued: **2 . . . Qg4 3. Rxg4 Bxg4 3. Bxg6**, and White's aggressive pieces and dangerous pawn soon led to recapturing the exchange. White won. **(1-0)**

Arthur Bisguier vs Bobby Fischer

NEW YORK, 1966-67
U.S. CHAMPIONSHIP
BLACK'S 69TH MOVE

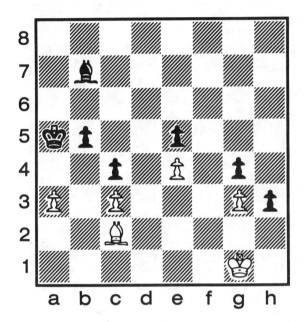

CLUE: White has everything secured, and Black's King is kept out of the game by White's Bishop at c2 guarding a4. An opaque situation that requires an explosive move to break things open.

SOLUTION: The deflecting sacrifice **1 . . . Bxe4!** lets through the light of day. After **2. Bxe4 Ka4 3. Bf5 Kb3 4. Bxg4 e4 5. Bxh3 Kxc3 6. g4 Kd2,** White resigned. There's no way White can stop both the e-pawn and the c-pawn from going in. Note that at d2, Fischer's King ideally guards the c1 and e1 promotion squares. **(0-1)**

Bobby Fischer vs Mr. Beach

NEW YORK STATE OPEN 1963
WHITE'S 21ST MOVE

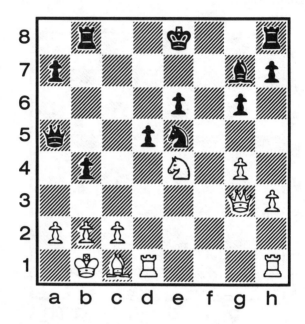

CLUE: The dark squares are the weak links in Black's chain, and the steadfast Bishop at g7 holds them together. How to knock it off is the name of the game.

SOLUTION: Fischer struck at the underpinnings with **1. Bh6!,** when 1 . . . Bxh6 is answered by 2. Qxe5, forking two Rooks and the e-pawn. Black tried to glue things together with **1 . . . Qc7,** but a new bolt **2. Nd6 + !,** created fresh problems (if 2 . . . Qxd6, then 3. Bxg7 nails the Knight at e5 and the Rook at h8 simultaneously). Black recoiled his King out of check **2 . . . Kd8,** losing his Knight after **3. Bxg7 Qxg7 4. Qxe5!.** Black resigned, for 4 . . . Qxe5 is met with the forking 5. Nf7 + and 6. Nxe5, putting Fischer a piece ahead. **(1-0)**

Sven Johannessen vs Bobby Fischer

HAVANA, 1966
BLACK'S 26TH MOVE

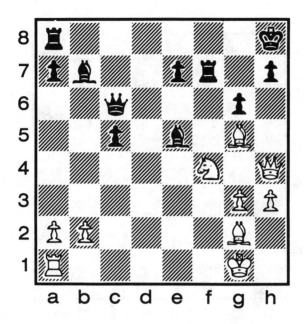

CLUE: White's attack has so far failed and he's an exchange down, but Fischer must defend accurately or White can still generate pesky counterplay. An incisive move is called for.

SOLUTION: Nothing's more pointed than **1 . . . Rxf4!,** reducing the position to bare bones. White resigned in view of 2. Bxc6 Rxh4 3. Bxb7 Rxh3 4. Bxa8 Rxg3+, and after the White King moves Black takes the Bishop at g5, leaving Fischer several pawns ahead; or 2. gxf4 (or 2. Bxf4) Qxg2 mate. **(0-1)**

Bobby Fischer vs Ludek Pachman

LEIPZIG, 1960
14TH OLYMPIAD
WHITE'S 38TH MOVE

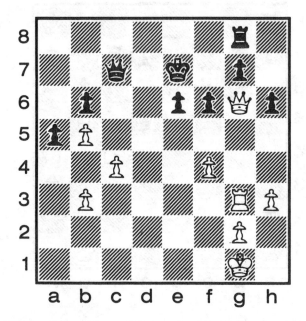

CLUE: It's a principle that if you're ahead in material, you should exchange pieces with a view to the endgame and eliminating counterplay. How banal, yet how sagacious in this case.

SOLUTION: Wholesale exchanges were initiated with **1. Qxg7 + !**. After **1 . . . Rxg7 2. Rxg7 +** (skewering Queen and King) **2 . . . Kd6 3. Rxc7 Kxc7 4. g4,** Black soon abandoned the losing endplay. **(1-0)**

Bobby Fischer vs Olivio Gadia

MAR DEL PLATA, 1960
WHITE'S 23RD MOVE

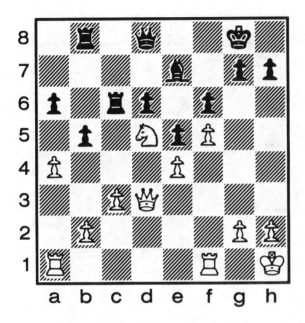

CLUE: Black's pieces are not coordinating well, and White's unassailable Knight sits powerfully in the center. Compare it to Black's Bishop, a blocked piece with no scope. Against these drawbacks, however, it's not the Knight that cemented White's superiority.

SOLUTION: Good Knight or not, Fischer readily ceded it **1. Nxe7 + !,** for if 1 . . . Qxe7, then 2. Qd5+ picks off the misplaced Rook. **(1-0)**

Bobby Fischer vs Miguel Najdorf

VARNA, 1962
15TH OLYMPIAD
WHITE'S 14TH MOVE

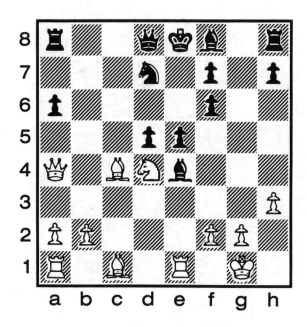

CLUE: Fischer's ready for business. His King is safely castled and he's better developed than Black, whose King may suddenly find itself stuck in the center. Quick, quick, before Black has a chance to complete his development and get his King to safety!

SOLUTION: Fischer demolished Black with the timely **1. Rxe4!**. The game continued: **1 . . . dxe4** (1 . . . dxc4 is answered by 2. Nf5, and Black doesn't even have material compensation for his troubles) **2. Nf5! Bc5** (else White plays 3. Qb3 with an irresistible attack against the f-pawn) **3. Ng7+** (so that Najdorf loses the right to castle) **3 . . . Ke7 4. Nf5+ Ke8 5. Be3,** and Fischer's powerful position was transmuted into a win after **5 . . . Bxe3 6. fxe3 Qb6** (to protect d6 from checks) **7. Rd1 Ra7 8. Rd6 Qd8 9. Qb3 Qc7 10. Bxf7+ Kd8 11. Be6.** A grandly conceived campaign! **(1-0)**

Bobby Fischer vs Mr. Bennet

SAN FRANCISCO, 1957
U.S. JUNIOR CHAMPIONSHIP
WHITE'S 38TH MOVE

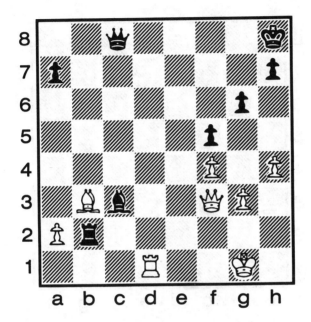

CLUE: Two open diagonals are involved: the light-squared b3-g8 and the dark-squared c3-h8. Your move, Bobby.

SOLUTION: Fischer dispatched his opponent with **1. Rd8 + !,** which wins the Queen or mates (as in the game) after **1 . . . Qxd8 2. Qxc3 +** (White's domination of both long diagonals is crushing) **2 . . . Qf6 3. Qxf6 mate. (1-0)**

Donald Byrne vs Bobby Fischer

NEW YORK, 1956
ROSENWALD TROPHY TOURNAMENT
BLACK'S 17TH MOVE

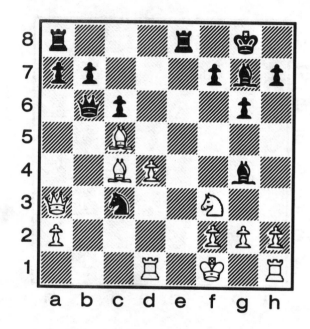

CLUE: Black's Queen and Knight are both under attack, and perhaps if he saves one he loses the other. These threats didn't deter the then thirteen-year-old Bobby Fischer from triumphing in what has been called the "Game of the Century."

SOLUTION: He played the out-of-this-world **1 . . . Be6!!**. The game continued: **2. Bxb6** (2. Bxe6 loses to 2 . . . Qb5+ 3. Kg1 Ne2+ 4. Kf1 Ng3++ 5. Kg1 Qf1+! 6. Rxf1 Ne2 mate) **2 . . . Bxc4+ 3. Kg1 Ne2+** (to win the d-pawn with a gain of time, clearing the g7-a1 diagonal) **4. Kf1 Nxd4+ 5. Kg1 Ne2+ 6. Kf1 Nc3+ 7. Kg1 axb6,** and Fischer subsequently won in five-star fashion. Undoubtedly, the greatest combination ever germinated by a child prodigy. **(0-1)**

Bobby Fischer vs Mikhail Tal

BLED, 1961
WHITE'S 23RD MOVE

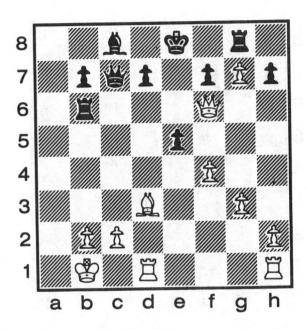

CLUE: Black has just uncovered an attack to White's Queen by the Rook at b6 (his pawn moved from e6 to e5). Fischer could swap down to an ending (1. Qxe5+ Qxe5 2. fxe5 Rxg7), but Tal, though a pawn down, would have some drawing chances. Time to pluck a rabbit out of a hat, or an outrageous move.

SOLUTION: Fischer divined the remarkable **1. fxe5!!**, appreciating that 1 . . . **Rxf6 2. exf6** (with Bxh7 on the agenda) **2 . . . Qc5 3. Bxh7 Qg5** (trying to win White's expansive pawns) **4. Bxg8 Qxf6 5. Rhf1 Qxg7 6. Bxf7+ Kd8 7. Be6** gives White a conquering hand. Bobby won in 47 moves. **(1-0)**

Bobby Fischer vs Dr. Reuben Fine

NEW YORK, 1963
SKITTLES GAME
WHITE'S 17TH MOVE

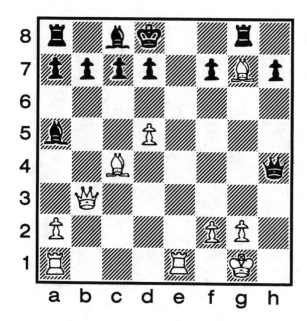

CLUE: The opening was an Evans Gambit (1. e4 e5 2. Nf3 Nc6 3. Bc4 Bc5 4. b4), one of the most exciting and romantic ways to start a game. The ending, though, was bluntly realistic.

SOLUTION: Fischer left Black tongue-tied and without a good move by **1. Qg3!**. Dr. Fine resigned, unable to both save his Queen and stop mate. If 1 . . . Qxg3, then 2. Bf6 mate follows. Otherwise, White simply captures the hanging Queen. **(1-0)**

Bobby Fischer vs Mr. Finegold

BAY CITY, MICHIGAN, 1963
WESTERN OPEN
WHITE'S 49TH MOVE

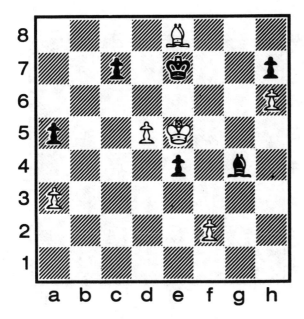

CLUE: White's Bishop, attacked, will be captured if it moves along the e8-h5 diagonal. Yet retreating on the a4-e8 diagonal may be too slow, giving Black time to defend. Never fear, the right move is already here.

SOLUTION: The shot heard round the board was **1. Bg6!**. Taking White's Bishop allows the h-pawn to Queen. Fischer won a couple of pawns and the game after **1 . . . Bd7 2. Bxh7 c5 3. dxc6 e.p. Bxc6 4. Bxe4 Bxe4 5. Kxe4 Kf6 6. f4.** (1-0)

Bobby Fischer vs Hans Ree

NETANYA, 1968
WHITE'S 17TH MOVE

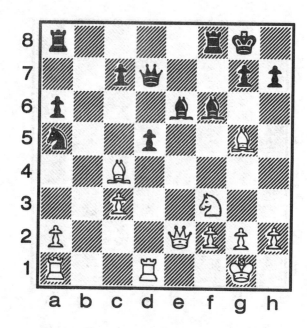

CLUE: Sure, Black is developed, but isn't he vulnerable along the a2-g8 diagonal? White jarringly wins a pawn.

SOLUTION: Fischer sacked his Queen **1. Qxe6 + !**, but after **1 . . . Qxe6,** won it back and gained a pawn with **2. Bxd5.** Black's Queen can't run away because it's pinned. Fischer won shortly thereafter. **(1-0)**

Arthur Bisguier vs Bobby Fischer

NEW YORK, 1960-61
U.S. CHAMPIONSHIP
BLACK'S 29TH MOVE

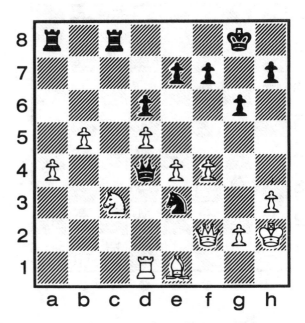

CLUE: White has approximate equality, with a Bishop and two connected (though attackable) passed pawns. He's menacing Fischer's Queen, and all White's pieces seem guarded. If 1 . . . Nxd1, then Black loses his Queen to 2. Qxd4, but therein lies a combination to be unlocked.

SOLUTION: The key is **1 . . . Qxc3!,** swapping the Queen for Rook, Bishop, and Knight. Play continued: **2. Bxc3 Nxd1** (forking the Queen and Bishop) **3. Qd4 Nxc3,** and Black eventually won. **(0-1)**

Bobby Fischer vs Dr. Erwin Nievergelt

ZURICH, 1959
WHITE'S 17TH MOVE

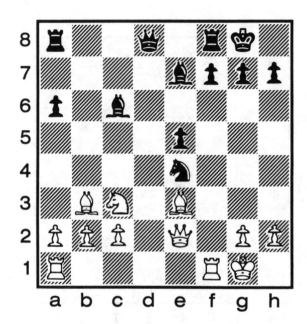

CLUE: There are a number of loose pieces and pawns in Black's position and it's simply a matter of determining the most advantageous way of devouring them.

SOLUTION: The Bishop at c6 is unguarded and vulnerable as **1. Rxf7! Rxf7 2. Bxf7 +** shows. Black responded **2 . . . Kh8** (instead of taking the Bishop), for on 2 . . . Kxf7, White plays 3. Qc4 +, also threatening the c6-Bishop. Fischer ended up a pawn ahead and subsequently won. **(1-0)**

Bobby Fischer vs Peter Dely

SKOPJE, 1967
WHITE'S 16TH MOVE

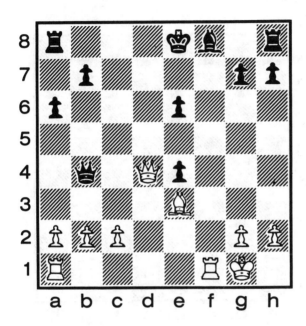

CLUE: Fischer's pieces are poised for the kill, and Black is just barely holding on, with his Queen, defended by the Bishop at f8, plugging the gap. Fischer's move changes everything.

SOLUTION: Black's game fell apart after **1. Rxf8 + !**, forcing **1 . . . Qxf8** in order to save the undefended Black Queen. Black gave up when he saw Fischer's **2. Qa4 +**. He can't play 2 . . . Ke7 because of 3. Bc5 +, skewering the Queen diagonally; nor can Black play 2 . . . Kf7 because of 3. Rf1 +, skewering the Queen vertically. On 2 . . . Kd8, White has a number of winning continuations, including 3. Bb6 + Kc8 4. Qc4 + with a penetrating attack. Finally, 2 . . . b5 is too weakening, as Black's position collapses after 3. Qxe4. **(1-0)**

Bobby Fischer vs Samuel Reshevsky

NEW YORK, 1958-59
U.S. CHAMPIONSHIP
WHITE'S 10TH MOVE

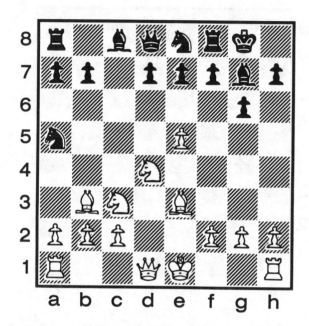

CLUE: Black is really cramped on the back rank and his Knight on a5 is out on a limb. Fischer's superior mobility and central concentration zooms doom.

SOLUTION: The winning sacrifice was **1. Bxf7 + !!.** In all lines Black loses his Queen for insufficient material: 1 . . . Rxf7 2. Ne6, and Black's Queen doesn't have a safe square, while the d-pawn is pinned by White's Queen; 1 . . . Kh8 2. Ne6 with the same result as before; and **1 . . . Kxf7** (which is what Reshevsky played) **2. Ne6!** (if 2 . . . Kxe6, then 3. Qd5 + Kf5 4. g4 + Kxg4 5. Rg1 + Kh4 6. Bg5 + Kh5 7. Qd1 + Rf3 8. Qxf3 mate) **2 . . . dxe6 3. Qxd8** and Fischer won the ending. **(1-0)**

Jose Agdamus vs Bobby Fischer

BUENOS AIRES, 1970
BLACK'S 35TH MOVE

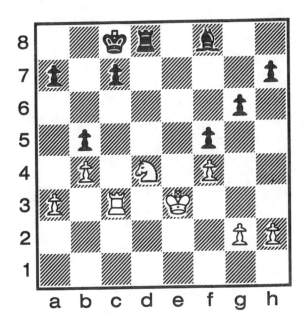

CLUE: Fischer has a pawn more than his opponent, but White's pieces could counterthreat if given the chance. There's an almost simplistic method to stop them.

SOLUTION: Black could have exchanged pieces by 1 . . . Bg7 2. Rd3 Bxd4+ 3. Rxd4 Rxd4 4. Kxd4, but White's King is too well centralized. The surest way is **1 . . . Rxd4! 2. Kxd4 Bg7+**. Though all the pieces get traded off, White's King ends up one square back on c3, and Bobby wins. **(0-1)**

A Collection of 101 Fischer Games in Algebraic Notation

The following are the complete game scores in algebraic notation for *Bobby Fischer's Outrageous Chess Moves* presented in this book. They should provide great pleasure and instructional value.

GAME 1

1. e4	c5	17. Re1	Qxe4	33. Bc3	Rdxc4
2. Nf3	d6	18. Rxe4	d5	34. Bxc4	Rxc4
3. d4	cxd4	19. Rg3	g6	35. Kd3	Rc5
4. Nxd4	Nf6	20. Bxd5	Bd6	36. Rxa5	Rxa5
5. Nc3	Nc6	21. Rxe6	Bxg3	37. Bxa5	Bxb2
6. Bc4	e6	22. Re7	Bd6	38. a4	Kf8
7. Bb3	Be7	23. Rxb7	Rac8	39. Bc3	Bxc3
8. Be3	O-O	24. c4	a5	40. Kxc3	Ke7
9. O-O	Bd7	25. Ra7	Bc7	41. Kd4	Kd6
10. f4	Qc8	26. g3	Rfe8	42. a5	f6
11. f5	Nxd4	27. Kf1	Re7	43. a6	Kc6
12. Bxd4	exf5	28. Bf6	Re3	44. a7	Kb7
13. Qd3	fxe4	29. Bc3	h5	45. Kd5	h4
14. Nxe4	Nxe4	30. Ra6	Be5	46. Ke6	(1–0)
15. Qxe4	Be6	31. Bd2	Rd3		
16. Rf3	Qc6	32. Ke2	Rd4		

GAME 2

1. e4	c6	13. c4	Rad8	25. Rxd5	f5
2. Nc3	d5	14. Bc2	Bxc2	26. Ne5 +	Bxe5
3. Nf3	dxe4	15. Kxc2	f5	27. Rxe5	Nf6
4. Nxe4	Nf6	16. Rhe1	f4	28. Rxe8	Nxe8
5. Nxf6 +	exf6	17. Bd2	Nf6	29. Be5	Kh5
6. Bc4	Bd6	18. Ne5	g5	30. Kd3	g4
7. Qe2 +	Qe7	19. f3	Nh5	31. b4	a6
8. Qxe7 +	Kxe7	20. Ng4	Kg7	32. a4	gxf3
9. d4	Bf5	21. Bc3	Kg6	33. gxf3	Kh4
10. Bb3	Re8	22. Rxe8	Rxe8	34. b5	axb5
11. Be3	Kf8	23. c5	Bb8	35. a5	Kh3
12. O-O-O	Nd7	24. d5	cxd5	36. c6	(1–0)

GAME 3

	White	Black		White	Black		White	Black
1.	e4	e5	19.	Bc2	Bd7	37.	Qxg4	Qe6
2.	Nf3	Nc6	20.	Bh6	Rfe8	38.	Qxe6	Rxe6
3.	Bb5	a6	21.	h4	Bg7	39.	Red1	Rd8
4.	Ba4	Nf6	22.	Bg5	f6	40.	a4	bxa4
5.	O-O	Be7	23.	Bc1	Bf8	41.	Rxa4	Nb7
6.	Re1	b5	24.	h5	g5	42.	Rd5	Rc6
7.	Bb3	d6	25.	Qg3	Qg7	43.	c4	Kg8
8.	c3	O-O	26.	Nh2	h6	44.	c5	Kf7
9.	h3	Nd7	27.	Ng4	Qf7	45.	Rb4	Rb8
10.	d4	Nb6	28.	Qf3	Bg7	46.	Rd7+	Ke6
11.	dxe5	Nxe5	29.	Ne3	Be6	47.	Rh7	Rb6
12.	Nxe5	dxe5	30.	Nf5	Bf8	48.	cxb6	Bxb4
13.	Qh5	Bf6	31.	b3	Rad8	49.	bxc7	Rc8
14.	Nd2	g6	32.	Be3	Rd7	50.	Nf5	Bf8
15.	Qf3	Qe7	33.	Qh3	Kh7	51.	g4	Na5
16.	Qg3	Bh4	34.	Bd1	Nc8	52.	b4	Bxb4
17.	Qh2	Bf6	35.	Bg4	Nd6	53.	Bd2	(1–0)
18.	Nf3	Be6	36.	Ng3	Bxg4			

GAME 4

	White	Black		White	Black		White	Black
1.	e4	e6	15.	Qh4	Nd5	29.	g4	Ke8
2.	d3	c5	16.	Qxd8	Rxd8	30.	Rf1	Rd5
3.	Nf3	Nc6	17.	a4	Rad7	31.	Rf3	Rd8
4.	g3	g6	18.	Bf1	Bxf1	32.	Rh3	Bf8
5.	Bg2	Bg7	19.	Kxf1	Nde7	33.	Nxa5	Rc7
6.	O-O	Nge7	20.	Nc4	Nc8	34.	Nc4	Ra7
7.	c3	O-O	21.	Bg5	N6e7	35.	Nxb6	Nxb6
8.	d4	d6	22.	Nfd2	h6	36.	Rxb6	Rda8
9.	dxc5	dxc5	23.	Bxe7	Rxe7	37.	Nf6+	Kd8
10.	Qe2	b6	24.	Ra3	Rc7	38.	Rc6	Rc7
11.	e5	a5	25.	Rb3	Rc6	39.	Rd3+	Kc8
12.	Re1	Ba6	26.	Ne4	Bf8	40.	Rxc4+	Kxc7
13.	Qe4	Ra7	27.	Ke2	Be7	41.	Rd7+	Kc6
14.	Nbd2	Bd3	28.	f4	Kf8	42.	Rxf7	(1–0)

GAME 5

	White	Black		White	Black		White	Black
1.	e4	c6	13.	Bxe7	Qxe7	25.	Rhe1	Rxc6
2.	d4	d5	14.	Kb1	Rd8	26.	Re5	Ra8
3.	Nc3	dxe4	15.	Qe4	b5	27.	Be4	Rd6
4.	Nxe4	Nd7	16.	Bd3	a5	28.	Bxa8	Rxd1+
5.	Nf3	Ngf6	17.	c3	Qd6	29.	Kc2	Rf1
6.	Nxf6+	Nxf6	18.	g3	b4	30.	Rxa5	Rxf2+
7.	Bc4	Bf5	19.	c4	Nf6	31.	Kb3	Rh2
8.	Qe2	e6	20.	Qe5	c5	32.	c5	Kd8
9.	Bg5	Bg4	21.	Qg5	h6	33.	Rb5	Rxh3
10.	O-O-O	Be7	22.	Qxc5	Qxc5	34.	Rb8+	Kc7
11.	h3	Bxf3	23.	dxc5	Ke7	35.	Rb7+	Kc6
12.	Qxf3	Nd5	24.	c6	Rd6	36.	Kc4	(1–0)

GAME 6

1. e4	c5	19. Re1+	Kf8	37. Ka3	Qc2		
2. Nf3	d6	20. c3	h5	38. Nd3+	Kf6		
3. d4	cxd4	21. f5	Rh6	39. Nc5	Qc1		
4. Nxd4	Nf6	22. f6	gxf6	40. Rxa4	Qe3		
5. Nc3	a6	23. Nf4	h4	41. Nxa6	f4		
6. Bg5	e6	24. Rd8+	Kg7	42. Rd4	Kf5		
7. f4	Be7	25. Ree8	Qg1+	43. Nb4	Qe7		
8. Qf3	Qc7	26. Kd2	Qf2+	44. Kb3	Qxh4		
9. O-O-O	Nbd7	27. Ne2	Rg6	45. Nd3	g5		
10. Be2	b5	28. g3	f5	46. c4	Qg3		
11. Bxf6	Nxf6	29. Rg8+	Kf6	47. c5	f3		
12. e5	Bb7	30. Rxg6+	fxg6	48. Kc4	f2		
13. exf6	Bxf3	31. gxh4	Qxh2	49. Nxf2	Qxf2		
14. Bxf3	Bxf6	32. Rd4	Qh1	50. c6	Qxb2		
15. Bxa8	d5	33. Kc2	Ke5	51. Kc5	Qc3+		
16. Bxd5	Bxd4	34. a4	Qf1	52. Kd5	g4		
17. Rxd4	exd5	35. Nc1	Qg2+	53. Rc4	Qe5 mate		
18. Nxd5	Qc5	36. Kb3	bxa4+	(0–1)			

GAME 7

1. e4	e5	11. d3	Bxh3	21. f4	Nd4	
2. Nf3	Nc6	12. gxh3	Qd7	22. Qc4	Qg6	
3. Bc4	Nf6	13. Bf3	Qxh3	23. c3	Nf5	
4. Ng5	d5	14. Nd2	Rad8	24. fxe5	Rxe5	
5. exd5	Na5	15. Bg2	Qf5	25. Bf4	Re2	
6. Bb5+	c6	16. Qe1	Rfe8	26. Be4	Rxb2	
7. dxc6	bxc6	17. Ne4	Bb6	27. Be5	Re8	
8. Be2	h6	18. Nxf6+	Qxf6	28. Rxf5	Rxe5	
9. Nh3	Bc5	19. Kh1	c5	29. Rxe5	(1–0)	
10. O-O	O-O	20. Qc3	Nc6			

GAME 8

1. e4	e5	16. Qc2	Ne7	31. Bc4	Kf7	
2. Nf3	Nc6	17. Ba3	Ng6	32. Bxe6+	Kxe6	
3. Bc4	Bc5	18. Rfd1	Nf4	33. Re1+	Kf7	
4. b4	Bxb4	19. Bf1	Kg8	34. Qc4+	Kg6	
5. c3	Ba5	20. Ne5	Qc7	35. Re7	Rhg8	
6. d4	exd4	21. Nc4	Be6	36. Rae1	h5	
7. O-O	d6	22. Nxd6	Rd8	37. Qf7+	Kh6	
8. Qb3	Qd7	23. e5	f6	38. R1e6	Rdf8	
9. cxd4	Bb6	24. Bxc5	Bxc5	39. Rxf6+	gxf6	
10. Bb5	Kf8	25. Nce4	Bxd6	40. Qh7+	Kg5	
11. d5	Na5	26. exd6	Qc8	41. h4+	Kg4	
12. Qa4	c6	27. Nc5	Bd5	42. Re4+	Kh3	
13. dxc6	bxc6	28. d7	Qc7	43. Qf5+	Rg4	
14. Bd3	Nb7	29. g3	Ne6	44. Rxg4	hxg4	
15. Nc3	Nc5	30. Nxe6	Bxe6	45. Qd3	(1–0)	

GAME 9

1.	b3	d5	16.	Rg3	Bxe5	31.	dxe4	c4
2.	Bb2	c5	17.	fxe5	f5	32.	b4	Bg4
3.	Nf3	Nc6	18.	exf6	Rxf6	33.	Ke3	Rd7
4.	e3	Nf6	19.	Qxg7+	Qxg7	34.	g6+	Kf8
5.	Bb5	Bd7	20.	Rxf6	Qxg3	35.	gxh7	Rxh7
6.	O-O	e6	21.	hxg3	Re8	36.	Ng6+	Ke8
7.	d3	Be7	22.	g4	a4	37.	Nxe5	Bc8
8.	Bxc6	Bxc6	23.	Nf3	axb3	38.	Nxc4	Kd8
9.	Ne5	Rc8	24.	axb3	Kg7	39.	Nd6	Rg7
10.	Nd2	O-O	25.	g5	e5	40.	Kf2	Kc7
11.	f4	Nd7	26.	Nh4	Bd7	41.	Nxc8	Kxc8
12.	Qg4	Nxe5	27.	Rd6	Be6	42.	Rd6	(1–0)
13.	Bxe5	Bf6	28.	Kf2	Kf7			
14.	Rf3	Qe7	29.	Rb6	Re7			
15.	Raf1	a5	30.	e4	dxe4			

GAME 10

1.	d4	Nf6	11.	Nxd2	e5	21.	exd4	Qe4
2.	Nf3	g6	12.	Nb3	O-O	22.	Qg4	Qc2
3.	Bf4	Bg7	13.	Qc3	Rc8	23.	g3	Qxa2
4.	Nbd2	c5	14.	Qb4	Re8	24.	Bb5	Qd5
5.	c3	cxd4	15.	Be2	exd4	25.	Bxe8	Qxh1+
6.	cxd4	d5	16.	Nxd4	Qh4	26.	Ke2.	Rxe8+
7.	Bxb8	Rxb8	17.	Qxb7	Bxd4	27.	Kd3	Be1
8.	Qa4+	Bd7	18.	Qxd7	Bxb2		(0–1)	
9.	Qxa7	Ne4	19.	Rd1	Bc3+			
10.	e3	Nxd2	20.	Kf1	d4			

GAME 11

1.	e4	e6	12.	Nb5	Qb6	23.	Bf2	Rfc8
2.	d4	d5	13.	O-O-O	Bd7	24.	Bd3	Na2+
3.	Nc3	Nf6	14.	Nd6	Na4	25.	Kd1	Nc3+
4.	e5	Nfd7	15.	Bb5	Nd4	26.	Kc1	Rc5
5.	f4	c5	16.	Be3	Ne2+	27.	Qh4	Ra5
6.	dxc	Bxc5	17.	Bxe2	Qxb2+	28.	Kd2	h6
7.	Qg4	O-O	18.	Kd2	Qb4+	29.	g4	fxg4
8.	Bd3	f5	19.	Kc1	Nc3	30.	Rxg4	Kh8
9.	Qh3	Bxg1	20.	Rde1	Nxa2+	31.	Qxh6+	(1–0)
10.	Rxg1	Nc5	21.	Kd1	Nc3+			
11.	Bd2	Nc6	22.	Kc1	d4			

GAME 12

1. d4	Nf6	18. a5	f6	35. Nd1	Ke6
2. Nf3	c5	19. axb6	axb6	36. Qxa2	Rxa2
3. c3	g6	20. Nd3	e5	37. Rb2	Ra1
4. g3	b6	21. Nf2	e4	38. Be1	Kd7
5. Bg2	Bb7	22. f4	Ra8	39. Bd2	Kc6
6. O-O	Bg7	23. Bd2	Rxa1	40. Be1	Na3
7. Nbd2	O-O	24. Qxa1	Ra8	41. Kd2	Kb5
8. Re1	d5	25. Qb1	Qc6	42. Bf2	Ka4
9. Ne5	Nc6	26. b3	Ba6	43. Be1	Be7
10. Ndf3	Rc8	27. Qb2	Bxf1	44. Bf2	Nb5
11. Nxc6	Bxc6	28. Rxf1	c4	45. Kc2	Ka3
12. Bh3	Bd7	29. b4	Qa4	46. Rb1	Ra2+
13. Bf1	Bc6	30. Rb1	Bf8	47. Rb2	Nxc3
14. Ne5	Bb7	31. Kf1	Nb5	48. Kxc3	Ra1
15. a4	Ne4	32. Ke2	f5	(0–1)	
16. f3	Nd6	33. Nd1	Kf7		
17. e3	Qc7	34. Nf2	Qa2		

GAME 13

1. e4	e6	15. Bxd7	Bxf3	29. Qh8	Re7
2. d4	d5	16. gxf3	Qxd7	30. h6	Kf7
3. Nc3	Nf6	17. Rdg1	f6	31. Qh7+	Kf8
4. Bg5	dxe4	18. Rxg7	Qxg7	32. Qd3	Kf7
5. Nxe4	Nbd7	19. Rxg7	Kxg7	33. h7	Rh5
6. Nf3	Be7	20. Qf4	Rac8	34. Qd5+	Re6
7. Nxf6+	Bxf6	21. h5	c5	35. f4	f5
8. h4	h6	22. Qg4+	Kf7	36. fxe5	Rxh7
9. Bxf6	Qxf6	23. Qg6+	Ke7	37. Qd7+	Re7
10. Qd2	O-O	24. dxc5	Rxc5	38. Qxf5+	Ke8
11. O-O-O	b6	25. Qxh6	Rg5	39. f4	Kd8
12. Bb5	Qe7	26. b3	e5	40. e6	(1–0)
13. Rh3	Bb7	27. Kb2	Rf7		
14. Rg3	Kh8	28. a4	Ke6		

GAME 14

1. e4	c5	14. f3	Rc8	27. Qf3	Qe6
2. Nf3	d6	15. Kb1	Nd7	28. Rc7	Rde8
3. d4	cxd4	16. h4	b5	29. Nf4	Qe5
4. Nxd4	Nf6	17. Bh3	Bxh3	30. Rd5	Qh8
5. Nc3	a6	18. Rxh3	Nb6	31. a3	h6
6. h3	Nc6	19. Bxb6	Qxb6	32. gxh6	Qxh6
7. g4	Nxd4	20. Nd5	Qd8	33. h5	Bg5
8. Qxd4	e5	21. f4	exf4	34. hxg6	fxg6
9. Qd3	Be7	22. Qxf4	Qd7	35. Qb3	Rxf4
10. g5	Nd7	23. Qf5	Rcd8	36. Re5+	Kf8
11. Be3	Nc5	24. Ra3	Qa7	37. Rxe8+	(1–0)
12. Qd2	Be6	25. Rc3	g6		
13. O-O-O	O-O	26. Qg4	Qd7		

GAME 15

1. e4	c5	11. Be4	Nc6	21. Re1	Nxc2
2. Nf3	Nf6	12. Qe2	c3	22. Rxe7 +	Rd7
3. Nc3	d5	13. bxc3	Bxc3	23. Bf4 +	Kc8
4. Bb5 +	Bd7	14. Rb1	O-O-O	24. Rxd7	Kxd7
5. e5	d4	15. Qc4	f5	25. Rd1 +	Kc8
6. exf6	dxc3	16. Qxc3	fxe4	26. Nf5	Rxg2 +
7. fxg7	cxd2 +	17. Ng5	Rhg8	27. Kf1	b6
8. Qxd2	Bxg7	18. Nxe4	Nd4	28. Ne7 +	Kb7
9. Bd3	Qc7	19. Qxc7 +	Kxc7	29. Nxc6	Rg4
10. O-O	c4	20. Ng3	Bc6	(1–0)	

GAME 16

1. e4	e6	15. h4	Qxc5	29. a4	a6
2. d4	d5	16. Qe4	f5	30. Rd7 +	Kh6
3. Nc3	Nf6	17. Qe2	b5	31. Rd6	Bxb2
4. Bg5	dxe4	18. Ng5	Bf6	32. Kxb2	axb5
5. Nxe4	Be7	19. Nxe6	Bxe6	33. a5	Ra8
6. Bxf6	Bxf6	20. Qxe6 +	Kh8	34. a6	Kh5
7. Nf3	Nd7	21. Kb1	Qxf2	35. Kb3	g5
8. Qd2	Be7	22. Qxf5	Qxf5	36. Kb4	Kg4
9. O-O-O	Nf6	23. Bxf5	g6	37. Kxb5	Kg3
10. Bd3	O-O	24. Bd3	Rad8	38. Rd7	g4
11. Nxf6 +	Bxf6	25. h5	Kg7	39. a7	(1–0)
12. Qf4	c5	26. hxg6	hxg6		
13. dxc5	Qa5	27. Bxb5	Rxd1 +		
14. Qc4	Be7	28. Rxd1	Rb8		

GAME 17

1. e4	d5	9. Nge2	Nbd7	17. Bf5	Nb6
2. exd5	Qxd5	10. O-O	e6	18. Nce4	Nxd5
3. Nc3	Qd8	11. Bxf6	gxf6	19. Rfd1	c6
4. d4	Nf6	12. d5	e5	20. Nc3	Qb6
5. Bc4	Bf5	13. Bb5	Be7	21. Rxd5	cxd5
6. Qf3	Qc8	14. Ng3	a6	22. Nxd5	Qxb2
7. Bg5	Bxc2	15. Bd3	Qd8	23. Rb1	Qxa2
8. Rc1	Bg6	16. h4	h5	24. Rxb7	(1–0)

GAME 18

1. e4	c6	6. Nf3	Bg4	11. Bb5 +	Nxb5
2. d4	d5	7. cxd5	Nxd5	12. Qc6 +	Ke7
3. exd5	cxd5	8. Qb3	Bxf3	13. Qxb5	Nxc3
4. c4	Nf6	9. gxf3	e6	14. bxc3	Qd7
5. Nc3	Nc6	10. Qxb7	Nxd4	15. Rb1	Rd8

16.	Be3	Qxb5	23. a4	Bg7	30. Bb8	Rc8
17.	Rxb5	Rd7	24. Rb6+	Kd5	31. a6	Rxc3
18.	Ke2	f6	25. Rb7	Bf8	32. Rb5+	Kc4
19.	Rd1	Rxd1	26. Rb8	Bg7	33. Rb7	Bd4
20.	Kxd1	Kd7	27. Rb5+	Kc6	34. Rc7+	Kd3
21.	Rb8	Kc6	28. Rb6+	Kd5	35. Rxc3+	Kxc3
22.	Bxa7	g5	29. a5	f5	36. Be5	(1–0)

GAME 19

1. d4	Nf6	13. Nf3	Nxf3+	25. b4	cxb4
2. c4	e6	14. Bxf3	h6	26. Qb2+	Qe5
3. Nc3	c5	15. Bd2	a6	27. Qxb4	Nf4
4. d5	exd5	16. Be2	Qe7	28. Rd1	b6
5. cxd5	d6	17. Rae1	Qe5	29. Rf2	Nd3
6. Nf3	g6	18. Kh1	Qd4	30. Qxb6	Nxf2+
7. e4	Bg7	19. f3	Nh5	31. Qxf2	Rxa4
8. Be2	O-O	20. Nb5	axb5	32. Kg1	Ra1
9. O-O	Re8	21. Bxb5	Qe5	33. Qe1	Ra2
10. Nd2	Nbd7	22. Bc3	Qe7	34. Qg3	Qb2
11. a4	Ne5	23. Bxe8	Qxe8	35. h4	Ra1
12. Qc2	g5	24. Bxg7	Kxg7		(0–1)

GAME 20

1. d4	Nf6	7. Bd3	dxc4	13. Ng3	Bb7
2. c4	e6	8. Bxc4	Qc7	14. Rc1	Qc6
3. Nc3	Bb4	9. Bb3	b6	15. f3	Qb5
4. e3	d5	10. Ne2	O-O	16. Ba4	Qxb2
5. a3	Bxc3+	11. Bb2	Nc6		(0–1)
6. bxc3	c5	12. O-O	Na5		

GAME 21

1. d4	Nf6	17. dxe5	f6	33. e4	Qc6
2. c4	g6	18. Rb2	Be6	34. Rd7	Qxe4
3. Nc3	d5	19. Rd2	Qc7	35. h3	a4
4. Bg5	Ne4	20. Bg4	Qc8	36. Bf2	Kf8
5. Bh4	Nxc3	21. Bf3	Rb8	37. c4	a3
6. bxc3	dxc4	22. Qe2	Rd8	38. Qxa3	Ra8
7. e3	Be6	23. Rfd1	Rxd2	39. Qb2	Ke8
8. Rb1	b6	24. Qxd2	Qe8	40. Qb5	Kf8
9. Be2	Bh6	25. Qd6	exf6	41. Rd1	Qxf4
10. Nf3	c6	26. Qd6	Rc8	42. Bxc5	Bxc5+
11. Ne5	Bg7	27. a5	Bf8	43. Qxc5+	Kg7
12. f4	Bd5	28. Qd2	Be7	44. Rf1	Qe4
13. O-O	Nd7	29. Bd5	Qf7	45. Qc7+	Kh6
14. Nxc4	O-O	30. Bxe6	Qxe6	46. Rxf6	Qd4+
15. a4	c5	31. Qd7	Kf7		(0–1)
16. Ne5	Nxe5	32. Qxa7	bxa5		

GAME 22

1.	c4	c5	20.	Nxe4	Qxe4
2.	Nf3	g6	21.	Bd3	Qd4+
3.	d4	cxd4	22.	Kh1	Rce8
4.	Nxd4	Nc6	23.	Be3	Qc3
5.	e4	Nf6	24.	Bxh6	Qxd2
6.	Nc3	d6	25.	Bxd2	Be5
7.	Be2	Nxd4	26.	Bf4	Bxf4
8.	Qxd4	Bg7	27.	Rxf4	gxf5
9.	Bg5	h6	28.	Rxf5	Kg7
10.	Be3	O-O	29.	Rg5+	Kh6
11.	Qd2	Kh7	30.	h4	e6
12.	O-O	Be6	31.	Rf1	f5
13.	f4	Rc8	32.	Rb1	Rf7
14.	b3	Qa5	33.	b5	axb5
15.	a3	a6	34.	cxb5	Bd7
16.	f5	Bd7	35.	g4	Ra8
17.	b4	Qe5	36.	gxf5	exf5
18.	Rae1	Bc6	37.	Bc4	Ra4
19.	Bf4	Nxe4	38.	Rc1	Bxb5

39.	Bxf7	Rxh4+
40.	Kg2	Kxg5
41.	Bd5	Ba6
42.	Rd1	Ra4
43.	Bf3	Rxa3
44.	Rxd6	Ra2+
45.	Kg1	Kf4
46.	Bg2	Rb2
47.	Rd7	b6
48.	Rd8	Be2
49.	Bh3	Bg4
50.	Bf1	Bf3
51.	Rb8	Be4
52.	Ba6	Ke3
53.	Rc8	Rb1+
54.	Kh2	Kf4
	(0–1)	

GAME 23

1.	e4	e5	11.	Nd2	Ne7
2.	Nf3	Nc6	12.	Nc4	O-O-O
3.	Bb5	a6	13.	Rd3	b5
4.	Bxc6	dxc6	14.	Na5	Bb4
5.	O-O	f6	15.	Nb3	Rxd3
6.	d4	Bg4	16.	cxd3	Ng6
7.	dxe5	Qxd1	17.	Kf1	Rf8
8.	Rxd1	Bxf3	18.	Ke2	Nf4+
9.	gxf3	fxe5	19.	Bxf4	Rxf4
10.	Be3	Bd6	20.	Rg1	Rh4

21.	Rxg7	Rxh2
22.	a3	Bd6
23.	f4!	exf4
24.	d4	Kd8
25.	Na5	c5
26.	e5	Bf8
27.	Nc6+	Ke8
28.	Rxc7	(1–0)

GAME 24

1.	Nf3	c5	18.	Ne1	g6
2.	b3	d5	19.	cxb5	axb5
3.	Bb2	f6	20.	Bb2	Nb6
4.	c4	d4	21.	Nef3	Ra8
5.	d3	e5	22.	a3	Na5
6.	e3	Ne7	23.	Qd1	Qf7
7.	Be2	Nec6	24.	a4	bxa4
8.	Nbd2	Be7	25.	bxa4	c4
9.	O-O	O-O	26.	dxc4	Naxc4
10.	e4	a6	27.	Nxc4	Nxc4
11.	Ne1	b5	28.	Qe2	Nxb2
12.	Bg4	Bxg4	29.	Qxb2	Rfb8
13.	Qxg4	Qc8	30.	Qa2	Bb4
14.	Qe2	Nd7	31.	Qxf7+	Kxf7
15.	Nc2	Rb8	32.	Rc7+	Ke6
16.	Rfc1	Qe8	33.	g4	Bc3
17.	Ba3	Bd6	34.	Ra2	Rc8

35.	Rxc8	Rxc8
36.	a5	Ra8
37.	a6	Ra7
38.	Kf1	g5
39.	Ke2	Kd6
40.	Kd3	Kc5
41.	Ng1	Kb5
42.	Ne2	Ba5
43.	Rb2+	Kxa6
44.	Rb1	Rc7
45.	Rb2	Be1
46.	f3	Ka5
47.	Rc2	Rb7
48.	Ra2+	Kb5
49.	Rb2+	Bb4
50.	Ra2	Rc7
51.	Ra1	Rc8

52.	Ra7	Ba5	57.	Ne2	Kb3	62.	Ke3	Bc5 +
53.	Rd7	Bb6	58.	Rb7	Ra8	63.	Ke2	Rh1
54.	Rd5 +	Bc5	59.	Rxh7	Ra1	64.	h4	Kc4
55.	Nc1	Ka4	60.	Nxd4 +	exd4	65.	h5	Rh2 +
56.	Rd7	Bb4	61.	Kxd4	Rd1 +	66.	Ke1	Kd3
								(0–1)

GAME 25

1.	e4	e5	8.	Nxd5	Bd6	15.	Nf6 +	Kh8
2.	f4	exf4	9.	d4	g5	16.	Qh5	Rd8
3.	Bc4	d5	10.	Nxg5	Qxg5	17.	Qxh3	Na6
4.	Bxd5	Nf6	11.	e5	Bh3	18.	Rf3	Qg6
5.	Nc3	Bb4	12.	Rf2	Bxe5	19.	Rc1	Kg7
6.	Nf3	O-O	13.	dxe5	c6	20.	Rg3	Rh8
7.	O-O	Nxd5	14.	Bxf4	Qg7	21.	Qh6 mate	(1–0)

GAME 26

1.	e4	c5	15.	Bc4	Rhg8	29.	Re3	Nc2
2.	Nf3	e6	16.	Rd1	Bf5	30.	Rh3	Rxe5
3.	d4	cxd4	17.	Bd3	Bxd3	31.	Nf3	Rxd5
4.	Nxd4	Nc6	18.	Qxd3	Nd4	32.	Rxh7	Rxd3
5.	Nb5	d6	19.	O-O	Kb8	33.	h4	Ne3
6.	Bf4	e5	20.	Kh1	Qxa3	34.	Rxf7	Rd1 +
7.	Be3	Nf6	21.	f4	Rc8	35.	Kh2	Ra1
8.	Bg5	Be6	22.	Ne4	Qxd3	36.	h5	f4
9.	N1c3	a6	23.	cxd5	Rc2	37.	Rxf4	Rxa2
10.	Bxf6	gxf6	24.	Rd2	Rxd2	38.	Re4	Nxg2
11.	Na3	d5	25.	Nxd2	f5	39.	Kg3	Ra5
12.	exd5	Bxa3	26.	fxe5	Re8	40.	Ne5	(1–0)
13.	bxa3	Qa5	27.	Re1	Nc2			
14.	Qd2	O-O-O	28.	Re2	Nd4			

GAME 27

1.	e4	e5	12.	Bg5	a6	23.	dxe5	Be7
2.	Nf3	Nc6	13.	Ba4	Bd7	24.	Rxe7 +	Kxe7
3.	Bb5	f5	14.	Bxf6	gxf6	25.	Qb7 +	Ke6
4.	Nc3	fxe4	15.	Qxe4 +	Kf7	26.	Qd7 +	Kxe5
5.	Nxe4	d5	16.	Ne5 +	fxe5	27.	Qd5 +	Kf6
6.	Nxe5	dxe4	17.	Rf1 +	Ke7	28.	Rf1 +	Kg6
7.	Nxc6	Qg5	18.	Bxd7	Kxd7	29.	Qe6 +	Kg5
8.	Qe2	Nf6	19.	Rf7 +	Ke8	30.	Rf5 +	Kg4
9.	f4	Qxf4	20.	Rxc7	Bd6	31.	Rf4 + +	Kxg3
10.	d4	Qh4 +	21.	Rxb7	Rc8	32.	Qg4 mate	(1–0)
11.	g3	Qh3	22.	O-O-O	Qxh2			

GAME 28

1. e4	e5	11. Be3	Nd7	21. Bb5	Rxb5
2. Nf3	Nf6	12. O-O-O	O-O	22. Nxa4	Rb4
3. d4	exd4	13. g4	Bb4	23. Nc3	Bb7
4. e5	Ne4	14. Ne2	Nb6	24. Rhe1	Kh8
5. Qe2	Nc5	15. Nd4	Qe8	25. f6	Bd8
6. Nxd4	Nc6	16. c3	Be7	26. Bg5	Rd4
7. Nxc6	bxc6	17. f5	c5	27. fxg7+	Kxg7
8. Nc3	Rb8	18. Nb5	d4	28. Bf6+	Kg8
9. f4	Be7	19. Bf4	dxc3	29. Qh4	Rxd1+
10. Qf2	d5	20. Nxc3	Na4	30. Nxd1	(1–0)

GAME 29

1. c4	c5	17. Rb5	Qe7	33. Nc6	Qc3
2. Nf3	Nc6	18. a4	Be6	34. Rb1	Qc2
3. d4	cxd4	19. Qa1	Qf6	35. Ne7+	Kh8
4. Nxd4	Nf6	20. Kg2	Na5	36. Nxd5	Rc8
5. Nc3	e6	21. Nd4	Nb7	37. Nc3	Rxc3
6. e3	d5	22. Rb4	Nd6	38. Qxh5+	Kg8
7. cxd5	exd5	23. a5	Ne4	39. Rb8+	Rc8
8. Be2	Bd6	24. axb6	axb6	40. Rxc8+	Bxc8
9. O-O	O-O	25. Qb2	Nxc3	41. Kf1	Ba6+
10. Nf3	Bg4	26. Ba6	Rc5	42. Ke1	Qc3+
11. g3	Bb4	27. Kg1	Bh3	43. Kd1	Qd3+
12. Bd2	Ne4	28. Ra1	b5	44. Kc1	Qc3+
13. a3	Bxc3	29. Bxb5	Nxb5	45. Kd1	Bc4
14. Bxc3	Nxc3	30. Rxb5	Rxb5	46. Qf3	Bb3+
15. bxc3	Rc8	31. Qxb5	Qe5	47. Ke2	Qc4+
16. Rb1	b6	32. Re1	h5		(0–1)

GAME 30

1. e4	e6	11. h5	h6	21. Nf4	Ke7
2. d4	d5	12. Rh4	Ba6	22. Nxd5+	Kd8
3. Nc3	Bb4	13. Bxa6	Nxa6	23. Ne3	Nxe3
4. e5	c5	14. Rf4	Qd7	24. Bxe3	Rc7
5. a3	Bxc3+	15. Qf3	Nc6	25. dxc5	Nxc5
6. bxc3	Qa5	16. Nh3	Rc8	26. Rd1+	Ke7
7. Bd2	Qa4	17. g4	Qe8	27. Bxc5+	bxc5
8. Qg4	Kf8	18. g5	Ne7	28. Rxe6+	(1–0)
9. Qd1	b6	19. gxh6	gxh6		
10. h4	Ne7	20. Rf6	Nf5		

GAME 31

1. e4	c6	5. Qxf3	Nf6	9. Nb1	Qb6
2. Nc3	d5	6. d3	e6	10. b3	a5
3. Nf3	Bg4	7. g3	Bb4	11. a3	Bxd2+
4. h3	Bxf3	8. Bd2	d4	12. Nxd2	Qc5

13. Qd1	h5	22. bxa5	Rxa5	31. Qf4	Ra8
14. h4	Nbd7	23. Rfb1	b5	32. Rh1	Rg8
15. Bg2	Ng4	24. Nf3	Ra4	33. a4	bxa4
16. O-O	g5	25. Bh3	Nxf3+	34. Rb1	e5
17. b4	Qe7	26. Qxf3	Kd7	35. Rb7+	Kd6
18. Nf3	gxh4	27. Kg2	Qg7	36. Rxg7	exf4
19. Nxh4	Nde5	28. Rb4	Rga8	37. Rxg8	f3+
20. Qd2	Rg8	29. Rxa4	Rxa4	38. Kg1	Kc5
21. Qf4	f6	30. Bxg4	hxg4	39. Rb8	(1–0)

GAME 32

1. d4	Nf6	13. Nxe4	Rxe4	25. Be2	Bxf4+
2. c4	c5	14. Bg5	Qe8	26. Bxf4	Rxf4
3. d5	e6	15. Bd3	Bxf3	27. Rb6	Rxf1
4. Nc3	exd5	16. Qxf3	Rb4	28. Bxf1	Rd8
5. cxd5	d6	17. Rae1	Be5	29. Rxa6	Kg7
6. e4	g6	18. Qd1	Qxa4	30. Bb5	Kf6
7. Bf4	a6	19. Qxa4	Rxa4	31. Bc6	Ke5
8. a4	Bg7	20. f4	Bd4+	32. Ra7	Rf8
9. Nf3	O-O	21. Kh1	Nd7	33. Re7+	Kd4
10. Be2	Bg4	22. Re7	Nf6	34. Rd7	Nf6
11. O-O	Re8	23. Rxb7	Nh5		(0–1)
12. h3	Nxe4	24. Kh2	Be3		

GAME 33

1. e4	c5	10. Kh1	Na5	19. Nh5	f5
2. Nf3	Nc6	11. Bg5	Qc5	20. Rad1	Qe5
3. d4	cxd4	12. f4	b5	21. Nef6+	Bxf6
4. Nxd4	Nf6	13. Ng3	b4	22. Nxf6+	Qxf6
5. Nc3	d6	14. e5	dxe5	23. Qxf6	Nc5
6. Bc4	Qb6	15. Bxf6	gxf6	24. Qg5+	Kh8
7. Nde2	e6	16. Nce4	Qd4	25. Qe7	Ba6
8. O-O	Be7	17. Qh5	Nxb3	26. Qxc5	Bxf1
9. Bb3	O-O	18. Qh6	exf4	27. Rxf1	(1–0)

GAME 34

1. e4	e5	15. Bf4	Bxf4	29. Re2	Bc8
2. Nf3	Nc6	16. Rxf4	Bd7	30. Qc4+	Kh7
3. Bb5	a6	17. Re1	Qc5	31. Ng6	Rxe2
4. Bxc6	dxc6	18. c3	Rae8	32. Qxe2	Bd7
5. O-O	f6	19. g4	Qd6	33. Qe7	Qxe7
6. d4	exd4	20. Qg3	Re7	34. Nxe7	g5
7. Nxd4	Ne7	21. Nf3	c5	35. hxg5	hxg5
8. Be3	Ng6	22. e5	fxe5	36. Nd5	Bc6
9. Nd2	Bd6	23. Rfe4	Bc6	37. Nxc7	Bf3
10. Nc4	O-O	24. Rxe5	Rfe8	38. Ne8	Kh6
11. Qd3	Ne5	25. Rxe7	Rxe7	39. Nf6	Kg7
12. Nxe5	Bxe5	26. Ne5	h6	40. Kf2	Bd1
13. f4	Bd6	27. h4	Bd7	41. Nd7	c4
14. f5	Qe7	28. Qf4	Qf6	42. Kg3	(1–0)

GAME 35

1. d4	Nf6	16. Nc4	b5	31. Bc6	Nxc6
2. c4	g6	17. Nd2	Qb6	32. Rc1	Qa7
3. g3	Bg7	18. Bb2	f5	33. Qxa7	Nxa7
4. Bg2	O-O	19. Ra3	Bh6	34. Rc7	Nb5
5. Nc3	d6	20. e3	Rac8	35. Rb7	Nc3
6. Nf3	Nc6	21. axb5	axb5	36. Nc4	Kf6
7. O-O	e5	22. Qa2	Bg7	37. b5	Ne5
8. d5	Ne7	23. Ra1	e4	38. Nxd6	Rd8
9. c5	Nd7	24. Bf1	Nd8	39. Rb6	Kg5
10. cxd6	cxd6	25. Ra6	Qb8	40. Ra6	Nxd5
11. a4	Nc5	26. Ra7	Rc7	41. b6	Nb4
12. Nd2	b6	27. Rxc7	Qxc7	42. Ra4	Rxd6
13. b4	Nb7	28. Nxb5	Bxb5	43. Rxb4	Rd1 +
14. Qb3	Bd7	29. Bxb5	Nf7	44. Kg2	Nf3
15. Ba3	a6	30. Bxg7	Kxg7	(0–1)	

GAME 36

1. d4	Nf6	11. Be2	Be6	21. Rfc1	Qa6
2. c4	g6	12. Nd5	b5	22. Rxc8 +	Rxc8
3. Nc3	Bg7	13. cxb5	axb5	23. Nc3	Bc4
4. e4	d6	14. Bxb5	Nxd5	24. f4	d5
5. f3	O-O	15. exd5	Bxd5	25. Bd4	Bxd4 +
6. Be3	Nbd7	16. a4	e6	26. Qxd4	Qb7
7. Qd2	c5	17. O-O	Qh4	27. Qf2	Ba6
8. Nge2	a6	18. Ne2	Rfc8	28. Rd1	Rc4
9. Ng3	cxd4	19. Be3	Nc4	29. Rd2	Rxc3
10. Bxd4	Ne5	20. Bxc4	Qxc4	(0–1)	

GAME 37

1. e4	c6	14. Be3	c5	27. Qa4	Rb7
2. d3	d5	15. a5	e5	28. Bb5	Nb8
3. Nd2	g6	16. Nd2	Ne8	29. Ra8	Bd6
4. Ngf3	Bg7	17. axb6	axb6	30. Qd1	Nc6
5. g3	Nf6	18. Nb1	Qb7	31. Qd2	h5
6. Bg2	O-O	19. Nc3	Nc7	32. Bh6 +	Kh7
7. O-O	Bg4	20. Nb5	Qc6	33. Bg5	Rb8
8. h3	Bxf3	21. Nxc7	Qxc7	34. Rxb8	Nxb8
9. Qxf3	Nbd7	22. Qb5	Ra8	35. Bf6	Nc6
10. Qe2	dxe4	23. c3	Rxa1	36. Qd5	Na7
11. dxe4	Qc7	24. Rxa1	Rb8	37. Be8	Kg8
12. a4	Rad8	25. Ra6	Bf8	38. Bxf7 +	Qxf7
13. Nb3	b6	26. Bf1	Kg7	39. Qxd6	(1–0)

GAME 38

1. e4	e5	12. Rxd1	Re8	23. Kg2	cxd5
2. Nf3	Nc6	13. f3	Ne7	24. exd5	Kb8
3. Bb5	a6	14. Nc3	Kc8	25. Re1	Bf8
4. Bxc6	dxc6	15. Be3	f5	26. Rf1	Rg7
5. O-O	f6	16. Rac1	fxe4	27. Bf6	Rg8
6. d4	Bg4	17. fxe4	g6	28. Rce1	Rd7
7. c3	exd4	18. Bf4	Bg7	29. d6	cxd6
8. cxd4	Qd7	19. d5	Rd8	30. Bxe7	Bxe7
9. h3	Bh5	20. Na4	Rhf8	31. Rf7	(1–0)
10. Ne5	Bxd1	21. g3	g5		
11. Nxd7	Kxd7	22. Bxg5	Rf7		

GAME 39

1. d4	Nf6	11. O-O	Ncxe5	21. Bd3	Re1 +
2. Nf3	d5	12. Nxe5	Nxe5	22. Kh2	Qg1 +
3. e3	g6	13. Be2	c6	23. Kg3	Rfe8
4. c4	Bg7	14. f4	Ng4	24. Rb1	gxf5
5. Nc3	O-O	15. h3	Bf5	25. Bd2	Rxb1
6. Qb3	e6	16. e4	Qd4 +	26. Qxb1	Qxb1
7. Be2	Nc6	17. Kh1	Nf2 +	27. Bxb1	Re2
8. Qc2	dxc4	18. Rxf2	Qxf2	(0–1)	
9. Bxc4	e5	19. exf5	Bxc3		
10. dxe5	Ng4	20. bxc3	Rae8		

GAME 40

1. e4	e6	11. O-O	c4	21. f5	Nd8
2. d4	d5	12. Be2	f6	22. Re3	Qf4
3. Nc3	Bb4	13. Ba3	fxe5	23. Rf3	Qe4
4. e5	c5	14. dxe5	Nxe5	24. a5	Nc6
5. a3	Bxc3 +	15. Re1	N7c6	25. axb6	axb6
6. bxc3	Ne7	16. Nxe5	Nxe5	26. Qb1	Kc7
7. a4	Qc7	17. f4	Nc6	27. Bc1	Qe1 +
8. Nf3	b6	18. Bg4	O-O-O	28. Rf1	Qxc3
9. Bb5 +	Bd7	19. Bxe6	Bxe6	29. Bf4 +	Kb7
10. Bd3	Nbc6	20. Rxe6	Rd7	30. Qb5	(1–0)

GAME 41

1. e4	e5	9. d4	Bxe4	17. Nxd6	cxd6
2. Nf3	Nc6	10. Nbd2	Bg6	18. Bf4	d5
3. Bb5	a6	11. Bxc6 +	bxc6	19. Qb3	hxg4
4. Ba4	d6	12. dxe5	dxe5	20. Qb7	gxh3 +
5. O-O	Bg4	13. Nxe5	Bd6	21. Bg3	Rd8
6. h3	Bh5	14. Nxg6	Qxg6	22. Qb4 +	(1–0)
7. c3	Qf6	15. Re1 +	Kf8		
8. g4	Bg6	16. Nc4	h5		

GAME 42

1. d4	d5	13. Kb1	O-O-O	25. Nf3	Qf6
2. c4	e6	14. Na4	Kb8	26. Bxf5	fxe3
3. Nc3	Nf6	15. Nc5	Bc8	27. Bxe6	Nxe6
4. cxd5	exd5	16. Nc1	Ng7	28. Qc3	c5
5. Bg5	c6	17. N1b3	b6	29. Rd1	cxd4
6. Qc2	Na6	18. Na4	Bb7	30. Nxd4	Nxd4
7. e3	Nc7	19. Rhe1	Nge6	31. Qxd4	Qg6+
8. Bd3	Be7	20. Rc1	Rhe8	32. Rc2	Re4
9. Nge2	Nh5	21. a3	f5	33. Qc3	Rc8
10. Bxe7	Qxe7	22. f4	Qh4	34. Qb3	Rxc2
11. O-O-O	g6	23. Re2	g5		(0–1)
12. h3	Bd7	24. Nd2	gxf4		

GAME 43

1. e4	c5	9. Rb1	Qa3	17. Rxf8 +	Bxf8
2. Nf3	d6	10. e5	dxe5	18. Qf4	Nc6
3. d4	cxd4	11. fxe5	Nfd7	19. Qf7	Qc5 +
4. Nxd4	Nf6	12. Bc4	Bb4	20. Kh1	Nf6
5. Nc3	a6	13. Rb3	Qa5	21. Bxc8	Nxe5
6. Bg5	e6	14. O-O	O-O	22. Qe6	Neg4
7. f4	Qb6	15. Nxe6	fxe6		(0–1)
8. Qd2	Qxb2	16. Bxe6 +	Kh8		

GAME 44

1. e4	e5	15. Ne3	Rd8	29. Nf6 +	Kh8
2. Nf3	Nc6	16. Qe2	Be6	30. Nd5	Qd7
3. Bb5	a6	17. Nd5	Nxd5	31. Qe4	Qd6
4. Ba4	Nf6	18. exd5	Bxd5	32. Nf4	Re7
5. O-O	Be7	19. Nxe5	Ra7	33. Bg5	Re8
6. Re1	b5	20. Bf4	Qb6	34. Bxd8	Rxd8
7. Bb3	d6	21. Rad1	g6	35. Nxe6	Qxe6
8. c3	O-O	22. Ng4	Nc4	36. Qxe6	fxe6
9. h3	Na5	23. Bh6	Be6	37. Rxe6	Rd1 +
10. Bc2	c5	24. Bb3	Qb8	38. Kh2	Rd2
11. d4	Nd7	25. Rxd8 +	Bxd8	39. Rb6	Rxf2
12. dxc5	dxc5	26. Bxc4	bxc4	40. Rb7	Rf6
13. Nbd2	Qc7	27. Qxc4	Qd6	41. Kg3	(1–0)
14. Nf1	Nb6	28. Qa4	Qe7		

GAME 45

1. e4	c5	12. O-O-O	b5	23. g6	e5
2. Nf3	d6	13. Kb1	b4	24. gxf7 +	Kf8
3. d4	cxd4	14. Nd5	Bxd5	25. Be3	d5
4. Nxd4	Nf6	15. Bxd5	Rac8	26. exd5	Rxf7
5. Nc3	g6	16. Bb3	Rc7	27. d6	Rf6
6. Be3	Bg7	17. h4	Qb5	28. Bg5	Qb7
7. f3	O-O	18. h5	Rfc8	29. Bxf6	Bxf6
8. Qd2	Nc6	19. hxg6	hxg6	30. d7	Rd8
9. Bc4	Nxd4	20. g4	a5	31. Qd6 +	(1–0)
10. Bxd4	Be6	21. g5	Nh5		
11. Bb3	Qa5	22. Rxh5	gxh5		

GAME 46

1. e4	e6	12. Bf4	a4	23. Bf6	Qe8
2. d3	d5	13. a3	bxa3	24. Ne4	g6
3. Nd2	Nf6	14. bxa3	Na5	25. Qg5	Nxe4
4. g3	c5	15. Ne3	Ba6	26. Rxe4	c4
5. Bg2	Nc6	16. Bh3	d4	27. h5	cxd3
6. Ngf3	Be7	17. Nf1	Nb6	28. Rh4	Ra7
7. O-O	O-O	18. Ng5	Nd5	29. Bg2	dxc2
8. e5	Nd7	19. Bd2	Bxg5	30. Qh6	Qf8
9. Re1	b5	20. Bxg5	Qd7	31. Qxh7+	(1–0)
10. Nf1	b4	21. Qh5	Rfc8		
11. h4	a5	22. Nd2	Nc3		

GAME 47

1. e4	c5	12. O-O-O	Nc4	23. Qd3	Bxc3
2. Nf3	Nc6	13. Qe2	Nxe3	24. Nxc3	Nxf4
3. d4	cxd4	14. Qxe3	O-O	25. Qf3	Nh5
4. Nxd4	Nf6	15. g4	Qa5	26. Rxh5	gxh5
5. Nc3	d6	16. h4	e6	27. Qxh5	Be8
6. Bc4	Bd7	17. Nde2	Rc6	28. Qh6	Rxc3
7. Bb3	g6	18. g5	hxg5	29. bxc3	Rxc3
8. f3	Na5	19. hxg5	Nh5	30. g6	fxg6
9. Bg5	Bg7	20. f4	Rfc8	31. Rh1	Qd4
10. Qd2	h6	21. Kb1	Qb6	32. Qh7+	(1–0)
11. Be3	Rc8	22. Qf3	Rc5		

GAME 48

1. e4	c5	25. Bf1	a5	49. Be8+	Kb7
2. Nf3	Nc6	26. Bc4	Rf8	50. Kb5	Nc8
3. d4	cxd4	27. Kg2	Kd6	51. Bc6+	Kc7
4. Nxd4	Qc7	28. Kf3	Nd7	52. Bd5	Ne7
5. Nc3	e6	29. Re3	Nb8	53. Bf7	Kb7
6. g3	a6	30. Rd3+	Kc7	54. Bb3	Ka7
7. Bg2	Nf6	31. c3	Nc6	55. Bd1	Kb7
8. O-O	Nxd4	32. Re3	Kd6	56. Bf3+	Kc7
9. Qxd4	Bc5	33. a4	Ne7	57. Ka6	Ng8
10. Bf4	d6	34. h3	Nc6	58. Bd5	Ne7
11. Qd2	h6	35. h4	h5	59. Bc4	Nc6
12. Rad1	e5	36. Rd3+	Kc7	60. Bf7	Ne7
13. Be3	Bg4	37. Rd5	f5	61. Be8	Kd8
14. Bxc5	dxc5	38. Rd2	Rf6	62. Bxg6	Nxg6
15. f3	Be6	39. Re2	Kd7	63. Kxb6	Kd7
16. f4	Rd8	40. Re3	g6	64. Kxc5	Ne7
17. Nd5	Bxd5	41. Bb5	Rd6	65. b4	axb4
18. exd5	e4	42. Ke2	Kd8	66. cxb4	Nc8
19. Rfe1	Rxd5	43. Rd3	Kc7	67. a5	Nd6
20. Rxe4+	Kd8	44. Rxd6	Kxd6	68. b5	Ne4+
21. Qe2	Rxd1+	45. Kd3	Ne7	69. Kb6	Kc8
22. Qxd1+	Qd7	46. Be8	Kd5	70. Kc6	Kb8
23. Qxd7+	Kxd7	47. Bf7+	Kd6	71. b6	(1–0)
24. Re5	b6	48. Kc4	Kc6		

GAME 49

1.	d4	Nf6
2.	c4	c5
3.	Nf3	cxd4
4.	Nxd4	e6
5.	Nc3	Bb4
6.	e3	Ne4
7.	Qc2	Nxc3
8.	bxc3	Be7
9.	Be2	O-O
10.	O-O	a6
11.	f4	d6
12.	f5	exf5
13.	Nxf5	Bxf5
14.	Qxf5	Nd7
15.	Bf3	Qc7
16.	Rb1	Rab8
17.	Bd5	Nf6
18.	Ba3	Rfe8
19.	Qd3	Nxd5
20.	cxd5	b5
21.	e4	Bf8
22.	Rb4	Re5
23.	c4	Rbe8
24.	cxb5	axb5
25.	Kh1	Qe7
26.	Qxb5	Rxe4
27.	Rxe4	Qxe4
28.	Qd7	Qf4
29.	Kg1	Qd4 +
30.	Kh1	Qf2
	(0–1)	

GAME 50

1.	d4	Nf6
2.	c4	c5
3.	d5	e6
4.	Nc3	exd5
5.	cxd5	d6
6.	Nf3	g6
7.	e4	Bg7
8.	Bg5	h6
9.	Bf4	g5
10.	Bc1	O-O
11.	Nd2	Nbd7
12.	Be2	Ne5
13.	Nf1	b5
14.	Bxb5	Qa5
15.	Ng3	c4
16.	O-O	Rb8
17.	Qa4	Qxa4
18.	Bxa4	Nd3
19.	Bb5	Ng4
20.	Nge2	Nxc1
21.	Raxc1	Ne5
22.	b3	cxb3
23.	axb3	a6
24.	Ba4	Nd3
25.	Rc2	f5
26.	Ng3	f4
27.	Nge2	f3
28.	Ng3	fxg2
29.	Kxg2	Bg4
30.	Nf5	Nf4 +
31.	Kg3	Bxf5
32.	exf5	Bxc3
33.	Kf3	Be5
34.	Ke4	Rb4 +
35.	Rc4	Rfb8
36.	f6	Kf7
37.	Kf5	Rxc4
38.	bxc4	Ne2
39.	Re1	Nd4 +
40.	Kg4	h5 +
41.	Kh3	Kxf6
	(0–1)	

GAME 51

1.	Nc3	c5
2.	Nf3	Nf6
3.	e4	d6
4.	g3	g6
5.	Bg2	Bg7
6.	O-O	Nc6
7.	d3	O-O
8.	h3	Rb8
9.	a4	a6
10.	Be3	b5
11.	axb5	axb5
12.	e5	dxe5
13.	Bxc5	Qc7
14.	Re1	b4
15.	Na4	Rd8
16.	Nd2	Nd4
17.	Nc4	Nd5
18.	Bxd4	exd4
19.	b3	Bb7
20.	Qd2	e5
21.	Nab2	Ra8
22.	Kh2	h5
23.	Bxd5	Bxd5
24.	Qxb4	Rxa1
25.	Rxa1	Qd7
26.	Qe1	Qf5
27.	Nd2	h4
28.	Nbc4	hxg3 +
29.	fxg3	Qe6
30.	Ne4	f5
31.	Qa5	Ra8
32.	Qxa8 +	Bxa8
33.	Rxa8 +	Bf8
34.	Ned6	Qd5
35.	Re8	Qf3
36.	h4	Qf2 +
37.	Kh3	Qg1
	(0–1)	

GAME 52

1.	d4	Nf6	11.	cxd4	b6	21.	Bb5	Qd6
2.	c4	g6	12.	Qd3	O-O	22.	Ne2	exd5
3.	Nc3	d5	13.	Bd2	Bb7	23.	exd5	Qxd5
4.	cxd5	Nxd5	14.	O-O	e6	24.	Qxd5	Bxd5
5.	e4	Nxc3	15.	Rfd1	Qd7	25.	Rxd5	Rb1 +
6.	bxc3	Bg7	16.	Bxa5	bxa5	26.	Nc1	Rxc1 +
7.	Bc4	Nc6	17.	Bc4	Rab8	27.	Bf1	Re8
8.	a4	Na5	18.	Ra2	Bc6	28.	f4	Ree1
9.	Ba2	c5	19.	Nc3	Rb4	29.	Rf2	Bf8
10.	Ne2	cxd4	20.	d5	Bb7		(0–1)	

GAME 53

1.	e4	c5	16.	Bd4	Re8	31.	Rxe8 +	Kh7
2.	Nf3	d6	17.	Rd1	Ng4	32.	c5	Qf6
3.	d4	cxd4	18.	h3	Qh4	33.	Re1	bxc5
4.	Nxd4	Nf6	19.	Rdf1	Bxd4	34.	bxc5	Qb2
5.	Nc3	Nc6	20.	Qxd4	Rad8	35.	Rff1	Qxa2
6.	Bc4	e6	21.	Nxd5	Bxd5	36.	c6	Qa5
7.	Bb3	Be7	22.	Bxd5	Nf6	37.	Rc1	Qc7
8.	O-O	Nxd4	23.	c4	Rd7	38.	Rfd1	g5
9.	Qxd4	O-O	24.	Re3	Red8	39.	fxg5	Kg6
10.	f4	b6	25.	Qe5	h6	40.	gxh6	Kxh6
11.	Kh1	Ba6	26.	Bf3	Rd2	41.	Rd6 +	Kg7
12.	Rf3	d5	27.	b4	Rf2	42.	Rd4	Kg6
13.	exd5	Bc5	28.	Ree1	Rxf3	43.	Ra4	(1–0)
14.	Qa4	Bb7	29.	Rxf3	Re8			
15.	Be3	exd5	30.	Qxe8 +	Nxe8			

GAME 54

1.	d4	Nf6	9.	Be2	Bxf3	17.	Bd2	exf4
2.	c4	g6	10.	Bxf3	e5	18.	Bxf4	Ne5
3.	Nc3	Bg7	11.	d5	Ne7	19.	Bc2	Nd4
4.	e4	d6	12.	Be2	f5	20.	Qd2	Nxc4
5.	Nf3	O-O	13.	f4	h6	21.	Qf2	Rxf4
6.	Bd3	Bg4	14.	Bd3	Kh7	22.	Qxf4	Ne2 +
7.	O-O	Nc6	15.	Qe2	fxe4	23.	Kh1	Nxf4
8.	Be3	Nd7	16.	Nxe4	Nf5		(0–1)	

GAME 55

1.	e4	c5	10.	Qe1	Bb7	19.	Rfd2	Nc5
2.	Nf3	d6	11.	Nh4	g6	20.	Bf1	b4
3.	d4	cxd4	12.	Nf3	Bg7	21.	Nd5	Bxd5
4.	Nxd4	Nf6	13.	Qh4	O-O	22.	exd5	Ne4
5.	Nc3	a6	14.	fxe5	dxe5	23.	Qe1	Nxd2
6.	f4	e5	15.	Bh6	Nh5	24.	Qxd2	Nxd5
7.	Nf3	Qc7	16.	Bxg7	Kxg7	25.	c4	bxc3
8.	Bd3	Nbd7	17.	Rad1	Nf4		(0–1)	
9.	O-O	b5	18.	Rf2	f6			

GAME 56

1. d4	Nf6	13. Bd3	f5	25. h3	f4
2. c4	e6	14. Qxa8	Nc6	26. Kh2	a6
3. Nc3	Bb4	15. Qxe8+	Qxe8	27. Re4	Qd5
4. e3	b6	16. O-O	Na5	28. h4	Ne3
5. Ne2	Ba6	17. Rae1	Bxc4	29. R1xe3	fxe3
6. Ng3	Bxc3+	18. Bxc4	Nxc4	30. Rxe3	Qxa2
7. bxc3	d5	19. Bc1	c5	31. Rf3+	Ke8
8. Qf3	O-O	20. dxc5	bxc5	32. Bg7	Qc4
9. e4	dxe4	21. Bf4	h6	33. hxg5	hxg5
10. Nxe4	Nxe4	22. Re2	g5	34. Rf8+	Kd7
11. Qxe4	Qd7	23. Be5	Qd8	35. Ra8	Kc6
12. Ba3	Re8	24. Rfe1	Kf7	(0–1)	

GAME 57

1. e4	c5	12. Qe2	Qa5	23. Rxf2	Qb6
2. Nf3	Nc6	13. f5	e5	24. Rg2	d5
3. d4	cxd4	14. Bf2	Bd8	25. Bxd5	Rad8
4. Nxd4	Nf6	15. Rad1	Bb6	26. Qh5	g6
5. Nc3	d6	16. g4	h6	27. Qxh6	Rxd5
6. Bc4	e6	17. h4	Nh7	28. exd5	e4
7. Bb3	Be7	18. Rd3	Kh8	29. Rdg3	Qd6
8. O-O	O-O	19. g5	Bd4	30. h5	Rg8
9. Be3	Bd7	20. Kh2	Bb5	31. hxg6	fxg6
10. f4	Nxd4	21. Nxb5	Qxb5	32. f6	Qxd5
11. Bxd4	Bc6	22. c3	Bxf2	33. Qxh7+	(1–0)

GAME 58

1. e4	c5	10. Qd2	Nf6	19. Bxc6	Qxc6
2. Nc3	d6	11. Kh1	O-O-O	20. Nf7	Rde8
3. g3	Nc6	12. Rae1	Kb8	21. Nxe5	Rxe5
4. Bg2	g6	13. Bg1	fxe4	22. Qf4	b5
5. d3	Bg7	14. dxe4	Ba6	23. a3	b4
6. f4	b6	15. Ng5	Bxf1	24. axb4	cxb4
7. Nf3	Bb7	16. Bxf1	Rhe8	25. Bd4	Rf5
8. O-O	Qd7	17. Bb5	e5	(0–1)	
9. Be3	f5	18. fxe5	Rxe5		

GAME 59

1. d4	Nf6	10. Nd2	Qh4	19. Kxf1	c5
2. c4	e6	11. f3	Nxd2	20. Kg1	Ba6
3. Nc3	Bb4	12. Bxd2	Nc6	21. Bg3	cxd4
4. e3	b6	13. Rae1	Na5	22. cxd4	exd4
5. Bd3	Bb7	14. Rb1	d6	23. Bxd6	Qe3+
6. Nf3	Ne4	15. Be1	Qg5	24. Qxe3	dxe3
7. Qc2	f5	16. Qe2	e5	25. Re1	Bxc4
8. O-O	Bxc3	17. e4	fxe4	26. Rxe3	Bxa2
9. bxc3	O-O	18. fxe4	Rxf1+	27. e5	Be6

28. Re1	Nb3	34. Kf2	Nc1	40. Kxg4	Rxg2+
29. Ba6	Nc5	35. Re3	Rb8	41. Kh3	Rg1
30. Be2	a5	36. Bc5	Rb2+	42. e6	Nf5
31. Bc7	a4	37. Kg3	Nb3	43. Rd3	g5
32. Bxb6	Nb3	38. Bd6	Nd4	44. Bg3	h5
33. Bd1	Rc8	39. Bg4	Bxg4	(0–1)	

GAME 60

1. d4	Nf6	10. Nh4	h6	19. Rbf2	Qe7
2. c4	e6	11. f4	Ng6	20. Bc2	g5
3. Nc3	Bb4	12. Nxg6	fxg6	21. Bd2	Qe8
4. Nf3	c5	13. fxe5	dxe5	22. Be1	Qg6
5. e3	Nc6	14. Be3	b6	23. Qd3	Nh5
6. Bd3	Bxc3+	15. O-O	O-O	24. Rxf8+	Rxf8
7. bxc3	d6	16. a4	a5	25. Rxf8+	Kxf8
8. e4	e5	17. Rb1	Bd7	26. Bd1	Nf4
9. d5	Ne7	18. Rb2	Rb8	27. Qc2	Bxa4 (1–0)

GAME 61

1. e4	c5	13. Bf4	Na5	25. Rxc8+	Nxc8
2. Nf3	e6	14. Rc1	b5	26. h5	Qd8
3. d3	Nc6	15. b3	b4	27. Ng5	Nf8
4. g3	g6	16. Ne2	Bb5	28. Be4	Qe7
5. Bg2	Bg7	17. Qd2	Nac6	29. Nxh7	Nxh7
6. O-O	Nge7	18. g4	a5	30. hxg6	fxg6
7. Re1	d6	19. Ng3	Qb6	31. Bxg6	Ng5
8. c3	O-O	20. h4	Nb8	32. Nh5	Nf3+
9. d4	cxd4	21. Bh6	Nd7	33. Kg2	Nh4+
10. cxd4	d5	22. Qg5	Rxc1	34. Kg3	Nxg6
11. e5	Bd7	23. Rxc1	Bxh6	35. Nf6+	Kf7
12. Nc3	Rc8	24. Qxh6	Rc8	36. Qh7+	(1–0)

GAME 62

1. d4	Nf6	9. O-O	b6	17. Kg1	Nxe3
2. c4	g6	10. b3	Ba6	18. Qd2	Nxg2
3. g3	c6	11. Ba3	Re8	19. Kxg2	d4
4. Bg2	d5	12. Qd2	e5	20. Nxd4	Bb7+
5. cxd5	cxd5	13. dxe5	Nxe5	21. Kf1	Qd7
6. Nc3	Bg7	14. Rfd1	Nd3	(0–1)	
7. e3	O-O	15. Qc2	Nxf2		
8. Nge2	Nc6	16. Kxf2	Ng4+		

GAME 63

1.	e4	e5	15.	dxe5	dxe5	29.	Be3	Qxa5
2.	Nf3	Nc6	16.	Nh2	Rad8	30.	a4	Ra8
3.	Bb5	a6	17.	Qf3	Be6	31.	axb5	Qxb5
4.	Ba4	Nf6	18.	Nhg4	Nxg4	32.	Rhb1	Qc6
5.	O-O	Be7	19.	hxg4	Qc6	33.	Rb6	Qc7
6.	Re1	b5	20.	g5	Nc4	34.	Rba6	Rxa6
7.	Bb3	d6	21.	Ng4	Bxg4	35.	Rxa6	Rc8
8.	c3	O-O	22.	Qxg4	Nb6	36.	Qg4	Ne6
9.	h3	Na5	23.	g3	c4	37.	Ba4	Rb8
10.	Bc2	c5	24.	Kg2	Nd7	38.	Rc6	Qd8
11.	d4	Qc7	25.	Rh1	Nf8	39.	Rxe6	Qc8
12.	Nbd2	Bd7	26.	b4	Qe6	40.	Bd7	(1–0)
13.	Nf1	Rfe8	27.	Qe2	a5			
14.	Ne3	g6	28.	bxa5	Qa6			

GAME 64

1.	e4	e5	14.	Nf5	Bxf5	27.	Rg6	Bd6
2.	Nf3	Nc6	15.	exf5	Qc7	28.	Rag1	Bf8
3.	Bb5	a6	16.	g4	h6	29.	h6	Qe5
4.	Ba4	Nf6	17.	h4	c4	30.	Qg4	Rdd7
5.	O-O	Be7	18.	Bc2	Nh7	31.	f3	Bc5
6.	Re1	b5	19.	Nf3	f6	32.	Nxc5	Qxc5
7.	Bb3	d6	20.	Nd2	Rad8	33.	Rxg7	Rxg7
8.	c3	O-O	21.	Qf3	h5	34.	hxg7+	Kg8
9.	h3	Nb8	22.	gxh5	Nd5	35.	Qg6	Rd8
10.	d4	Nbd7	23.	Ne4	Nf4	36.	Be4	Qc8
11.	Nh4	Nb6	24.	Bxf4	exf4	37.	Qe8+	(1–0)
12.	Nd2	c5	25.	Kh1	Kh8			
13.	dxc5	dxc5	26.	Rg1	Rf7			

GAME 65

1.	e4	g6	8.	Qxf3	Nc6	15.	Qg3	Kh8
2.	d4	Bg7	9.	Be3	e5	16.	Qg4	c6
3.	Nc3	d6	10.	dxe5	dxe5	17.	Qh5	Qe8
4.	f4	Nf6	11.	f5	gxf5	18.	Bxd4	exd4
5.	Nf3	O-O	12.	Qxf5	Nd4	19.	Rf6	Kg8
6.	Bd3	Bg4	13.	Qf2	Ne8	20.	e5	h6
7.	h3	Bxf3	14.	O-O	Nd6	21.	Ne2	(1–0)

GAME 66

1.	d4	Nf6	14.	Nxb5	Bxb5	
2.	c4	g6	15.	cxb5	Rfb8	
3.	g3	Bg7	16.	Bf3	Nf6	
4.	Bg2	O-O	17.	a4	a6	
5.	Nf3	d6	18.	bxa6	Qxa6	
6.	O-O	Nc6	19.	Ra3	Qxd3	
7.	Nc3	Bf5	20.	exd3	Rb4	
8.	d5	Na5	21.	a5	Rb5	
9.	Nd4	Bd7	22.	Bd2	Rxb2	
10.	Qd3	c5	23.	Bc3	Rb7	
11.	Nb3	Ng4	24.	Re1	Ne8	
12.	f4	b5	25.	Bd2	Kf8	
13.	Nxa5	Qxa5	26.	Bd1	Rb2	

27.	Bc1	Bd4+				
28.	Kh1	Rf2				
29.	Bg4	Nf6				
30.	Bh3	Rc2				
31.	a6	Ra7				
32.	Bc8	Nxd5				
33.	Rb3	Nb4				
34.	f5	gxf5				
35.	Bg5	e6				
36.	Bd8	Ra8				
37.	Bb6	Rxc8				
	(0–1)					

GAME 67

1.	e4	e5	10.	d5	b5	
2.	Nf3	Nc6	11.	Qe2	Na5	
3.	Bb5	a6	12.	Bd1	Be7	
4.	Ba4	d6	13.	g3	O-O	
5.	c3	Bd7	14.	h4	Rfc8	
6.	d4	Nge7	15.	Bg5	hxg5	
7.	Bb3	h6	16.	hxg5	Qxg5	
8.	Qe2	Ng6	17.	Nxg5	Bxg5	
9.	Qc4	Qf6	18.	Na3	c6	

19.	dxc6	Be6	
20.	Qh5	Bh6	
21.	Bg4	Bxg4	
22.	Qxg4	Nxc6	
23.	Rd1	b4	
24.	Nc4	bxc3	
25.	bxc3	Nd4	
26.	Nb6	(1–0)	

GAME 68

1.	d4	Nf6	10.	Ne2	Bxd5	
2.	c4	g6	11.	exd5	Nbd7	
3.	Nc3	Bg7	12.	O-O	Ne5	
4.	e4	O-O	13.	f4	Nxd3	
5.	Bg5	d6	14.	Qxd3	h6	
6.	Qd2	c5	15.	Bh4	Re8	
7.	d5	e6	16.	Rae1	Qb6	
8.	Bd3	exd5	17.	Bxf6	Bxf6	
9.	Nxd5	Be6	18.	f5	g5	

19.	b3	Qa5	
20.	Rc1	Qxa2	
21.	Rc2	Re3	
22.	Qxe3	Qxc2	
23.	Kh1	a5	
24.	h4	a4	
	(0–1)		

GAME 69

1.	e4	c5	10.	f5	Bc4	
2.	Nf3	d6	11.	a4	Be7	
3.	d4	cxd4	12.	Be3	O-O	
4.	Nxd4	Nf6	13.	a5	b5	
5.	Nc3	a6	14.	axb6	Nxb6	
6.	Be2	e5	15.	Bxb6	Qxb6+	
7.	Nb3	Be6	16.	Kh1	Bb5	
8.	O-O	Nbd7	17.	Bxb5	axb5	
9.	f4	Qc7	18.	Nd5	Nxd5	

19.	Qxd5	Ra4	
20.	c3	Qa6	
21.	h3	Rc8	
22.	Rfe1	h6	
23.	Kh2	Bg5	
24.	g3	Qa7	
25.	Kg2	Ra2	
26.	Kf1	Rxc3	
	(0–1)		

GAME 70

1. e4	c5	31. Bxc3	Rxc3	61. Bc2	Nf7 +
2. Nf3	Nc6	32. Kb2	d3	62. Kg4	Ne5 +
3. d4	cxd4	33. Kxc3	dxe2	63. Kf4	Kd4
4. Nxd4	e6	34. Re1	Nd6	64. Rb4 +	Kc3
5. Nb5	d6	35. Bh5	Nb5 +	65. Rb5	Nf7
6. Bf4	e5	36. Kb2	axb4	66. Rc5 +	Kd4
7. Be3	Nf6	37. axb4	Rd4	67. Rf5	g5 +
8. Bg5	Qa5 +	38. c3	Rh4	68. Kg4	Ne5 +
9. Qd2	Nxe4	39. Bxe2	Nd6	69. Kxg5	Rg6 +
10. Qxa5	Nxa5	40. Rd1	Kc7	70. Kxh4	Rxg2
11. Be3	Kd7	41. h3	Rf4	71. Bd1	Rg8
12. N1c3	Nxc3	42. Rf1	Re4	72. Bg4	Ke4
13. Nxc3	Kd8	43. Bd3	Re5	73. Kg3	Rg7
14. Nb5	Be6	44. Rf2	h5	74. Rf4 +	Kd5
15. O-O-O	b6	45. c4	Rg5	75. Ra4	Ng6
16. f4	exf4	46. Kc3	Kd7	76. Ra6	Ne5
17. Bxf4	Nb7	47. Ra2	Kc8	77. Kf4	Rf7 +
18. Be2	Bd7	48. Kd4	Kc7	78. Kg5	Rg7 +
19. Rd2	Be7	49. Ra7 +	Kd8	79. Kf5	Rf7 +
20. Rhd1	Bxb5	50. c5	bxc5 +	80. Rf6	Rxf6 +
21. Bxb5	Kc7	51. bxc5	Ne8	81. Kxf6	Ke4
22. Re2	Bf6	52. Ra2	Nc7	82. Bc8	Kf4
23. Rde1	Rac8	53. Bc4	Kd7	83. h4	Nf3
24. Bc4	Rhf8	54. Rb2	Kc6	84. h5	Ng5
25. b4	a5	55. Bb3	Nb5 +	85. Bf5	Nf3
26. Bd5	Kb8	56. Ke3	Kxc5	86. h6	Ng5
27. a3	Rfd8	57. Kf4	Rg6	87. Kg6	Nf3
28. Bxf7	Bc3	58. Bd1	h4	88. h7	Ne5 +
29. Bd2	d5	59. Kf5	Rh6	89. Kf6	(1–0)
30. Rd1	d4	60. Kg5	Nd6		

GAME 71

1. e4	c5	14. Kb1	Rc8	27. Rxg6	Nf8
2. Nf3	e6	15. a3	Nxd3	28. Rg4	Rf7
3. d4	cxd4	16. cxd3	Nc5	29. Qg2	Qb7
4. Nxd4	a6	17. Nd4	Ba8	30. Bg5	Bxg5
5. Nc3	Qc7	18. f5	e5	31. Rxg5	Rh6
6. Bd3	Nc6	19. Nde2	Bd8	32. Nd4	Ne6
7. Nb3	Nf6	20. Rhg1	Qb8	33. Nxe6	Rxe6
8. Be3	d6	21. g6	hxg6	34. Qg4	Rh6
9. f4	b5	22. fxg6	Rc7	35. Rc2	Kd8
10. Qf3	Bb7	23. d4	exd4	36. Rf5	Rxf5
11. g4	Be7	24. Rxd4	Rd7	37. Qxf5	Rh8
12. O-O-O	Nb4	25. Nd5	Ne6	38. Qg5 +	Ke8
13. g5	Nd7	26. Rd2	fxg6	39. Rc8 +	(1–0)

GAME 72

1. e4	e5	5. O-O	Be7	9. h3	h6
2. Nf3	Nc6	6. Re1	b5	10. d4	Re8
3. Bb5	a6	7. Bb3	d6	11. Nbd2	Bf8
4. Ba4	Nf6	8. c3	O-O	12. Nf1	Bb7

13. Ng3	Na5	**21.** Qd2	Nh7	**29.** f3	Nf8
14. Bc2	Nc4	**22.** Kh2	Be7	**30.** h4	gxh4
15. b3	Nb6	**23.** Nf5	Bg5	**31.** Rxh4	Rh7
16. a4	c5	**24.** Nxg5	hxg5	**32.** Rah1	Rxh4
17. d5	c4	**25.** g4	g6	**33.** Rxh4	g5
18. b4	Bc8	**26.** Ng3	f6	**34.** Rh6	Kg7
19. Be3	Bd7	**27.** Rh1	Rf8	**35.** Rxf6	(1–0)
20. a5	Nc8	**28.** Kg2	Rf7		

GAME 73

1. e4	e5	**13.** dxc5	dxc5	**25.** Rxd1	Rd8
2. Nf3	Nc6	**14.** Nf1	Be6	**26.** Rxd8 +	Qxd8
3. Bb5	a6	**15.** Ne3	Rad8	**27.** b3	cxb3
4. Ba4	Nf6	**16.** Qe2	c4	**28.** Bxb3	Nf8
5. O-O	Be7	**17.** Nf5	Rfe8	**29.** c4	Qd7
6. Re1	b5	**18.** Bg5	Nd7	**30.** Qc2	Qb7
7. Bb3	d6	**19.** Bxe7	Nxe7	**31.** cxb5	axb5
8. c3	O-O	**20.** Ng5	h6	**32.** Ng4	N6d7
9. h3	Na5	**21.** Nxe6	fxe6	**33.** Qd3	Qc6
10. Bc2	c5	**22.** Ne3	Ng6	**34.** Qe3	Kf7
11. d4	Qc7	**23.** g3	Nf6	**35.** Nxe5 +	Nxe5
12. Nbd2	Nc6	**24.** Red1	Rxd1 +	**36.** Qf4 +	(1–0)

GAME 74

1. c4	g6	**24.** Rxc5	Bxc5	**47.** e4	a4
2. Nc3	c5	**25.** Nd3	Bxd3	**48.** Kg2	Ra2
3. g3	Bg7	**26.** Qxd3	Rd8	**49.** Rxf7 +	Kxf7
4. Bg2	Nc6	**27.** Bf3	Qc7	**50.** Bc4 +	Ke7
5. Nf3	e6	**28.** Bg2	Be7	**51.** Bxa2	a3
6. O-O	Nge7	**29.** Bxe7	Qxe7	**52.** Kf3	Nf6
7. d3	O-O	**30.** Qd4	e5	**53.** Ke3	Kd6
8. Bd2	d5	**31.** Qc4	Nb6	**54.** f4	Nd7
9. a3	b6	**32.** Qc2	Rc8	**55.** Bb1	Nc5
10. Rb1	Bb7	**33.** Qd3	Rc4	**56.** f5	Na6
11. b4	cxb4	**34.** Bg2	Qc7	**57.** g4	Nb4
12. axb4	dxc4	**35.** Qa3	Rc3	**58.** fxg6	hxg6
13. dxc4	Rc8	**36.** Qa5	Rc5	**59.** h5	gxh5
14. c5	bxc5	**37.** Qa3	a5	**60.** gxh5	Ke6
15. bxc5	Na5	**38.** h4	Nc4	**61.** Kd2	Kf6
16. Na4	Bc6	**39.** Qd3	Nd6	**62.** Kc3	a2
17. Qc2	Nb7	**40.** Qd7	Kg7	**63.** Bxa2	Nxa2 +
18. Rfc1	Qd7	**41.** Rd1	Ne8	**64.** Kb2	Nb4
19. Ne1	Nd5	**42.** Qd7	Qxd7	**65.** Kc3	Nc6
20. Nb2	Bb5	**43.** Rxd7	Nf6	**66.** Kc4	Nd4
21. Ned3	Bd4	**44.** Ra7	Ng4 +	(0–1)	
22. Qb3	Nxc5	**45.** Kg1	Rc1 +		
23. Nxc5	Rxc5	**46.** Bf1	Ra1		

GAME 75

1. d4	Nf6	**9.** cxd6	exd6	**17.** f4	Nf6
2. c4	g6	**10.** Ne4	Bf5	**18.** Be2	Rfe8
3. Nc3	Bg7	**11.** Ng3	Be6	**19.** Kf2	Rxe6
4. e4	O-O	**12.** Nf3	Qc7	**20.** Re1	Rae8
5. e5	Ne8	**13.** Qb1	dxe5	**21.** Bf3	Rxe3
6. f4	d6	**14.** f5	e4	**22.** Rxe3	Rxe3
7. Be3	c5	**15.** fxe6	exf3	**23.** Kxe3	Qxf4 +
8. dxc5	Nc6	**16.** gxf3	f5	(0–1)	

GAME 76

1. c4	g6	**12.** Nf4	Nbd7	**23.** Kg1	Bxf4
2. Nc3	Bg7	**13.** a4	Nf8	**24.** exf4	Kg7
3. g3	e5	**14.** c5	d5	**25.** f5	Rh8
4. Bg2	d6	**15.** b5	N8h7	**26.** Bh6 +	Rxh6
5. e3	Nf6	**16.** Bd2	Ng5	**27.** Rxh6	Kxh6
6. Nge2	O-O	**17.** Rb2	Qd7	**28.** Qd2 +	g5
7. O-O	c6	**18.** Kh2	Bh6	**29.** bxc6	Qxf5
8. d4	Re8	**19.** a5	Bg4	**30.** Nd1	Qh3
9. Rb1	e4	**20.** hxg4	hxg4	**31.** Ne3	Kg6
10. b4	Bf5	**21.** Rh1	Nf3 +	(0–1)	
11. h3	h5	**22.** Bxf3	gxf3		

GAME 77

1. e4	e5	**9.** c4	Nc7	**17.** Bxf4	Qxf4
2. f4	exf4	**10.** d4	O-O	**18.** g3	Qh6
3. Bc4	Ne7	**11.** Bxf4	Ne6	**19.** Kg1	Bh3
4. Nc3	c6	**12.** Be3	Bb4 +	**20.** Ne5	Bxf1
5. Nf3	d5	**13.** Kf2	Nd7	**21.** Rxf1	Bd2
6. Bb3	dxe4	**14.** c5	Nf6	**22.** Rf3	Rad8
7. Nxe4	Nd5	**15.** Nxf6 +	Qxf6	**23.** Nxf7	Rxf7
8. Qe2	Be7	**16.** Rhf1	Nf4	**24.** Qe7	(1–0)

GAME 78

1. c4	e6	**15.** dxc5	bxc5	**29.** Qg3	Re7
2. Nf3	d5	**16.** O-O	Ra7	**30.** h4	Rbb7
3. d4	Nf6	**17.** Be2	Nd7	**31.** e6	Rbc7
4. Nc3	Be7	**18.** Nd4	Qf8	**32.** Qe5	Qe8
5. Bg5	O-O	**19.** Nxe6	fxe6	**33.** a4	Qd8
6. e3	h6	**20.** e4	d4	**34.** R1f2	Qe8
7. Bh4	b6	**21.** f4	Qe7	**35.** R2f3	Qd8
8. cxd5	Nxd5	**22.** e5	Rb8	**36.** Bd3	Qe8
9. Bxe7	Qxe7	**23.** Bc4	Kh8	**37.** Qe4	Nf6
10. Nxd5	exd5	**24.** Qh3	Nf8	**38.** Rxf6	gxf6
11. Rc1	Be6	**25.** b3	a5	**39.** Rxf6	Kg8
12. Qa4	c5	**26.** f5	exf5	**40.** Bc4	Kh8
13. Qa3	Rc8	**27.** Rxf5	Nh7	**41.** Qf4	(1–0)
14. Bb5	a6	**28.** Rcf1	Qd8		

GAME 79

1.	d4	Nf6	6.	Nf3	Nc6	11.	exd4	bxc6
2.	c4	e6	7.	O-O	dxc4	12.	Bg5	Re8
3.	Nc3	Bb4	8.	Bxc4	Bd6	13.	Qd3	c5
4.	e3	O-O	9.	Bb5	e5	14.	dxc5	Bxh2+
5.	Bd3	d5	10.	Bxc6	exd4		(0–1)	

GAME 80

1.	e4	c5	16.	Bxc1	Bxb5	31.	bxc3	Rxe5+
2.	Nf3	d6	17.	Nd5	Bh4+	32.	Kd2	Rxe1
3.	d4	cxd4	18.	g3	Bxf1	33.	Kxe1	Kd5
4.	Nxd4	Nf6	19.	Rxf1	Bd8	34.	Kd2	Kc4
5.	f3	Nc6	20.	Bd2	Rc8	35.	h5	b6
6.	c4	e6	21.	Bc3	f5	36.	Kc2	g5
7.	Nc3	Be7	22.	e5	Rc5	37.	h6	f4
8.	Be3	O-O	23.	Nb4	Ba5	38.	g4	a5
9.	Nc2	d5	24.	a3	Bxb4	39.	bxa5	bxa5
10.	cxd5	exd5	25.	axb4	Rd5	40.	Kb2	a4
11.	Nxd5	Nxd5	26.	Ke2	Kf7	41.	Ka3	Kxc3
12.	Qxd5	Qc7	27.	h4	Ke6	42.	Kxa4	Kd4
13.	Qb5	Bd7	28.	Ke3	Rc8	43.	Kb4	Ke3
14.	Rc1	Nb4	29.	Rg1	Rc4		(0–1)	
15.	Nxb4	Qxc1+	30.	Re1	Rxc3+			

GAME 81

1.	e4	e5	13.	h3	Bxf3	25.	Ne3	gxh3
2.	Nf3	Nc6	14.	Qxf3	O-O	26.	g3	Bg5
3.	Bb5	a6	15.	Bc5	Qe6	27.	Nf5	h5
4.	Ba4	d6	16.	Nd2	Rad8	28.	Kxh3	Rd7
5.	c3	Bd7	17.	Bxc6	bxc6	29.	Kg2	Qd8
6.	d4	g6	18.	Qe2	Rb8	30.	Qe2	h4
7.	O-O	Bg7	19.	Qxa6	Bf6	31.	Rxd7	Qxd7
8.	Bg5	Nge7	20.	b4	Rfd8	32.	Qg4	Qd8
9.	dxe5	dxe5	21.	a4	g5	33.	Rd1	Qf6
10.	Qe2	h6	22.	Kh2	g4	34.	gxh4	Bxh4
11.	Be3	Qc8	23.	Qc4	Qc8	35.	Be7	(1–0)
12.	Rd1	Bg4	24.	Nf1	Ng6			

GAME 82

1.	e4	c5	9.	f5	Nfxe4	17.	Qe2+	Be6
2.	Nf3	d6	10.	fxe6	Qh4+	18.	Nf4	Kd7
3.	d4	cxd4	11.	g3	Nxg3	19.	O-O-O	Qe8
4.	Nxd4	Nf6	12.	Nf3	Qh5	20.	Bxe6+	Nxe6
5.	Nc3	a6	13.	exf7+	Kd8	21.	Qe4	g6
6.	Bc4	e6	14.	Rg1	Nf5	22.	Nxe6	(1–0)
7.	Bb3	Nbd7	15.	Nd5	Qxf7			
8.	f4	Nc5	16.	Bg5+	Ke8			

GAME 83

1.	c4	g6	13.	a5	Nf6	25.	Be4	Nf5
2.	Nf3	Bg7	14.	Qa4	Bd7	26.	Rc6	Qg7
3.	d4	Nf6	15.	Qa3	Bh6	27.	Rb1	Nh4
4.	Nc3	O-O	16.	Bd3	Qc7	28.	Qd3	Bf5
5.	e4	d6	17.	bxc5	bxc5	29.	Kh1	f3
6.	Be2	e5	18.	exf5	gxf5	30.	Ng3	fxg2+
7.	O-O	Nc6	19.	Bc2	a6	31.	Kg1	Bxe4
8.	d5	Ne7	20.	Nde4	Bxc1	32.	Qxe4	Nf3+
9.	Nd2	c5	21.	Nxf6+	Rxf6	33.	Kxg2	Nd2
10.	Rb1	Ne8	22.	Rfxc1	Raf8		(0–1)	
11.	b4	b6	23.	Rb6	Bc8			
12.	a4	f5	24.	Ne2	f4			

GAME 84

1.	e4	e6	17.	Re3	O-O-O	33.	f3	Bd7
2.	d4	d5	18.	Rg3	Kb8	34.	a5	Kc7
3.	Nc3	Bb4	19.	Rf3	f5	35.	Kf2	Rf7
4.	e5	c5	20.	exf6	e5	36.	Ke3	Kd6
5.	a3	Bxc3+	21.	Qg3	Nxd4	37.	g3	Kc5
6.	bxc3	Qc7	22.	Re3	e4	38.	f4	Bg4
7.	Nf3	Nc6	23.	Rxe4	Qxg3	39.	Rb1	Re7+
8.	Be2	Bd7	24.	Rxd4	Qg4	40.	Kd2	b6
9.	O-O	Nge7	25.	Rxg4	Bxg4	41.	axb6	axb6
10.	a4	Na5	26.	Bxg6	Rhg8	42.	h3	Bd7
11.	Re1	cxd4	27.	Bh7	Rh8	43.	g4	d4
12.	cxd4	Nc4	28.	Bd3	Rde8	44.	f5	Re3
13.	Bd3	h6	29.	f7	Re7	45.	f6	Rf3
14.	Nd2	Nxd2	30.	f8/Q+	RxQ	46.	Rf1	Rxf1
15.	Bxd2	Nc6	31.	Bb4	Rff7	47.	Bxf1	Be6
16.	Qg4	g6	32.	Bxe7	Rxe7		(1–0)	

GAME 85

1.	e4	c5	19.	Bg5	Qxd1+	37.	Bg5	Bxg5+
2.	Nf3	d6	20.	Rxd1	Rfe8	38.	hxg5	Kg7
3.	c3	Nf6	21.	Bb3	c4	39.	Ke3	Kg6
4.	Bd3	Nc6	22.	Bc2	Ne6	40.	Kf4	Nc5
5.	Bc2	Bg4	23.	Be3	Reb8	41.	g3	Bd7
6.	d3	g6	24.	Rb1	a6	42.	a3	Be8
7.	Nbd2	Bg7	25.	Rff1	Be8	43.	Bb1	Na4
8.	h3	Bd7	26.	Kf2	Nd8	44.	Ne2	Nb2
9.	O-O	O-O	27.	Rxb8	Rxb8	45.	Nd4	Nd1
10.	Nh2	b5	28.	Rb1	Rb5	46.	Ne2	Nf2
11.	f4	b4	29.	Rxb5	axb5	47.	Ke3	Nh3
12.	Nc4	d5	30.	Ke2	h6	48.	Nf4+	Kxg5
13.	Ne5	bxc3	31.	Kd2	g5	49.	Ng2	f6
14.	bxc3	dxe4	32.	h4	g4	50.	exf6	Kxf6
15.	dxe4	Nxe5	33.	Nd4	e6	51.	Nh4	e5
16.	fxe5	Ne8	34.	Bf4	h5	52.	Bc2	Bd7
17.	Nf3	Nc7	35.	Bg5	Nb7	53.	Bb1	Ng5
18.	Rf2	Bb5	36.	Bf6	Bh6+	54.	Bc2	Nf7

55.	Bb1	Nh8	62.	Kh2	Ke7	69.	Kg1	Bxe4
56.	Bc2	Ng6	63.	Kg1	Kd6	70.	Bxe4	Ka4
57.	Nxg6	Kxg6	64.	Kf2	Kc5	71.	Bf5	Kb3
58.	Kf2	Kg5	65.	Kg1	Kb6	72.	Bxg4	e4
59.	Kg2	h4	66.	Kh1	Ka5	73.	Bxh3	Kxc3
60.	Kh2	h3	67.	Kg1	Bc6	74.	g4	Kd2
61.	Kg1	Kf6	68.	Kh1	Bb7		(0–1)	

GAME 86

1.	e4	g6	9.	O-O-O	Ne7	17.	fxe6	fxe6
2.	d4	Bg7	10.	g4	Qa5	18.	Bc4	Nxe5
3.	Nc3	d6	11.	Kb1	Rb8	19.	Qg3	Bg7
4.	f4	c6	12.	e5	dxe5	20.	Bxd5	cxd5
5.	Nf3	Bg4	13.	dxe5	Nd5	21.	Bh6	Qc7
6.	Be3	Nd7	14.	Ne4	Bf8	22.	Nd6+	Kd8
7.	h3	Bxf3	15.	Bc1	b5	23.	Bxg7	Qxd6
8.	Qxf3	e6	16.	f5	b4	24.	Qxe5	(1–0)

GAME 87

1.	d4	Nf6	10.	Nxc4	Nbd7	19.	e5	dxe5
2.	Nf3	c5	11.	Re1	Ba6	20.	fxe5	Nxd5
3.	d5	b5	12.	Qa4	Qc8	21.	Nxd5	Qxc6
4.	c4	Bb7	13.	Na5	Nb6	22.	e6	Ne5
5.	g3	g6	14.	Qh4	Re8	23.	Rxe5	Bxe5
6.	Bg2	bxc4	15.	Bg5	Qc7	24.	exf7	Rf8
7.	Nc3	Bg7	16.	Nc6	Bb7	25.	h3	Rxf7
8.	O-O	O-O	17.	e4	Nbd7	26.	Nf4	Rxf4
9.	Ne5	d6	18.	f4	Kh8		(0–1)	

GAME 88

1.	e4	e6	16.	Ng5	h6	31.	h3	Rc8
2.	d4	d5	17.	Ne4	Nxe4	32.	Kf1	Ra8
3.	Nc3	Nf6	18.	Rxe4	Qd6	33.	Kg1	a5
4.	Bg5	dxe4	19.	Qh5	c5	34.	Qe4	Rd8
5.	Nxe4	Be7	20.	Rg4	Kf8	35.	Rg3	Kf7
6.	Bxf6	Bxf6	21.	Rd3	cxd4	36.	Qh7	Rg8
7.	Nf3	Nbd7	22.	Rgxd4	Qc7	37.	Qg6+	Ke7
8.	Bc4	O-O	23.	Qh4	Rxd4	38.	Qxg7+	Rxg7
9.	O-O	c6	24.	Qxd4	Re8	39.	Rxg7+	Kd6
10.	Qe2	b6	25.	Bb5	Bc6	40.	Rxc7	Kxc7
11.	Rad1	Qc7	26.	a4	Bxb5	41.	g4	Kd6
12.	Nxf6+	Nxf6	27.	axb5	f6	42.	h4	e5
13.	Qe5	Qe7	28.	c4	Rc8	43.	g5	(1–0)
14.	c3	Bb7	29.	b3	Re8			
15.	Rfe1	Rfd8	30.	f4	Ke7			

GAME 89

1. e4	c5	9. f4	Nc6	17. Bxc6	Rxc6
2. Nf3	d6	10. Nxc6	Bxc6	18. Rad1	Rfc8
3. d4	cxd4	11. f5	e5	19. Nd5	Qd8
4. Nxd4	Nf6	12. Qd3	Be7	20. c3	Be7
5. Nc3	a6	13. Bg5	Qb6+	21. Ra1	f6
6. Bc4	e6	14. Kh1	O-O	22. a4	Rb8
7. Bb3	b5	15. Bxf6	Bxf6	23. Nxe7+	(1–0)
8. O-O	Bb7	16. Bd5	Rac8		

GAME 90

1. e4	c5	9. c4	bxc4	17. Nf5+	Ke8
2. Nf3	d6	10. Bxc4	Bxe4	18. Be3	Bxe3
3. d4	cxd4	11. O-O	d5	19. fxe3	Qb6
4. Nxd4	Nf6	12. Re1	e5	20. Rd1	Ra7
5. Nc3	a6	13. Qa4+	Nd7	21. Rd6	Qd8
6. h3	b5	14. Rxe4	dxe4	22. Qb3	Qc7
7. Nd5	Bb7	15. Nf5	Bc5	23. Bxf7+	Kd8
8. Nxf6+	gxf6	16. Ng7+	Ke7	24. Be6	(1–0)

GAME 91

1. e4	c5	15. Nd5	Nc6	29. Bb3	f5
2. Nf3	Nc6	16. Ne3	Qc5	30. g3	Re8
3. d4	cxd4	17. c3	Rad8	31. Qc6	Qb8
4. Nxd4	Nf6	18. Qf3	Rd7	32. Rd7	Re1+
5. Nc3	d6	19. Rad1	Rd6	33. Kf2	Qe8
6. Bg5	g6	20. Rxd6	Qxd6	34. Qf3	Rb1
7. Bxf6	exf6	21. Rd1	Qc5	35. Rd1	Rxb2+
8. Bc4	Bg7	22. h3	b5	36. Kg1	Qc8
9. O-O	O-O	23. Rd5	Qb6	37. h4	Bxc3
10. Ndb5	f5	24. Rd6	Ne5	38. Rd8+	Qxd8
11. exf5	Bxf5	25. Qd5	Qc7	39. Qxc3+	Qf6
12. Nxd6	Ne5	26. f4	Nc4	40. Qxf6 mate	(1–0)
13. Bb3	Qd7	27. Nxc4	bxc4		
14. Nxf5	Qxf5	28. Bxc4	Kh8		

GAME 92

1. Nf3	Nf6	8. e4	Nbd7	15. Bc4	Nxc3
2. c4	g6	9. Rd1	Nb6	16. Bc5	Rfe8+
3. Nc3	Bg7	10. Qc5	Bg4	17. Kf1	Be6
4. d4	O-O	11. Bg5	Na4	18. Bxb6	Bxc4+
5. Bf4	d5	12. Qa3	Nxc3	19. Kg1	Ne2+
6. Qb3	dxc4	13. bxc3	Nxe4	20. Kf1	Nxd4+
7. Qxc4	c6	14. Bxe7	Qb6	21. Kg1	Ne2+

22. Kf1	Nc3 +	29. Qd8 +	Bf8	36. Kf1	Ng3 +
23. Kg1	axb6	30. Nxe1	Bd5	37. Ke1	Bb4 +
24. Qb4	Ra4	31. Nf3	Ne4	38. Kd1	Bb3 +
25. Qxb6	Nxd1	32. Qb8	b5	39. Kc1	Ne2 +
26. h3	Rxa2	33. h4	h5	40. Kb1	Nc3 +
27. Kh2	Nxf2	34. Ne5	Kg7	41. Kc1	Rc2 mate
28. Re1	Rxe1	35. Kg1	Bc5 +	(0–1)	

GAME 93

1. e4	c5	17. Nf6 +	Bxf6	33. Rde7 +	Kd8
2. Nf3	Nc6	18. Qxf6	Qc7	34. Rd7 +	Kc8
3. d4	cxd4	19. O-O-O	Rxa2	35. Rc7 +	Kd8
4. Nxd4	e6	20. Kb1	Ra6	36. Rfd7 +	Ke8
5. Nc3	Qc7	21. Bxb5	Rb6	37. Rd1	b5
6. g3	Nf6	22. Bd3	e5	38. Rb7	Qh5
7. Ndb5	Qb8	23. fxe5	Rxf6	39. g4	Qh3
8. Bf4	Ne5	24. exf6	Qc5	40. g5	Qf3
9. Be2	Bc5	25. Bxh7	Qg5	41. Re1 +	Kf8
10. Bxe5	Qxe5	26. Bxg8	Qxf6	42. Rxb5	Kg7
11. f4	Qb8	27. Rhf1	Qxg7	43. Rb6	Qg3
12. e5	a6	28. Bxf7 +	Kd8	44. Rd1	Qc7
13. exf6	axb5	29. Be6	Qh6	45. Rdd6	Qc8
14. fxg7	Rg8	30. Bxd7	Bxd7	46. b3	Kh7
15. Ne4	Be7	31. Rf7	Qxh2	47. Ra6	(1–0)
16. Qd4	Ra4	32. Rdxd7 +	Ke8		

GAME 94

1. e4	e5	7. O-O	dxc3	13. Bb2	Qg5
2. Nf3	Nc6	8. Qb3	Qe7	14. h4	Qxh4
3. Bc4	Bc5	9. Nxc3	Nf6	15. Bxg7	Rg8
4. b4	Bxb4	10. Nd5	Nxd5	16. Rfe1 +	Kd8
5. c3	Ba5	11. exd5	Ne5	17. Qg3	(1–0)
6. d4	exd4	12. Nxe5	Qxe5		

GAME 95

1. e4	e6	13. Ne2	O-O-O	25. h6	Qd6
2. d4	d5	14. c4	e5	26. Qg5 +	Qe7
3. Nc3	Bb4	15. dxe5	Nxe5	27. Qd5 +	Qd6
4. a3	Bxc3 +	16. Rxd8 +	Kxd8	28. Qg5 +	Qe7
5. bxc3	dxe4	17. Nf4	Rg8	29. Qg3	Bf5
6. Qg4	Nf6	18. Be2	Kc8	30. Qf4	Qe6
7. Qxg7	Rg8	19. Rd1	Rd8	31. g4	Bg6
8. Qh6	Rg6	20. Rxd8 +	Kxd8	32. Qg5 +	Qe7
9. Qe3	b6	21. Qg3	Ng6	33. Qd5 +	Qd6
10. Bb2	Bb7	22. h4	Nxf4	34. Be5	Qxd5
11. O-O-O	Nbd7	23. Qxf4	Ne8	35. cxd5	f6
12. h3	Qe7	24. h5	Bc8	36. Bg3	Ke7

37. Kd2	Nd6	43. Ba2	f5	49. Bg6	Bd7
38. Ke3	b5	44. gxf5	Bxf5	50. Bxh7	c5
39. Bxd6 +	Kxd6	45. Bb3	Bg6	51. dxc6	Bxc6
40. Kd4	a6	46. Ba4	Bf5	52. Bxe4	Bxe4
41. c4	bxc4	47. Be8	Ke7	53. Kxe4	Kf6
42. Bxc4	a5	48. Ke5	Bg4	54. f4	(1–0)

GAME 96

1. e4	e5	10. Rd1	O-O	19. Rxd5	Bxc3
2. Nf3	Nc6	11. c4	bxc4	20. Rc1	Bb4
3. Bb5	a6	12. Bxc4	Qd7	21. Rxc7	Rac8
4. Ba4	Nf6	13. Nc3	Nxc3	22. Ra7	Rc2
5. O-O	Nxe4	14. bxc3	f6	23. Rdd7	Bc3
6. d4	b5	15. exf6	Bxf6	24. Rac7	h6
7. Bb3	d5	16. Bg5	Na5	25. Be3	(1–0)
8. dxe5	Be6	17. Qxe6 +	Qxe6		
9. Qe2	Be7	18. Bxd5	Qxd5		

GAME 97

1. d4	Nf6	15. b3	Qc7	29. Rd1	Qxc3
2. c4	g6	16. f4	b5	30. Bxc3	Nxd1
3. Nc3	Bg7	17. cxb5	Qb6	31. Qd4	Nxc3
4. Nf3	O-O	18. Kh2	axb5	32. b6	Rc5
5. Bf4	c5	19. Nxb5	Bxa1	33. e5	Rxa4
6. d5	d6	20. Rxa1	Rfc8	34. b7	Rxd4
7. e4	Qa5	21. Qc4	Qa6	35. b8/Q +	Kg7
8. Bd3	Bg4	22. a4	Nb6	36. exd6	exd6
9. O-O	Nbd7	23. Qc2	c4	37. Qxd6	Rcxd5
10. h3	Bxf3	24. b4	c3	38. Qc7	Ne2
11. Qxf3	Ne5	25. Nxc3	Qc4.	39. f5	Rxf5
12. Qe2	Nxd3	26. b5	Qd4	40. Qa7	Rfd5
13. Qxd3	a6	27. Be1	Nc4	41. Qa8	Nf4
14. Bd2	Nd7	28. Qf2	Ne3		(0–1)

GAME 98

1. e4	c5	15. Be3	a6	29. Rd1	Qf6
2. Nf3	Nc6	16. Nc3	Nxe4	30. Rxd8 +	Qxd8
3. d4	cxd4	17. Rxf7	Rxf7	31. Bxa6	Qd5
4. Nxd4	Nf6	18. Bxf7 +	Kh8	32. a3	h5
5. Nc3	d6	19. Qc4	Bg5	33. b4	Qd1 +
6. Bc4	e6	20. Nxe4	Bxe3 +	34. Kh2	h4
7. Bb3	Be7	21. Kh1	Qd7	35. Qf4	Qe1
8. O-O	O-O	22. Bh5	Bb5	36. b5	Bd5
9. Be3	Bd7	23. Qb3	Qd4	37. b6	e3
10. f4	Nxd4	24. Nd6	Qxd6	38. b7	Bxb7
11. Bxd4	Bc6	25. Qxe3	Bc6	39. Qf8 +	Kh7
12. Qe2	b5	26. Bf3	e4	40. Bd3 +	g6
13. Nxb5	e5	27. Be2	Rd8	41. Qf7 +	Kh8
14. fxe5	dxe5	28. h3	h6	42. Qxg6	(1–0)

GAME 99

1.	e4	c5	7.	Bb3	a6	13.	f5	Qb4
2.	Nf3	d6	8.	f4	Qa5	14.	fxe6	Bxe6
3.	d4	cxd4	9.	O-O	Nxd4	15.	Bxe6	fxe6
4.	Nxd4	Nf6	10.	Qxd4	d5	16.	Rxf8 +	Qxf8
5.	Nc3	Nc6	11.	Be3	Nxe4	17.	Qa4 +	(1–0)
6.	Bc4	e6	12.	Nxe4	dxe4			

GAME 100

1.	e4	c5	15.	Bf4	Nc4	29.	Rxd6	Bf5
2.	Nf3	Nc6	16.	Qe2	Bxf4	30.	b4	Rff8
3.	d4	cxd4	17.	Qxc4	Kg7	31.	b5	Nd8
4.	Nxd4	g6	18.	Ne4	Bc7	32.	Rd5	Nf7
5.	Nc3	Bg7	19.	Nc5	Rf6	33.	Rc5	a6
6.	Be3	Nf6	20.	c3	e5	34.	b6	Be4
7.	Bc4	O-O	21.	Rad1	Nd8	35.	Re1	Bc6
8.	Bb3	Na5	22.	Nd7	Rc6	36.	Rxc6	bxc6
9.	e5	Ne8	23.	Qh4	Re6	37.	b7	Rab8
10.	Bxf7 +	Kxf7	24.	Nc5	Rf6	38.	Qxa6	Nd8
11.	Ne6	dxe6	25.	Ne4	Rf4	39.	Rb1	Rf7
12.	Qxd8	Nc6	26.	Qxe7 +	Rf7	40.	h3	Rfxb7
13.	Qd2	Bxe5	27.	Qa3	Nc6	41.	Rxb7	Rxb7
14.	O-O	Nd6	28.	Nd6	Bxd6	42.	Qa8	(1–0)

GAME 101

1.	d4	Nf6	13.	Qc2	Qc6	25.	e5	R6d7
2.	c4	b6	14.	Bd3	Qxc2	26.	Nc1	Bf8
3.	Nc3	Bb7	15.	Bxc2	O-O-O	27.	b4	Nc4
4.	f3	d5	16.	Kf2	Rd6	28.	Ra2	Nxe5
5.	cxd5	Nxd5	17.	b3	Nc6	29.	Rc2	b5
6.	Nxd5	Qxd5	18.	Rd2	Rhd8	30.	Ne2	Nc4
7.	e4	Qd7	19.	Rhd1	Nb4	31.	Rc3	e5
8.	Bc4	g6	20.	Bb1	Ba6	32.	f4	exd4
9.	Qb3	e6	21.	a3	Nc6	33.	Rxd4	Nxe3
10.	Ne2	Bg7	22.	Bd3	Bxd3	34.	Kxe3	Rxd4
11.	Be3	Nc6	23.	Rxd3	f5	35.	Nxd4	Rxd4
12.	Rd1	Na5	24.	R3d2	Na5			(0–1)

About the Author

Bruce Pandolfini is the author of fourteen instructional chess books, including *Beginning Chess; Pandolfini's Chess Complete; Chessercizes; More Chessercizes; Checkmate; Principles of the New Chess; Pandolfini's Endgame Course; Russian Chess; The ABC's of Chess; Let's Play Chess; Kasparov's Winning Chess Tactics; One-Move Chess by the Champions; Chess Openings: Traps and Zaps; Square One;* and *Weapons of Chess.* He is also the editor of the distinguished anthology *The Best of Chess Life & Review,* Volumes I and II, and has produced, with David MacEnulty, two instructional videotapes, *Understanding Chess* and *Opening Principles.*

Bruce was the chief commentator at the New York half of the 1990 Kasparov-Karpov World Chess Championship, and in 1990 was head coach of the United States Team in the World Youth Chess Championships in Wisconsin. Perhaps the most experienced chess teacher in North America, he is co-founder, with Faneuil Adams, of the Manhattan Chess Club School and is the director of the New York City Schools Program. Bruce's most famous student, six-time National Scholastic Champion Joshua Waitzkin, is the subject of Fred Waitzkin's acclaimed book *Searching for Bobby Fischer.* Bruce Pandolfini lives in Manhattan.